...aybe he had turned into a werewolf, but he wouldn't ...hat.

...e paused, his tail swinging out of reach. *Why not?*

Bradley sat down on his haunches, cleared his throat, pointed his nose toward the moon, and launched into the best howl he could muster. "A-woo—ha ha ha ha!"

The mournful sound was so at odds with how good he felt that he started laughing in the middle of it. He pulled himself together.

No, seriously, he told himself. *Howl*. He took another breath. "A-wooooo!"

That was better. With a little practice, he could be really good at it.

His legs began to twitch. His altered body got impatient at sitting in one place. He had to run some more. He ran, loving every mile. He thought he could never grow tired of the joy of the wind in his face. No wonder dogs with their heads hanging out of car windows looked so happy.

He suddenly knew the secret they never talked about in any of the horror movies or TV shows or books. Being a werewolf was So. Much. *FUN!*

"Howl!"

Strip Mauled

Edited by
Esther M. Friesner

STRIP MAULED

Introduction copyright © 2009 by Esther M. Friesner.

Copyright © 2009 by Tekno Books and Esther M. Friesner.

A Baen Books Original

Baen Publishing Enterprises
P.O. Box 1403
Riverdale, NY 10471
www.baen.com

ISBN: 978-1-4391-3320-0

Cover art by Clyde Caldwell

First Baen paperback printing, October 2009

Distributed by Simon & Schuster
1230 Avenue of the Americas
New York, NY 10020

Printed in the United States of America

10 9 8 7 6 5 4 3 2 1

Additional Copyright Information

Contents

Leader of the Pack

Esther M. Friesner

Alas, poor werewolves, forever doomed to be Avis to the vampire's unassailable fang-hold on Hertz, Pepsi to their Coke, Burger King to their McDonalds!

(Note to any litigation-happy corporate types out there: The preceding metaphor is merely one lone ink-stained wretch's personal perception of brand-name pecking orders and is in no way intended as either an outright statement or an insinuation of any kind that might conceivably affect—positively or negatively—the public image, good name, market share or income of the commercial entities mentioned. So don't start whining; it demeans us both.)

Okay, where was I? Oh, yeah . . .

Pity the werewolf indeed, always forced to ride in the back seat of the Sexy/Hot/Cool Monster car while the vampire gets to sit up front and choose the radio station. To what may we ascribe this unfortunate situation? How did werewolves get swatted across the snout with the

Rolled-up Newspaper of Second-Class Citizenship? There are no easy answers.

Oh heck, *yes* there are: Let's blame the media!

Think back to the earliest horror movies involving such supernatural critters. Once you get past *Nosferatu*'s presentation of the vampire as overgrown gnome, the bloodsuckers are inevitably portrayed as suave, seductive, and snappily dressed. Slap your actor into a swooshy, utterly fabulous cape and presto, you've got a cinematic vampire ready to go, no Transformation Scene required. (What about when Dracula turns into a bat? No biggie. A **poof** of flash powder and a rubber *Fledermaus* on a wire and you're done.)

But werewolves? Major Transition Scene nightmare, people, especially in the early days of the monster movie, long before CGI or its poorer but passable predecessors. The on-screen metamorphosis from human to werewolf was a lot of stop-action-add-another-tuft-of-fake-fur tedium resulting in a final product that was—let's be honest—pretty chintzy. Wolves have fangs, but underbites? *Tusks*? Face it, some of the first wolfmen on screen were Wookies with bad pompadours.

Over the years, werewolves have seen their image improve. Not only are movie Transformation Scenes smoother and the make up and facial prostheses at the end of the T.S. tunnel more terrifying and less snort-and-giggleworthy, but there's even been been some attempts to help those monthly moon-howlers lay claim to a little of the vampire's sex appeal. Yet for all that progress, they're still #2, thus going to show that you never really get over a bad start, especially when it's a matter of something as shallow yet societally key as personal appearance.

If you don't believe this, let's talk about our high school experiences, shall we? Zits and braces or better to open, player.

It is therefore my great pleasure as someone with my thumb on the pulse of the media (somewhere around the carotid artery) to be able to do something towards helping our long-suffering lycanthropic brethren to lay claim to their rightful bite of the American Dream, namely market share. And where better to get a grip on the throat of a national audience than in the still-demographically-influential suburbs?

Werewolves and the suburbs are a natural go-together. Okay, so they're not the Obligatory/Iconic Suburban Golden Retriever or Chocolate Labrador, but they've got a much better chance of taking home the Best in Show ribbon than their Undead rivals. In some suburban households, if it brings home a trophy, who cares if it also brings home bloody chunks of the neighbors every time the full moon shines? And let's not forget one more advantage to the suburban werewolf: If his lupine side does something nasty on your lawn, his human side can come by later with the Pooper Scooper. In your *face*, Dracula!

Therefore, welcome to the fur-sprouting, mall-browsing, moon-howling, latté-sipping world of *Strip Mauled*. I think you'll like what you find.

Sit.

Stay.

Good reader.

Jody Lynn Nye lists her main career activity as "spoiling cats." She lives northwest of Chicago with two of the above and her husband, author and packager Bill Fawcett. She has published more than thirty-five books, including six contemporary fantasies, four SF novels, four novels in collaboration with Anne McCaffrey, including *The Ship Who Won*; edited a humorous anthology about mothers, *Don't Forget Your Spacesuit, Dear!*; and written over a hundred short stories. Her latest books are *A Forthcoming Wizard* (TOR Books), and *Myth-Fortunes*, co-written with Robert Asprin (Wildside Books).

Howl!

Jody Lynn Nye

Bradley Newton turned one of the silver objects over in his hands. The Eastern European man with shiny black hair and a pockmarked face slumping in the Naugahyde armchair on the other side of the utilitarian desk looked deliberately insouciant. Bradley wanted to wipe that smirk off his face, and off the lawyer's, too. He kept his own round face expressionless.

"So, Mr. Elanovitch is willing to pay whatever fine you assess, inspector," the attorney offered. "We maintain that he did not understand that his import of these items was considered to be excessive."

"Import? Smuggling is the word I would use, counselor," Bradley retorted. That jerked the European man to attention, but only for a moment. He was not threatened by the plump inspector on the other side of the desk. Bradley picked up another silver artifact from the heap before him, this one long and thin like a fountain pen, but with a knob shaped like a snail shell on the top. "Customs and Excise is vigilant about these things. Your client has lived in the United States for six years, and traveled in and out of the country over twenty-eight times a year. He must know the limits on imports. If he never read Form I-6059B, then he's one of the few who hasn't."

"Fine me and release my goods," Elanovitch intoned, bored, plucking at the armrest with idle fingertips. "Either you arrest me, or you don't. We offer to pay. Take it or leave it. Or unless you want something for yourself, eh?" His weaselly black eyes fixed on Bradley's hazel ones. "Your annual pay is probably much less than my business makes in a day."

That made Bradley's blood pressure shoot up, but he kept his temper down. His supervisor and at least one other credible witness were on the other side of the two-way mirror that occupied much of the fourth wall in a largely featureless interview room, and the interview was being recorded on videotape. If they made him react, they won, and they knew it. "Bribing a federal official is a felony," he said, shaking the knobby cylinder at Elanovitch. "This is a serious matter, and . . . ouch!"

He looked down at his hand. Blood dripped from the web of skin between his thumb and forefinger. A curved, triangular blade no longer than his thumbnail had popped out of the bottom of the silver artifact. He snatched out his handkerchief and squeezed the area to stop the bleeding. The blade had left a crescent-shaped mark in the skin. He looked up at the horrified men on the other side of the table. "The importation of concealed weapons is another crime, Mr. Elanovitch."

"I did not know that was there!" the European bellowed, actually alarmed. "It is an accident! Nothing I bring in is illegal. It is household instruments, historical of age. I pay fine and I get you bandage. I even say please."

"We won't debate the extenuating circumstances," the lawyer interjected, "if we may settle this matter swiftly, without the government bringing charges?"

"What about physical assault on a government agent?" Bradley countered.

"That's just an owie, inspector," the lawyer said. "A little Bactine and a Scooby Doo bandage will make you all better. What will it take to get us out of here before dinnertime?"

Bradley realized, not for the first time, that he disliked the lawyer much more than his client. He wanted to break out of his own skin, leap over the desk and throttle the attorney, then hammer the importer to death with his own suitcase of contraband. If it wouldn't punish him more than the other two, he would have kept them there until midnight.

"I can't promise that there will be no charges pressed in the future, but this time United States Customs is willing to accept a substantial fine, plus the customs on each item over the legal allowance." Coolly, he pulled the printing calculator to him from the side of the desk and began to tap in numbers. *Large* numbers. This fine would be substantial, partly to make Elanovitch think a thousand times before doing it again, and partly because his attorney was such a jerk. It was the only revenge he was permitted to take.

Bradley hunched over the wheel of his subcompact in the traffic leaving O'Hare Airport. Another day, another criminal who thought of him as a patsy. He had worked for Customs for fifteen years. At forty-two, he had twenty-three years more before he could retire. Another 54.7 percent of his life facing the same endless conflict with petty criminals, the pugnaciously ignorant and the downright exploitive criminals who passed before him day after day after day.

Bradley walked into the house and almost called out before he remembered that Angela was in Columbus with the kids, visiting her folks. They would be gone for a week. It was spring break. A twinge of regret made him ache for the carefree college days and just after when the two of them had been able to run off to Florida during spring break. For the hell of it. Just for fun. It seemed like nothing he did these days was just for fun. Not even sex. Even sex was getting to be boring. The relic of the teenager buried deep within him was shocked. He never in a million lifetimes thought he would ever feel that way, and he loved Angie. He adored her. It didn't stop the miserable cycle of his day-to-day life from grinding him down.

Over a dinner made up of leftovers from the refrigerator, he watched the Discovery Channel on television. He felt like going away from it all, leaving the suburbs and his boring job and becoming a deep-sea fisherman. On television pulling up cages full of king crabs looked dangerous, disgusting, cold, and terrifying. All of that was better than what he had to do now. Pull in a half-ton net with his bare hands? Great! As long as he didn't have to enumerate each crab on a form in triplicate.

"It's a midlife crisis," he told himself, as he sorted the recyclables from the non-recyclable trash and threw them into separate garbage bins. "That's all."

Knowing that was his problem didn't help. He had always laughed off the notion he might have a midlife crisis, but it was worse than he had dreamed. He thought he would just have an urge to buy a red sports car and hang out with a blonde half his age, but there was no joyful anticipation in the prospect. He felt gloomy to the depths of his soul. Was this what he was going to do for the rest of his life? He wished he could talk to Angela, but even more, he wished she could understand what he was going through.

Three more days of Elanovitches, TV dinners and missing his family dragged by. Bradley didn't like sleeping alone. He missed the kids. He missed the noise and the chaos and the feeling that he belonged to something better than he was.

He woke with a start and scanned the bed for Angela's familiar body that ought to have been there beside him, half-curled on her side under the light quilt, warm and comforting by her mere presence. She wasn't there. He remembered again. Three more days until his family returned. Soon. He tried to settle down, but he was too restless. It felt as if the sheet was rucked up under his rear end. He wriggled to settle the lump. It wouldn't smooth out.

The light of the full moon shone between the bedroom curtains he had forgotten to close before he fell asleep. He kicked off the comforter. He had to get out of the bedclothes. They were stifling, smothering him in their pillowy bonds. Bradley fumbled for the bedroom light.

"Aah!" he yelled.

Someone was in the room with him!

"Who are you?" he screamed at the black-bearded man.

The other's mouth moved at the same time his did. The intruder was wearing *his* boxer shorts! He realized suddenly that he was looking at his own reflection.

"No!" Bradley cried. He must be still dreaming. He slapped his hands against his body, refusing to believe in the black hair that covered him everywhere except his eyes, lips and palms, wiry and coarse as a terrier's. He flung himself off the bed, trying to run away from his horrible image, but it seemed that the whole house was full of mirrors and shiny surfaces. The hairy man leaped out at him again and again. Bradley stumbled down the stairs, through the living room and the kitchen, and out into the night.

He had to get away from the nightmare. Something must help him to wake up. He raced along the street, covering ground faster than he ever could in the daylight. Bradley looked down to see curving claws between his toes. His feet looked twice as long as usual. Something slapped him in the backside. He glanced behind, and saw a two-foot-long tail.

Run away! his brain shrieked.

He plunged in between houses, crashing through bushes and trees, trampling garden plots. Blue-flowered stalks grabbed at his legs in the Sullivans' yard. Why were there hydrangeas in his dream? He hated hydrangeas!

The beam of the streetlight at the corner struck glints off the shining hair on his hands and arms. To get away from the sight, he dashed across the street and into the forest preserve.

Part of his mind shouted at him that the preserve closed at sunset. Trespassing on state land wasn't allowed. The rest of him, the wild part, laughed at restraint. It forced him to open up his stride, until he was running flat out across the prairie. He panted in terror, gasping in oxygen until it felt as if the top of his head would come off. His legs carried him faster and faster. He started laughing. The pure adrenaline exhilarated him. He felt giddy. He dropped to all fours and discovered he could gallop still faster, leaping over streams and paths, bounding over benches. Bradley found an open patch of grass and rolled around on it. That felt good! He flipped over and ran in a circle, chasing the tail. It eluded his snapping jaws.

What had happened to him? What *was* he?

All he could think over and over again was *werewolf*. The spooky books his son loved to read at night talked about mystical transformation, the fear of silver bullets, and how the man-wolf beast howled at the moon.

Maybe he had turned into a werewolf, but he wouldn't do *that*.

He paused, the tail swinging out of reach.

Why not?

Bradley sat down on his haunches, cleared his throat, pointed his nose toward the moon, and launched into the best howl he could muster.

"A-woo—ha ha ha ha!"

The mournful sound was so at odds with how good he felt that he started laughing in the middle of it. He pulled himself together.

No, seriously, he told himself. *Howl.* He took another breath.

"A-wooooo!"

That was better. With a little practice, he could be really good at it.

His legs began to twitch. His altered body got impatient at sitting in one place. He had to run some more. Flipping onto his long feet, he ran, loving every mile. He thought he could never grow tired of the joy of the wind in his face. No wonder dogs with their heads hanging out of car windows looked so happy.

He suddenly knew the secret they never talked about in any of the horror movies or TV shows or books. Being a werewolf was So. Much. *FUN!*

Bradley sped up a hill, his pads pounding on the dirt path. A browsing deer he surprised leaped up and away from him. The scent excited him. He fell into pursuit, racing after its shape in the cold blue moonlight. He had an urge to bury his teeth in its throat. He wanted the taste of its blood on his tongue.

The deer wasn't waiting around to satisfy his urges. It increased its lead on him by lengths, leaping effortlessly over park benches and around the reeking outhouses. Bradley galloped, his tail straight out behind him. He never realized how fast deer could run. He gave it all he could, even pulling within ten feet of it, but the deer took a sharp left and dashed across the well-lit main road next to the forest preserve. Bradley windmilled to stay upright as he veered to follow, but headlights struck him. He got off the road just in time. A pickup truck roared past him, honking its horn in irritation. The deer disappeared into the trees on the other side. Bradley watched it go. The wild part of him felt dismay.

He tottered back into the woods. He was more exhausted than he could have believed. It had been years since he had gone running. He preferred to jog on the treadmill or around the track at the health club, at no more than 3.5 miles an hour. He was exhausted, and his feet and palms hurt. Gingerly, Bradley picked his way back to a park bench and curled up underneath it in the comforting dark.

Just a short rest, he told himself.

"Awright, mister!" a harsh voice roused him out of sleep. "I suppose you're gonna tell me your prescription medications make you sleepwalk, huh? Get up!"

Bradley blinked at a pink sky and a black silhouette shining a yellow circle of light in his face. He tried to remember where he was and failed. The police officer grabbed him by the arm and hauled him to his feet. Bradley realized with a start that the black fur that had covered him was gone. As was most of the pair of underpants he had been wearing when he left home. Modesty was just barely preserved by the scrap of cloth around his belly. The rest of his shorts had been torn to shreds by the bushes. His skin was covered with scratches and bruises.

"I'm all right, officer," he said, straightening his back to try and look dignified. The officer eyed him. Obviously, he failed.

"Don't need to go to the emergency room?" the officer asked. "Did someone dump you here?"

"Uh, no," Bradley said. "I . . . uh, sometimes I sleepwalk," he added. The policeman shook his head as though disappointed he hadn't come up with a more colorful explanation. Bradley wished he sounded more original, but he didn't want to be branded a kook. No one would believe he had been transformed into a werewolf. In the cold light of dawn, he didn't completely believe it himself.

"Come on," the officer sighed. "Get in the cruiser. I'll take you home."

Bradley let himself in the unlocked back door and took a long, hot shower. It was a good thing his wife and kids weren't there. They might have bought the werewolf explanation, but Angela would have been mortified that he had to be brought home by the cops.

The matter of his transformation distracted him throughout the day. He was pretty sure that lycanthropy didn't run in his family. He hadn't eaten or drunk anything unusual, unless he counted a couple of exotic frozen entrées from the food store. He'd never had a reaction to Chicken Madras before, especially not breaking out in fur and a tail. No, the only possible vector of transmission of his werewolfness had to be that artifact that cut him: Mr. Elanovitch's contraband. He wanted to get a second look at it.

Casually, so as not to draw special attention to his query, Bradley checked the confiscated goods locker first thing the next morning. To his disappointment, all the Elanovitch articles were gone. The importer's lawyer had reclaimed everything as soon as the Customs Office had opened. Bradley hesitated to contact the importer. He couldn't think of a good excuse. He didn't want to seem weak by bringing up the minor injury, nor appear to be asking for the artifact as a bribe. The object didn't seem to have had an on/off switch anyhow, nor did it have a plainly visible "reverse werewolf curse" setting on it. Bradley wished he could find out more about it. His practical mind pushed all speculation to the rear. Flights had been arriving since before dawn from foreign countries. He had a backlog of queries to cover.

The memory of the night's adventure kept his spirits up as he faced a dozen Mr. Elanovitches over the course of the day. They all lied to him. They all acted cocky and bored. He was forbidden by the rules to threaten them. They frustrated him because they enjoyed being dishonest, enjoyed making an illicit profit off the government that protected them. They laughed at him, a plump, middle-aged man, and at the United States of America that employed him to help protect its economy. Bradley concentrated on doing his job. He just kept thinking of that rush of air in his face. More than once, he caught himself smiling a little. The expression unnerved more than one of his opponents on the other side of the desk. *If they could only have seen me,* he thought, imagining the terrified look on their faces. *Pay your fine,* he imagined his employers saying, *or our werewolf will rip out your throat.* That would make it worthwhile getting up in the morning again.

He couldn't wait for the evening.

Bradley gulped down his TV dinner hot right out of the microwave, not even bothering to sit down. Eagerly, he watched for moonrise. As the orange edge of the pocked, full globe peered up over the horizon, Bradley felt his ears prick up. Literally. He felt them with his fingertips as the rounded pinnae stretched up and became pointed. He ran to the mirror to watch. Fur sprouted all over his skin from five o'clock shadow to bearskin rug in moments. His teeth turned to fangs in a long, underslung jaw. His hands and feet lengthened noticeably, and the tail pressed against the back of his underwear. Bradley lowered the band to make way for it. He was going to have to have special shorts with a hole for the tail. His chest bulged forward, and his waist curved in against his spine. He patted the new convexity with delight.

This time he was aware of the animal nature trying to impose its will on his human senses. The stale smells of the house made him feel claustrophobic. The walls seemed to move in on him, trapping him. He wanted the sweet scent of the woods. Before he knew it, he was racing for the back door on all fours. He had to reach up to turn the knob, then he was out across the backyard into the leaf-dappled twilight.

Bradley had never had an athlete's physique before. It felt as good as it looked. He ran faster than Michael Johnson or any Olympic star. He would give up everything if he could do this night after night forever. He dashed all over the neighborhood until the moon was at its height, dousing everything in pale blue light.

The scents were everywhere. They overpowered his conscious mind. He tasted the smell of warm blood on the air. Living animals were all around him. He wanted something—no, craved it. He wanted to feel life. He wanted to feel it between his hands, between his teeth, tearing the heart out of a living creature. Part of him was horrified, but it was overtaken by the wild sensation of the forbidden. What could they do to him? He was power incarnate! He would have prey!

Bradley galloped through the streets on all fours, seeking that prey. That musky smell had to be the raccoons that turned over the neighborhood garbage cans. He ran towards the strongest concentration of smells.

Unfortunately, smelling went both ways. They detected him long before he arrived at the place they had just been. They had fled up trees, where he could not follow, or into their well-defended burrows, claws and teeth facing out. He didn't want to dig for blood. He wanted to leap upon his victim!

He went to the park, where the playground equipment swung empty. The scent of young, sweet human blood floated to his nostrils, but the taste was old. It was after ten o'clock. The children had a curfew, imposed only that spring by the state legislature. They were all inside. Even the tough kids got tired of being rousted out of the parks by the cops night after night. Bradley turned away from the swing set in disgust. How inconvenient! Someone had to be out walking *somewhere*.

He smelled fresh blood and headed toward it, trotting from thin grass onto tarmac. The convenience store, yes! People came and went from it all night long. He slunk around the side of the building on all fours, and watched for a stray, unwary human.

His eyes were dazzled by the parking lot lights. He had never noticed it before, but the convenience store had lights more powerful than those in a ballpark. To his heightened senses, it was like getting slapped in the face with a flashlight over and over again. He saw cars pull up to the six spaces near the door. Humans hopped out of them, but they were inside the store before he could make himself spring toward them through the glare. Within moments, they emerged again with slushies and hot dogs. They got back into their cars and drove away.

One looked promising. A girl in a low-cut tank top that revealed her slender throat came out to a convertible with a bag in one hand. Forcing himself to ignore the lights, Bradley wiggled his backside, and sprang. As she pulled out of the space, he thundered toward her. The car lurched out of reverse and shot out of the parking lot with Bradley in pursuit. Wait until she stopped at a light. He'd leap over the back of her car and tear her to pieces!

The speed limit on the road was only thirty-five, but the girl had to be doing at least ten over the limit. Bradley cursed all lawbreakers as he chased her through several stoplights, including one she sailed through on amber. Her posture remained easy, and she swayed her head to the music blaring out of her radio. She didn't see him. How could she miss a full-grown wolfman, unless she never looked in the rearview mirror. Kids! He let out a howl. In response, the girl in the car turned her radio up.

Bradley galloped around the streets, looking for a victim on foot. He tried the shopping mall. At that hour it was closed and empty. The grocery had just shut. Even the cart boys had left. The schools and the junior college were desolate. Not one single warm body was out on the sidewalks where he could kill them.

It was the suburbs. No one *walked* anywhere. They drove out of their attached garages already in their cars, and rode around in parking lots until they found a space close to the door. How was he to find prey to satisfy his urge?

He turned back toward his neighborhood, ready to give up in dismay. Then, his keen hearing picked up the distant sound of hysterical barking. He knew that yap! He turned on one foot and hurtled in that direction.

The Lermans on the corner of his street had an obnoxious little dog. Bradley had despised it from the moment it had arrived. He stopped in the shadow of a bush and sank to his belly. Narrowing his eyes, he focused on the yard. He saw the dog through the trees lit up like a fluorescent glow stick. Now was time for revenge for all the times it piddled on him, attacked his ankle, yipped incessantly for hours out on its chain in the yard. He would tear it to tiny, quivering pieces!

Bradley hurtled toward it on all fours. It saw him. At first it dashed toward him, barking frantically. His scent hit it. The dog yelped and turned around. It scampered in the direction of the back door of the house. It couldn't possibly make it before Bradley descended on it. He bared his teeth and leaped, cutting off the dog's escape. It froze. Bradley laughed.

"Die, you miserable Beanie Baby!"

He lunged. The dog cowered, its legs shaking.

Good sense brought Bradley barreling to a halt in spite of himself. What was he thinking? It was his neighbor who left the dog out all the time and wouldn't get it obedience training.

No, he should *terrify* the pesty little monster, not kill it! That is what it deserved.

Bradley stood over the small dog and howled. The animal stood its ground for a moment, but the primal sensation of predator meets much, much larger predator kicked into its small wad of neural tissue. It let out a sound that was the canine equivalent of *Ayieeeee!* It circled around Bradley and went tearing back toward the house. It scrabbled hysterically at the door with its little claws, yelping to be let in.

Satisfied, Bradley galloped away. When the door opened, he heard with his extended hearing Mr. Lerman swearing. The dog raced into the house, still crying in terror. He bet he wouldn't see it outside again until its bladder was bursting.

Bradley returned to the house happy but exhausted. So he wasn't going to find live prey. He could put up with that. He could not wait to show Angela his new shape. She'd be knocked out. In the meanwhile, he had one more night of wild freedom until she returned.

He got home from work in time to greet the family as the car pulled into the driveway. Bradley kissed them all and carried the luggage inside. He kept looking at them while they ate dinner at a local family restaurant, doting on them, wondering how he got along for seven whole days without them. He was dying to tell them about his transformation. Twelve-year-old Mark would be thrilled. He wasn't too sure about ten-year-old Elizabeth, who covered her eyes during scary scenes in the movies. But Angie had to know.

"What are you looking at?" his wife asked him, squirting mustard on her hamburger.

"Uh, just glad you're back," he said, hastily picking up French fries and stuffing them into his mouth. This wasn't the place to tell them.

Mark had to go to band practice. Instead of griping that he had had a long day at the office, Bradley cheerfully volunteered to drive him to the junior high. Angela gave him a strange look, but she didn't say anything. He decided he wouldn't tell them, not yet. He wanted to show Angela first.

Just before moonrise, he pulled her into their bedroom and locked the door.

"What are you doing?" Angela demanded.

Bradley sat down on the bed and patted the mattress beside him. She shook her head and stood with her arms crossed and worry on her face. Not a good start, but he had to tell her. He took a deep breath.

"Honey," he began, "I have something I have to tell you."

"You're gay?" she blurted out.

Bradley gawked at her. "No! Where did you get that? Figure skating makes me sick. No. I'm . . . a werewolf."

Her expression turned from concern to naked disbelief. "Yeah, right. I've got laundry in." She started for the door. He jumped up and took her arm.

"No, really, honest, honey! It happened a couple of days after you left." He told her about the silver object, about Mr. Elanovitch, about the transformation and racing through the forest preserve. He skipped the part about the girl in the convertible.

She listened, searching his face as if trying to decide whether he was crazy or deluded.

"Brad, I don't know what to say. I mean, I don't know whether you're crazy or trying to pull something on me. Just tell me what it is, all right? I know you're bored out of your mind with your job. Are you telling me you want to quit your job and go into acting? Is that it?"

Bradley threw up his arms in frustration. "Forget it! Wait until moonrise. You'll see."

They stayed together at opposite ends of the room, waiting for the edge of the lunar globe to appear over the trees. Against Angie's objections, he opened the window so he could jump away from her if he felt some urge to harm her.

The moon rose. Bradley braced himself . . . and nothing happened. He ran to the mirror and stared at his face. *Grow!* he thought at the stubble on his chin. But it didn't. He ran back to the window. The moon *was* rising, wasn't it?

The tension in Angela's body melted away.

"Uh-huh," she said.

"But . . ." he said. Angela shook her head and unlocked the door, leaving him staring out of the window.

What was wrong with him? For three days he had been a man-beast, a creature out of legend. He was an ordinary person again, overweight, with thinning hair and a 401k account.

He ran into Mark's room and thumbed through the books on the shelf. In the story he pulled out, it said that the werewolf only roamed during the full moon.

The moon was no longer full. It had dwindled at its right-hand edge to a shape like a face. It reproached him. Bradley moaned. The magic couldn't be over!

He got up several times that night to consult the mirror. The bland, ordinary face that stared back at him refused to transform. He wanted that sense of transformation. He had to have it back, but it wouldn't come back. He returned to work more miserable than he had ever been. When he got home at night, he did his chores and played with the kids, but he found it hard to find anything to be enthusiastic about. The midlife crisis came back so bad that not even three red sports cars or a dozen blondes could help.

Angela regarded him with pity and exasperation as she watched him mope around the house.

"Honey," she said, as he hoisted the full garbage bag out of the kitchen can, "I want you to find someone to talk to. Is there such a thing as Werewolves Anonymous? Because you are an addict."

Bradley regarded her with suspicion. "You don't believe me."

Her expression was kind, not cynical. "No, not really. But you've imagined yourself into something powerful. I know you hate your job. You always talk about how it's killing you. Maybe it is. Start looking for something else. That'll help. Or how about a hobby? You're always talking about taking up a hobby. I love you. I hate to see you being miserable."

"It was so great," he said sadly, as he took the white bag out to the trash can.

Angie was right. He had to snap out of it. Maybe he *had* been dreaming for three nights in a row. Shellfish gave him weird dreams. Maybe this time the combination of stress, TV dinners and the Ambien he had to take to put himself to sleep gave him hallucinations. He settled back into their ordinary life, resolved to find a counselor and take up woodworking, or something.

Life at work continued to be miserable. One so-called international businessman who had been caught with ten containers full of designer knockoffs had had the nerve to threaten him personally with a lawsuit for restraint of trade. The government ombudsman assured Bradley he was not individually liable for government regulations, but it still kept him from sleeping at night. It got so bad that he took a double dose of sleeping pills against the warning on the front of the bottle. Sleep dragged him deep into his pillow, but his dreams were active and weird.

He felt a fierce nudge in the ribs.

"Brad! Brad, wake up!"

He tried to crawl out of the dream, where he was being prodded into a corner by a barber holding a rattail comb.

"Brad! Wake up! You're hairy!"

"I am?" The drug haze receded, and he realized he could see her in the dark. He felt his jaw and his ears. Thrilled, he leaped up and turned on the lights. They flooded his brain, much more light than he needed, but he wanted her to see. "See?" he said. "I told you." It came out "Grrr grrr gghhh." He tried again, but he didn't need to. Angela screamed, but more with delight than fear.

"Oh, my God, you're not going crazy!"

Bradley got control of his tongue, palate and vocal chords. "You thought I was?"

"Well, naturally I thought you were. Who believes in werewolves?"

"I do. You should, too. *Look* at me." He pounded his bulging chest.

Angela surveyed him up and down. Her eyes widened, then she got a coy look on her face.

"Who is this *big*, hairy creature in *my* bed? I certainly hope he's not going to *attack* me." She threw herself down among the pillows, arms up over her head. "Is he?"

Bradley could never resist it when she lay like that. He dived for her and wrapped her in his arms, mouthing her neck. She let out a shriek of delight.

Leaving her limp and satisfied, he jumped out of the window and ran through the neighborhood. He couldn't help bellowing his delight, hearing echoes in the deserted streets. There were some annoyed shouts and barking from distant dogs, but he didn't care. He felt great. The curse hadn't gone away. In fact, it had some fabulous fringe benefits.

Three days of the lunar month helped keep him sane at his job and managing the kids' full schedule of activity during the other twenty-five. Enthusiasm for Angela's new, hairy suitor made the marriage bed a more interesting place than it had been in years. Bradley also discovered his senses were boosted during the non-wolf times. He found things the kids had lost by smell. He cleared pests out of the yard, including the gopher he had been unable to unseat for years. The Endangered Species Act wouldn't let him kill or harm it, but never said a damned thing about werewolf eviction. He had never been in better shape in his life. Three days of intense physical activity per month started to whittle away the suburban paunch. His muscle tone improved to the way it had been when he played soccer in school.

"I have to admit I'm envious," Angela said one evening, admiring his trim solar plexus. "Is there a way I can get in on this?"

"Should we have two . . . you-know-whats in the family?" Bradley asked.

"Why not? Frankenstein had his bride. How about the Wolfman?" She tickled the whiskers at the side of his jaw. He just couldn't resist that.

"I'll figure something out," Bradley promised. He would find Elanovitch. It was what Customs and Excise was best at, after all.

They had not told the kids yet. He was still trying to figure out how, but since Angela had taken the news so readily, he doubted the kids would have problems. It only interfered with their social life a little.

As the keeper of their social calendar, Angela was the one who coordinated with their friends for nights out. "No, sorry, we can't get together on Saturday," she told someone on the phone. "That's one of Brad's hairy days and we've got a date that night. Can you imagine what a mess he'd make of the Olive Garden? How about Tuesday instead?"

Bradley was a changed man at work. Instead of slinking in in the morning, he strutted. His supervisor noticed the boost in his confidence, handing him the tough cases. Instead of dreading them, Bradley came to enjoy them. He just pictured the head of his interviewee on the body of the yappy little neighbor dog, racing toward its house. His success rate soared.

"Newton," his boss barked at him. "Got a big problem for you. I want you to handle it yourself."

Brad was instantly on guard.

"What is it, sir?"

The supervisor's mouth went up in the corner. "Mr. Elanovitch is back," he said. "The guy just doesn't know when to quit. This time we've really got him."

Bradley matched his grin, and he felt the wild blood rising in his veins. But the practical side of him made itself felt, too.

"Say, sir, can we keep him until after moonrise?" Bradley asked, hoping he didn't sound too eager. "Mr. Elanovitch and I have a lot to talk about."

K.D. Wentworth has sold more than seventy pieces of short fiction to such markets as *The Magazine of Fantasy & Science Fiction*, *Alfred Hitchcock's Mystery Magazine*, *Realms of Fantasy*, *Weird Tales*, *Sword and Sorceress 23*, *Witch Way to the Mall*, and *Return to the Twilight Zone*. Four of her stories have been Finalists for the Nebula Award for Short Fiction. Currently, she has seven novels in print, the most recent being *The Course of Empire*, written with Eric Flint and published by Baen. She lives in Tulsa with her husband and a combined total of one hundred sixty pounds of dog (Akita + Siberian Husky) and is working on several new novels with Flint. Website: *http://www.kdwentworth.com*.

Special Needs

K.D. Wentworth

"When will I get my Howling badge?" eight-year-old Hunter demanded as he came in through the back door, bringing a surge of crisp fall air with him. He was swinging the road-kill raccoon that Annemarie had tied on a string. "Paco already has his."

"Paco is almost a year older," Annemarie said from the table while she opened the packages of blue and gold plastic cups. "Daddy told you—howling comes to the Sharp-Toothed Folk when it's ready. It can't be rushed."

"I just don't want to be the last in my den." He held up the dead raccoon like a stringer of fish and grinned. "What should I do with this?"

Annemarie had spent all week checking out road kill on local streets, trying to locate just the right carcass, one that smelled strongly enough to help the boys earn their Cub Scout Tracking badge. Her nose twitched. She'd found this one two days ago, and it was marvelously odorous, if she did say so herself. "Did you lay the scent trail around the backyard?"

"Yes." He jiggled the string so that the expired raccoon danced just above the kitchen's blue-flowered tiles. Its dead eyes stared and it looked almost alive again in a tantalizing sort of way. She felt half inclined to pounce on it herself.

"Then hide the carcass out in the trash can—and no rolling on it! I don't care how good it smells. Wash your hands when you come back in so you don't give the game away." She glanced at the clock. "They'll be here any minute."

The door creaked as her son ducked back outside. Patiently, she filled the little plastic cups with cherry Kool-Aid and arranged them on the snacks table, alternating blue with gold for the traditional Cub Scout colors. She thought they looked nice though the pattern wouldn't survive the den meeting's initial feeding onslaught. Still, the effort at stylishness cheered her. Martha Stewart would have approved—if she wasn't in stir.

Hunter had just finished washing his hands when the doorbell rang. He dashed to the front door. "Paco!" she heard him say as she set the brownies next to the platter of raw chicken legs, then, "Justin!" Feet pounded into the house, accompanied by giggling. Voices mumbled, then Hunter shouted, "Mom!"

Sighing, Annemarie brushed a brownie crumb off the table and headed to the door. To her surprise, a red-haired woman with the predatory smile of a lynx stood there. She wore an elegantly cut ivory business suit, three inch matching spike heels, and had a restraining hand on the shoulder of a fidgety, doughy-cheeked boy in full Cub Scout uniform.

The woman thrust out a hand with manicured blood-red nails. She had a manic gleam in her eye. "I'm Sheila

Wilson. We moved into the red-brick house down the street last week. I hope you don't mind us dropping in on you like this, but my son, Eric-Hayden, is in your boy's class at school and Hunter said you were having a den meeting today." She glanced over her shoulder at a gleaming ice-blue Chevy Tahoe idling at the curb. A silver-haired man rolled down the window and pointed at his massive gold wristwatch.

"Yes, but—" Annemarie said.

"Eric-Hayden was a Cub Scout back in Lansing before we moved," the Wilson woman went on in a rush, "and he's working on his Wolf badge, just like Hunter. He's dying to join a new den so that he doesn't get behind." Sheila urged the stocky boy into Annemarie's white tile vestibule which seemed to immediately shrink. "Say hello, darling."

Eric-Hayden only scowled and ducked his head. His hair was cut so close to the scalp, she couldn't tell its color. "This . . . is a . . . a special needs den," Annemarie said hastily as the boy spotted the snacks table and lurched past her, gathering speed with each step like a small locomotive. "We're invitation-only."

"Special needs?" the woman said. Her brow knitted in distress. "Oh, I'm so sorry, but you'll find that Eric-Hayden is not the least bit prejudiced against, well, *slower* children."

"It's not that—" Annemarie said.

"It will be good for Eric-Hayden to deal with the less fortunate," Sheila said. "In fact, there's probably a badge for it." Her fixed smile broadened, which Annemarie would have bet was impossible, then the woman leaned around her. "Have a lovely time with your new friends, darling!"

Annemarie shook her head. "I'm sorry! You—you can't—"

"I'll pick him up at five." Sheila Wilson whirled and dashed back down the steps, her spike heels clicking on the pavement, just as the last two members of Sharp-Toothed Den 1410, Spense and Topher, arrived and gave Annemarie the special Den Snarl, complete with clawing fingers.

Numbly, she returned the sign as the Tahoe drove off. In the dining room, she could hear shouting. "Hey, Butt-Face, we don't eat snacks until Mom says!" Hunter was telling Eric-Hayden, whose cheeks already bulged with brownie.

Annemarie took a deep calming breath and joined the fray. "We don't call each other Butt-Face here," she said firmly. "Cub Scouts are always courteous."

Hunter circled the intruder, head cocked to one side. A low growl rattled in his throat as he took in the new scent, then, to her relief, settled into his dad's recliner. Her mind whirled. Once the meeting was over, she would convince the boy's parents to find another, more conventional den. There had to be at least three out here in Windsor Heights Rancho Estates. For now, they would all just do their best to get through the next hour without betraying any hint of the "special" nature of Den 1410.

She maneuvered Eric-Hayden into an extra chair, then picked up her list. "Everyone, sit down," she said. "As you can see, we have a visitor today, Eric-Hayden Wilson from Lansing."

"Call me Smudge," the boy said. He had chocolate smeared on his nose. "Everyone back home did."

Paco and Spense laughed. Annemarie gave them her best shut-up-or-I'll-rip-your-throat-out look. "Now," she said, straightening her blue and gold Scout neckerchief, "Is everyone ready for the Mom and Me Moonlight Run on Sunday night?"

The five heads nodded.

"Great," she said. "I'll be calling your mothers with the details." She ticked that item off her list. "Don't forget that the district Pack meeting will be on the fifteenth." They nodded again. "Did you all have a good week?"

Justin, pale, tow-headed, and the smallest member of the den, gave them all a joyful gap-toothed grin. "I howled last night!"

Hunter bolted to his feet, the hair on the back of his neck bristling. "Did not!"

"Yes, I did!" Justin said, rising. "You can ask my dad."

"Liar!" Hunter bellowed. His eyes flashed the fiery orange of impending *change* as he launched himself across the room, growling and snapping, and knocked Justin to the floor.

Not here and now, especially in front of an outsider! It was the nearness of the full moon, Annemarie told herself as she pulled her snarling son off Justin. That always brought out their wildness. She held onto Hunter's struggling body with both arms. "It doesn't matter!" she whispered. "It *will* come."

"No, it won't," Hunter said. He turned in her arms and his eyes faded from dangerous orange back to safely blue. "Everyone else will get their howl and I'll just be a voiceless nothing!"

She smoothed his black hair. "We'll talk about it later. Now, sit down and behave yourself!"

Head hanging, Hunter retrieved his Cub Scout cap and returned to his seat.

Eric-Hayden was watching the scene with startled gray eyes, but Annemarie saw that he hadn't been too alarmed to lose the opportunity to score another brownie. "Aren't we going to say the Cub Scout Promise?" he said, crumbs dribbling from his mouth to the freshly vacuumed beige carpet. "That's how my old den always started a meeting."

Paco and Topher obligingly bolted to their feet and raised their right hands in the traditional Cub Scout salute. "I promise—to do my best—not to bite anyone," they recited in singsong fashion, "claw the upholstery—mark my territory inside the house—or—"

"We're going to skip that this week," Annemarie said hastily. "Our Promise is a little different from the one that most dens do. We don't want to confuse Eric-Hayden."

"Smudge!" the boy said. "I hate being called Eric-Hayden!"

"So," she said, "any other achievements to report?"

Topher waved his hand. He was a lanky boy with a thatch of unruly brown hair that always reminded her of a pelt, a perfect example of a child of the Sharp-Toothed Folk. "I chased an old lady across the street."

The other boys giggled.

"That's not exactly the way it's supposed to go," Annemarie said, reaching deep for patience. "You're supposed to *help* her."

"I was helping," Topher said. "She was so slow, she'd never have made it across before the light changed without me snapping at her heels."

She folded her hands, striving for calm. "Good intentions do count, but, next time, *escort* the elderly person, no matter how long it takes. Chasing and snapping are considered very rude by ordinary people. You'll never get your Wolf badge that way."

"Told you!" Justin whispered under his breath and Topher bristled. The two stared defiantly into one another's eyes.

Annemarie sighed and stepped between them. Den meetings this close to a full moon were always a bit tetchy. "Now," she said with a determined smile, "we're going to work on our Tracking badges."

"What kind of tracks?" Eric-Hayden said. "Bear prints?"

"Not that kind of tracking, dodo," Hunter said, his head cocked scornfully. "Scent tracking, you know, with your nose."

"Oh." Eric-Hayden looked longingly at the table. "Can I have another brownie?"

"Not yet," Annemarie said. "Let's go outside and see how well we do with the scent Hunter put down." With a whoop, the five Sharp-Toothed boys dashed out to the backyard.

Eric-Hayden just stared at her. "Outside?" he said, as though she'd proposed hiking down into the Grand Canyon.

"Come on," she said. "It will be fun."

He hung back, head low. "I'm not very good at games."

"You can just watch," she said, pulling on a thick blue sweater. "Hunter can't play either because he laid the trail." She reached for his hand. The child hesitated, then took hers.

Outside, the October light was fading and the wind was gloriously brisk. The boys were wrestling, play-snarling, and covering themselves in bits of dead grass and leaves. "That's enough," she said and they all, more or less, quit, save for a few final surreptitious punches. "Now, who wants to go first?"

"Me!"

"Me!"

"No, me!" Spense and Justin got into a shoving match.

"Stop that!" she said, separating the boisterous pair. She had to admit, despite his size, Justin gave as good as he got. He probably *had* howled last night. "Topher can have the first run." She motioned him forward. "Try to pick up the scent."

Topher closed his eyes as he prowled the yard. "Here!" he said triumphantly by the porch steps. "Raccoon! Really really dead raccoon!"

"Very good," she said. "Now—"

Eric-Hayden tugged at her hand. "Can I try?"

"Not today," she said, knowing his human senses would fail miserably. She turned to the rest and pulled the stopwatch out of her pocket. "Now, Topher, follow the trail through the yard and I'll time you. Everyone else turn around." Justin, Spense, and Paco obeyed without an argument. Scent games were only fun, of course, if you sniffed out the trail yourself. Otherwise it was like working a crossword in which someone had already written all the answers. "Go!" She clicked the stopwatch.

Topher swung his head back and forth, then pounced on the scent. She could almost see his ears quiver. The full moon was coming on fast. Thank heavens the meeting hadn't fallen on the very day. They'd all probably be squabbling over the steaming remains of Eric-Hayden's carcass by now and then there would have been hell to pay with the local Boy Scout Council. Her own ears, in fact, felt a bit mobile at the moment and Eric-Hayden smelled far more like *warm hamburger* to her than *boy*.

Topher dashed around the yard, losing the scent at the swing set, then picking it back up by the hose reel. She clicked the stopwatch off as he ended at the north fence gate. "Two minutes, twenty seconds! Excellent! Now, Paco, it's your turn."

One by one, the remaining three ran the scent trail, with bonus points going to Justin, who even smelled out the dead raccoon in the trash can. She let them remove the lid so that everyone got a good long sniff. Eric-Hayden watched in silence.

"Paco had the best time, but all of you did very well," she said as they trooped, rosy-cheeked with the chill, back inside. They were happily punching one another as she handed out plates and cups, letting the boys serve themselves from the snacks. She sat down and bit into a brownie, listening to them chatter.

Five minutes later, the doorbell rang. Hunter ran to answer it, then reappeared with Sheila Wilson.

"Eric-Hayden, darling, did you have a good ti—" Mrs. Wilson stopped in midstride, one ivory pump suspended in the air. She gazed in shock at a half-eaten raw chicken leg on Justin's plate.

Great Devourer! Annemarie had forgotten about the platter of chicken *au naturel*. This close to the full moon, the den preferred their meat ultrafresh, but she should have put it back in the refrigerator after their unexpected guest arrived. "My goodness, we—must have had an oven malfunction!"

Smiling grimly, she circled the living room, retrieving the chicken legs, piling them on her own plate over the scouts' protests, coming last to Justin. When she reached for his chicken, the boy sank his teeth into the uncooked flesh and growled. His eyes glimmered orange. "Justin, let me have that," she said, wondering if she was going to get bitten.

He only growled louder.

"They're so territorial at this age," Annemarie said over her shoulder to Sheila Wilson as though all boys behaved like this. She turned and concealed the plate behind her back. Fortunately, Eric-Hayden's portion had been untouched. Justin worried at his chicken leg, still snarling. She eased in front of him to block Sheila's view. "It was lovely to have Eric-Hayden as a visitor," Annemarie said, when the woman didn't respond. "But I'm sure that we can find him another, more appropriate den."

"My name is Smudge!" Eric-Hayden said. "And I like this den! They do really cool stuff. I want to stay!"

"Your stepfather is out in the car," Sheila said. Her face was wooden. "And you know how he hates being kept waiting."

"What about the Mom and Me Moonlight Run?" Hunter asked. "Is Smudge going on that?"

"No," Annemarie said. "He—"

"A run?" Sheila seized Eric-Hayden's hand and levered him onto his feet. "How lovely! I've been competing for years, especially 5K's."

"It's been—um—cancelled!" Annemarie knew she was babbling. "I just hadn't had the chance to tell the boys."

"Oh." Sheila's crimson lipstick smile was poisonous. She gazed at Hunter, her carefully made-up eyes narrowed. "So sad about the special needs," she said, then dragged her unwilling son to the door. "That one looks almost normal."

Later, after the rest of the boys had gone home, Annemarie and Monty, her husband and Hunter's father, had a little talk with Hunter over dessert.

"You know everyone in your den is from the Sharp-Toothed Folk." Annemarie passed Hunter a slice of blood-chocolate cake.

He took it, his eyes downcast. "Yes."

"So, if we are going to have the kind of activities we like, we can't invite ordinary people. They won't understand."

"I didn't invite him, Mom." Hunter only picked at his cake, even though Annemarie knew it was his favorite, the batter having been enriched with a full cup of chicken blood. His fork clinked on the plate. "He heard me on the playground talking to Topher."

"Then don't mention den meetings at school," Monty said. "We can't have this kind of slipup again."

"Sorry, Dad," Hunter said as the phone rang.

Annemarie rose and went to the kitchen to answer. "Hello?"

"Mrs. Donohue, this is Sheila Wilson."

"Yes?" she said, heart racing. Had the boy eaten some of the raw chicken after all and fallen ill?

"Eric-Hayden still wants to join your den."

"But—"

"The special needs stuff doesn't matter to him," Sheila said. "In fact, just between you and me, there's been some talk from his teachers from time to time that he might be a trifle on the special needs side himself."

"I—"

"Not that I ever believed it for a second!" Sheila said. "His biological father was a flake, but he wasn't a moron. The child is just an underachiever. He could make A's if he wanted."

"We'll find him a regular den," Annemarie said, desperate to get in a word or two herself. "I'm sure there are some—"

"For whatever reason, he likes *this* one," Sheila said. "If you won't accept him, I'll just have to file a complaint with the local Boy Scout Council. That little *faux pas* with the undercooked chicken would have to be mentioned under those circumstances. I'm sure you understand."

Annemarie's pulse was thundering. She felt distinctly furry behind the ears and could almost smell Sheila's hot prey scent through the phone line. "I—see."

"Nothing personal," said Sheila, "but I have to look out for my darling boy's interests. I expect you to provide a full schedule for the den's activities in the coming weeks via Hunter tomorrow at school, and of course I will be glad to take my turn providing *healthy* snacks at the meetings. You'll find that I make an exquisite fruit-cup."

Annemarie felt her fingernails lengthening into claws, her hair standing on end. A growl rattled deep in her throat.

"Let me know when the Mom and Me Moonlight Run has been rescheduled." The connection clicked off.

Annemarie hung up and prowled back to the dining room table.

"Wow, Mom, your eyes are way cool!" Hunter bounced in his seat.

"That must have been some conversation," her husband said, leaning back in his chair.

"You could say that." Unable to settle, Annemarie went to the refrigerator and rummaged for the leftover raw chicken legs, then microwaved one just long enough to simulate living body temperature. When the timer dinged, she snatched it out and tore off a bite. The uncooked flesh tasted simply delicious, a treat she rarely allowed herself during the darker nights of the month.

So. Chewing, she stared out the kitchen window into the inviting darkness. Light from the filling moon silvered the swing set and garbage cans. Every fiber of her being longed to rush into the night and chase down something small and terrified, then tear it to quivering bits.

Patience, she told herself, ripping off another mouthful of raw chicken. The full moon was only three days away and it seemed they were to have company.

Annemarie volunteered at the Boris Karloff Elementary School library on Fridays, so she took a den schedule by the boys' class and used the opportunity to observe Eric-Hayden. He was a plodder, it turned out, the kind who just put his head down and soldiered on, completing the assignment even though he obviously had no idea what the lesson was about.

She had to admire that kind of tenacity. Sharp-Toothed children were not always the best of students either, especially close to the full moon. They tended to be distractible and crotchety, not to mention extremely touch-and-scent-dominant, relying on their noses and hands for information rather than eyes and ears. Educators often didn't know how to handle them.

When their teacher, Mrs. Solly, brought the class to the library after lunch, Hunter was positively bristling. Annemarie left the check-out desk to take him aside. "What's the matter?"

Hunter glared at Eric-Hayden who was sitting at a table, thumbing through a kindergarten level picture book about balloons titled *Poppie's Big Date*. "He's telling everyone!"

"About what?" she whispered.

"About the dead raccoon!" A growl rattled low in her son's throat. His eyes glimmered orange for a second, then subsided.

"I'll talk to him," she said, patting his shoulder. Hunter nodded, the hair on the back of his neck still standing on end, and returned to prowl the bookshelves.

Annemarie sat down next to the boy. "Eric-Hayden," she said.

"Smudge!" he said, clasping the book to his chest as though she would take it away.

"Smudge," she said, "I hear you're telling other students about yesterday's den meeting."

"So?" He opened the book and stared at the illustration of a prissy orange balloon decked out with a girlish hairdo. Annemarie thought it looked demented.

She pulled the book down to meet his gray eyes. "Didn't you have a good time?"

He sighed. "Yes."

"Well, if you tell everyone about the *special* things we do, then we can't do them anymore," she said. "Den 1410 keeps those kinds of activities to ourselves."

"You mean they're a secret," he said, turning the page to study a leering purple balloon jazzed up with a bow tie and top hat. It had, it seemed, designs on the orange balloon.

"Yes," she said, glancing over her shoulder to make sure the Mrs. Giles, the librarian, wasn't overhearing this conversation. "Things like tracking the dead raccoon are a secret."

"Secrets are bad," he said doggedly. "Kids aren't supposed to keep secrets."

"Not from your parents, no," she said, "but Cub Scouts keep each others' secrets."

"They do?" His eyes rose from the page to gaze up at her.

"If they want to belong to Den 1410, they sure do," she said. "Though, we can find you a different den where they don't have secrets, if that's what you want."

"No," he said in a small voice. His fingers tightened on the book. "We never had any fun in my old den. We just cut things out of stupid construction paper and ate carrot sticks."

Annemarie stood and realized there was a line of children waiting over at the check-out desk. She had to get back to work. "Do you want to take that book home?"

"No," Eric-Hayden said. "I've read it before. It's really scary. At the end, there's a girl with a pin."

On Sunday, the night of the full moon, Annemarie packed a cooler with raw hamburger and liver, her contribution to the den picnic scheduled after the traditional Mom and Me Moonlight Run. Monty was going howling up on Bartlett Hill first with the other Cub Scout dads, then would meet them later at the picnic grounds.

Her ears had already gone distinctly pointed. It always felt so darned good to lose the cumbersome human form and revel in her pent-up energy.

Hunter's eyes were a glimmering orange and the backs of his hands furred. He bounced in his seat in the car. "This is going to be so great!" he said. "I can't wait!"

Last year, the moms and Scouts had flushed a coyote, any number of rabbits, and three deer. The deer had led them through the greenbelt skirting the suburbs for an hour, their hot scent like ambrosia in the night. Hunter's legs had been even shorter then, but he'd done a great job of keeping up.

"Maybe we'll actually run something down this year!" he said, his voice low and growly.

She smiled and felt how sharp her teeth had become in the last few minutes. "Maybe!"

They parked their Toyota SUV in the park's lot which adjoined the suburb's main greenbelt. Hunter shucked his clothes in the back seat, *changed* into his adorably furred shape, and then she opened the door for him. The other boys had already transformed and were scuffling in the grass in their wolf forms, play-mauling one another. Snarling happily, he leaped into the fray.

Overhead, the moon was rising, gloriously full. Stars glittered and the whole night world was limned with silver. The other four moms, already *changed*, waited at the trees' edge, ears eager. Annemarie locked her purse in the trunk, hung the car key around her neck on a chain, then headed for the park Ladies Room to *change*. Her human shape felt stodgy and stiff-legged. She so looked forward to this moment each full moon.

An ice-blue Tahoe pulled up. Annemarie stopped, alarmed as the front doors swung open. Sheila and Eric-Hayden Wilson climbed out. Sheila was wearing a velvet dark-blue jogging suit. Eric-Hayden was shivering in a hoodie and sweat pants.

"Hi!" Sheila waved at her, then bent at the waist to touch her toes. "Where's the starting point?"

Annemarie glanced at the five scuffling wolf cubs. "How—?"

"Not with your help, that's for sure!" Sheila snapped. "There was certainly nothing about tonight on the information sheet you gave Eric-Hayden. Topher Cooney had to tell us."

One by one, the cubs stopped playing and oriented on the newcomers. Their eyes gleamed orange and at least one of them was growling. Their mothers sensibly faded into the trees.

"I'm afraid everyone else has already started," Annemarie said, trying to make her startled brain think. "Hunter went ahead with them. I'm—staying behind to watch the cars."

"Where did all those puppies come from?" Eric-Hayden said, his eyes wide. "Can I play with them?"

"They're—strays," Annemarie said. "Shoo, puppies!" She waved them toward the hidden moms, but they didn't take the hint. "Go home!"

"Stay away from the nasty things, darling," Sheila said. "They probably have fleas and all kinds of diseases."

Several of the Sharp-Toothed cubs yipped at the insult.

"Well, we'd better get started," Sheila said, pulling a leg up behind her thigh to stretch her quadriceps. "I'm pretty fast, though, so I bet we can catch up. Where's the path?"

"Over there." Annemarie pointed at the easement which had been long ago cleared for the high tension lines. "It's a mile run to the end and then back again." And by the time the two of them returned, the den could be safely gone, she thought.

"Come on, Eric-Hayden!" Sheila said, then jogged toward the open corridor through the trees. Giving the cubs one last longing look, the boy lowered his head and plodded after her.

Annemarie sat on the bumper of her Toyota as they disappeared into the greenbelt. That had been entirely too close! Another five minutes and Sheila would have caught her trotting out of the Ladies Room in full wolf form.

Darla Cooney, Topher's mother, loped up and then transformed back so that she was crouched at Annemarie's feet in her naked skin. "What was that all about?"

"Evidently Topher told Eric-Hayden about the run tonight," Annemarie said. "We have to call it off."

The Sharp-Toothed cubs turned to Topher, who was a bit taller at the shoulder than the rest, then all four leaped on him, biting in earnest this time.

"No, no, stop that!" Annemarie and Darla waded in, pulling them off by the scruff of their necks. "It doesn't matter whose fault it is now. We just have to fix it."

Darla stalked off to the Ladies Room to retrieve her clothes, obviously smoldering from the stiff set of her shoulders. Annemarie wouldn't have wanted to be in Topher's furry hide at that moment. "*Change* back, all of you," she told the den.

Four of them did so that Topher, Spense, Justin, and Paco knelt by the picnic table, but her own son, Hunter, remained stubbornly wolf. "You, too, mister," she said, "on the double!"

Hunter snarled, ears pinned, then dashed toward the greenbelt, disappearing into the cleared corridor where the Wilsons were jogging to catch up with people who weren't there.

Darla returned, pulling on a sweat shirt. "Where's Hunter?"

"The little wretch followed the Wilsons," she said, thoroughly vexed. "I guess I'll have to go after him."

The other three mom wolves walked out of the trees, bristling. Darla shook her head. "Go ahead. We'll alert the dads not to show up in their fur."

Annemarie left her clothes in the Ladies Room, *changed*, and dashed after Hunter. It did feel good to stretch out and run on all fours. The scent was laid down, hot and fresh. She would give that boy such a thrashing when she caught up!

Fifteen minutes later, she found her cub prowling through the trees along the greenbelt. Sheila Wilson was still jogging, but Eric-Hayden had slowed to a walk and was rapidly falling behind. She poked Hunter with her nose. "Get back to the park!"

His orange eyes turned to her. "Something's weird, Mom."

She bared her teeth, resisting the urge to seize him by the scruff of his neck. "No excuses!"

"Smell him," he said, glancing back at Eric-Hayden.

Hackles raised, she snarled.

Hunter dropped to the ground, eyes turned away, submitting wolf-fashion. "Mom, I mean it! Smell him!"

She inhaled and let the scent molecules dance through her head. An instant later, recognition clicked into place. Her tail drooped. *That*—couldn't be right.

"You smell it, too, don't you?" Hunter said.

"He's not—" He couldn't be. She would have known right away, the moment Eric-Hayden walked through the door.

"He's Sharp-Toothed Folk," Hunter said, "though the scent is not very strong."

"He must not be pureblood," Annemarie said as they watched the boy fall more and more behind. "Not even halfblood, I think, maybe only a quarter or an eighth." Diluted blood meant he could have gone through his entire life never knowing the potential locked up in his genes if he hadn't come in contact with the den's intense Sharp-Toothed pheromones under the full moon.

Sheila disappeared around the bend and Eric-Hayden stopped, thoroughly winded, staring after his mother resentfully.

"I'll get him," Hunter said and loped out of the trees before she could stop him.

Sighing, she padded after him. The proverbial fat was really in the fire now.

"Puppy!" Eric-Hayden said to Hunter and sagged to his knees, arms open. "You followed me!" His eyebrows had gone distinctly shaggy and his teeth and ears were a bit pointy.

Good thing his mom was far ahead, Annemarie thought. She would have been hysterical if she'd gotten a good look at this. Eric-Hayden must have inherited the connection to the Sharp-Toothed Folk from his absent father's line.

"Puppy, you smell good!" Eric-Hayden was *changing* faster now, fur springing up on his face and hands. Obviously the Sharp-Toothed pheromones were doing their job.

Annemarie felt a sudden rush of tenderness towards this lost cub. What would it be like to grow up experiencing even a hint of what she felt each full moon without understanding what it meant or what to do about it? "Eric-Hayden," she said, "I know it feels good to *change*, but we can't let your mom see this."

"Yeah," Hunter said. "She would totally freak out!"

"My name is Smudge," the boy said automatically, then stared at the two wolves. "You can talk!"

"Big deal," Hunter said. "So can you."

"But—" The boy's mouth gaped and he gazed around the moon-silvered trees and undergrowth, seeming to realize suddenly he was alone with two wild animals. He stumbled back. "Mom!"

Annemarie nosed him gently. "Look at your hands."

His gaze dropped to his fur-covered hands. "Whoa!"

"Dude, you're part of the Sharp-Toothed Folk," Hunter said. "Didn't you ever *change* like this before?"

"In—in my dreams sometimes I dream that I'm a wolf," Eric-Hayden whispered, his eyes glimmering a faint orange. "Mom even took me to a doctor about it. He said it's not real."

"It's totally real," Hunter said. "This is so cool!" He frisked around the boy, play-bowing, then nipping his ear.

"Eric-Hayden!" Sheila's voice came through the night.

"*Change* back now!" Annemarie said. She could hear the woman's running feet.

"I—don't know how!" The boy's eyes filled with tears.

"Show him," she told Hunter.

Hunter's furry outline shimmered, then he was a boy again, albeit a completely naked one.

"Hey, what happened to your clothes?" Eric-Hayden said.

"Eric-Hayden!" Sheila called, her panicked voice closer now.

"Close your eyes and think *human!*" Annemarie said.

"Come on, Smudge, you can do it!" Hunter said.

She *changed* back herself and then put her hands on his shoulders. "Breathe slowly," she said. "Concentrate on being ordinary, perfectly perfectly ordinary."

His orange-tinted eyes closed obediently. She felt his breath slow. The fur . . . retracted. His teeth and ears rounded back into normal configurations.

"Great!" she hugged him, then slipped again into wolf form. "Bring your mom to the park when she gets here."

Hunter *changed* back too and then mother and son raced away through the night, nipping at one another in their exuberance at being out in their true skins under a glorious full moon.

Monty and the other dads were already there sitting at a concrete picnic table, when the two of them got back, all the men in human form again and decidedly miffed. It wasn't often they were able to get together for a fun night of howling. Annemarie loped on to the Ladies Room where she *changed* and dressed.

The boys were playing a half-hearted game of catch when Eric-Hayden and Sheila walked out of the greenbelt. "Oh, there you are," Sheila said with a tight forced smile. "You said the course was just down and back. Why didn't we pass anyone?"

"The others decided to return through the trees," Annemarie said. "They didn't know you were trying to catch up."

"Well, it certainly wasn't much of a run," Sheila said, "and I have some phone calls to return, so we should just go home."

"Mom, no!" Eric-Hayden turned to Annemarie, hands fisted.

"We could take him home in our car after the picnic and games," Annemarie said, "if you like."

"I don't know," Sheila said. "He seemed a little peaked out there. He couldn't keep up with me at all."

"I'm fine!" Eric-Hayden said, hopping on one foot in demonstration. "Let me stay, please!"

Sheila's cellphone rang and she pulled it out of her pocket. "It's your stepfather," she said, checking the number. "All right, but don't be late. Tomorrow is a school day." She flipped the phone open and talked all the way back to the Tahoe.

Hunter watched until the blue SUV drove away, then turned to her. "Now, Mom?"

When the tail lights rounded the corner, she smiled. "Yes, go ahead and *change* back." The five boys dashed into the trees to discard their clothes. Eric-Hayden watched them.

"First you have to undress," she said softly. "You won't need clothes—after."

He bit his lip, then lumbered toward the trees.

The five Sharp-Toothed cubs emerged, running and leaping, growling, bowling each other over in the moon-silvered grass. Eric-Hayden pulled off his hoodie and entered the woods. Annemarie held her breath. He'd had a dose of pheromones as well as exposure to the full moon, but would he be able to *change* all the way with his diluted blood? Maybe Monty should coach him through his first time. She turned to her husband. "Could—"

A wolf cub edged out of the forest, big-shouldered and a bit paunchy in the middle, awkward and shy. He lifted his feet one at a time as though unsure what to do with them. The other five Scouts halted their play-brawl and stared, eyes bright, ears pricked. Paco raised his head and howled in welcome, joined after a second by tiny Justin. Spense and Topher hung their heads, mute. Like Hunter, their howls hadn't come yet.

Hunter, though, circled the newcomer, tail high, eyes a brilliant full-moon orange, then threw back his muzzle and let loose with a marvelous deep-throated howl that sent tingles down Annemarie's spine. All the parents erupted in applause.

She dropped to her knees and held out her arms. Hunter leaped, knocking her down. Laughing, she buried her face in his silken fur as her clever boy nipped her ear in Sharp-Toothed joy.

On a good day, Tracy S. Morris has photographed two of the Presidents of the United States. On a bad day, she's been dragged behind a speedboat on an icy lake in freezing rain. She's been a photographer, reporter, writer, fencer, historian, costumer and gardener. She is a black belt in tae kwon do, and a self-confessed kamikaze speller. Tracy is the author of the "Tranquility" novellas, which are available from Yard Dog Press, and writes paranormal articles for Firefox News. She currently lives in Fort Smith, Arkansas with her husband and two dogs. Find her on the web at *http://www.tracysmorris.com*.

Fish Story

Tracy S. Morris

"Be glad I came along, Celeste. I know how these suburbanites are. They'll wait until you're not looking, then sneak up and bite you. Before you know it, you'll crave half-caf mocha lattes and drive a minivan when the moon is full."

Celeste looked from her notes to the well-manicured lawns and cookie-cutter red brick houses of *Branson Estates*, as the rented silver Taurus glided past. Then she shot a sideways glance at Lucky. His lip was curled up into a sneer.

City wolf goes to the country. She shook her head. "You're a sensitive man, Lucky."

"I'm in touch with my feminine side." Lucky put one hand over his heart. "Every lunar cycle I become very moody."

"Moody. That's one way of looking at it." Celeste frowned. "You also try to eat the face off anyone who'll come within reach."

"All part of my charm," Lucky said. "Why do you think I have so many werewolf groupies?"

"Why did I bring you along again?"

Lucky smirked at her. "Because I'm cute and fuzzy and you like to scratch my ears."

"No, that's why *you* like me. You're the guy who keeps showing up on my doorstep when there's something unseelie you want me to go step on like I'm some kind of arcane Orkin man."

"I thought *you* asked for *my* help on this trip." Lucky showed off his razor-sharp canine teeth when he smiled. "Something about a story that was going to get you off the copy editing desk and onto the front page at your newspaper? What was it you said? 'I need a fuzzy armored tank to back me up.'"

"So you keep reminding me," Celeste muttered as she turned back to her map.

An uncomfortable silence fell over the car until eventually, Lucky cleared his throat. "Three disappearances?"

"That's what my cousin, Elvis, said. Something out in Table Rock Lake sucked a couple of fishermen and a tourist down. They still haven't found the bodies. It could just be giant catfish, but it might be something more."

"Wait—your cousin is named Elvis?"

"Yes."

"Who names their child Elvis?"

"The Presley family?"

"You guys really are from Dogpatch, aren't you?"

Celeste tilted her head. "Got it in one."

Lucky blinked. "Really? I was joking, but . . . there's really a Dogpatch?"

"Not anymore," Celeste shook her head. "It was in Arkansas. There used to be an amusement park. Uncle

Merle played Li'l Abner." She shifted her gaze to the road ahead. "Turn here."

Lucky steered the rental onto a rocky dirt road. Low-hanging tree branches hung like claws, scraping the roof of the vehicle as they passed. When Lucky's foot moved from the gas to the brake, Celeste leaned over to get a better look at the speedometer. With a stab of annoyance, she realized that they were only going five miles per hour. "You know, we can speed up."

"Not if I want to get my deposit back on this rental," Lucky said. "They take money off for a damaged paint job."

"I told you we were going to the suburbs."

"Yeah, but I was thinking Bree Van de Kamp, not Jed Clampett. Does your cousin live out here?"

"He lives closer to the strip. We're going to Table Rock Lake first. I want to scry around. Pull off here."

The road wound past a clearing on the lakefront with a picnic table. Lucky pulled up next to the table and parked. The sounds of cicadas filled Celeste's ears and heat and humidity saturated her the moment she opened the car door.

Before them, Table Rock Lake stretched out like a giant mirror. The weedy embankment sloped gently away from the picnic table. Celeste and Lucky hiked down to a point where the land extended in a long thin finger out into the placid water.

Her eyes remained fixed on the surface as she felt the area with her extra senses. Somewhere out in the lake she felt a dark presence. Something out there had intelligence and malevolent will. Despite the heat, an arcane chill raised gooseflesh up her arms. She rubbed her hands up and down them.

"Do you sense something?" Lucky asked.

She nodded slowly as she tested the feel of the thing. Under the force of her attention it twisted away.

She growled in frustration. "I can't get a lock on it. I need to get closer."

Lucky nodded to the spit of sandy dirt that stretched out into the water. "Maybe out there?"

"It's worth a try."

The sandy ground sank under their feet as they walked onto the stretch of land. Once they reached the very tip, she stretched out her senses again. To her dismay, Celeste couldn't sense the dark presence.

"It's not here anymore."

"That's a good thing, right?" Lucky asked.

"Maybe," she shrugged. "It may have moved on to a deeper part of the lake. Or maybe it's just lurking. Waiting for us to leave."

"That's comforting." His own head turned slowly as he scanned the area. Suddenly, he paused and squinted while shading his eyes from the sun.

"What?"

Lucky frowned. "I thought I saw something." He craned his neck and stared out at the still water.

Without warning, a large shape erupted from the depths. It arrowed up the shore at them with preternatural speed. Celeste had the briefest impression of water glistening as it streamed from the body of a dark, angular creature. Even as she jerked away from the thing, she snapped an arcane shield around herself.

Then Lucky was between her and the creature, a solid, safe barrier of muscle and bone.

With distance, she could see that it resembled a shark: bulbous eyes, row upon row of sharp teeth, nose like an arrow. Lucky locked his arms around it. His biceps bulged through the shirt he wore as he tried to wrestle it back into the water.

Celeste's heart sped up as she watched her best friend tangle with the beast. She knew that he didn't have nearly enough strength now—with the full moon several weeks away—to combat the shark.

I've got to do something. She scanned up and down the beach for some kind of weapon that she might use to help Lucky. Then her eyes fell on a large rock. She chewed on her bottom lip as she watched the two grapple for mastery. *Aren't sharks supposed to be sensitive at the tips of their noses?* She picked up the rock, ran up to the struggle and pelted it at the beast.

The rock sailed as if guided by an unseen hand directly into the shark's nose. The monster flinched, worked its massive jaws in obvious pain and then slid ponderously back into the water.

In the wake of its leaving, Lucky stumbled. He would have fallen if Celeste hadn't been there. She locked her arms around him and pulled him to her. Where her hand touched his side she felt stickiness.

"Side hurts," he muttered.

Blood coated her hand when she pulled it away. She held her breath and glanced up the hill where they'd parked the rental.

"Lucky, can you get back to the car?"

"I'll try," he said. He leaned most of his weight on her as they shuffled back to the car.

Celeste's lungs burned as she struggled with her burden. By the time she opened the car and let him flop into the passenger seat, her legs wobbled from exhaustion. She looked down at him as he sprawled across the seat, leaking blood onto the floorboards.

I don't think we're going to get our deposit back.

She rounded to the driver's side and readjusted the seat to fit her smaller frame. *The first time he lets me drive would be when he's bleeding to death.*

Once they were under way, she did her best to keep one eye on the dirt road and one on Lucky, as she whipped the car around a turn. The car fishtailed and gravel fanned out from the back wheels. Celeste bit her lip, as she wondered if they were going to spin out. But she'd grown up on country lanes just like this one and she knew how to baby a car back onto course.

"Lucky?" She leaned over and prodded him. "Lucky!"

"What?" He opened his good eye to glare at her.

"Just wanted to let you know that if you die on me—I'm going to take up Necromancy. Then I'm going to bring you back so that I can kill you myself."

He chuckled, then winced and grabbed his side. "Are you hurt? Make sure you don't get any blood on you. Last thing we need is for you to go furry too."

Celeste ran a mental diagnostic on the thin arcane barrier she'd conjured when this whole mess started. "Not to worry. My magic shield is still up."

"You know, for someone who hates magic—you use it a whole lot."

"Yeah? And for someone who's bleeding to death—you sure talk a whole lot."

She could see a blacktop highway up ahead. Celeste set her jaw and punched the gas. The car bounced once as it crossed onto the new road and then rocketed onward.

"Where are we going?" Lucky asked.

"I'm taking you to see my cousin. He's a vet. He'll know what to do."

"A vet?"

"I'd take you to a hospital, but . . ." She flapped a hand in his direction. "Werewolf."

"I hate you."

"I know." Celeste rolled her eyes. She wondered how she got into these messes in the first place.

The sign in front of Elvis' clinic said VET, TAXIDERMY AND PET GROOMING. NO MATTER WHAT YOU GET YOUR DOG BACK. She parked the vehicle at a lopsided angle in the driveway and left the keys in the ignition and her own door open when she arrived at the clinic.

The door burst open and a man in a Lynyrd Skynyrd T-shirt and greasy black mullet came running out. Celeste squinted at him and realized that it was Elvis. Her cousin must have seen her roar up the driveway like Dale, Jr. He stopped at the edge of the lawn, and pointed a .45 at her. Immediately, she threw up her hands. Although she trusted the arcane barrier to protect her, she knew Elvis had a twitchy trigger finger.

"Cese? That you?" He squinted at her.

"It's me, Elvis. Lower the peacemaker. I got a were-wolf in the passenger seat who needs stitching up."

Before she could lift a finger to help, Elvis went to the car, put his shoulder under Lucky's arm and had him halfway back to the house.

Celeste watched as the two of them disappeared through the doorway. She stared blankly at the puddles of blood that had dripped onto the sidewalk. Through the haze of shock, she felt the prickle of eyes on her back.

She turned to see a portly man in Bermuda shorts, a wife beater and orthopedic socks staring at her with wide eyes and an open mouth. He had obviously been water-ing his azaleas when they'd pulled up. Now he was absently watering his left shoe.

Celeste jerked her thumb toward the clinic and gave Elvis' rubbernecking neighbor a shaky smile. "Mauled by a poodle," she explained. Then she turned on her heel and walked to the house. When she shut the door, he was still watering his left shoe.

Inside, Elvis had sat Lucky up on the stainless steel table and was busily stitching up his side.

"Good thing you're a werewolf, otherwise whatever it was would've bit you in two," Elvis said.

Lucky winced as Elvis stuck the needle in his ribs again. "That's what they said when I lost the one eye."

Celeste sighed in relief. "How did you lose it?" she asked.

"Jumping in front of a damsel in distress." He smiled at her lopsidedly. "The experience didn't seem to have taught me anything."

"I put up an arcane shield, you idjit." Celeste smiled to soften the meaning of her words. "Next time you jump in front of someone, try to make sure they're a little more damselish."

"I'll keep that in mind next time I've got the opportunity to jump in front of Bruce." Lucky winced again as Elvis tied off his stitches.

"You know not to lick these? Or do I have to put a giant lampshade around your neck?" Elvis asked.

Lucky rolled his eyes. "I'm sure I can manage." Then he turned to face Celeste again. "Did you get a better look at that thing? All I saw was teeth."

She scratched her nose as she remembered the attack. "Looked like a tiger shark. Pointy face, gills, stripes on the side of its body."

"It didn't behave like any kind of shark I've ever heard of," Lucky said. "It crawled up on land to get at us. What kind of shark acts like that?"

"I think I know what it was," Elvis said. He crossed the room to the counter where his cash register sat. From underneath it, he pulled out a thick book. Then he held it up so that the others could see it.

Celeste squinted at the cover. *Ozark Legends.*

"I found this at the library while waitin' on ya'll to show up," he said. "It says here that before Table Rock Lake was built, this area had a lot of logging camps. They used to buy draft horses from Scotland."

"Of course!" Celeste snapped her fingers. "A kelpie! Legends say that if you can bridle one you can force it to serve you."

Elvis nodded. "Those old Celtic tales are full of people who forced one of those unseelie things to haul the stones to build this or that castle. They probably could pull a wagonload of logs better than a whole heard of oxen."

"Kelpie?" Lucky wrinkled his forehead. "Like an Australian sheepdog?"

"No," she scoffed. "Like the Jethro Tull song."

"Oh." Lucky drew out the single syllable. "But in the song, the kelpie was a horse. Jabberjaw back there was definitely not. And for that matter, why hasn't it attacked anyone before now?"

"Who knows?" Celeste shrugged. "Maybe it just now got free. I bet if we check along the shoreline around there somewhere, we'll find a bridle washed up somewhere. The important thing is to stop it. We need to get back out to that lake," Celeste said. "This time loaded for bear."

"Thought you might say that." Elvis reached back under the counter and pulled out a couple of fireplace pokers. "The unseelie in New York hate cold iron too?" he asked Lucky.

"Can't abide it," Lucky said.

"Good. Then you know what this is for." Elvis handed him a poker.

"Why don't we just shoot it?" Lucky took the poker between his thumb and forefinger.

Elvis scoffed. "You've been watching too much TV, city boy."

"Iron is too light for small caliber weapons," Celeste explained. "It's a nice idea—but not practical. We've got to do our killing up close and personal."

Elvis led them out the front door and over to the garage. Inside sat a black four-wheel-drive pickup truck and a trailer with an aluminum fishing boat.

Lucky stopped and stared at the boat. "Wait! We are *not* going out on that lake in that!"

Celeste put her hands on her hips. "Why not?"

"Why not?" He waved at the flat-bottomed boat. "Look at it, Cese! In case you didn't notice, we're going up against a kelpie with a fire poker. We're going to need a bigger boat!"

Celeste fought off a stab of annoyance. "It's a johnboat," she said. "They were invented for poling around the rivers up here in the Ozarks. It's got a wide bottom, so it won't tip over, even if the kelpie tried to crawl up in it with us."

She turned away to climb into the truck next to Elvis. "Besides." She threw back over her shoulder at Lucky. "You want safety? Stick out your thumb and see if you can't hitch a ride on that great big paddle boat that the tourists love so much. But I'm going back out there."

She heard Lucky huff in annoyance. Then the werewolf climbed with stiff movements into the passenger seat of the truck. She looked down to hide the smug grin that battled its way onto her face.

This time, Elvis steered them through a dusty, red-dirt campground. At the one end, the road terminated with a boat ramp that sloped down to disappear into the lake.

Celeste and Lucky got out of the truck to watch as Elvis launched the boat into the water and then beached it into the red clay lakeshore. They held it there at the beach as the vet parked the truck.

Then Lucky helped the two of them into the boat and pushed it back out into the water. When he leaped into the end, the flat-bottomed boat barely rocked.

"See? Stable!" Celeste crossed her arms.

Lucky mimicked her pose. "We'll see. We haven't taken it through the sudden death match yet."

"You're a cheerful ray of sunshine," Elvis said.

"Injured. This morning," Lucky snapped.

Elvis picked up a set of controls for the trolling motor and steered it out into the lake. As they slid into deeper water, Lucky touched Celeste's arm, and pointed to the water.

She turned in time to see the water off to their right swirl a little.

"What did you see?" she peered into the dark, green depths of the water.

Lucky shrugged. "It was gone before I could get a good look."

Celeste chewed her bottom lip nervously. "Do you think it was a fish?" *Please, let it be a fish.*

"You know, I watched *Jaws* when I was little," Lucky said. "My dad told me it was based on a true story. There was a shark that swam upstream into a freshwater outlet in New York sometime around the turn of the century and killed a bunch of swimmers. After that, I wouldn't take a bath for months. Only showers."

"What got you over it?" Celeste asked.

"Dad made me watch *Psycho*," Lucky said.

Celeste blinked. "That explains a lot."

"Here," Elvis reached under his seat and produced a red nylon bag. He threw it to Lucky. The werewolf opened it to reveal a half-dozen glow sticks. Lucky raised an eyebrow.

"Might have just been a fish," Elvis said. "Also might have been a kelpie. The water is pretty shallow here. So if we light up the lakebed, we'll know."

Lucky snapped a glow stick and threw it overboard.

As the stick drifted downward it illuminated a large streamlined shape, a shape that was hurtling toward the bottom of the boat at an alarming speed. Reflexively, Celeste threw up her arcane shield again.

The boat bucked like a wild bronco. One moment she was thrown from her seat and into the bottom of it, the next she was in the air, looking down on the water. Then she plunged below the surface.

The water was icy cold. It stung like a thousand needles over the surface of her skin before fading to a chilling numbness. Celeste came up, coughing and spluttering. Water streamed from her eyes. She had just a moment to register the sounds of Lucky and Elvis shouting before the feeling of something razor-sharp clamping onto her ankle and pulling her under.

If not for the arcane shield that wrapped her skin like lightweight body armor, she might have been severely lacerated. Instead she felt the bone-grinding pain of being held in a viselike grip and pulled downward.

She kicked out with her free leg, and connected with something solid. Abruptly, the hold on her ankle vanished. She surfaced and looked around frantically.

The johnboat lay upside down, floating a few feet away. Its trolling motor rose to the sky like a rude salute. Lucky knelt on the upturned boat, clinging stubbornly with one hand to the motor and clutching the poker in the other.

As soon as he saw her, he waved frantically. "Cese! Get up here!"

Celeste scanned for Elvis, but her cousin was nowhere to be found.

With her heart hammering in her chest, she swam to the boat with long strokes that splashed whitecaps around her. Lucky extended the poker to her. She took the end, and let him hoist her onto the upturned flat bottom.

"Where's Elvis?" She jerked her head from one side of the boat to the other with wide eyes, hoping that the vet would surface.

"Over here!"

Celeste followed the sound of his voice to the lakeshore and saw Elvis standing there.

"How did you get over there?"

"Swam!" Elvis said.

"The wonders of adrenaline," Lucky muttered to her.

Celeste searched the lake for signs of whatever had attacked them. But the surface was still and no shadow flitted between the boat and the glowing light below. She grasped the trolling motor just as Lucky released it and crawled over to the edge of the boat to yell at Elvis. "Did you get a good look at it?"

"This time," he said.

"What did you see?"

"Looked like the thing that attacked us before," Lucky said. "Like a casting reject from *The Discovery Channel*:

grey skin, stripes along the sides. Lots of nasty, pointy teeth."

"Behind you!" Elvis' plaintive warning carried across the stillness of the lake. Celeste turned in time to see the kelpie arrow toward them through the water like a knife through hot butter.

Lucky recoiled, then crawled to the spot where Celeste clutched the trolling motor. He wrapped his arms around her and the motor just as the kelpie shot over the edge of the boat and started crawling toward them.

The capsized vessel rocked and pitched, but they held fast to the motor as if they were glued.

When the boat threatened to sink under their combined weight, Lucky suddenly released her and held the poker high over his head like a warrior in a bad medieval movie.

This is usually the part where the guy with the bad sword technique gets cut in two, Celeste thought. With a quick gesture and a hastily spoken word she sent a bolt of pure energy at the kelpie. The creature recoiled, causing the boat to rock unsteadily and throwing Lucky back down to the hull.

" 'It's got a wide bottom, so it won't tip over, even if the kelpie tried to crawl up in it with us,' " Lucky parroted as he tried to rise to his knees again. "Why do I ever listen to you?"

"Shut up!" Celeste snapped.

As if throwing off a stupor, Lucky shook his head. Then he lifted himself back onto his knees, held the poker aloft like a lance and aimed for the kelpie's bulbous eye.

When he threw the improvised weapon, it sailed true, striking the creature's vulnerable socket. The kelpie jerked once and shook its head. Lucky lunged for it and seized onto the poker. In one fluid motion, he pulled the weapon free, swung it in a momentum-building arc and bludgeoned the creature. This time, it jerked again and slid into the water.

Celeste compressed her lips, crawled to the side of the boat and peered into the water. In the phosphorescent light of the glow stick she saw the kelpie's body sink through the shallow water. A dark stain leaked from its head.

A clatter of metal told her that Lucky dropped the poker. Seconds later he lay next to her on the edge of the boat peering over. He stuck his tongue out to one side and smiled around it. "Candygram?"

"If you make any more shark jokes, I'm going to beat you with that poker," Celeste said.

"No worries," Lucky said.

Now that the immediate danger was over, she felt the frigid water that soaked her to the skin. Lucky released the side of the boat to run shaking hands through his wet hair. Celeste realized that her hands were also shaking.

"Celeste?"

"Yeah?"

"You got your story yet?"

"I think so." Celeste looked up as she thought about what she would need to finish the story. "I've got to get some more background information and a couple of pictures of the carcass. But page one here I come."

"Good. Because I'm done with this guest shot on shark week. I want to go back to New York where things don't eat you."

"What about the sewer alligators?"

Lucky winced as he eased himself into the water. Then, pushing the boat ahead of him, he doggie-paddled to the shore. "They aren't hurting anyone," he said. "They can stay in the sewers."

Elvis met them at the beach. "Thanks for bringing the boat back," he said. "I reckon ya'll want to use the shower back at the clinic."

"Actually, I think we want to cut this visit short," Celeste said. "You know the old saying, guests are like fish."

"They eat tourists when they're not looking?" Elvis scratched his head.

"Never mind," Celeste said. "I think we just want to drop our rental off and fly home."

"If you say so," Elvis said. Then he grinned at Celeste. "Ya'll think I can have that kelpie carcass?"

"Elvis." Celeste threw her hands up. Her eyebrows climbed her forehead. "What the heck do you want with a kelpie?"

"I thought I'd stuff it and mount it on the wall," Elvis said. "You gotta admit, this is a heck of a fish story."

Tim Waggoner's latest novels include *In the Shadow of Ruin, Stargate SG1: Valhalla,* and *Cross County.* He's published over one hundred short stories, some of which are collected in *Broken Shadows* and *All Too Surreal.* His articles on writing have appeared in *Writer's Digest, Writers' Journal* and other publications. He teaches creative writing at Sinclair Community College in Dayton, Ohio, and is a faculty mentor in Seton Hill University's Master of Arts in Writing Popular Fiction program. Visit him on the web at www.timwaggoner.com.

Blame It on the Moonlight

Tim Waggoner

Bill ran through the nightwood, branches snagging his clothes, scratching his fur-covered face and hands. Light from the full moon filtered down through the branches, providing more than enough illumination for his lupine eyes to see. The moonlight healed his cuts almost instantly, but each time he was wounded small amounts of his blood were exposed to the air. Not for very long, but long enough. The sharp coppery tang was strong in his nostrils, and if *he* could smell it . . .

From somewhere behind him in the woods, Bill's preternatural hearing picked up a rustling, followed by an excited insectine chittering. The sound hit him on a deeply instinctive level, stirring a feeling within him unlike anything he had ever known.

She was coming.

"Fear of the number thirteen . . . which one is that?"
"Not hydrophobia. That's fear of sailing."
"No, you dope, it's fear of water in general."

"What about triskaidekaphobia? It's got tri in it, and that means three, right?"

"Three's not thirteen."

"I know that, but it's the closest choice up there."

Bill sat at the end of the bar, a bottle of light beer in front of him. He was doing his best to ignore Ryan and Luis. The two men sat nearby and were deeply into the trivia game currently displayed on the four flat-screen video monitors mounted around the bar so that every customer was afforded a clear view of whatever happened to be playing at any given moment. Bill could've done without the screens, just as he could've done without Ryan and Luis tonight. They both worked out at the airport loading freight onto planes, and they wore identical uniforms: light blue short-sleeved shirts, dark blue slacks, black shoes, dark blue ball caps. But despite their menial jobs, Ryan and Luis fancied themselves masters of all knowledge, whether mundane or arcane, and when it came to trivia, they could be annoying as hell.

An image flashed through Bill's mind then: clawed, fur-covered hands ripping down one of the screens and using it to bash in the two morons' skulls.

He heard a throaty rumbling, and it took him a moment to realize he was making the sound. He stopped growling and took a sip of his beer, hoping that no one had noticed.

I hate full moons, he thought.

My Office—as in "I'm going to my office, honey, don't wait up"—was a small, unprepossessing bar located in a strip mall in downtown Ash Creek, Ohio. Nestled between a hobby store called Playin' Around and a restaurant with the exceptionally unimaginative name of Fond-oooo!, My Office consisted of a square bar area in the center of the building, a dozen or so tables with chairs placed around the bar, the aforementioned video screens, and not much else. You could get the usual assortment of beers and alcoholic drinks—nothing imported or too fancy, though—and something to eat off the appetizer menu, if you didn't mind stomach cramps. Light jazz music played softly in the background, the sort of music that's supposed to be atmospheric but which just ends up being depressing.

Bill wore a gray suit jacket, blue tie, gray pants, and polished black shoes. He'd come to the bar straight from work, as he always did when the full moon fell on a weeknight. He was the only patron in the establishment that actually looked like he belonged in a place called My Office. Not that there were many others here; it was slow tonight, even for a Wednesday. Besides Bill and the trivia twins, the only people present were Mark—My Office's owner and chief bartender, a literature professor with the improbable name of Jimmy Love who looked something like a clean-shaven Santa Claus, and a woman Bill didn't recognize. Bill sat at the north side of the bar, Ryan and Luis to his right on the west side, and Jimmy Love directly opposite Bill on the south side. Bill noticed that despite the early hour, Jimmy was already working on a brandy. Usually he had a beer or two first.

Must've had a rough day, Bill thought.

The woman—a slender, pretty blonde who looked to be in her early to mid thirties—sat alone at a table. She wore a brown sweater, jeans, and black boots. Her hair fell past her shoulders, and she had an . . . interesting scent. Bill inhaled deeply through his nostrils to get a better fix on it. There was something at once familiar and exotic about her scent, something that equally intrigued and disturbed Bill, though he wasn't sure why.

The woman sipped a glass of red wine as she followed the trivia game on one of the screens. As if becoming suddenly aware of Bill's scrutiny, she turned to look at him. She locked gazes with him for a moment, smiled, and then turned her attention back to the trivia screen.

Bill's growl was softer this time.

Mark gave Ryan and Luis—who were now snapping at each other for not going with triskaidekaphobia as the correct answer—fresh mugs of beer. A new question came up on the monitors asking which planet Phobos was a moon of. Bill could've answered that. He knew a lot about moons. Ryan and Luis immediately began arguing, and Mark left them to come over and check on Bill.

"Full moon tonight, eh?"

Mark was rail-thin, in his early forties, with jet black hair and a neatly trimmed mustache and goatee. Women found him irresistible, which was too bad since Mark was gay.

Bill swallowed another mouthful of beer then set his bottle on the counter.

"What makes you say that?" Bill said.

"Besides the calendar? For one thing, you hardly ever come in here on any other night." Mark grinned. "And I heard you growling a minute ago."

Bill felt his cheeks redden with embarrassment, and he had to resist glancing over again at the blonde. "Don't worry. I have it under control."

Mark reached down and tapped the bar surface near Bill's right hand—his currently human right hand. Five deep furrows had been carved into the wood, and from the look of them, they'd been there awhile.

"That happened months ago, Mark. I offered to pay for the damage."

"And I told you not to worry about it." Mark positioned his fingers over the furrows then slowly drew his hand along them. "I like them. They give the place a little character, you know?" He gave Bill a sideways look. "Course, I could've done without having to clean up the mess you left that night. I had to replace a whole section of flooring. Bloodstains don't come out of wood."

"And you *did* accept my money for *that* repair, didn't you?"

"And happily so." Mark paused for a moment before going on. "Whatever happened to that guy who pissed you off that night? He never did come back in here."

"He tried to sue me for the nerve damage he received when I raked his face, but his lawyer refused to believe I was a werewolf, and he was forced to drop the suit."

"Good for you. Far as I'm concerned, the creep deserved it considering the sort of comments he made about your wife." Mark glanced at Ryan and Luis, who—along with Jimmy Love—were now debating whether golf originated in Scotland or France. "But don't get any ideas tonight. If you started attacking every jackass that came in here, I'd run out of customers."

Bill remembered the guy, and he remembered what he'd said.

I envy you, Bill; I really do. It must be great to really cut loose, to let go, to express your primitive side. I imagine your wife gets a little . . . curious when the moon comes up. Am I right? Let me ask you something: does your dong get hairy too? Is it a man's dong, a wolf's dong, or a cross between the two? Does it get bigger when you change? I bet your wife loves that! Bet she howls louder than you do!

And that was when Bill changed and took half the man's face off with a single swipe of his claws.

"Guess there wasn't a whole lot of point in defending Joan's honor that night," Bill said. "Considering she left me less than a week later." He felt his teeth ache, grow sharper, and he took another swig of beer to calm himself.

"You told me she left because her allergies were making her miserable, even when you were human."

"Yeah. It was either stay married to me or be able to breathe. She chose breathing. I understand, but it still sucks, though."

"Sure does." Mark glanced over at the blonde, who was still watching the trivia game. "You dating anyone right now? If not, you might think about going over to chat up Claire. She was in the other night, and we got to talking. Seems like a real great girl."

Mark believed in the long-hallowed tradition of bartenders being sympathetic listeners, but he took it a step further. He believed in actually doing things to make his customers' lives better. Mark claimed he was a Samaritan. Bill figured that was just another way of saying *annoying busybody*. Of course, if Mark hadn't been so sympathetic, he might not have allowed a reluctant werewolf to hang out in his bar every month during the cycle of the full moon. So Bill supposed he shouldn't complain.

Bill felt an itching on the back of his right hand. He looked down at thick tufts of brown fur beginning to sprout from his skin. He concentrated and the fur slowly receded.

Bill looked up at Mark. "I don't think it's a good idea tonight."

Mark shrugged. "Suit yourself. But being a werewolf gives you a certain mystique, you know. You ought to put it to good use."

"Hey, Mark!" Jimmy Love brandished his empty snifter. "Hit me again?"

"You got it." Mark gave Bill a parting wink and went over to serve Jimmy another brandy.

Bill glanced at his watch and sighed. It wasn't even eleven o'clock yet. He had hours left to go until dawn, and already he'd had several flare-ups. Maybe if he started drinking something harder than beer . . . it was easier to maintain control when he was relaxed, and he was always mellow after a few drinks.

I bet your wife loves that! Bet she howls louder than you do!

Usually mellow, he amended.

"Excuse me?"

Bill was so startled to hear the woman's voice next to him that his upper canines instantly lengthened, piercing his bottom lip. The wounds immediately began to heal, and his teeth slowly retracted, though they remained somewhat longer than normal.

The blonde—Claire, he remembered—had walked over to the bar and now stood next to him. She smiled, somewhat shyly, "I don't mean to be nosey, but is it true? Are you really a . . . a werewolf?"

Bill liked that smile, almost as much as he liked her deep blue eyes. A thought passed through his mind: how had she been able to sneak up on him like that? His senses were always preternaturally heightened, even in human form, and no more so than during the cycle of the full moon. But he hadn't heard Claire approach. Maybe he was just distracted by his thoughts, and maybe the beer he'd drank so far was already having an effect on him. Maybe.

Bill smiled at Claire, keeping his lips closed to avoid displaying his teeth. "Where did you hear a wild story like that?"

Claire nodded toward the other end of the bar. "From Jimmy Love. I was in here a few nights ago and we got to talking. He told me that you always come in here during the nights of the full moon—and he told me why."

Bill scowled at Jimmy, but the professor merely lifted his brandy and gave Bill a boozy smile as if to say, You're welcome.

"I'm Claire Avery, by the way." She held out her hand for him to shake.

"Bill Severt." He took her hand, concentrating to keep his nails normal length and his palm free of unwanted hair. Her grip was gentle but with an underlying strength, and she maintained physical contact with him a few seconds longer than necessary. Despite himself, the contact excited him, and Bill felt fur sprout on the back of his neck and the tips of his ears take on sharp points. If Claire noticed, she was too polite to mention it.

"Do you mind if I join you?" Claire said.

Bill gestured to the empty stool next to him. "Please."

She sat down and put her half-empty wine glass on the bar in front of her. She then turned to Bill and gave him a warm smile.

"So it's true?" she asked.

Bill considered telling her that it was just a drunken joke Jimmy had been playing on her, but when he looked at her smile, he found that not only couldn't he lie to her, he didn't want to.

"Yes. I'm a werewolf."

She leaned toward him, eyes gleaming with excitement. "That's fascinating! When did you first find out?"

"When I was a kid. It runs in the family."

"And you come in here to . . . what? Hide out when you change?"

"Not exactly. As you might imagine, being a werewolf is more than a little problematic at times, and life is much easier when you can resist the change and remain human during the cycle of the full moon. Some werewolves lock themselves in cages, others practice meditation techniques to control the change. Me, I come here. Just like the show's theme song: 'Where Everybody Knows Your Name.' It's relaxing here, and the people are for the most part nonjudgmental, even if—"

"Hey, Bill!" Ryan interrupted. "What's the plant that werewolves are allergic to? Luis says it's belladonna, but I say it's wolfsbane."

"It *can't* be wolfsbane!" Luis protested. "It's too obvious!"

Bill sighed. "Or maybe not obvious enough. Wolfsbane is the right answer."

Ryan punched Luis on the shoulder. "See? I told you!"

Luis glared at Ryan as he entered the correct answer into the trivia console.

Bill turned back to Claire. "I was about to say, even if they *are* irritating sometimes."

Claire laughed. There was a pause in the conversation as each took a sip of their respective drinks.

"So what happens when the bar closes?" Claire asked.

"Mark usually lets me stick around, and I give him a hand cleaning up. After that, it's close enough to dawn for the moon's influence to have waned, and I can go home." He smiled, hoping his teeth weren't too sharp to be intimidating. "Some wild animal I am, huh?"

Mark was at the other side of the bar talking to Jimmy Love. Both men glanced at Bill and gave him disappointed looks. Bill knew what they were thinking. He should be making the most of Claire's interest in his lycanthropic life-style to impress her. He should tell her stories of racing through moonlit fields, heart pounding, blood thrumming through his veins as he ran his prey to ground. But he wasn't the type to feed a woman a line just to get her into bed, no matter how attractive she was. Though he had to admit he was tempted. Not only was Claire beautiful, there was something special about her that he couldn't put his finger on. Though they'd only spoken for a few minutes, he felt a definite connection to her, a connection that seemed to be deepening quickly.

Of course, now that he'd confessed to being a wimpy werewolf, she'd probably lose interest and leave, and he wouldn't blame her one bit.

So Bill was surprised when Claire said, "I think that's very responsible of you. Sure, hanging out here might make your life easier, but it also protects anyone you might, uh . . . go after. I admire that." She leaned even closer. "A lot."

Bill felt a certain part of his anatomy begin to change in a way that had nothing to do with lycanthropy. "Thanks."

After that, he expected Claire to continue asking him questions about being a werewolf, but instead she asked what he did for a living—he was an accountant—and told him about her job as a phlebotomist. The conversation moved on from there, and they talked about where they'd gone to college and high school, where they'd grown up, what movies and TV shows they liked, what sort of restaurants they enjoyed, places they liked to go on vacation . . . The time flew by, and though Bill knew it was way too early to be thinking like this, he couldn't help wondering if he was falling in love with Claire.

"Last call. You two want anything else?"

Bill turned to Mark, startled. He'd forgotten about the bartender, about the bar, about everything else except Claire. He looked around and saw that Jimmy Love was so soused he could barely stay awake—Mark would call a cab to take Jimmy home, as he always did—and though Ryan and Luis were still playing video trivia, they were too tired to argue about it anymore. Bill glanced at his watch and was surprised to see it was 1:45 in the morning.

"Nothing for me," Claire said. "Bill?"

"I'm fine."

"Looks to me like the two of you are quite fine indeed." Mark grinned and moved off to check on the others.

Bill reddened in embarrassment, but Claire just laughed. Somewhere along the line she'd taken to holding his hand, and she gave it a squeeze now.

"I'm not the type of gal who picks up men in bars, Bill, but I've had a wonderful time tonight. I hope you have too."

"I have." Bill was about to ask her if she'd like to have dinner with him—maybe not tomorrow or the night after, but when the cycle of the full moon was over—but before he could do so, she lowered her eyes and as she spoke her voice took on a wistful tone.

"I really like you, Bill. Very much." She gripped his hand tighter. "And that makes what I'm about to tell you so difficult to say."

Oh god, she's married! Bill thought. *Or worse, she used to be a man!* But it couldn't be either of those. He'd have smelled another man's scent on her, and if she was a transsexual, she'd still smell male to him. She *did* have that odd scent that he couldn't place, but whatever it was, it wasn't remotely male, he was certain of that.

"There's a reason I came in here tonight, Bill. Why I started coming here in the first place." A pause. "I was looking for you."

He frowned. "I'm not sure what you mean."

"You said being a werewolf runs in your family, right? Did your parents ever tell you about other creatures that change shape?"

"Sure. There are varieties of shapeshifters other than werewolves, though they tend to be rare." A thought occurred to him then. "Are you trying to tell me that you're a shapeshifter too?"

She nodded, still unable to meet his gaze.

"But that's wonderful! It means we can understand each another in a way humans can't. It'll bring us even closer."

"No, Bill, it won't. Not all types of shapeshifters are compatible. Did you parents ever warn you about certain kinds?"

Bill tried to remember. Like him, his parents had strived to live as normal a life as possible, and the times they spoke about their lycanthropic heritage were rare.

"They told me that were-bears tend to have foul tempers, and that I should stay away from were-rats or else I might catch something. But the only really dangerous shapeshifter they ever told me about was . . . " He trailed off as horrified realization set in.

Claire looked up and met his gaze. "That's right, Bill. I'm a were-flea."

Bill yanked his hand away from Claire. It all made sense now. Her strange scent, her career as a phlebotomist . . .

Laughter erupted from the other four men in the bar.

"Sorry you two," Mark said. "We couldn't help overhearing. All right, I admit it; we were eavesdropping. But a were-*flea*? Come on!"

Mark, Jimmy, Ryan, and Luis burst into another round of laughter.

"What's she going to do?" Ryan said. "Make you itch to death?"

"I've heard of dates that suck, but this is ridiculous!" Luis added.

More laughter. But Bill wasn't amused, not in the slightest.

He began speaking in a hushed, frightened voice. "A were-flea is the only true predator that other shapeshifters have. They are extremely rare, created only when a flea bites a shapeshifter in animal form and then turns around and bites a human."

Claire nodded. "It happened on a camping trip when I was twelve."

Mark and the others had stopped laughing and were now listening intently. Bill continued.

"Like other shapeshifters, were-fleas transform during the cycle of the full moon. They are driven to seek out other shapeshifters and—"

"Feed on their blood," Claire finished. She gave Bill a sad look and said, "I'm sorry. I truly am."

Jimmy Love belched loudly then and said, "That has got to be the most idiotic thing I have ever—" and then he screamed as Claire began to change.

Her skin became a shiny reddish-brown as exoskeletal armor replaced flesh. Numerous hairs and short spines extruded from her shell, tearing through the fabric of her sweater. The upper half of her body remained roughly humanoid, but her bottom half became entirely insectine, and her jeans shredded to make way for a large abdomen and four long segmented legs. Her blonde hair retreated into the shiny surface of her reddish-brown head, and her eyes became large and black. Her nose flattened until only two small nostril holes remained, and her teeth sharpened to fine points. Her arms grew longer and leaner, and her hands transformed into wicked curved claws perfectly designed for grabbing and holding onto prey.

Bill had never seen anything so terrifying—and in her own way magnificent—in his life.

She lunged for him, and Bill threw himself off the barstool just in time to avoid Claire's claws. He spun in midair as he fell and landed gracefully on all fours. He'd instinctively changed into his own lycanthropic form—half-man, half-wolf—on the way down, which was a damn good thing, for only his lupine speed saved him from Claire's next attack. With a single thrust of her four powerful insect legs, she became a blur as she shot toward Bill. He swiftly rolled to the side, but not quite fast enough to avoid Claire raking his back and tearing his suit jacket and the shirt beneath it to ribbons—not to mention gouging bloody furrows into his fur-covered flesh. But Claire's ferocious momentum kept her moving past, and she skidded across half the bar, knocking over a number of tables and chairs before managing to bring herself to a stop.

Bill leaped to his feet, tore off the ragged remnants of his jacket and shirt, and cast them to the floor. The wounds on his back burned like fire, but already the pain was lessening as his lycanthropic metabolism worked swiftly to repair the damage. Bill turned to see how the others were, and he wasn't particularly surprised to discover that all four of them—Mark, Jimmy, Ryan, and Luis—were staring at Claire with various mixtures of horror and disbelief.

"Get out of here!" Bill yelled. "She only wants me!" At least, that's what he *tried* to say. His werewolf throat was no longer designed to produce human speech, not to mention that it was a real bitch to enunciate properly with a mouthful of fangs. So his warning, instead of coming out as words, came out as a series of snarls and growls.

Mark, Jimmy, Ryan, and Luis tore their gazes off Claire, looked at Bill, then started their own nonsensical yelling—only theirs was spurred by sheer terror.

Great, Bill thought. *They think I'm a bloodthirsty monster too.*

His friends were frozen with fear, and he knew that if he and Claire continued to fight inside the bar, one or more of the others was bound to get hurt in the crossfire. And while Bill was fairly confident were-fleas only drank the blood of other shapeshifters, he wasn't entirely sure on that point. What if, once she had drained him dry, she decided to have one of his friends for dessert? Bill had no choice. He had to draw Claire away from the others, and fast.

He ran toward the door.

She tried to intercept him halfway across the bar, but as she leaped toward him, he jumped straight up, and she sailed beneath him. Chittering in frustration, she once more crashed into tables and chairs, reducing them to so much kindling. Bill landed easily and kept running.

He reached the door, yanked it open, and plunged out into the parking lot.

The cool night air welcomed him, and the light from the full moon overhead washed down on him like a restorative balm, healing the last of his wounds and infusing him with a fresh strength and vitality. The strip mall that housed My Office was located next to a small strand of woods—another reason why Bill liked coming here during full moon nights. If he could reach the woods, he might be able to escape Claire. The trees were thick and close together, and they'd interfere with her jumping. Bill knew he could outrun her in a strict footrace, for there were few things on Earth faster than a terrified werewolf running for his life. He fixed his gaze on the line of trees on the other side of the parking lot and poured on the speed.

He heard the sound of My Office's door being smashed open, followed a second later by triumphant chittering as Claire slammed into his back. The two of them skidded across the parking lot, reopening the slash wounds on Bill's back and giving him a nasty case of road rash on his belly and chest. As soon as they came to a stop, he tried to crawl away from Claire, but she grabbed hold of him with her claws and flipped him over onto his back. He grimaced as his wounds ground against the blacktop, and he attempted to slash out at Claire with his own claws, but she grabbed hold of his arms with her middle set of legs and pinned them to his side. He was helpless.

She bowed the humanoid half of her body down until her head was only inches away from Bill's. Her black insect eyes shone with reflected moonlight, and even though he knew he was about to die, Bill couldn't help but think of how strangely beautiful they looked.

Bill expected Claire to sink her fangs into his neck, but instead she opened her mouth wide and stuck out her tongue. It was longer than a human's and it tapered to a needlelike tip. *Efficient design,* Bill thought.

She leaned closer and her tongue darted toward Bill's neck, the needle-tip sinking into his flesh. It stung, but it didn't hurt as badly as he'd feared. He felt the pull as his blood was suctioned into Claire's tongue, and she chattered softly in a kind of satisfied ecstasy.

He soon began to feel lightheaded and his vision started to grow hazy around the edges. His werewolf physiology could heal almost any wound, but there was no way it could replace his blood supply as quickly as Claire was draining it. Another few moments, and it would all be over.

Without thinking, and not quite understanding why he did so, Bill lifted his head and gave Claire a kiss on her carapaced cheek.

"It's okay," he said. "I know you can't help it."

Bill lowered his head back to the ground and waited for darkness to claim him.

The suction stopped.

Claire's eyes gleamed even more brightly now, and at first Bill couldn't understand why. But then he realized: it was because they were filled with tears. She was crying.

Her needle-tongue withdrew from his neck and receded into her mouth. She gazed down at him, and though her face was utterly inhuman, Bill had no trouble at all reading her expression of loving sorrow.

A series of clicks and pops came out of her mouth, and though it didn't sound very much like human speech, Bill still understood her words.

I'm so sorry.

He rose to his feet and she pulled him into an embrace. He hugged her back, his strength swiftly returning now that she had stopped draining his blood.

He glanced to the right and saw Mark, Jimmy, Ryan, and Luis standing on the sidewalk in front of My Office, watching.

"That," Mark said, "has got to be either the sickest thing I've ever seen or the sweetest."

"I vote for both," Jimmy said.

Ryan and Luis agreed, and the four of them went back inside the bar, presumably for another last round of drinks.

Bill grinned and hugged Claire even tighter. She hugged him back with two arms and two legs, softly thrumming a sound like a kitten's purr into his ear.

Bill continued running through the woods, weaving between the trees. If he could manage to keep enough obstacles between them, he just might be able to avoid her. All he had to do was make it to the other side of the woods, and then—

He heard her chittering a half second before she landed on him, driving him to the forest floor. He lay there as her tongue slithered forth from her mouth and gently touched its needle-tip to the back of his neck. She drank several swallows, not enough to seriously deplete him, and then drew her tongue back into her mouth.

"Tag," she chittered. "You're it!"

Then she hopped off of him, spun around, and jumped away in the opposite direction, laughing.

I love full moons, Bill thought.

Grinning, he gave chase.

Lucienne Diver has written short stories and a romantic comedy under her pseudonym, Kit Daniels, but is finally ready to come out of the authorial closet with "Imaginary Fiend" and her debut young adult novel, *Vamped* (think *Clueless* meets *Buffy the Vampire Slayer*), a May 2009 trade paperback from Flux.

Imaginary Fiend

Lucienne Diver

"Did you see that?" I asked Bob. I'd gotten pretty good making myself understood with little to no lip movement, since Bob, aka Kneebob, aka Bobbin, aka the bane of my existence, was a Tinkerbell-sized piskie and invisible, except when he chose not to be, to those without the Sight. Lucky me—oh joy, oh rapture—I was *blessed*. But my recent run-in with a werewolf had left me periodically feral, not stupid. Talking to myself didn't fit with my macho cop image. At least the werewolf who'd attacked me, unlike the pesky piskie, hadn't stuck around to insist on the politically correct form of his name. Or to annoy me into an early grave.

"The girl with 'Luscious' written across her butt?" Bob asked, bouncing up and down on my shoulder. "You think there's truth in advertising?"

"Down, boy. Fifteen'll get you twenty."

"Huh?"

I rolled my eyes skyward. "Never mind. I meant beyond the girl."

"The boy who's talking to himself?"

"Or is he?" I asked.

Bob looked askance at me. If you've never had your sanity questioned by a pint-sized pain in the ass, I highly recommend it. Good for raising the heart rate and really getting the blood pumping.

"Look closer," I added through clenched teeth.

Bob squinted his beady little eyes. "All I see is a blur, like a CGI effect or someone using the wrong speed film. Is that it? Are we on candid camera?"

"That's it. No more late night TV for you. Real world, Bob. Focus. I think this boy's 'imaginary friend' may be a klepto. I swear I saw something disappear off the shelf just now, and if this thing is doing a double blind— focusing his visibility on the boy and blurring himself to other eyes, you know who's going to get blamed if anyone else notices the vanishing merchandise."

Bob's eyes got as big as saucers, but not in empathy, I knew. "Oh no. No, no, NO. We're just here to get a birthday present for Jezi. You know, your *girlfriend*."

"My partner," I growled.

"Whatever. Anyway, you promised—in, out, ice cream. *Ice cream*, Vic. Do those words mean nothing to you?"

He flitted right up in front of my face and waved his arms around. The werewolf part of me instinctively twitched as if to swat him aside, but I beat down the impulse. Not quite so easy with the full moon a mere day away.

"If you want to cause trouble," I bit out, "do it over there." I cocked my head to the side, heedless of "Luscious" and her friend, who quickly scurried into another aisle. Men who stood in jewelry aisles twitching and talking to themselves were suspect. I didn't take it personally. Much. Giving Bob the green light for mischief was risky, but the distraction would take any unwanted attention off the boy and give me the chance to make things right.

"Really?" he asked, eyes alight. "Never mind. If you're kidding, I don't want to know."

He flitted off toward the girl with the invitational backside, who'd conveniently stopped with her friend to look at a purse not far away.

Bob promptly bit her on the butt.

She screeched, her friend squawked. The rack she'd been examining teetered, sending purses flying through the air.

Everyone turned to stare, including the mother of the boy with the imaginary friend. I used the distraction to sneak up behind the blur, leaving a single rotating rack of shirts between us. Since the mall trip wasn't official business, I didn't have any of my gear—not a cuff or a weapon on me. My reflexes were going to have to do. I reached through the rack and clamped my hands on some invisible, but excessively furry shoulders. The thing thrashed and its blurring flickered as I yanked it into the rack among the clothes. I got the impression of purple shag and that was all before it winked out again. The demented little DJ in my head insisted on playing "One-Eyed, One-Horned Flying Purple People Eater" as a soundtrack to our scuffle.

"Hey!" yelled the boy, instantly on alert. His grey eyes met mine. "Leggo my friend!"

His cry called his mother's attention back from projectile purses. She whirled on me, just as her son dove into the rack. He grabbed his purple pal and put up a heck of a tug-of-war for his furry, thieving friend. I could win, of course, but maybe not without knocking over the rack and hurting the boy.

"Help!" his mother screamed, as if I was kidnapping her boy and *he* hadn't just charged in after *me*. "Security!"

I could flash my badge and all, but that would mean a) letting go of my prey and b) somehow explaining what I'd seen, risking the men in white suits coming to take me away—ho ho!

The woman added her weight to her son's in our strange tug of war, and rather than tear him in half I let her have him, even though it meant allowing Hairy to slip through my fingers.

"Bob, to me," I yelled.

He appeared, grinning like a fiend. "Not luscious," he informed me. "Too much chemical in the wash. Soft, though!"

"ID and then escape," I ordered.

He blinked and suddenly we were in another part of the store, staring as security ran past.

"Wow, what did you do?" Bob asked, impressed.

"Forget it. Did you get the ID?"

Bob nodded.

"Well, hand it over."

He started shaking his head . . . vigorously. "That's going to take ice cream. I'm thinking triple fudge ripple with marshmallow topping. Maybe caramel. And sprinkles! I love sprinkles!" He smacked his lips.

"Remind me again why we're stalking this kid?" Bob asked from his perch atop my steering wheel.

When I'd asked for ID, I'd meant a license or some-thing with an address, but Bob, in typical *Bob* fashion, hadn't gotten things quite right. He'd·ended up with the kid's school ID, which meant a trip back to my place and some Internet research based on the kid's name and school district to track down his home address. The research had turned up other interesting tidbits, like the fact that the place had a history. Just months ago, the former owner had died under questionable circum-stances, apparently slipped in the shower and knocked herself senseless, bleeding out on the floor. If it hadn't come up in the search, I would never have connected the address, since it hadn't been my case. There'd been some discussion around the department about declaring it murder vs. accidental death. The grandniece who lived with her had a juvie record and was considered a person of interest, but with no hard evidence of foul play and the daughter pushing to close the case, probably to inherit and collect on the double indemnity clause of her mother's insurance, the death had finally been ruled acci-dental.

Interesting that the same house would be the site of a second intrigue so hard on the heels of the first. Almost as mysterious as how Bob had gotten marshmallow all the way up into his ear and why with access to washcloths and hot-and-cold running water he didn't do a thing about it.

"I'm saving it for later," he said when I asked. I should have known better.

Anyway, I was way more interested in the well-cared-for Victorian in front of us with enough gingerbread to feed a horde of ravenous elves.

"The two things have to be linked," I mused out loud. "It's too much of a coincidence otherwise. But what does an old lady's death have to do with a boy's larcenous imaginary friend? And why would something with the power of invisibility waste it on penny-ante pilfering?"

"Lar-what? Pilfering? Jeez, Vic, who talks like that? Small words, few syllables, 'kay?"

"Larcenous, Bob, like in larceny. You know, the reason you're on the run from the big bad dwarves and I'm stuck playing your bodyguard?"

"My hero!" he chirped, rising on fluttering wings like he might come in for a hug.

"Touch me and die," I warned.

"Fine. Whatever," he said, face falling into a pout. "More than meets the eye. Yada, yada, yada. I think you're just trying to get out of shopping."

Bob wasn't the brightest bulb in the bunch, but sometimes even a blind man hit the nail on the head.

"Shh, they're coming out," I said, as if Bob's chatter could be heard across the street, even with the windows rolled down to take advantage of the spring breeze.

The boy was dressed in a monkey suit, pulling at the collar and looking all around miserable.

"I still don't understand why Mr. Mudge couldn't come," he whined to his mother.

She was busy catching at the sheer blue shawl the wind tried to whip away from her, revealing a satiny gown and a figure I wouldn't have given her credit for this afternoon. Not that I'd been paying much attention. I'd been a wee bit distracted.

"Stacio, for the last time, Mr. Mudge is not real. You're seven years old, you should know this," she answered distractedly. "Plus, even nice monsters don't belong at Gabe and Tina's wedding."

"If he's so fake, I don't see what trouble he could cause," the boy muttered rebelliously. "It's not fair."

His mother gave a long-suffering sigh I'd grown way too familiar with in my short time with Bob.

They got into mom's shiny red Mercedes, the kid sitting in the passenger seat in violation of safety and New York State law and off they went.

"Aren't you going to bust 'em?" Bob asked, having heard me rant on this very topic maybe once or twice.

"Not right now. *Now* you're going to pop in there and open the door." Bob might have been able to magic me to another part of the store earlier, but getting my mass through solid walls into a locked house was a little beyond his abilities. Plus, old houses like this sometimes had residual warding from more believing times. A little something extra that never got written up in the sales specs.

"Won't *Mr. Mudge* notice something like that?"

"Not if you're quiet."

"Oh!" he said, like that had never occurred to him. "I can do quiet. I'll show him that two can play at invisibility."

I didn't bother to point out the flaw in his logic. If Bob was feeling cooperative, I wasn't going to mess with it.

He disappeared, and a half second later, the front door snicked open. Unlike Bob, I had to use human means to cross to the door, and I did it as though I had business at the house. At six-foot-two, looking exactly like a Tony or Vic or Vito, except for the blue eyes that had somehow crept into my family line, I could easily be mistaken for a wise guy by *Sopranos*-minded folks, but more often I was instantly pegged as exactly what I was—a cop. Something in my look or my walk, I guessed. I didn't know, but I wasn't too worried about making the neighbors nervous. I reserved that for mall security.

Once inside, I locked the door behind me.

"See anything yet?" I asked Bob, who hovered at eye level.

"Vic!" he cried, clutching both hands to his heart. "I wouldn't start without you."

"No, really."

Bob gave me back one of my sighs. "Fine. He's in the den . . . . I took a quick peek."

"Lead the way."

I followed Bob past a chef's kitchen that Jezi would probably kill for, past a formal dining room with cherrywood table and crystal chandeliers, a marble bathroom that seemed too grand to pee in and finally to a closed door. Instinct was raising the hairs on the back of my neck.

If I'd been with Jezi rather than Bob, we'd have done the silent three-count and gone in flashing guns and badges. As it was . . .

"Bob, whatever's in there, I want it sneezing its brains out—and I don't mean that literally!" I added quickly, already envisioning the splatter.

It was a cheap trick, but easy to get the drop on something when its eyes were squeezed shut and its heart momentarily stopped. I burst in as the first sneeze rattled the door.

Mr. Mudge whirled on us as we entered. He looked like something a kid would have come up with—like someone had given a bulldog tusks, put its head on an orangutan body and covered it with purple fur. A convulsion overtook it the second it made eye contact and it blew itself back a foot with a sneeze momentous enough to rattle windows and transform it into a woman with orange hair—not red, *orange*. It sneezed again and flipped back to the monster. A third time and . . . well, you get the idea.

I dodged a blast of projectile snot only to see it steam as it shattered a lamp and scarred a table. It was roughly the color and consistency of guacamole. There was no comparison for the smell. Not with my overactive lupine sensitivity.

"Worst idea ever," I muttered to myself. "Give yourself up and the sneezing stops!" I called out, feeling dumber than dumb. I hadn't uttered such a stupid line since Jezi had come across a woman beating her father with his own prosthetic limb and I'd offered, "Put down the leg and no one gets hurt."

Mudge . . . er, the woman . . . snorted, and it was a bad, bad thing. "Clearest—ah-ah-choo—my sinuses have ever been!"

I dodged another nose bullet.

"Bob, for God's sake, recall on the sneezing!"

Instantly it stopped, leaving Mr. Mudge as a petite woman, flaming in orange-headed fury.

"What are you doing here?" she demanded, hands going to her hips.

"We could ask you the same question," Bob said, getting right up in her face.

"I live here," she answered. It was hard not to notice that her eyes were the same color as her nasal nuggets—guacamole. On someone else the green eyes might have worked, but together with the orange hair, it looked like someone had colored her with crayons—and not from the hundred count box.

"You or *Mr. Mudge*?" I asked.

She shrugged. "Same difference."

"I don't think Stacio's mom would think so."

"What about Stacio's mom?" asked a new voice from behind me.

I stiffened. In the wake of nasal warfare I hadn't even heard the door open. I turned slowly, catching sight of the look on *Ms*. Mudge's face as I did—shock and a feral kind of fear. Something was definitely going on here.

Stacio's mother wasn't looking at me, but staring right into Mudge's guacamole gaze. "Imagine my surprise when the alarm company called me just as I hit the church. An oversight, I told them. But I knew—as soon as I put two and two together. That scuffle at the mall. That was *you*, wasn't it?" Great, I'd been thinking about wards and completely ignoring the more mundane danger of silent alarms. Clearly, I'd been spending too much time with paranormal pests.

Speaking of little devils, Bob zipped from his hiding place at that moment to flit in front of my face. "Uh, Vic, I'm confused."

"That makes two of us," I said, before remembering that they couldn't see him. Ah, well, they wouldn't be the first to think I'd lost my mind.

"And you!" Stacio's mom hissed, turning on me at the sound of my voice. "What do *you* have to do with all this? I have half a mind to call the police."

"I *am* the police," I told her.

She recoiled physically. I could almost see the wheels spinning in her mind, rethinking whatever it was she thought she understood about the situation and her approach.

"Good. Arrest this woman."

"On what grounds?" I asked, pleased she'd fast-forwarded past the whole question of my presence without warrant or backup.

"Murder."

"What?" Mudge and I said at once.

"This woman murdered my mother. Clearly she's come back for us."

I looked from her to Mudge, whose face was going red with rage.

"Did not. *You* did," she fired back.

Stacio's mom looked calm and a little unimpeachable in her satiny dress. I didn't trust her for a second. But then, I wasn't sure I trusted either one as far as I could throw them. "*I* had an alibi," she stated.

"You have *power*," Mudge countered. "You didn't have to be there to do it."

"Too true," she admitted. "But it helps."

Almost faster than I could track, Stacio's mom raised her hands and fired a blast at Mudge, who ducked and rolled, landing up against a table that lurched, dangerously rocking the stained glass lamp Bob had hidden behind earlier. The lady of the house cried out, like the lamp was far more precious than Mudge's hide, which seemed to be true from her perspective.

"Home invasion," she called to me. "You're my witness."

Her trolley had slipped the rail if she thought that was going to justify cold-blooded murder, but just at that moment it didn't matter. I had problems of my own. Big, hairy, toothy problems. So close to the full moon, power crackling all around me, my instincts were instigating the Change. My skin rippled like a five G effect, and hair sprouted over my arms, face and neck like weeds.

"*Uh, Vic?*" Bob squeaked.

I reined it in, but just barely. Stopped at half man, half beast. Claws erupted from the tips of my fingers, shedding blood and skin. My teeth were wicked blades. The hunger for the hunt welled up in me until it became crucial to identify one of these women as prey.

Mudge fired back, both a power pulse that knocked society mom on her ass and an accusation. "Your mom knew all about you. She was leaving everything to me. The house, her book of shadows—"

"Liar!" shrieked monster mom, her eyes taking on the red of hellfire.

I'd heard enough. I jumped between them as both prepared to fire again and got hit by twin bursts of power—one icy cold and the other fiery hot. I felt like I was burning in frostbitten fire.

The wolfman in me howled, and I went into a frenzy, as if I could fight off the effects. Glass shattered. Furniture overturned. Only part of it was me. All around a battle raged.

"Bob, containment!" I growled, just barely understandable from my misshapen mouth.

Someone was quicker. He no sooner flitted out from behind the curtain, where he'd retreated when the action began again, then someone caught him with a fiery blast.

Right, that settled it then. I knocked everything in my path aside to get at the piskie and grabbed him up roughly by his tiny tunic.

I launched myself at the first combatant I saw—Mudge—and as she flinched, thinking I was about to strike, I shook Bob over her, shedding piskie dust everywhere. She subsided, lost in a fog of forgetfulness and bliss. For now, anyway.

A lance of pure agony hit me between the shoulder blades, and I went sprawling on the floor, losing hold of the pesky piskie, who slid to unconscious safety under a bookshelf.

I rolled over to face my final opponent, whose grin would have fit the face of the evilest evil stepmother.

"Well, Wolfman. Now you're *mine*. You can help me sniff out this book that Mudge is so anxious to get her hands on and I haven't been able to find . . . or die. Your choice."

"You did kill the old lady, didn't you?" I asked.

She shrugged, like I'd just asked her "paper or plastic." "I plead the fifth."

"In that case—" I rolled up onto my shoulders and used them as a springboard to launch myself onto my feet, claws reaching for and closing around her throat in the blink of an eye. "You have the right to remain silent. Anything you say can and will be used against you in a court of law—"

Her eyes looked about to pop out of her head. I felt badly for a second that I'd be depriving Stacio of his mom, but maybe he'd still be able to console himself with his imaginary friend . . . or his cousin once removed, or however that worked.

The bookshelf rattled, and Bob shot out from under, flitting mad. So bummed to have missed half the action that he didn't even give me any grief over a little memory manipulation to wipe out my shaggier side from the women's minds. Stacio's mom, aka Jordan Rinaldi, developed a sudden need to confess.

I sighed heavily afterward. "You know what this means, don't you, Bob?" I asked.

"Handcuffs?" Bob asked, hopefully.

I rolled my eyes. "I'll have to take them down to the station, process the arrest paperwork. *No time to shop.* Guess it'll be money again this year. Can't say I didn't try."

Bob rolled his eyes right back at me. "Some guys will do absolutely anything to get out of shopping."

It was so true.

Daniel M. Hoyt's short fiction has appeared in several leading magazines and anthologies since his first publication in *Analog*, most recently in *Witch Way to the Mall* (Baen), *Something Magic This Way Comes* (DAW), *Transhuman* (Baen) and *Space Pirates* (Flying Pen Press). After tangling with the suburban witches of Costwold Acres (aka Cauldron Acres) in "The FairWitch Project" (*Witch Way to the Mall*), Dan was shocked to find werewolves living in a nearby neighborhood, where this story takes place. (He has no doubt vampires are lurking about in yet another neighborhood!) In his own neighborhood, Dan coerces computer demons to do his bidding and writes short stories, edits anthologies (*Better Off Undead* and *Fate Fantastic*), and works on his second novel while marketing his first. Catch up with him at www.danielmhoyt.com.

Neighborhood Bark-B-Q

Daniel M. Hoyt

"So, you're the new pup?" A tiny, middle-aged woman with dirty blonde hair tied up in a librarian bun looked me up and down quickly and pushed her glasses up her aquiline nose. Flowers and a hint of musk clouded her red blouse and skirt. "Welcome to Loopy's. Did anyone tell you about the free haircuts?"

"Um . . . sure," I lied, more confident in my hair stylist's abilities than interested in what, if true, would have to rank as the oddest fringe benefit I'd ever been offered in my six-year career in computer programming. "I'm supposed to report to a Mr. Wiley?"

The blonde grinned and wagged a finger vaguely to her left. "I'll take you to him." She turned and scampered off immediately. "I'm Rose Hood, by the way," she said over her shoulder.

Quick-stepping to catch up with her fast-moving tiny legs, I fell in behind as she barreled down a narrow hallway lined with office doors. "Bryan Wolff."

Rose stopped abruptly and jerked her head around. "Bold." She pushed up her fallen glasses, twisted the doorknob nearest her and flung open the door, stepping through so quickly she gave the impression of leaping. I choked on a residual cloud of her woodsy perfume. "Wolff, the new database analyst, Mr. Wiley."

A transparently pale man at his desk looked up. He was younger than I expected, roughly my own age, with medium-length thick, tangled red hair atop his head and an equally tangled red beard, cut to about the same length.

I smiled, thrust out a hand and advanced as my new boss stood.

"Great to have you on board," he said, shaking my hand vigorously. Tangles of red hair escaped his long-sleeve button-down cuffs. "Wolff, was it? Bold." He glanced at Rose nervously, and she whisked past me, slamming the door behind her.

"I see you've met Little Red."

"Little Red Hood?"

Wiley stared blankly. "Her wardrobe is strictly red." He closed his eyes and drew in a deep breath. "Jovan White Musk for Women. I *love* that scent." He opened his eyes again, looking at me dreamily. "Did anyone tell you about the free haircuts?"

"I've got just the neighborhood for you, Mr . . . Wolff," said Harry Coates, Realtor, as I settled into his vintage Cadillac convertible. He'd come highly recommended at Lou Pines Data Mart, better known as Loopy's. "Bold. A lot of Loopy folks find a home in Black Forest—out by the lake, very secluded."

Pulling out a freebie *Local Homes* I'd picked up at a diner near my motel, I flipped to a page I'd marked. "What about this one?"

Harry glanced at the ad dismissively and turned the ignition. The big-block V8 roared to life. "Costwold Acres, by the golf course," he shouted over the revving engine.

"Exactly," I yelled back. "I like to golf. And I hear the lawns are fabulous."

Harry let off the gas. "True," he admitted with a slight shrug and put the Caddy in gear. "I can't *legally* tell you not to buy there, but I *can* legally tell you that there's no *proof* that there's witches there." He paused, while his implication sank in. "Tell you what," he said as he pulled onto a country highway. "We'll go out to Black Forest first; if you still want to go to Costwold Acres afterward, we'll go there."

"Fair enough," I muttered, sheepishly, since we were already headed toward Black Forest.

Ten minutes later, past more wall-to-wall developments than I'd ever imagined could be packed into such a small area, Harry pulled off the highway and sped directly toward a massive lake looming on the right. A wall of trees in the distance stretched either way as far as I could see.

"The lake, I presume?"

Harry nodded. "Black Forest proper is out there, but this set of developments is known as Black Forest as well. We'll start with a favorite of Loopy folks, Moonlit Thicket." He slued the Caddy around a curving lane and slammed to a halt in front of a cozy little ranch on a slight grade, half-hidden by trees. Jumping out, he bounded up the driveway.

Like the neighboring houses, the lawn was long and choked with weeds, mostly obscuring the inevitable garden gnomes peeking out from the hedges here and there. Dandelion seeds floated everywhere in a fuzzy mist. On a warm Saturday morning in the middle of summer, I expected to hear a dozen mowers, trimmers and hedge clippers, but . . . nothing. There were plenty of people outside: young couples in shorts chatting in their driveways, college girls in sweat pants walking their dogs, sleepy middle-aged men lurching out mid nap to check their mailboxes, families sipping lemonades on their front porches, staring at me and gesturing. It was just like the suburb I grew up in, except they didn't seem to care about their lawns.

Running to catch up with the Realtor, I recognized half a dozen of the neighbors I'd met over the previous week at Loopy's. Still, it didn't feel like *my* kind of neighborhood. "I don't know about this place."

Harry raised an eyebrow. "Really? I was *sure* you'd love it. Well, since we're here, why not take a look inside?"

I grimaced, but went on. The house itself was immaculate, inside and out, quite a contrast with the unkempt lawn surrounding it. A well-appointed kitchen with stainless steel appliances and black marble countertops included an eat-in area adjacent to a glass patio door opening to the backyard. The kitchen bled over an eating counter with barstools into a great room with a massive built-in plasma TV.

"There's a second bedroom with all the wiring for a home office," Harry said. "Loopy folks telecommute for a few days every month, if you know what I mean."

I didn't, but I let it pass. The truth was, I'd been fantasizing about that plasma TV in the great room. But that yard would take a lot of work.

"I don't know, Mr. Coates. The lawn—"

Harry scowled, but his Realtor's smile quickly reappeared. "But you like the house?"

Subconsciously, I glanced toward the great room. "It's okay, I guess."

"Tell you what," Harry said, smiling conspiratorially, "I know the owner. Let me talk to her about a rent-to-own. Get you out of that motel, at least."

"That *would* be nice. There's no microwave there. I have to go to work for breakfast, but *someone* always smells up the kitchen first with something dreadfully foul, like kidneys or liver. Still, I don't know—"

"I'm pretty sure she'll leave the TV," Harry said casually.

"How much?"

"Heard you found a place in the Thicket?" Mr. Wiley asked on my two-week anniversary at Loopy's, poking his redness around my cube wall without warning. "Nice place."

"Yes, Mr. Wiley." My boss had told me to call him by his first name, but I couldn't bring myself to do it. Coyote Wiley? Get real. I hoped we didn't have to order office supplies from Acme.

"Good, good. Just wanted to say I'll need those schemas Friday instead of next Monday, okay?"

"Sure."

"Good, good," Wiley said. He glanced at my wall calendar. "Looks like a full moon this weekend—we'll be working from home next week, of course, so be sure it's done Friday. Did anyone tell you about the telecommuting?"

"Rose—uh, Little Red—explained."

"Good, good," he said and vanished.

That conversation with Rose had been even stranger than our first one. For a week every month, on a schedule that I couldn't quite pin down, we all worked from home. As near as I could tell, it was one of the major perks that drew people to Loopy's, and the company made a big deal of the environmental and economic impact in their literature. But Rose hinted the telecommuting policy was in place for quite a different reason—wink, wink. It was all very confusing, but I was excited to work at home, so I kept mum.

Wiley's head popped around my cube wall again. "Don't forget to come in sometime next week for that free haircut."

"Wolff, right? Bold." Rex Canaan, a database programmer from work, greeted me in my driveway the next morning.

"Bryan Wolff," I said. "Aren't you Rex?"

Grinning, he said, "Sure am. I see you're settling in okay."

"Thanks. You live around here, I take it?"

"Just up the street a bit," he said, motioning with his head. "Listen, I was wondering if you wanted to join our carpool? Bingo Leapps retired last month, and we've got a spot open. Save you some gas money, if you're interested."

"Sure, that sounds good." And neighborly. Maybe the Thicket would be okay after all.

At a wave from Rex, a red sedan pulled into my driveway. "Hop in."

Rex made introductions as I climbed in the seat behind the driver.

Seconds later, we were on the highway in bumper-to-bumper traffic that I knew from recent experience would stretch a peaceful ten-minute drive into a half hour of frazzled nerves and white knuckles. I was glad to have a break.

The driver, Scotty Terrier, turned to Rex. "How about that video conference with Coffee Corner? 'Can we have it next week?' "

Rex, in the front passenger seat, slapped his thigh and stomped his foot on the floorboard. Boomer Sheepskin, the other passenger in the rear—inexplicably munching the last bite of a milk bone—howled and stomped both feet. Scotty howled, too. For a moment, I thought it was dinnertime at the dog pound. I jerked away instinctively and smashed my head on the door frame.

"You okay, Wolff?" Boomer said, loudly. The din ceased immediately.

"Fine," I said, rubbing my head.

"Hey, you weren't at the video, were you?" asked Rex. "Wiley should have sent you. I mean, they *are* your customer. Want me to talk to him?"

Shaking my head, I said, "Thanks, but I'll do it."

Over six years in the tech field, I'd found that when you let other people do things for you, they tended to grab the credit as well. Blame, on the other hand, always seemed to find its way to you, no matter how many people were between you and the accuser. The only way to get ahead was to take the initiative yourself, as well as accepting the consequences. In the end, you'd be credited with both wins and losses. The poor saps that let others talk for them always ended up with only losses.

Shrugging, Rex said casually, "Did I tell you guys that Rebecca Furr in Accounting asked about the carpool again last week?"

Boomer made a guttural sound like a choked-off bark and said, "Really? What'd you tell her this time?"

Scotty twisted his head around and glanced at me. "How are you going to explain Wolff? We don't need HR breathing down our necks."

"Relax," said Rex. "I told her last week Wolff was already riding with us."

Choking off another bark, Boomer said, "Good move." He turned to me. "Thanks; you really saved our bacon here."

Puzzled, I asked as innocently as I could, "What's wrong with Rebecca Furr?"

Rex howled briefly. "She's a *girl!* Can't have another *girl!*"

"Not after Sally, no," muttered Scotty solemnly.

"No way," Boomer added.

"Who's Sally?" I asked.

We rode in embarrassed silence for a couple minutes. Boomer and Rex stared out the window pointedly; Scotty focused on his driving, narrowly avoiding a fender bender once as he changed lanes.

I wondered if they meant Sally Mange. She was a local legend at Loopy's, a nineteen-year-old administrative assistant who'd gotten in the family way by someone at work the year before. The rumor was that she was actually carrying on with *three* guys at once and didn't know which one was the father. She refused DNA tests, and was raising the kid by herself—with financial help from Lou P. himself, in a kind of tacit admission of responsibility for the people in his employ. Loopy folks thought of this as a grand gesture, almost paternal, and spoke of the incident in hushed, reverent tones. The story was always a tiny bit different each time I heard it, so he assumed it was one of those rumors that crop up periodically, spin freely for a while, picking up more and more outlandish details, until it's left with only a kernel of truth.

"Hey, Boomer," Rex said brightly, finally. "Do you have visitation with Cubby this weekend?"

"No," Boomer said, glancing nervously at me. "He's with Scotty."

I'd have to look into this Sally business.

Boomer sighed. "You know, I could *really* go for another milk bone right now."

"How's that schema coming along?" Wiley asked Thursday morning, his head perched on my cube wall. I glanced up. Wiley's red mess of hair and beard looked noticeably longer than it had on Monday.

"Almost finished. I'll have it for you in the morning."

"Good, good," he said.

Normally, he'd just pop away as quickly as he'd come, but this time Wiley stayed, scrutinizing me, flashing a scowl now and then.

"Is there anything else, Mr. Wiley?"

"I told you about the free haircuts, right?"

"Are you going to mow your lawn, mister?" a teen kid with long shoulder-length blond hair asked me on Saturday morning, as I pushed the primer button on my brand new lawn mower. A red 20" Huffy lay on its side at the bottom of my driveway. "It's a full moon tomorrow."

"Yeah, so?" I yanked the starter cord, and the engine coughed.

The kid cocked his head to one side. "It's not . . . you know . . . *scratchy* when it's cut short. It's soft. I *hate* that. Don't you?"

I stared at him and yanked the starter cord again. The lawn mower coughed again.

"That's how I like my lawn." I returned my attention to the mower. The engine caught, a high-pitched whirr shattering the Saturday morning silence.

A couple of my neighbors bolted out their front doors a few seconds later, staring at me in horror.

The mower barely kept up with the long grass and tough weeds, choking to a halt almost immediately. A half dozen people congregated in the middle of the street half a block away, having an animated conversation. The blond kid on the Huffy was there, staring at me.

Let them talk. If I wanted a decent lawn, I could have a decent lawn. There was always some guy in every neighborhood obsessing over his lawn; in *this* neighborhood, the bar was set so low that even a lazybones like *me* could be the obsessive schmo.

By the time I finished a half hour later—I'd only get a few feet before the mower would choke out again and I'd have to restart it—most of the neighborhood was in the street, watching me curiously.

Rex was at the front of the crowd, cradling a baby. He handed the infant to a short, dark-haired woman next to him and moved away rapidly, as if he didn't know her.

Oh, well. Now was as good a time as any to get to know the neighbors. I didn't want to be that mean guy down the street whose house the kids egged and TP'd.

After stowing the mower in the garage, I screwed up my courage and headed for the crowd. Several people cut out and ran back to their houses when they saw me approach, but the majority waited. The dark-haired woman turned at someone's call and bustled off to a house—not Rex's as I'd expected—in that curious waddle-and-hop-skip that only a first-time mother can do, when she holds her infant close to her chest and tries to run without jostling the babe. I thought I saw a butterfly trailing her, before I realized it was a full-color tattoo on her exposed left shoulder.

"Good morning," I said. "Bryan Wolff. I thought I'd mow the lawn this morning; is that okay?"

Heads nodded amidst murmuring.

The blond kid said, "He *likes* it short."

"I do. I was going to weed and feed next. There's no neighborhood association regulation against that, is there?"

Heads shook nervously.

Someone at the back stifled a guttural bark. I knew that sound. Boomer came around to the front. "Man wants to mow his lawn. Fine by me. Anyone else feel like being neighborly?"

Boomer made introductions. It turned out that the neighborhood wasn't just a favorite of Loopy folks, it was *entirely* Loopy folks. After some friendly chats, I felt a lot better about the neighborhood. Pretty soon it was just me and Boomer.

"Whose house is that?" I pointed where I'd seen the dark-haired woman with the baby go.

Glancing over, Boomer stifle-barked. "That's Scotty's," he said without a trace of bitterness. "He's got the cub this weekend, so he couldn't come out."

"Was that your ex-wife? The dark-haired woman with the tattoo?"

Boomer barked. "Sally? Cubby's mom? She's not my ex-wife; I've never been married. Where'd you get *that* idea?"

"The carpool," I said, sure I'd touched a nerve. "You said Scotty had visitation with Cubby this weekend?"

"Oh, right," he said, forcing a smile. "No, I just help them out; watch the cub sometimes. We were friends back in college."

"Her name is Sally? Didn't you guys mention a Sally in the carpool?"

Boomer's eyes flashed a look of danger I'd never seen in him. "Different Sally," he said through gritted teeth.

I didn't mention that I'd seen Rex holding the cub. It didn't seem very neighborly right then.

"How's the new place, Bryan?" my mother asked over the phone Sunday night. "I worry about you that close to the woods. Who knows how many wild animals roam around there at night."

"Look, Mom," I slurred, "I got up this morning, attacked the backyard, then soaked the entire lawn, front and back, with weed and feed. I spent the whole day doing yardwork, and I just came to bed without dinner, tired beyond belief."

"No dinner?" my mother shrieked through the tinny receiver. "Go eat something right now!"

"I will, Mom," I lied. "Right after I get off the phone."

"You do that, young man. You need to keep up your strength."

I cut the conversation short, quite unintentionally, by falling asleep to my mother's droning outrage. I woke to the loud *Eep! Eep! Eep!* of a disconnected line, hung up the phone and set it on the nightstand. Later, I'd lie to my mother about eating. Now, I'd sleep.

The full moon shone sunlike through my bedroom window, bright enough to pierce my eyelids. I tossed and turned, but couldn't sleep, between my eyelids telling me it was morning and the argument I was having with my mother in my head.

Have a steak with that! I'm a vegetarian, Mom.

Don't you want to be a big strong man like your father? He's 400 pounds, Mom, and he gets winded punching buttons on the TV remote.

Your cousin Alfie wouldn't drink his milk and now he has to pee into a bag! Alfie's your uncle, Mom, and he's 92!

Reluctantly, I dragged myself out of the bed to fix myself a snack—a *small* snack, just enough to get Mom out of my head. It was nearly midnight, after all.

Stumbling into the kitchen, I didn't bother flicking the light on—it seemed redundant with the eye-burning moonlight. I passed by the patio door to admire my handiwork—moonlight really suited the in-progress yard: light enough to look well-trimmed; dark enough to hide the flaws.

A movement in the neighbor's backyard caught my eye next door. My redheaded neighbor, Jenny Timberland, stood stock-still in a white bikini, staring up at the moon. I'd met her the day before, one of the lawn mowing spectators. She and her husband, Brad, moved in only last year, and were trying to start a family. The door behind Jenny opened, and Brad emerged—

—stark naked, his manhood dangling in full view in the moonlight! I blinked, and looked again, but it was still dangling free. Only then did I notice that Jenny was naked as well. She'd turned sideways; now that I could see her full-on, it was clear that her white bikini was really her untanned skin. Jenny grabbed Brad's hand and stretched up to kiss him, then the two of them stood, starkers, staring up at the moon.

Great. Naked moon freaks next door. I shook my head and headed back to the fridge.

A howl in front drowned out the low hum of the refrigerator. I'd never heard a sound like that before, not even in a neighborhood of dogs. Was Mom right about the wildlife here? I raced to the front, but couldn't see anything past the shrubs out the front windows. Cautiously, I cracked open the front door.

There was nothing furry on the front porch, so I slipped out for a better look.

I got a better look, all right. It looked like *all* of my neighbors were milling around in the nude. Young couples like Jenny and Brad, old geezers with walkers, families with naked toddlers running around, even a muscular guy in a wheelchair. All naked, adults staring up at the moon.

Had they all come out to see where the howl had come from? And they all just happened to sleep in the nude? Or were they *all* moonworshipping nudists? The entire neighborhood?

I backed into the house and shut the door quietly. Back in my bedroom, I stacked my pillows against the window to keep out the moon's searchlight and crumpled onto my bed, facing away from the window.

Another howl, farther off, startled me. A chorus of howls nearby answered it.

Dogs. It had to be dogs. The Thicket was *full* of dogs. Right now, howling dogs, casual nudists and a lighthouse-bright moon were more than I could bear.

A loud dog fight broke out next door, in the backyard.

Snatching my MP3 player from the nightstand, I jammed the earbuds in my ears and cranked the volume.

It was going to be a long night.

We didn't see you out last night, Rex IM'd Monday morning.

I froze. How to answer that? Carefully, I typed, *What?*

A few minutes passed before Rex responded. *Never mind. We'll catch up Monday.*

The rest of the week, I stayed inside, afraid to go out. Not for groceries to replenish my rapidly-depleting food stock, not even to the mailbox. By day, I pulled the blinds and holed up in my office, pretending nothing was wrong. After work, I watched the big plasma TV and carefully avoided looking out the windows, especially in the kitchen. The pillows remained in my bedroom window, separating me from the neighborhood.

As for telecommuting, everyone at work seemed no-nonsense, one-hundred-percent devoted to their jobs. Not a single joke came across my IM or email. I wondered if this was normal behavior.

The rest of the week passed without anything else unusual—except for one cryptic IM from Boomer on Thursday:

Don't forget your free haircut this week.

"I see you got your free haircut," Wiley said, poking his red tangles around my cube wall. "Good, good."

I looked over and stared. His hair and beard were shorter than I'd ever seen—clearly he'd gotten *his* free haircut—but they still managed to tangle. "Yes," I lied and returned to my work.

For the next few weeks, I was the consummate professional, completely focused on my work, on time with my assignments, absolutely on my game. It wasn't just me that had changed, either; I noticed that my co-workers seemed to be walking on eggshells around me, and even the carpool talk was restricted to pleasant chitchat. I did nothing to dissuade this behavior.

I noticed that Wiley's hair and beard grew awfully fast. He'd pop in every few days to check on me or get a progress report, and I could see a difference each time. In fact, *everyone's* hair grew significantly faster than mine. *I* hadn't had *my* hair cut since I'd started working at Loopy's.

I half expected Wiley to pop in and warn me about getting *too many* free haircuts.

"Hi, Mr. Wolff, I brought you a cake," said a plain, dark-haired woman when I answered my doorbell on Tuesday of the next Loopy Telecommuting Week. She pushed a cake tin at me. A nauseating waft of greasy bacon and cheese escaped from the tin.

I stood frozen, my hand on the doorknob, my heart pounding in my chest. It had been nearly a month, and I hadn't talked to any of my neighbors since. I was considering moving soon. These people were *weird*.

"I'll just put it over here, okay?" she said and ducked under me to leave the cake on a nearby end table. On her way past, I noticed a full-color butterfly tattoo on her shoulder.

Turning, I said tentatively, "You're Sally?"

She set down the cake tin carefully and turned around, treating me to a smile that lit up her face. "Yes! Did Rex tell you?"

"No, Boomer."

Sally blushed a little. "Well, don't believe everything they say about me at work. The boys couldn't help themselves; we all worked late one Friday before a telecommuting weekend, went out for drinks, had a bit too much and got caught in the car under a full moon, that's all. It was all perfectly consenting, considering. I'm not complaining; the boys take care of everything—not Loopy, as I'm sure you've heard." She rolled her eyes. "What would Cubby do with a *fourth* daddy, anyway?"

She winked at me and brushed past me, then turned, inches away, looking up expectantly. "You should come and see us tonight. It's the full moon, you know. I'm sure Rex won't mind, and little Cubby loves company."

Rex? And Boomer? *And* Scotty? All in some kind of bizarre fourway with the legendary Loopy Sally?

"Mr. Wolff?"

"Bryan."

"Bryan. Please consider joining us for the baying. We're all worried about you, staying inside. It's dangerous."

"I'll . . . think about it," I said slowly, desperately trying to keep my face blank. I hadn't realized it was the full moon tonight; based on the last month, I was pretty sure being outside with the nude moonies was more dangerous than staying inside, but Sally seemed very *committed* to her version.

I closed the door quickly after Sally left and watched her through the peephole. She went straight to Rex's house.

Shaking my head, I tried to convince myself it was all a hallucination. It would have worked if I hadn't seen the cake tin on my end table.

I took it to the kitchen eating counter and opened the tin. It still smelled like cheesy bacon. I tasted it. Yup. Bacon and cheese *cake*.

These people were *weird*.

"Wolff? What are you doing here this late?" Rex looked so shocked when he opened the door that I could easily imagine him clutching his chest and collapsing right there.

Frankly, *I* didn't know what I was doing there. I could have stayed home, watching TV. But I grew up in the suburbs, and some things were "just not done," according to my mother—things like avoiding your neighbors. It wasn't, well, neighborly. I'd been a hermit for a good month, and they'd let me sulk without complaining. I owed them an apology, at least. Maybe they weren't that bad. I'd had worse neighbors—like the guy who cleaned his Uzi on the front porch at 3:00 A.M. *These* neighbors probably just howled at the moon for a while, then went to bed.

Besides, I seriously doubted they were going to ask me to strip naked for my first baying. Wasn't the idea to get me to *want* to join the cult? I was sure it would be okay to howl at the moon fully clothed.

Screwing up my courage, I announced, "I've come for the . . . baying. Sally invited me."

Rex blanched.

Sally called from the kitchen. "He came?"

"He did," said Rex, a bit woodenly. He stepped aside to let me in.

"It's almost time," Sally called. "We should go outside now; you know how much Cubby likes to watch the other children play, even if they have to go inside before the change." She emerged through the kitchen door holding Cubby in her arms and handed the baby to Rex. She leaned toward me and whispered, "I'm glad you came," in my ear as she unbuttoned her blouse and stripped right in front of me, without a hint of modesty. Unbundling the baby and pulling off his diaper, she took the naked baby and sauntered out the front door.

"You coming?" Rex left, naked, leaving the door wide open.

I followed, dumbly.

"You sure you want clothes on?" Rex asked. "They look new. Shame to ruin them."

"Oh, stop it," Sally said, giggling. "Let him be. Maybe that's the way they did it where he grew up." She shifted Cubby to one arm and patted my shoulder with her free arm. "You be as comfortable as you want. Did you remember to leave your front door unlocked?"

"Yes," I lied, jamming my hand in my pocket to feel for my key.

Across the street, several naked children circled a sprinkler, laughing. A few doors away, the blond teenager with the Huffy writhed happily in the knee-length grass. A sudden high-pitched howl from the Timberlands' backyard made me jump. It was followed by a yelp and a loud growl that rose in intensity to a howl.

"They're so cute," Sally whispered to Rex and giggled. "Jenny told me she's late, but she doesn't want to tell Brad because she's afraid he won't want to mate in the backyard any more. Isn't that silly?"

Rex made a low guttural sound. Sally belted out a yowl so loud I jumped back. One or two of the neighbors a few blocks away answered her, hopefully, as if she'd made a lewd proposition. Rex howled out a warning, and they stopped abruptly. He shot her a sharp look and she giggled.

"What? Just because I have a baby, I can't flirt a little? Scotty and Boomer don't mind." She yowled again, defiantly.

Fifteen minutes and hundreds of howls later, Sally bent down to Cubby and cooed, "Bedtime, Cubby. Your time will come soon enough." She turned and breezed past without noticing me.

Rex arched his back violently, then hunched over, as if in severe pain. I ran to help him, kneeling beside his crumpled body. His face twisted toward me, his eyes glowing yellow in the full moonlight, framed by a face that looked like he'd been beaten to an inch of his life. I watched in horror as his nose lengthened to a sharp snout, with razor-sharp canines lining his mouth, and hair thickened all over his face and body. His skin appeared alive, as if something were crawling under it, making its way down his back, along his arms and thighs. The sound of crunching bones accompanied his grunts of pain.

I looked away for a moment, hoping it was all a trick of my mind, but the scene was the same in every yard. People in pain, changing, transforming into—

Werewolves!

I ran, fast. My lungs burning, I fumbled my key out before I hit the porch, unlocked the door and flashed inside. Glancing back, I saw something hairy streak out Rex's front door on four legs, yowling like Sally. Slamming and locking the door, I collapsed against it, my chest heaving.

The next howl I heard sounded from my living room; I nearly hurled myself down the basement stairs before I realized I'd left the TV on when I'd gone out.

An American Werewolf in London was on.

"Mr. Wolff?" Sally called in a little-girl voice through the closed door after ringing my bell the next morning.

"Won't you try my cookies?" She giggled and pounded on the door. "Oh, come on, Bryan, I won't bite."

I wasn't so sure. "What do you want?" I yelled from the safety of the hallway.

"Just to talk. I think we need to talk. Don't you?"

Sally kept ringing and pounding and cajoling. I inched to the door and peeked out the peephole. Her hair was a mess and her face looked battered, but at least she was wearing clothes—a sundress with several slashes across the belly clinging to patches of wetness all over her, no doubt thrown on after a long night of romping around naked and lupine.

I cracked open the door.

Sally forced a smile. "You're not really one of us, are you?" She looked disappointed. She smelled of wet fur, though I couldn't see any wolf coat remaining.

"It's just my name." At least now I understood why everyone thought I was bold; they envied my supposed brashness in announcing my *condition* openly. Living together in secret packs—werewolf neighborhoods— they isolated themselves so they wouldn't accidentally harm their human friends. In a way, it was kind of noble. Creepy, but noble.

"I'm so sorry, Bryan. Rex said you looked terrified, but you don't have to worry—we'd *never* hurt you. You're probably thinking of leaving, aren't you? Please stay."

"*Why* would I stay?" I was considering leaving *right now*.

"I thought we were neighbors. Doesn't that count for something?"

"Yeah, hi-how're-you-doin' neighbors, not owooo- let's-eat-some-sheep neighbors!"

Sally looked crestfallen. "I suppose I deserved that. But we're really not bad. I talked it over with the others;

they were all pretty shocked after last night, but most of them don't mind you staying, if you promise not to tell anyone about us."

"Or what? You'd have to kill me?" My hands started shaking.

"That's not very nice. I *told* you we wouldn't hurt you. And I don't think you'd tell people, anyway."

Sally was right. Nobody had harmed me, and they certainly were *trying* to help me fit in, even though *they* probably thought *I* was a little weird. From their perspective, *I* was the one being a difficult neighbor.

I inched open the door. "Is Cubby okay? Does he turn—"

"Not yet; he's just a baby." She picked a twig out of her hair. "We don't . . . change until our teens. He's just like any other human baby right now. I *do* worry, you know, leaving him all alone like that, even if it's only one night a month."

"Why not get a babysitter?" I asked without thinking, and opened the door a bit more.

Sally pushed a stray clump of hair and dirt from in front of her eyes. "Usually, the older kids in the litter watch the young ones. But I only have Cubby, and he's so tiny right now."

My heart went out to Cubby, all alone at that age for a long night, month after month. I couldn't let it pass; it wasn't neighborly, and my mother raised me to be a good neighbor. The words came out of my mouth before I could stop them. "Are you sure? I could watch Cubby, so you don't have to worry."

"Would you? That's so nice! I *told* Rex you'd be a *good* neighbor!" She leaped forward, arms outstretched; I jumped back, staring down at her still-damp body, wrinkling my nose.

"Oh, don't worry, silly," she said. "I know how I smell, but there's no fur left; it falls off in the morning. Do I need to shower before giving you a hug?"

You want a good neighbor? Today, I hugged a wet were-wolf, and set myself up as the neighborhood's pet human. Well, so long as they didn't want me neutered . . .

Tomorrow, I might even get a free haircut.

Laura J. Underwood is a fantasy author with a number of tales in print, including *Song Of Silver* (Dark Regions Press), *Bad Lands* with Selina Rosen (Five Star Press 2007), *The Lunari Mask* (Yard Dog Press 2007) and *The Green Women* (Sam's Dot Publishing 2008). Her short fiction has appeared in *Sword And Sorceress*, *Catfantastic*, *Such A Pretty Face*, *Turn The Other Chick* and various other anthologies and magazines. When not writing, she's First Assistant at the Carter Branch of the Knox County Public Library System. Occasionally she plays harp and wields swords as a member of the SFWA Musketeers. She lives in East Tennessee with a cat of few grey cells and her folks. For more information visit her web page at *http://www.sff.net/people/keltora*.

That Time of
the Month

Laura J. Underwood

"Have you seen my son Charlie?"

Morgan looked up from the book she was reading and spied Mrs. Briggs at the hedge with a leash in one hand and a rolled-up newspaper in the other. The old woman was sniffing the air as though she scented something rotten.

Morgan resisted the urge to flare her nostrils. Instead, she shook her head and pretended to have no interest in what her neighbor was doing. Since the Briggs had moved into the house next door three moons ago, Morgan had considered building a ten-foot fence to reclaim her privacy. Not, she suspected, that any barrier short of the Great Wall of China would keep that woman at bay. Mrs. Briggs was always out there sniffing around, trying to see what was happening in Morgan's backyard. Privacy was an issue Morgan prized above all else, and it annoyed her that she now had neighbors who couldn't keep to their own territory.

"Here, Charlie," Mrs. Briggs called and started to whistle. "Come on, boy. I haven't got all day. Supper's getting cold, son."

Morgan rolled her eyes. She continued to pretend to read now as Mrs. Briggs moved towards the back of the yard and then suddenly shouted, "Charlie! Bad boy!"

As Morgan peered over the top of her now forgotten novel, Mrs. Briggs rushed into the area between the shed and the hedge and laid into something out of sight with the newspaper. There was a yelp akin to a dog, and then a more human, "Gad, Mom! Okay, stop it!"

Charlie stood up, giving Morgan a view of his bare chest, which was not as hirsute as she would have thought or even liked, and a shaggy head of a long mullet. Morgan considered him cute, except for that serious underbite. Even from here, he smelled like a wet dog.

"You fool, how many times have I told you to stop doing that where the neighbors can see!" Mrs. Briggs snapped like a rabid hound.

Charlie glanced in Morgan's direction. His face turned a little red as he waved and said, "Oh, hi, Morgan!"

His mother whapped him across the nose with the newspaper, snagged his mullet and started dragging him towards the house.

"Ow, Mom, stop it, that ain't cool, I . . ."

"Just shut up and get in there!" she snarled. "I swear, boy, you'll be the death of me and the rest of our kinfolk if you don't learn how to behave in civilized parts!"

They disappeared through the back door of the bungalow. Morgan heard the slam of the screen and the rattle of voices going faint as they moved into another part of the house.

She put her book aside, and watching the Briggs' house to make sure no one was watching—yes, she had seen Charlie peeping out at her when she sunbathed—she hurried towards the back end of her own yard. Reaching the hedge, she looked over it in the area between the greenery and the garage.

There was a bone, bloody and gnawed, lying in the small pathway that led to the back gate.

Morgan eyed it, and then glanced at the house and muttered, "Stupid backwoods werewolves . . . just what I needed."

She turned and headed back for her own house.

When the Briggs first moved in, Morgan had suspected even then that they were a bunch of common hillbilly werewolves. In this day and age, no one really believed in such things, and just calling the police to report them for being lycanthropes would get her put in a loony bin. So she watched for the signs, and as soon as the first full moon started to shine, she began to find the bones of dead rabbits and the remains of cats scattered about the hedgerows of their small suburban neighborhood. *Sloppy, lazy, shiftless . . .* It angered her that they were so careless with their kills. Fortunately, some folks thought the coyotes were to blame. Morgan had examined every kill she discovered before disposing of it, and she knew the telltale signs of long claws and teeth were larger than anything a coyote could do. Besides, the coyotes didn't come near this place. They knew better.

Stupid hicks, she had thought. *Leaving your kill out where the whole world can see.*

The Briggs were clearly out of place here in the suburbs of Fenderbank City. They tended to keep dead cars in the driveway (even though they got cited for them more than once) and Mrs. Briggs actually dangled laundry on a line to dry in spite of having bought a home with all the most modern conveniences left by the late and not so lamented previous owner, Mr. Corwin. His relations had wanted a quick sale and had even lowered the price since selling a house with blood splatters on the walls wasn't easy. Nor had Corwin's relatives wanted anything out of the house where their uncle had died so brutally. They were too creeped out by the whole experience.

As far as Morgan was concerned, Corwin got exactly what he deserved. He was always too darn nosy for his own good.

She had rather hoped, however, that someone quiet and less intrusive would move in. Instead, she got the Briggs. They acted like a bunch of hillbilly wannabes. Papa Briggs was a big hairy man who sat on the front porch pulling slugs from a bottle of moonshine and whose chewing tobacco splats adorned the sidewalks like ugly starfish. Mama Briggs reminded Morgan of Ma Kettle in the way she was built and talked.

And then there was Charlie, a thirty-year-old son who should have been off on his own. He was definitely not an alpha. Morgan had almost taken a liking to him, mainly because he did seem awful docile for a werewolf, but Charlie was as ignorant as dirt and subtle as a chin zit. Now and again, Morgan saw him watching her from the house, and she could practically smell the feral lust visible in his eyes. But the moment she actually looked straight at him to see if he could put his money where his mouth was—so to speak—he would duck and cower and if he'd had a tail, it would have been between his legs.

Every time the moon rose, Morgan knew it was that time of the month for the neighbors. There had been reports of three large shaggy dogs seen wandering around the local Low-Mart parking lot down on the main road; one black, one grey and one sort of sandy brown—the color of Charlie's mullet. They had chased down a deer one time, and another time, they were seen scrambling after someone's cat.

At first, Morgan had been angry. The last time a pack moved into her neighborhood, they had been a group of young Hispanics. They pissed and pooped on Morgan's yard and tore up her flowerbeds, and had it not been for her own allergies, she would have planted wolfsbane and roses to teach them a lesson. Things reached a pitch when someone dumped the remains of a deer right behind Morgan's house. That was the last straw. Morgan had nosed around until she found out where the pack lived, and then she had called the INS. The pack quickly disappeared when it turned out they didn't have green cards.

With the Briggs, it was going to be different. She couldn't just keep calling the police about the old cars, and since the Briggs were clearly American born, it was impossible to sic any of the government offices on them. Charlie was too old for Social Services to take an interest in his constant abuse by his mother. Somehow, Morgan was going to have to figure out a way to break up the pack.

And then, Morgan decided, she knew a way.

It was still afternoon when Mrs. Briggs yelled at Mr. Briggs to get off his sorry behind and take her down to the Low-Mart.

"We're going to be there tonight, woman," he snapped back.

"I need to go now!" Mrs. Briggs retorted. "They got them extra large flea collars on sale, and you know they'll run out by dark. Don't know where that boy's getting them fleas, but he's a-needing a collar right now."

"Just dip him again," Mr. Briggs said.

"That messes up his skin," Mrs. Briggs retorted. "You know how sensitive he is."

With much grumbling, Mr. Briggs came out, swinging his keys on a chain. He and Mrs. Briggs trundled into the truck. It roared to life, a metal dragon belching black smoke out of the tail pipe.

Morgan stood by the curtained front window and watched them head on down the street. She glanced over at their house, and sure enough, Charlie was at the window. He couldn't see her because of the angle and the shadows, but she could see him, and she smiled.

Charlie, she figured, was going to be easy. Typical of a backwoods hick, he had no idea how to act among the more civilized. She had seen him pissing on her back gate just the other day, but only on the outside. It was as though he wanted to mark the territory without being too obvious.

She would remedy that. With the right training, he would adjust. The problem as she saw it would be to get him away from Mama.

We'll show you who's alpha, Morgan thought. She headed out the back of the house, wandering over to the fence, wearing the tightest pair of cutoff jeans and tube top she had. She pretended to be watering the herbs, and then she dropped the hose and bent over, making certain her tightly clad backside was directed at the Briggs house and in full view.

She heard the screen door slam and the thump of feet across the grass. Picking up the hose, she played with the spout then turned.

Charlie was right there at the fence, his tongue hanging out, his eyes bugged.

"Something wrong, Charlie?" she asked and looked him right in the eye.

He went back into the submissive posture she had become so used to seeing, tucking his chin, grinning, his cheeks turning red. And panting.

"Nothing, Miss Morgan," he said. "I just thought you'd fallen and . . ."

"Well, how sweet of you, Charlie," she said and stepped closer to the fence, letting the water trail down her leg and into her tennis shoes. "No one ever cared whether or not I fell before."

He looked up, startled. Before, she had always told him to get lost, and it must have startled him to have her being so forward and friendly.

"I . . . uh . . ."

"Come on, Charlie. Don't be bashful."

He practically melted when she reached over and stroked his cheek with one hand.

And then she realized he was peeing through his pants. He looked down, embarrassed, and ran back towards the house.

"Charlie, wait!" she called.

He stopped on the porch, obedient as a lamb, ducking his head and looking back at her.

"I am sorry," she said sweetly. "I seem to have gotten you all wet with my hose."

His head snapped up. He looked down at the stain and his tongue lolled out of his head.

"Come on back," Morgan said. "I never get to just talk to you without your Mama being around."

"That's because Mama's afraid—" Charlie stopped.

"Afraid of what," Morgan asked. "Afraid a silly girl like me is gonna steal her handsome son?"

Charlie was suddenly at the fence again, leaning over. The wafting odor of raw meat was on his breath. "You think I'm handsome?"

"Of course, I do. I thought it the day you moved in," Morgan said. She leaned over the fence, her lips close to his. He looked uncertain, but then she nuzzled his neck, steeling herself against the fact that he clearly didn't wash it, and then nipped him. He yipped just a bit.

"I could use a guy like you on my side," she said.

Charlie grinned and nipped her back. She growled in her throat, and he fell down, rolling over on his back, one leg thumping.

And she knew then that he was hers to command.

In Hollywood, Morgan reflected, the way of the wolf said that the moon was always full when the lycanthrope changed. Scientifically, there were "full" moons for nearly three nights in a row.

In reality, she had learned over the years of dealing with werewolves that the moon had nothing to do with it. True lycanthropes could change at will. Even dumb hick werewolves had that power.

Morgan was sitting by the window in the dark, watching the Briggs' house for movement, when she heard the creak of the back screen. Quickly, she charged into the kitchen and stood at the open back door just in time to see the shapes of three large canines trotting across the backyard and bounding across the fence.

Dressed in a black exercise suit, Morgan stole out of her house and followed. She had let her long dark hair down, and it now draped like a cowl about her head and face as she dashed across her back lawn and leapt over the fence. She landed quietly in the soft-soled boots and kept up the pace, trotting down the alley in the wake of the three forms, staying downwind.

Fortunately, they were not that difficult to keep track of. Charlie was stopping and marking nearly every bush and fence. The black beast kept going, but the grey one would stop and snarl at the younger. At least once, Morgan had to duck behind some garbage cans when the grey wolf attacked the younger, grabbing his throat. He went down in a submissive posture and she snarled and growled, and then meekly, he followed with less marking.

The local Low-Mart was set on the edge of an old wooded pasture that already had signs up about future development and condos. The three wolves raced around the edge of the parking lot to head for that territory. There they began to scare up rabbits and other rodents.

Morgan edged along until she was as close as she dared to get, still keeping downwind. She watched them gathering their kills into a pile in the center of a clearing. Now and again, Charlie would eagerly snag up one of those kills and attempt to scarf it down whole. But the grey wolf—and Morgan could now see that she was definitely a female—nearly bit his head off when he tried.

Waiting only until the pile was a goodly size, Morgan stood up and stepped out of the shadows. Three heads turned. The grey wolf snarled. The black one lowered his head and growled.

Only Charlie, the brown wolf with the underbite, ducked his head and sauntered towards Morgan, tentatively wagging his tail.

"Evening, Charlie," Morgan said and stared at the other two. "Did you make up your mind which pack you wanted to be in?"

"Charlie!" the grey wolf barked in a hoarse manner. "Get your sorry tail back over here, boy, or I'll . . ."

"Or you'll what?" Morgan interrupted. "Whap him on the nose with a newspaper like he was a common dog? You disgust me, Mrs. Briggs. You and yours don't know the first thing about being civil."

The grey wolf rose up on hind legs and shook until the fur fell away, leaving her plump Ma Kettle figure exposed under the light of the moon. Morgan resisted the urge to say "Ewwwww," and kept her gaze on the steady yellow eyes that the old woman still displayed. Her bun had pulled free, and long grey hair cascaded down across her rolls of exposed flesh.

Sloppy and out of shape, Morgan thought.

"Civil?" the old woman snarled. "You think we give a damn about being civil? This is survival, little girl, and you just learned our secret. We can't let you live now. Charlie, get your sorry hide back over here now."

Charlie stayed just behind Morgan like a heeled pup.

"Bill, go get your boy," Mrs. Briggs said.

The black wolf snarled, "He ain't no boy of mine, and you well know it, woman."

Mrs. Briggs snarled and snapped a blow across the black wolf's skull with her fist. "You sorry son of a . . . Charlie, this is your last chance! You get back over here, or I'll take you down when I kill her."

"Kill me?" Morgan said and put a hand to her chest. "What make you think you can kill me, old woman?"

"I've killed bigger mortals than you, girlie," Mrs. Briggs replied. "I'm the leader of this here pack, and what I say goes, and Charlie might find you attractive, but he ain't gonna have no pups with the likes of you after I eats your heart out."

"Really?" Morgan sneered at the old woman as she began to remove her exercise suit and casually tossed it aside. Charlie's eyes practically bugged out of his head and he thumped his tail in appreciation. "Maybe it is time you learned that you're not the only alpha bitch around," Morgan said.

"Why you little tramp! I'll chew up your bones!" Mrs. Briggs dropped to all fours and changed rapidly back into a grey wolf and lunged. But even as the old woman was shifting, Morgan dropped to the ground as well, took a deep breath and let the change take over. But instead of a fat, grey, paunchy werewolf, Morgan was a sleek beast of prey, every black hair laid perfectly against her muscular body.

Mrs. Briggs lunged and tried to snap jaws closed on Morgan's throat, but Morgan ghosted out of the old woman's reach, and before Mrs. Briggs could turn and renew the attack, Morgan was on the grey wolf, closing jaws down on the back of the old woman's neck and snapping hard.

Bone crushed under Morgan's massive jaws. Mrs. Briggs yelped once and then fell silent to the ground. Morgan heard snarling and snapping to her back and turned in time to see the black male and Charlie head to head, nose to nose, lips pulled back, canines exposed. Neither attacked, but neither withdrew.

Morgan sighed and, like smoke, she shifted back into her human form. Naked, she walked over to step between them, pushing both males back. Charlie immediately went into a submissive posture, wagging his tail. Mr. Briggs hesitated, then backed away and paced nervously at the edge, wandering over to the corpse of his wife now slowly shifting back to that of an old woman. Satisfied that he would keep his distance, Morgan collected her exercise suit and pulled it back on.

"As I see it, *Bill*, you have an easy choice," Morgan said. "You can join *my* pack, or you can get the hell out of town and never show your face in these civilized parts again. There's only room for one alpha lycanthrope in these parts, and I am not about to let it be anyone but me . . . and Charlie here is going to be my new alpha male. So are you with us or against us?"

Bill sat back on his haunches and changed into a man—a hirsute, naked man—and scratched his neck thoughtfully.

"Can I take what's left of Nellie here if I agree to leave?" he asked.

"Nellie?" Morgan said.

"My wife. Her name was Nellie," Mr. Briggs said. "Her kinfolk will want to give her a proper wake back in the hills. They'll also wanna know who killed her and why."

"You can tell them she made the mistake of messing with a younger alpha," Morgan said and nodded. " But you better not be getting any ideas about bringing the pack here." Morgan snarled and showed sharp canines to make her point.

Mr. Briggs pulled himself upright and started to haul Mrs. Briggs' corpse over his shoulder.

"You'd best watch yourself, boy," Mr. Briggs said, tossing an admiring glance at Morgan. "She's one tough alpha. Don't think for a minute she'd ever gonna let you be top dog."

Charlie grinned a wolf's grin.

Mr. Briggs disappeared into the shadows with his wife.

Morgan turned to look down at Charlie. "You're not very good at shifting quick, are you?" she asked.

He shook his head.

"We'll work on that," she said and patted him on the head, and his back leg drummed the ground. "Come on, big boy."

Morgan turned, snagging up a couple of the dead rabbits as she started towards the suburban lights. Charlie grabbed a couple as well and trotted after her.

After a youth which included lighting smudge pots in orchards in the middle of the night, being assistant librarian in a research library and News Director at a radio station, and being taught to kayak by the Polish secret police, Berry Kercheval has been herding computers in Silicon Valley for many years. After two technical books, he's recently started writing fiction since you can make it all up. Recent stories have appeared in *Helix*, a quarterly specfic e-zine, and *Witch Way to the Mall*. He lives in Palo Alto, CA, with his wife, kids and too many British sports cars.

Pack Intern

Berry Kercheval

Justin got off the bus and looked across the parking lot at the Tri-City Mall. Today was the first day of his summer internship with mall security. Mater Ruth, his Witch School teacher, had arranged for him to work here over the summer "for the experience." She had been pretty cagey about just what kind of experience he was supposed to get. It wasn't magic, that was clear. At the thought, he patted his pocket where he kept his silver athame and wand. Mater Ruth said it was important to keep them with him at all times so they'd get "attuned to his aura" or something. Still, the money would be nice even if it was barely above minimum wage. It would certainly be different working in the mall instead of just hanging out there.

As he started across the lot to the mall entrance, he saw Veronica, the nice lady from Pizza Barn, walking ahead of him. Justin liked Veronica; she always remembered he liked extra mushrooms on his slice and would often have it warming in the oven before he had crossed the length of the food court to the pizza stand.

As he watched, Veronica passed behind a van, but didn't come out on the other side. Justin heard a scream. He ran to one of the "panic button" posts the mall management had installed that spring and pulled the handle. A Klaxon began to honk and a blue light flashed at the top of the post.

Justin ran over to the van to see what had happened to Veronica. As he turned the corner, he saw her starting to sit up from the ground. A very large dog was backing away. Justin pulled out his wand, flourished it at the dog and shouted, "Stupefy!"

A stream of sparkles came from the end of his wand and fell to the ground near his feet. *This is harder to do when you know it's supposed to be hard,* he thought.

The dog lolled its tongue. Justin was sure it was laughing at him. It turned and went running down the aisle of the parking lot. As Justin knelt to help Veronica, it turned between two cars and vanished.

"Are you all right?" he asked.

"The dog, it attacked me! *Madre de Dios,* I was scared. I fell down, then he ran when the noise started. Thank you!" She hugged him and began to cry.

A pair of men dressed in the navy blue polo shirts and khaki trousers of Mall Security came running up. "Is everyone OK? What happened?" asked the one whose name tag read HI, MY NAME'S PHIL!

Between Veronica's outbursts, Justin explained what he had seen and pointed to where the dog had disappeared.

"Tom, go check it out. See if you can find any trace of this dog."

The other security man barked "Yes sir!" and trotted down the aisle, going back and forth across the dog's path, and turned at the same spot the dog had.

Phil turned his attention back to Veronica, who had stopped crying and was picking up her purse and sweater from the asphalt. "Will you be all right now, ma'am?" he asked.

She nodded, and then exclaimed "*Santa Maria*! I will be late!" and hurried off to the mall entrance.

"And you, sir," Phil said to Justin, "thanks for sounding the alarm."

"You're welcome, Mr. Harris," Justin replied. Phil raised one corner of his thick eyebrow and Justin continued, "I'm Justin, your new intern. Mat . . . Mrs. Thompson sent me."

"Oh, you're Ruth's young fellow! Welcome. Come with me to the office and we'll get you started."

Phil punched a code into the lock on the plain door at the end of a service corridor between Pottery Hut and Namaste Video, and let Justin into the Security office of Tri-City Mall. It was pretty plain. On one side, a rack of monitors showed views from security cameras in the mall and the parking lot. A couple of desks, a battered couch, and a few storage cabinets completed the furnishings. A white board had a list of names and shift assignments, and next to it a bulletin board held the legally mandated minimum wage poster and a collection of snapshots of people under the legend BANNED. An open door led to a locker room.

Besides the main room and the locker room, there was a storage room with neatly stacked equipment: spare radios, Mall Security polo shirts, and emergency gear—a portable defibrillator, some folding stretchers and a couple of industrial-sized—no, make that mall-sized—first-aid kits.

"I hope we never have to use these babies, but if we ever do we're ready," said Phil. "Do you have your first-aid certification with you?"

Justin produced the card from his wallet. The weekend class Mater Ruth had made him take had been a bit boring, but it was a good feeling to know that he could help people in a crunch. "I'm doing the advanced course this fall."

"That's great. We seldom get more than stumbles and bruises, or a cut or burn from the food court workers. They usually handle those themselves," said Phil. "OK, let's get you kitted out."

Phil collected a radio, a polo shirt, and a mysterious device about the size and shape of a small flashlight from the shelf, and showed Justin where his locker was.

"You met Tom, sort of. The rest of the day shift is out patrolling. Let's walk around, I'll show you the drill, and we'll meet them as we go, OK?" Phil looked Justin directly in his eyes. Slightly uncomfortable, Justin dropped his gaze and said, "Um, OK, sure." When he glanced back, Phil was smiling.

They left the Security office and walked out into the mall. As they toured the mall, Phil showed Justin how to hold the flashlight device over inconspicuous tabs attached to the walls of the mall. "RFID tags in the tabs register a time stamp in this gizmo. This way, the management can verify we've been doing our patrols."

Outside the Beach, Bar and Bed shop they found the other Security man from the parking lot watching the crowd.

"Tom," Phil said.

"Sir," Tom replied, looking down. "Apart from the parking lot incident, everything's quiet today."

"Good. This enterprising young fellow turns out to be Justin, the intern I mentioned yesterday."

Tom shook hands with Justin. "Glad to meet you, Justin. We're all interested to see how you work out." He had a strong grip, and Justin let go first to escape the discomfort. Tom rolled his shoulders and grinned.

"I'm showing Justin the ropes," said Phil. "See you in the office at the end of the shift."

They walked on into the mall atrium and passed the Tot Shot photo kiosk. Justin smiled, remembering how he and Mo had chased a demon there last spring.

Phil tapped Justin on the shoulder. "There, over by the fountain. What do you see?"

Justin looked. A man in a flannel shirt and jeans was talking with a young woman with long blond hair and a tight sleeveless top. The man was waving his arms and edging closer to the woman, who was trying to back away.

"Looks like they're having a fight. Could it be trouble?" Justin asked.

Phil nodded. "Yes, it could. This is one of the main things we have to watch out for. So far they're OK, but if he crosses the line . . . "

The man started poking the woman on the chest. She raised her arms to protect herself, and he shoved her back. She stumbled into a bench and sat down.

"You mean like that?" asked Justin. He turned to Phil, but the tall man was already halfway to the couple.

"Excuse me sir, ma'am. I'm with Mall Security. Are you folks all right?"

"Stay out of this, rent-a-cop. This is between me and my woman."

" 'Your woman,' " exclaimed the woman. "We're not even dating. He came over and started trying to pick me up, but I just want him to leave me alone," she said to Phil.

"Sir, the lady wishes to be left alone. I think it's time for you to leave now." Phil tried to edge between the man and the woman.

"I'll leave when I'm good and ready, jerk. And I'm not leaving without her." He shoved Phil with both hands. Phil took a step back, tripped over the edge of the fountain and fell in. The man stood laughing as Phil floundered in his unexpected bathtub.

Justin had been watching this exchange carefully. He stepped up behind the man, poked a knuckle in his back and said, "I'm Mall Security too. Freeze, dirtbag!"

The man stopped laughing and slowly raised his hands. He started to look around but Justin poked a little harder. "Freeze, I said. Don't move."

Phil stood up in the fountain pool and shook his shoulders back and forth, spraying water around him like a soaked dog. He was clearly angry, even growling. His frown brought his bushy eyebrows together. He closed his eyes and took a deliberate deep breath. Justin could see the anger dial back from a full boil to a slow simmer.

Phil stepped out of the pool and over to the man. "I don't think our friend here is going to cause any more trouble, Justin. Are you, friend?"

Between the barely controlled anger of Phil, and Justin behind his back, the man decided that Tri-City Mall was not the best place for him right now. "No more trouble, no, I was just leaving. Babe?"

The woman refused to look at him. Phil cleared his throat and the man walked rapidly to the nearest exit.

"Are you OK, ma'am? Do you have anyone to stay with?" The woman was unhurt and gratefully declined further assistance. She departed in the opposite direction, and Phil and Justin walked back to the Security office.

"I keep a change of clothes in my locker just in case something like this happens." He used his radio to call the maintenance staff to mop up the water before anyone slipped in it. As they walked, Justin noticed an odor coming from Phil, a sort of wet-dog scent, but not quite. *Phil must have a dog at home,* he thought. *I bet it shed on his pants.*

"That was some quick thinking, Justin. But don't do something like that again; what if he had known we don't carry weapons? You could have been hurt badly if he had a knife."

Justin blushed and patted the pocket holding his athame. *I never even thought of that.*

Back at the office, Phil said, "It's almost lunchtime. Why don't you grab a bite at the food court and meet me back here in an hour?"

Justin entered the Coffee Spot and approached the counter.

"Justin!" exclaimed Mo. "How was your first morning in Security?"

"Veronica was attacked by a dog in the parking lot. Big brute, he was. He ran off when I pulled the alarm, and then the Security crew came and made sure she was OK. Then Mr. Harris, I mean My-Name's-Phil, showed me around and we broke up an argument. Some sleaze-ball was trying to pick up a woman who didn't want the attention. And now it's lunchtime. Hungry?"

They strolled over to the food court and got pizza slices. Veronica wouldn't let Justin pay for his.

Over the slices, Justin told Mo more about the morning's events, and how his spell had failed. Mo was a witch too; in fact it was her sloppy witch-school homework that had released the demon—more of an imp, really—and led to Justin discovering his own powers. That time, he had improvised the same "stupefy" and frozen the mischievous imp, but why didn't it work when he had a proper wand and everything?

"That's a good question for Mater Ruth next class, but I think it has to do with how much you know you should be able to do; when you didn't know you had any Talent at all, you didn't know that spell was hard; now you do and sure enough, it is. Um. Does that make sense?" Mo frowned.

"I guess so. More studying, huh?" Justin said.

"Always more studying for us witches; even Mater Ruth still studies. There's always something to learn; that's what makes the world so wonderful, she says."

The rest of the day was pretty uneventful. Sent to patrol on his own, Justin made the rounds, clicking his gizmo at the RFID tabs, helping people pick up dropped packages, giving directions to bewildered shoppers. Once a group of middle-school boys were acting up outside Gamer Ground, the video game store, but Justin gave them his best hard-assed-Phil stare and they moved on without incident.

At the end of his eight hours, he went back to the Security office and reported to Phil. The rest of the day shift was there, filling out time cards and incident reports for the insurance company.

"How did you like your first day?" asked Phil.

"It was OK. The morning was a bit exciting, but the afternoon was quiet."

"That's the way we like it," put in Tom from the table where he was doing his paperwork. "Quiet means happy customers; happy customers mean happy management; happy management means we keep our jobs."

Phil turned to Tom and frowned. Tom gazed at the table and said, "Sorry, sir, didn't mean to interrupt."

"OK," said Phil. "Justin, I'm afraid you'll have to be on day shifts to start. The new guy never gets his pick. I hope you understand."

Justin was surprised. Day shifts? He had expected to be put on the graveyard shift as the new guy, not days. This was terrific; he would have evenings free for Mo. And for Witch School; there was no summer vacation for junior witches and wizards. Mater Ruth said if she gave them the summer off they'd have to start over in the fall. That sounded insulting but the way Mater said it you knew she was only partly serious. Besides, it was true: what little skill he had would start to go if he didn't keep up.

"No, days are fine. I'll do what's needed."

"Good attitude. Now tomorrow morning Tom will be in charge; I'm back on nights. Eight A.M. sharp, OK?"

With that, Justin was dismissed. He left the office and was walking to the exit near the bus stop when he remembered he'd left his day pack in his locker. He turned and went back to the office. He punched the code on the lock and pushed the door open. Crossing to the locker room, he called out, "I just forgot my . . ."

Justin stopped in the doorway. In the locker room was Tom, just pulling off his shirt, and two enormous wolves.

They turned to Justin and snarled. Justin backed into the main room—or he tried to. Bob was standing behind him, blocking his escape.

Tom finished pulling off his shirt and dropped it on the floor. He took a step toward Justin. "Just what do you think you're doing, you little sneak?"

Behind him, Bob closed the door. "We can make him disappear, Tom."

Justin thought fast. He remembered when he had first started Witch School, Mater Ruth had spent an amused hour telling him just what was real and what was fantasy. Witches: real. Elves: fantasy. Demons: real. Unicorns: fantasy. Werewolves . . .

Uh oh.

Real.

All the pieces fell into place: the team's strength and size, Phil's dominance of the others, even his doggy odor. They were werewolves, and he was in their nest. One in human form was behind him, Tom was in front, and two in wolf forms were approaching from the sides, growling. They crouched low and stepped closer, ready to spring. He could feel the heat of their bodies and smell the rank breath of carnivores.

Justin thought fast and took a risk. He dropped to his knees, put his hands behind his back and turned his head to the side, exposing his neck.

Tom stopped, surprised. He studied Justin for a moment and then reached out and cuffed him on the side of his head.

"OK, boy," he said, "where did you learn that submission will save you from wolves?"

Justin straightened up. "Discovery Channel. There was this special program . . ."

Everyone laughed. Even the wolves sat back on their haunches and lolled their tongues out.

"How did you know that would work on us?" asked Tom.

"Well, I figured that since I was only gone a minute, the wolves couldn't have come from outside, which meant they must be where; and given that, it's obvious you're high in the pack—Phil's the Alpha, right? So I figured since I was sort of a pack member—well, pack intern, OK—if I didn't want my throat torn out, submission was the only way to keep you guys from attacking me."

Phil opened the locker room door and stood in the doorway. He'd been listening since Justin came in.

"Smart kid," he said. "But why were you so quick to assume we're werewolves? Most people, it's hard to convince them even when you Change in front of them. You didn't see the Change but you figured it out anyway."

"Oh, that's easy," said Justin. "I've seen a few weird things. I'm a witch." He pulled out his wand, gestured, and a spray of flowers erupted from the wand's tip and then faded from sight.

"Wow!" said Tom.

"Yeah," said Phil. "Pretty cool, but I knew you were a witch; Ruth and I go way back. I was going to wait to see what you were like before fully briefing you, but events have forced matters. Still, no harm done, right, fellows?"

His voice took on an edge of command and the rest of the team, human and wolf alike, nodded obedience.

"Well, Justin, now that you know our little secret you can help with a problem we have. You remember that Veronica was attacked in the parking lot this morning."

"Veronica from Pizza Barn? I remember. She's OK, isn't she?"

"Yes, she's OK," said Phil. "When you hit the panic button, it scared off the perp, and our team was there in seconds."

"So what's the big deal? I mean, it's terrible that Veronica was attacked, but the dog was scared off, right? End of story."

"Not the end of the story." Phil tapped his nose. "We smelled him. Very distinctive."

"So if he shows up again you call animal control, right?"

"Well, no. You see, he's a were too. He wasn't after cash, or even rape—he wanted blood. We could smell the Hunger on his scent."

A couple of the guys from the night shift were nodding. "It's a werewolf thing," Bob said. "Even in human form we can smell things humans can't."

Phil explained that as Security, they had the run of the mall at night, and being able to Change and run more or less at will made the Hunger controllable; a rogue were that had to try to stay in human shape all the time got a bit crazy during the full moon.

"I get it," said Justin. "Apart from it being terrible if he killed Veronica, or anyone else, you guys could lose your sweet gig here at the mall. But wait . . ." Justin frowned. "What about the security cameras? If you guys are running around in wolf form, won't you show up on the tapes?"

The pack laughed. "Hey, we control the surveillance system. We've got a video file showing Bob in human form making his rounds, and if anyone asks for a tape, we update the time stamps, run off a tape, and give them that," said Phil.

"But what if someone breaks in? What happens to them?"

"In a mall full of werewolves? *We* happen to them. It's our job to protect the mall and everyone in it. We take it seriously." A couple of the guys growled agreement. Justin was suddenly glad he was on *their* side.

Justin thought for a moment. "Back to the rogue were. I'm going to guess tracking him didn't work, or we wouldn't be here."

"Right," said Tom, "We tracked him halfway across the lot and then his scent suddenly disappeared. We think he got into a car, Changed to human, and took off."

"So I guess we have to set a trap."

Phil looked at Justin and slowly smiled. "Good idea, kid. Here's what we're going to do."

Justin stood in the mall entrance. "Are you sure this is going to work?" he asked. The lapel mic on his hooded sweatshirt picked it up, and the radio squawked its reply into the earpiece hidden by the hood.

"Well, no, kid," replied Phil, "but it's our best shot, and you'll be perfectly safe; the guys are hidden in parked cars all the way to the bus stop and we're all listening."

"Well, OK, but I still don't see why I have to be the bait."

"No offense, kid, but you're the wimpiest of us all."

Justin sighed. He was in pretty decent shape for a senior, but Phil had a point: he wasn't a werewolf. He put his hands in his pockets to keep them warm in the cool night air and stepped off the curb.

"Here goes, then. I'm leaving the entry and heading for the bus stop."

"Roger that," replied Phil.

For the next hour, Justin trudged out to the bus stop with evening shoppers— "Try to look a little more vulnerable, kid!"—sat there as if waiting for a bus, and then got up and trudged back to the mall. "Slump more!"

On his sixth trip, Justin was beginning to wonder if the ploy was going to work, when as he passed a parked SUV, a hand reached out from underneath and tripped him. Hands still in his pockets. Justin fell to the pavement and the owner of the hand was out from under the SUV and on top of him in an instant. "Aaah!" Justin cried out, and in his earpiece heard Phil ask, "You OK, kid?"

"No! No, I'm not OK!" he cried as the man sat on top of him. He bent over and put a hand to Justin's throat as if looking for the best spot to rip it open. *Somehow, I don't think submission is going to work here*, Justin thought. He felt in his pocket for the athame. It was razor sharp—that was important, symbolically, and magic was big on symbols—and even better, it was silver. He wrenched it free from his pocket, but couldn't bring it to bear easily.

"That's OK," said the man. "I like it when you struggle. The fear makes the meat sweeter." His face started to lengthen. Hair grew out of his cheeks and forehead and a wolf's ripping fangs emerged from his mouth. He bent lower and growled in Justin's face.

As the rogue shifted his weight, Justin pulled his hand from under the creature's leg, and stabbed the athame into his calf.

"Aroooo!" His face snapped back to human and he howled in pain. Clutching his wounded leg, he fell off Justin. "What did you cut me with, you little bastard? It burns!"

Justin sat up and put the silver athame to the rogue werewolf's throat. A wisp of smoke from the rogue's throat spiraled up between them. "This is an athame, the sharpest knife a witch can use, and it's made of pure silver forged in the light of the full moon. Do you feel lucky?"

When Phil, Tom and the rest of the team came pounding up the parking lot lane, they found the rogue wolf cowering against the SUV, with Justin holding the silver knife at his throat. "I'll go quietly, whatever you want, but just get this crazy kid away from me!" he pleaded with Phil.

Phil took in the scene, and laughed. "Good work, kid!" he said. "We'll take it from here."

"What will happen to him?" Justin stood up. The rogue's nostrils flared as he smelled the crew and realized that not only was he in the hands of Mall Security, but that they were all werewolves except Justin.

"Oh, crap," said the rogue.

"Well, kid," Phil replied to Justin without breaking his stare with the rogue, "a wolf that enters another pack's territory and causes trouble has two options. Submit and join the pack, or die. Lucky for you, pal, you haven't really hurt anyone yet so you get to choose. Stand up, Justin, and let him make his choice."

Justin stood up and took a step back. The rogue were sighed, broke the gaze with Phil and rolled over onto his back. Phil knelt and nipped at his throat. "OK, we're good. Come on buddy, let's get you patched up and have a talk. If you want, we can help you stay out of trouble, or give you bus fare out of town. But if not . . . " He left the unspoken threat hanging.

They all started back to the mall. Justin said, "Is that it for the day? Can I go home? I'm feeling pretty tired."

"Yeah, the excitement will do that. Enjoy your first action, kid? You did pretty good for a witch."

"Is it always this exciting?" Justin asked.

Phil laughed. "No, this is unusual. Usually it's mostly lost kids and rowdy teenagers when the movies let out, but we need to be ready for anything. See you tomorrow."

"Thanks," said Justin. He entered the mall with the crew but turned toward the Coffee Spot where Mo was working the late shift.

"How was your day?" she asked, making him a cafe mocha.

"Hairy!" said Justin.

Karen Everson is a jack of all arts. She has published fiction, non-fiction and poetry and is currently working on a novel based on her story, "Incognito Ergo Sum," as well as a novel centered around Olwen's family of werewolves. Along with her writing, she runs Moongate Designs, a small business showcasing her art and needle-work designs. She lives in Michigan with her other great passions: her husband Mark, daughter Caitlyn, and numerous pets.

Support Your
Local Werewolf

Karen Everson

"Welcome to our humble abode," Kay said, as we bumped our bags over the threshold. She dropped her backpack on the floor and shut the front door with her rump. "It's not a mansion, but it's home."

"It's awesome," I said, looking around the cheerfully cluttered house. I slanted my eyes at her. "And my house is big and old, but it is not a mansion. At least in your house, plumbing wasn't an afterthought."

"Nope, the plumbing is fine." She gave me a strange look. "Um, is that why your nose is twitching? You checking the plumbing?"

Oops. "Sorry. Mr. Clean makes my nose twitch."

"Oh!" She sniffed, "Geez, Mom must have just washed the floor. We better take our shoes off."

One of the side effects of my peculiar heritage is that my sense of smell is extra-sensitive, and I tend to, literally, sniff things out. I quit trying to untangle all the animal scents—cat, fish tanks, and, oops, mice, let's *hope* they're pets—and gave Kay my best grin. "Seriously, Kay, I'm happy to be here. Thanks for putting me up over Thanksgiving break."

She grinned. "You just love me for my cable TV."

"Nah. It's the really big bookstore on the main drag, you spoiled suburbanite."

"Redneck refugee."

"It's a fair cop." I live in Landfair, Virginia, an hour and several decades from civilization as I wish to know it.

Kay's parental units were out, so Kay got me settled into the guest room, then took me on the obligatory tour of the house. Kay had described the decor as "Early Fantasy Writer," but I knew a Green-Witch's nest when I saw it. It was a lot like home, or like home might have been without Granddad's rule that he had to be able to do a 360 in his wolf without knocking something over with his tail.

Well-laden bookshelves loomed, squatted or squeezed into any space that could be made to hold one. Plants clustered in every source of sunlight, and statues of Gods, Goddesses, butterfly-wing fairies and animals, as well as candles, crystals, and a beach worth of seashells found display space in the interstices. My mom *collected* too. She'd never found her inner wolf, but Granddad used to joke that if we'd owned the secret of shifting to bird form, she'd have accessed her inner magpie, no problem.

"I think our mothers would have really liked each other," I said. Kay heard the wistfulness in my voice and put an arm around my shoulder.

"My dad isn't crazy about all the Elizabethan-style fairies," she said lightly, "Even though Mom tries to tuck them into the plants. He complained about them at work once and people started leaving Tinkerbell stuff in his cube."

I chuckled, allowing myself to be distracted. "He must be cool, though. You said he was Mr. Science-Guy, but hey, here he is married to a witch."

"He's great, and there goes *that* broom closet," Kay said.

"I'm down with it," I assured her. "My mom was Wiccan, too. She hid fairies in the plants, too, though they were more Brian Froud and less Amy Brown. Sometimes when I'm working in the solarium—I think you guys would call it a Florida room—I find one that I don't remember seeing before."

"That's kind of cool." She gave my arm a little squeeze. "Like your mom's reminding you she still loves you. Maybe she's looking out for you, O."

"The Welsh believe in that, you know," I said softly, "that our dead watch over us." I decided not to mention that my grandfather sometimes talks to my dead grandmother in the middle of the night, with pauses like he's listening to answers. Kay may be a witch's daughter, but I didn't want to strain her tolerances to the breaking point.

"So," I said brightly. "Take me for a walk. Show me the gardens, drag me around the neighborhood. My butt's asleep from that long drive. I need to walk."

Kay rolled her eyes. "Whatev', dude. You're the guest."

After I had sincerely admired the "National Wildlife Federation Backyard Habitat" gardens, the faux-stone bench, and the beautifully private and perfect for Changing back porch, we toured the small neighborhood. With exams and papers due before vacation, it had been the better part of a month since I'd been able to go for a run in my wolf shape. (Try finding a college with werewolf accessibility. It's not in the brochures.) My wolf needed *out*. The moon was waxing into full tonight, and that was NOT going to help.

My wolf is as much a part of my heritage as my brown eyes and hair. I Change at will, not according to the lunar cycle. But certain circumstances can bring the Wolf closer to the surface. Being in danger. Having someone I care about in danger. Or, if I've been neglecting my inner furball, a full moon.

Long story short, I needed to run, so I needed to know where the dogs were.

Dogs *notice* me. Some yip and run. Some go insane, barking and growling, while some recognize me as alpha and flop over on their backs, whining and waving their fours in the air.

Fortunately, the neighborhood seemed to run heavily toward yap dogs and pussycats.

Cats are no problem—*nobody* can predict what a cat will do. Whether the cat stares at me like I contain the mysteries of the universe and she's sussing them out, or if she hisses and runs, hey, dude, it's a *cat*.

I don't worry too much about little dogs, either. Little dog for "OMG! OMG! It's a WEREWOLF!" sounds pretty much like "OMG! OMG! It's a SQUIRREL!"

Big dogs are the worry. As a wolf I can handle myself. Mass translates directly, so I'm a well-fed 120-pound wolf. I've great teeth, (look, no cavities!) thick glossy fur, (that smells of rosemary shampoo, thank you), and my nails are sharper than a natural wolf's because I don't spend all my time trotting around on my fours. But wolfing out in the suburbs was not likely to be an option, and I'd just as soon not get bitten. Besides, I'd feel really bad if someone's pet was put down for biting me. In human form I don't smell like a wolf, but to a dog, I don't smell human, either. I smell *wrong*. Dangerous.

My first big dog was a flopper, a leashed German shepherd out for a walk with "Mom." As soon as it got close enough to really get my scent, it dropped to the ground with a whimper, offering its throat. Kay and the owner stopped dead, gaping.

"Oh, my, what a beautiful doggie!" I gushed. I knelt, grinning like an idiot at the owner. With one hand I did a quick muzzle squeeze, canid for "your submission has been accepted," while I made a big show of rubbing the dog's tummy with the other.

"Dogs just seem to know that I'm a champion tummy rubber," I babbled. I *do* give good tummy rubs, and the shepherd helped me out by giving a blissful wiggle. The view supplied a pronoun. "He's just gorgeous, and so well-socialized! How old is he?"

Nothing puts a dog owner at ease like having their baby praised. Fifteen minutes later, the dog remembered why he'd wanted to go walkies in the first place, and we all parted friends.

The next two encounters were a little more disconcerting. On the next street over a woman had just stepped out of her door, walking a fluff dog on a retractable lead. The little dog was trotting along the walk ahead of her, snuffling noisily. Then he caught a whiff of me.

The fluff ball gave a single yip and squatted, just missing his mistress's pristine pink sneaker. Then he did a 180, and shot between his mistress's legs, disappearing back in the house through the doggie door. His owner stood staring at the steaming heap on her nice white walkway. The leash stretched behind her like she was trying to take her house for a walk.

"Hi, Mrs. Krumm!" Kay called sweetly, waving. Mrs. Krumm shot us a dirty look.

"That's probably the first time Cookie has actually taken a dump in his own yard!" Kay whispered gleefully. "Mrs. Krumm's notorious for not picking up after him, but she has a fit if anyone else's dog soils her grass."

I had a moment of culture shock. Unless they happen to be raising *serious* hunting dogs, folks where I live don't do leashes, let alone scoop poop. Use the bathroom *before* run, check. Then I did a double take. "Her name is Krumm, and she named her dog Cookie?"

"Wondered if you'd catch that," Kay said.

Three doors down from the incontinent Cookie was a bigger problem. A young girl was kneeling in her front yard, playing tug-of-war with an enormous shepherd. The girl was, I guessed, about eight years old, and stunningly beautiful in pure Nordic fashion, with silky flaxen hair and big chicory-flower-blue eyes. But it was her dog that held my attention.

This dog was not going to be a flopper. If I'd been four-footed, I might have had to acknowledge *him* as dominant, a fact that was raising the hair on the back of my neck. I guessed him at 180 pounds, and he could easily have wrested the rope toy away from his small mistress if he'd wanted to. He probably could have picked her up in his jaws and walked off with her.

My first thought was that he might be a hybrid, part wolf. They're illegal in most states, but it's hard to tell without running DNA. His fur was thick, pale grey with darker grey markings, with a white ruff, belly and legs.

"Hey, Marley-Mouse," Kay called, genuine liking in her voice. "How's it going?"

The blonde girl raised a hand to return Kay's wave. The dog let go of the rope toy and moved to stand between his young mistress and us.

"It's okay, I guess." Marley said. She had to rise up on her knees to see us over her protector. She slapped his flank gently. "Get *down*, you silly dog. You know Kay."

Wolfie lay down but got right back up again. Kay went to him without hesitation. He gave her hand a sniff and greeted her pat with a tail sweep, but his attention was all on me.

"Nice dog," I said. I stayed on the sidewalk and kept my eyes steady. I didn't want to antagonize the big animal, but I wasn't going to concede dominance, either. Besides being a bad idea, it went against the grain. The dog's head was held just at shoulder level, tail straight out behind him, neither threatening nor submissive. His eyes, focused unblinking on my face, were an unnerving blue.

Husky blood, I told myself, and the browlike markings of darker grey were probably what made the blue seem so vivid. So *knowing*.

"His name is Wolfie," Marley said. "You can pet him, he won't bite. But you have to come in to the yard. Mom makes him wear one of those electric collars, and he knows just where the fence is. It's got a thing that opens the doggie door for him, too, so he can go in and out whenever he wants."

"Okay." I drew a careful breath as I stepped into his territory. He watched.

I held out my hand. He sniffed me carefully, then permitted me to stroke him. *Truce.* Kay had dropped into the grass beside Marley, so after a moment, I sat down, too. Wolfie lay down in the middle and settled his head on Marley's knee. After a while he decided that having three people to admire and pet him wasn't entirely a bad thing.

"Do you have another show soon?" Kay asked, her hand buried wrist-deep in Wolfie's fur. "Marley does Junior Beauty Pageants," she added for my benefit. "Hey, Marley, maybe O and I will come and see you strut your stuff."

"Oh, *puh-leese* don't!" Marley said immediately. "Seriously, it is so totally lame, I would die if anybody cool was there."

"Well, glad to hear I'm cool, anyway," Kay grinned. "You still singing and dancing?"

"Singing. I've got a kind of cowgirl rig for this talent set, and you *so* don't want to tap in cowboy boots. I tried it and my feet got all over blisters. And you won't *believe* what Mom's got me singing!"

"What?"

" '*Stand by Your Man*'! Do you *believe*? I'm like, *Mom*! I'm *nine*! If I have a man there's serious bad kink happening. And she got all bent and told me not to talk filth, it was just a song to show off my voice, like there aren't other songs that would do that."

"That sucks. She should at least let you help pick what you sing."

"I *like* singing," Marley sighed. She buried her hands in Wolfie's ruff like she needed something to hold onto. "The contests were fun when I was little. It was something Mom and I could do together after the divorce. But now Mom gets so completely *wound*. And I think it's mean for her to make me sing that song when *she* left my dad."

This was *way* more sharing than either Kay or I had bargained for, but Marley looked so grim that we hugged her and hung with her for a while. Kay asked her about Wolfie and Marley perked up talking about how smart he was. She asked me if I was named "O" for the lady in the movie, and after I unswallowed my tongue and quit blushing I explained that Kay called me "O" because she was too lazy to say Olwen. And yes, it was a funny name, it was Welsh and I was named after an ancestress back in Wales.

Then we all played with Wolfie until Marley's stage mom called her into supper.

When we got back to Kay's house her parents were home, and on the front porch there was a rabbit eating the last blossoms off a rather sad looking pot of petunias. "There's a bunny," I said to Kay. "It's eating your petunias."

"Yeah, that's Diamond," Kay said. "That's okay, you can have them," she said to the rabbit. "They're pretty much spent, and they never last indoors."

Green-Witch daughter, Green-Witch's house, I reminded myself. Kay went in. I paused, watching the rabbit watching me as it munched down the last flower. "Diamond," I said, "most of the folk back home would call you dinner."

The rabbit looked at me with its dark, liquid eyes, unconcerned. *You're not in Landfair anymore, Toto.*

The rabbit swallowed and hopped off the porch, disappearing into a mass of lilies. Every muscle in my body twitched with the desire to follow.

I *so* needed a run.

It helped that Kay's mom was a witch, and that Kay was too tired from driving for a pajama party.

I explained to Kay's mom that I have trouble sleeping, and could I go out and sit on the porch or walk around the yard if I got restless? "Of course, dear," she answered. She got a wry smile on her face. "But don't howl at the moon, or my neighbors will call the police."

I blanched, but Kay's mom didn't notice. Her eyes had gone distant. I was sure she'd once been the sort of witch to sing naked beneath the esbat moon. From the wistful sadness in her face, she missed it.

At two in the morning I slipped out onto the porch with its screen of turning trees. Though it was a clear night, the sky was alien looking, with a sickly greenish cast from the lights of the distant city. There were barely any stars, but the full moon bleached the grass silver, and painted black pools beneath the trees and shrubs. Moonlight spilled over the top of the trees, lighting me, making me feel exposed despite their shelter.

I thought of Kay's mom and her wistful eyes, and forced myself to strip. I hid my clothes in the shadows. Then, for a moment I simply stood, letting the night and the moon settle over my skin until they became all the garment I required.

I crouched, touched my palms to the cool wood, and bid my Wolf come.

I felt the soft fire of that other Self beneath my skin, felt the slight pressure of my canines growing just a little longer, a little sharper. I knew a flash of amber fire came and went behind my eyes. Then the Change took me completely, the Wolf flowing out and over and the human Olwen flowing within.

When the gift first came to me I tried to watch that transformation, Changing over and over in front of a mirror. I could see my eyes flash golden, and perhaps, just perhaps, my lips curl away from a first hint of fangs. Then my eyes—or my mind—would just slide away, cease to see, until the Wolf was all, and the only clue to the person within lay in the color of the wolf's fur and eyes.

As for the Change itself, imagine being dropped unprepared into an ocean wave, having it tumble you about so that you lose all sense of up and down, water flooding your nose and eyes and ears so that you lose all your senses, even the breath in your lungs, to that rush of alien element. Then, just as you believe you are drowning, the wave ebbs. You see the stars, and know *that is up,* and you find your head up and your feet down. Your breath returns and the world is comprehensible once more. That's what it is like. The wolf's senses, maybe the wolf's *brain*, tumble the world until somehow your human mind, your *self* that is human and wolf both, pulls the world aright again and makes sense of it all.

The chaos of scents and sounds resolved into clarity. That low grumble beneath the creeping juniper was a groundhog and a possum, objecting to each other and even more to me. I heard the *thump* of an alarmed rabbit, and the sonar stitches the bats sewed into the night. In the clear fall air every scent and sound was a cry of life against the coming of the cold.

I sprang out joyfully into the living night, and ran.

You would think that there would be more wildlife where I live, out in the country, than here in Kay's suburbs. But back home wildlife are "varmints," considered food or competition for food. It was nice being somewhere that a shotgun wasn't a standard home furnishing.

It was wonderful to run where people call animal control for a stray dog, instead of shooting at it.

Life was jubilant here. Beside cats and dogs my nose told me tales of life, from mice to foxes and sparrows to raptors. A concrete ditch channeled an ancient, twisted creek around the subdivision, coaxing the wide quiet water into a swift flow less hospitable to mosquitos. Where the subdivisions switched over to the commercial district, however, the creek had been allowed to be itself. There was one spot of perhaps an acre that was a "wetlands preserve" where I'd seen ducks and geese and herons. My nose was leading me there. I planned to follow my nose, get wonderfully filthy and perhaps have a swim. The wolf didn't mind the cool night, and the dirt would fall off when I Changed.

Then I crossed behind the Krumms' house, and suddenly found myself awash in floodlights. *Oops.*

I tucked my tail and ran. I was nearly clear of the lights when Cookie began to bark. By time Mrs. Krumm stepped out onto her patio, Cookie tucked under one arm and a large flashlight in her other hand, I had made it into Marley's backyard. Trying to ignore the fact that I was fleeing from a fluff dog and a middle-aged lady in curlers, I went to ground, ears flattened and eyes shut, trying my best to look like a hump of grass.

After a bit, both dog and mistress were satisfied that whatever had set off the motion sensors was safely gone, Cookie making that satisfied, "I am a brave protector" rumble. I waited a few minutes after I heard the sliding door shut before I lifted my head and glanced around. The floodlights had been extinguished, and the house was dark.

Marley's house was dark, too, which is why the sound of a door closing drew my attention. Curious, I crept around the side of the house, ears pricked.

A dark van was parked in the driveway of Marley's house, and a woman was loading a child-sized bundle into the back passenger seat. The woman's scent meant nothing, but I caught Marley's scent, and something else that had my hair rising and a growl starting in my throat, a sharp, acrid stink that did not belong in the clean autumn night.

The woman got into the driver's seat and shut the door. Silently, without headlights, the van began to roll backwards down the driveway into the street.

I began to run, snarling an alarm. In the street, the van's engine growled back and it pulled away, still without lights.

I smelled Wolfie before I saw him. I was going too fast to stop so I jumped the limp form and spun to snuffle at him. He was breathing, but his eyes were rolled halfway back in his head. His collar was missing, and a dart was lodged in his shoulder. I caught it in my teeth and jerked it out, but that was all the time I could spare him.

I turned my nose to the driveway. The tires on the van had been new or almost so, and whoever had last filled the tank had spilled when they withdrew the nozzle, for there was a smell of gasoline mixed with the scent of new rubber.

Fainter, but calling like the moon, was the scent of the child.

I followed.

I was lucky. With the late hour, there was no other traffic, and my quarry did not go too far before going to ground. It was still well dark when the trail took me into the drive of a house with a FOR SALE sign in the front yard, though my pads were sore from running on blacktop. The house was older and more isolated that the ones in Kay's neighborhood, and even in the moonlight, it looked badly kept.

The van was gone, but it had stopped here. My nose said the woman, Marley, and one other female had gotten out. The woman's scent was stronger than the other two, and I thought she might have returned to the van and driven away.

It was Marley I wanted. She'd been taken in the front door, but that was locked now. When I circled the house, however, I found a window had been broken and unlocked. A little effort raised the sash enough for me to squeeze through.

The third person, the one I hadn't seen, had come this way too. I followed the scent until it crossed and joined with Marley's, then followed both to a closed door that showed a light underneath. A key lay on the floor outside. I was trying the knob with paws and teeth when someone cried, "Go away!"

It was a girl's voice, but not Marley's. Was the damned woman starting a collection? I swallowed a growl at the thought, and sat down and scratched at the door, whining.

The door opened a crack. A girl of about Marley's age, and as dark as Marley was fair, peeked out at me. I whined again, ducking my head, trying to look harmless.

The door opened wider. "Wolfie? Are you Marley's Wolfie?" The door opened all the way and the girl threw her arms around my neck and pressed a tear-stained face into my fur. "Marley won't wake up and I'm really scared!"

I nuzzled her neck, then backed away, and Changed. "Take me to her," I said gently, and reached for her hand.

The girl's eyes went huge, but she bravely took my hand and drew me through the door into a windowless bathroom. In a moment I saw Marley.

She lay on the cracked yellow tile, but someone had tucked a blanket around her, and there was a girl's robe tucked under her head. The robe matched the dark-skinned girl's terry bedroom slippers.

"You took good care of her," I said. I knelt to check Marley. I could smell that sharp medicinal smell around her mouth and nose. But she breathed as though simply asleep, and her heartbeat was steady and strong. "She's drugged, but she'll be fine. We just have to be patient and wait for her to wake up. What's your name?"

"Talia. Why were you a dog, and why don't you have any clothes?"

"It's a long story." I took a quick glance around the room. The house smelled like it had been empty a while, but clearly the electricity was on. There was a roll of toilet paper and several bottles of water on the sink, as well as a couple of Snickers bars. The room was chilly, but it looked like whoever had put the girls here hadn't meant for them to be too uncomfortable. "Talia, why don't you tell me what happened? That's really what's important."

Talia looked like she was going to cry again, and she reached to take Marley's hand in her own. "My mom kidnaped Marley so that she can't go to the Junior Miss County Wide Beauty and Talent Pageant tomorrow. She said Marley was my only real competition. But I was afraid Marley would be scared, so I hid in the back of the van, and then I snuck in and waited until my mom left. I wanted Marley to know nobody would hurt her and that she'd be able to go right home after the pageant was over. But then she wouldn't wake up, and I got cold, and I got scared. I'm really glad you're here, even if you are naked. Maybe later, you can turn back into a dog and keep us warm." She eyed me. "Marley makes Wolfie sound kind of magical, but you aren't Wolfie, are you?"

"No. Wolfie is a boy, for one thing. And he's really a dog. What you saw me do—it's very rare, and very secret. I'll help you no matter what, but it would help me if you didn't tell anyone what I can do."

She smiled then. "Well, *duh!* Like anyone would believe me anyway! It's bad enough my mom makes me do this pageant stuff, I don't want to have to see a shrink on top of school and music lessons!"

"You don't like it either, huh?"

"It is *sooo* totally lame," Talia said, rolling her eyes and looking and sounding so much like Marley that I laughed. "I'd rather play soccer, or even just do my music without it having to be a contest all the time. But at least my mom isn't making me sing 'Stand By Your Man.'"

I smiled. "Listen, you stay here with Marley, and I'll see if I can find anything to keep us warm until she wakes up. Then we can figure out what to do."

Talia nodded. "Okay. I know my mom pulled a really bone-head move, but she's my mom, you know? I don't want her to get in trouble."

"I understand," I said. "I'll think real hard, okay? Why don't you see if you can't cuddle down with Marley under the blanket? I'm going to close the door to keep out the draft, but I'll be back soon."

The first floor, at least, was pretty stripped, but in the front closet I found a handful of hangers and a battered heater. I plugged the heater into the nearest outlet to test it. It worked. There was a smell of burning dust and a noisy rattle from the fan, but it would serve to warm the single room the girls were in.

I had unplugged it to take back to the girls when I heard glass crunch.

As quietly as possible I set the heater down and took a battered wooden hanger from the closet. I slipped toward the room with the broken window, hoping I wouldn't have to Change to defend myself and the children. I can't just slip back and forth between forms indefinitely—too often, too close together, and I could incapacitate myself.

I clutched my makeshift weapon, and peeked into the room.

The moon had shifted, throwing light through the broken window. Against that patch of moonlight something hulked. I saw the light glint off pale fur.

The shape was wrong for a dog—wrong for *anything* I could think of. It was taller and bulkier than a dog, but more squat than a man, and it was making a wet, snuffling sound. Its smell was a mix of wet dog and boys' locker-room funk. My mind conjured Lovecraftian visions as my neck prickled and adrenaline pumped through me.

Eyes shone briefly in the dark and the figure grew taller. It spoke, a snarl chopped into words.

"Bitch! What have you done with my child?!"

Slowly I straightened. *"Wolfie?"*

I fumbled for a light switch, found one, and flicked it on.

We stood there blinking at each other in the weak light of a dirty 40 watt bulb. Unlike me, Wolfie was not naked. His muscular legs were clad in heavy denim, and he had something like a diver's rubber-soled shoes on his feet. Thick greying chest hair peeked through the V-neck of a long-sleeved silk T-shirt. Over it all was the heavy mantle of his Wolf-Skin, the hollow-eyed pelt drawn up like a hood over his head. Blue eyes as vivid as chicory flowers glared at me.

"She's your daughter," I said. *D'oh!* "Marley's your daughter."

"Yes. *Now where is she? If you have hurt her, I will kill you.*"

"She's fine! Just sleeping. There's another girl with her, and if you use your nose, you know I'm not the one who took her. Look, I came to help, so can you put away the teeth? They're still, um, wolfy."

He ran his tongue over his fangs and winced. His face crunched up in a snarl as he concentrated, but when he relaxed again he had human teeth. "Sorry," he said in a more normal voice. "Is that better?"

"Much. Look, you *are* Wolfie, right? I'm Olwen. We played fetch today? I rubbed your belly?"

He colored, but recovered quickly. His eyes flicked down my body. "I can return the favor if you'd like," he said. He didn't quite manage not to smirk.

My turn to blush. I'd actually forgotten that I was naked. My family isn't big on modesty, it just isn't practical. And Wolfie was being a gentleman. He kept his eyes on my face. Mostly.

"In this shape I am Erik," he said. "An old name from an old heritage—like your own, I think. For seven years I've worn my other shape. It was all I could think of to stay close to my daughter and keep her safe. Because I did not think my heritage would carry another generation, I'd kept this side of me from my wife, Marley's mother."

I winced. "Bad move."

"As you say. And when I did show her the truth—" he shrugged—"she accused me of drugging her, making her hallucinate. She left me, as was her right, but someday Marley will need knowledge only I can give her."

"You're sure she inherited your . . . gift? In my family, we don't know until adolescence."

"There are signs for us. When Marley was born I asked the nurse for the placenta, and examined it privately. I've carried this ever since, against the day of her need." He reached up and pulled something from beneath his own Wolf-Skin. It was another, but this one was white, and of a size to cover a nine-year-old girl.

"It grows as she does," he said, tucking it away again. "Though she will not hear the moon for another three or four years. You have no Skin? I wondered about you today. I smelled your magic, but not your Wolf."

I shrugged. "I'm Welsh, not Norse. I carry my wolf inside."

He smiled, but his eye teeth were growing again, and it was a scary effect. "So we are both the bastard children of forgotten gods. Now, let me put on my other Self, and take me to my daughter."

I tried to watch him change, but it proved as impossible to watch as my own transformation. "Got a tip for you, Wolfie," I said when he was back on all fours. "When the time comes to tell Marley about her heritage, try to sound a little less like an escapee from *Lord of the Rings*."

I'm alpha enough to want the last word.

I took him to the girls, detouring for the heater. "Look who found us!" I said brightly. "Talia, this is Marley's Wolfie. Wolfie, this is Talia, who came to help Marley."

Talia ran wondering hands over Wolfie's back while Wolfie licked and nosed at his daughter. Marley responded enough to put her arm around his neck.

"Listen, now, before Marley wakes up," I told Talia. "I think I know what you need to do, but you'll have to do a little acting, okay?"

She nodded vigorously.

"Okay, this is what happened. You fell asleep at home, and then you woke up here with Marley. You don't have any idea how you got here. You tried to look through the keyhole and you saw that the key was in the lock, so you pushed toilet paper under the door and poked the key until it fell on the paper and you could pull it inside and unlock the door. Got that? Then Wolfie found you. As soon as it starts to get light, you and Marley and Wolfie walk to the police station. I'm not going to be able to go with you . . . ."

Talia nodded vigorously, "Because you're naked, and you're a dog." She considered that statement for a moment. "Sorry."

"No problem. If someone stops for you, have them call the police. *Absolutely* keep Wolfie with you, okay? He'll keep you safe. The police will get your moms."

"What about the pageant?" Talia asked timidly.

"By the time everything is done with the police, it will be over, or at least too late for you to go."

"Good!" Talia said firmly. Wolfie added a low bark, agreeing.

"Hopefully, your moms will be so happy that the two of you are safe they won't even care about the pageant."

"I hope so," Talia said. She gave me a sly, even wolfish grin. "If not, guess I have some pretty good blackmail material, huh?"

Esther M. Friesner dearly loves working in a field that has no trouble reconciling her role as the creator of the wildly popular *Chicks In Chainmail* series of anthologies, her Nebula Awards for some decidedly serious stories, and her latest vocation for YA novels (including *Nobody's Princess* and *Nobody's Prize* for Random House, *Temping Fate* for Penguin, and more on the horizon). Originally from New York until the siren song of Yale brought her to Ph.D.-land, she's been living in suburban Connecticut ever since and knows whereof she writes.

Isn't That Special

Esther M. Friesner

If she had to hold that stiff little smile in place for much longer, Donna Vincenzo was sure that her head would explode. That would never do. Belmont Acres was not zoned for explosions. The Homeowners' Association maintained order and decorum scrupulously, rooting out the nits of nonconformity with a singular focus found only in the most dedicated, devoted, otherwise useless and boring lives.

"—and then Nathaniel told us all about how things used to be different for his grampa, in the olden days." While Donna grinned and cringed, her pride and joy, little Gilda, nattered away. The kindergartener had been rambling on about the new child in her class for at least fifteen minutes, all the while slurping skim milk and turning cinnamon-dusted rice cakes to gummy ruin in her hands. She was unaware of the mounting tension vibrating through her mother's trans-fat-free body, and of the intensifying effect her words were having on said tension. "He said that his grampa had to live all by himself for

years and years and *years* in the forest until the war came
and he got to be a hero for killing Nazis and he married
this girl named Ilona and she was an orphan and they
came to 'Merica and—"

"Would you like a cookie, dear?" It was not an offer
made lightly. Donna would sooner give up her morning
cup of kelp broth than resort to baked goods bribery
when dealing with her trophy child. In her world, the
only truly obscene S-word was "sugar," and she moni-
tored her daughter's intake of the vile contaminant as
closely as possible without pushing Gilda's school into
taking out a restraining order, barring both mother and
child from the cafeteria. This, however, was an emergency. She needed time to process the atrocious information the girl had just dumped into her lap, and for that
she needed Gilda to shut the hell up for a while.

"Gimme!" Gilda dropped the rice cake like a dead
cockroach. Donna was so distracted by worry that she
didn't bother correcting her daughter's lack of good man-
ners. She stuck two cookies into Gilda's grasping paws
and flung herself onto her BlackBerry, skimming her
emergency contacts in a wild-eyed panic. By the time
Gilda had gobbled up the last crumb of chocolate chip
baksheesh, Donna had set up five distinct meetings to
handle the dreadful crisis. Breathing a bit more easily,
she dragged Gilda off to their in-home fitness studio and
made damned sure that her daughter did enough Bye-
Bye Baby Cellulite exercises to redeem her from a fat
[sic] worse than death.

The next morning, with her daily 5K run and Xtreem
Flabslayer workout behind her, Donna swooped into the
first of her seek-and-destroy tête-à-têtes, her lean limbs
reeking of honorable sweat, Chanel No. 5, and the I-
Can't-Believe-It's-Not-Money air freshener presently

perfuming the interior of her BMW SUV. She erupted through the door of Gilda's kindergarten classroom, a Puma sportswear-clad Valkyrie, and opened negotiations with a hoarse, aggrieved, "*What* are you going to do about it?"

Gilda's teacher, Ms. Randolph, stared at Donna's outstretched, accusatory finger and didn't so much as blink. She'd been teaching kindergarten to the spawn of the Overly Entitled for more than twenty years. By the simple ploy of dropping a dollar into a coffee can every time one of her student's parents used the words "special," "empowered," "creative," and of course "gifted" to describe their precious booger-eating treasure-from-a-gated-community-Heaven, she always saved more than enough to take a yearly posh Caribbean vacation every time spring recess rolled around. She dropped a fiver in the can whenever *dis*satisfied parents threatened to take legal action if all of their kidcentric demands were not met. An extra buck went in for every "Do you know who I *am*?" and two for each "My taxes pay your salary!" The coffee can was doing better than most folks' 401ks.

"What am I going to do about *what*, Ms. Vincenzo?" Ms. Randolph asked calmly. "You'll have to forgive me, but my pet ferret hid my PDA this morning and I'm not sure if you're here about the bake sale or the werewolf."

Donna ground her teeth, then took a deep, cleansing breath left over from her days as a yoga instructor. "I certainly hope you're joking. I've taken time away from my *vital* commitments to deal with an issue that should never have *been* an issue in the first place. I shudder to think that the person so many influential members of this community have entrusted with the educative guidance of our nation's most precious resource, our future, our *children*, would not be suitably informed of the reason for my extremely inconvenient rescheduling of today's agenda just to accommodate your supposedly limited schedule."

Ms. Randolph stared at Donna. "Gobsmacked" did not begin to describe her reaction to the spate of verbiage that had just escaped her antagonist's collagen-stuffed lips. Up to this point, Ms. Randolph's interactions with Donna had been limited to Parents' Night, where—this being kindergarten—if you didn't need to tell Mommy and Daddy that their li'l pumpkin was inadequately toilet trained, playing with bodily by-products, or overindulging in Comparative Anatomy, you were home free. The teacher had never suspected Donna capable of such a spate of aggressive gibberish. Ms. Randolph cursed inwardly. She was actually going to have to *deal* with this sinewy harpy rather than shoo her away with a nice take-home assortment of bland reassurances.

"I'm *so* sorry," Ms. Randolph replied, taking care to employ a tone that pretty much said *The hell I am, but try to prove it, bitch*. "Sometimes I forget that I'm not in a teaching situation. The latest authoritative research on elementary education indicates that the more often a child is exposed to humor—the more examples of *being able to take a joke* which that child encounters during the formative years—the greater the chances of said child being accepted to an Ivy League school. It's all quite fascinating and completely true." She grinned. "But I can see that this interview will go faster if we keep things simple. Obviously you're here about little Nathaniel Corbett."

"Corbett?" Donna echoed. She knew that name. It was a name that had the oomph needed to make her knees buckle and to force her to go from a position of on-her-feet-and-dominant to stunned-and-collapsed in the wobbly chair next to Ms. Randolph's desk. *Corbett* was the name of one of the town's preeminent families, the sort of people that Donna Vincenzo thought of as Worthwhile Social Contacts as opposed to those she regarded as servants, toadies, inconveniences, or meaty placeholders. With one foot planted on the verdant hills of the country club and the other sunk up to its creamy white thigh in the yacht basin, the Old Money colossus that was Clan Corbett bestrode Donna's narrow world. "*Those* Corbetts?"

Ms. Randolph switched off her smile. She knew almost to the neuron flash exactly what Donna Vincenzo must be thinking. To cross the Corbetts was to court a good old-fashioned down-home social status stompin', an unthinkable outcome abhorrent to any soul who actually gave a dodo's dookie about such things. This was no time to gloat.

Oh hell, *yes*, it was!

"My goodness, I thought you *knew*," Ms. Randolph purred.

"I—Gilda never told me Nathaniel's last name, just that his grandfather was—was a rather colorfully *ethnic* type of person."

"That's the first time I've heard a werewolf described as something one step away from a Morris dancer, but no matter. I'm just relieved to know there's a healthy reason why you didn't know Nathaniel's a Corbett. For a moment, I was afraid you weren't having *meaningful* communication with your child." Ms. Randolph launched the gratuitous psychobabble javelin straight at Donna's heart and kept a beautifully straight face when the overbearing shrew cringed.

"I *always* communicate with Gilda," Donna protested feebly. "Every single day. When she told me about Nathaniel's family history of—*physical otherness,* I simply assumed she was talking about his *paternal* grandfather."

"Well, she wasn't." Ms. Randolph's smile was sweet enough to rot a saber-toothed tiger's fangs to nubbins. "Although I do like the image of Burgoyne Corbett stripping off his Savile Row suit under the full moon, going hairy, and running across the golf course, munching the caddies." She laughed.

Donna didn't. She stood up shakily, but with a determined look on her face. "I'm sure you must find this situation very funny, Ms. Randolph, but I can assure you, you are the only one who does." With that, she turned on her heel and strode out of the classroom. The interview was over, and so what if it hadn't yielded the desired result? It was, as previously mentioned, merely the *first* of Donna's meetings that day.

Three weeks later, Gilda came home in tears. "What's wrong, darling?" Donna asked, embracing the heartsick five-year-old. "Does something hurt? Was someone mean to you at school today? Did you eat a donut and you're afraid to tell Mommy?"

Gilda tilted her head back and wailed, "My boyfriend's *gonnnnnnnnne!*" Then she buried her head on her mother's shoulder and sobbed bitterly.

"Now, now, precious, I'm sure he's just got a case of the sniffles. He'll be back in school tomorrow, you just wait and see." Donna patted Gilda's curls, then added: "I didn't even know you had a little boyfriend."

Gilda lifted her head and nodded vigorously. "I do and he's wonderful and we're going to get married and

he loves me and he gave me a candy bar and he said I'm
the only one who can call him Nate and he was even
going to let me watch him change into a werewolf later
this month and—"

"He gave you a *what*?" Donna demanded, aghast.

Thus did she learn that her prized offspring was not
just consorting with an unacceptable companion whose
lupine forebears were not known for either good temper
nor good nutrition habits, but had actually accepted a
gift of *refined sugar* from the miserable little son of a
bitch. The horror . . . the horror . . .

*I didn't get that brat the hell out of my baby's class a
moment too soon,* Donna thought, basking in the smug
comfort of an exclusionary job well done. *And there's no
way that Burgoyne Corbett will ever know this was all
my doing.*

She smiled, covered her daughter in an oily wash of
other-runny-nosed-fish-in-the-sea platitudes, and let the
child indulge herself with all the kelp wafers she could
eat until lunch was ready.

Donna was just setting their mother-daughter salad
plates on the kitchen table when the phone rang. A distraught Helen Norris was on the line, her voice shrill
and inconvenient. "Donna, you've got to help me! My
husband just called. He got e-mail from Nathaniel Corbett's grandfather and that man is *furious*. He found out
that we're the ones who got up that petition and forced
the Board of Ed. to hold a special session *and* who got
the Channel 3 Child Peril Patrol on speed dial! He said
that little Nathaniel is absolutely devastated to be banned
from his old kindergarten class and he's threatening all
sorts of terrible things unless we tell the authorities to
let the boy back in!"

Donna sighed. "Helen, dear, *breathe*. Your aura is positively jagged with stress. Meet me at Bistro Metrovia in fifteen minutes and we'll get this whole silly misunderstanding settled. My treat."

Helen consented to the meeting. Of course she did. Dining out in Belmont Acres was split among fast food franchise pit stops (accent on "pit"), diners, seafood shacks, "edgy" ethnic eateries (any place the spices were hot enough to make soccer moms shriek and giggle over how *daring* they were being, as if eating severely toned-down Pad Thai was the equivalent of juggling cobras while getting a butt tattoo in Bangkok), and the high-priced, high-pretense Dining Experiences whose dainty, overwrought dishes and condescending waitstaff permitted patrons to dream that they *were* still cosmopolitans (instead of merely *drinking* them).

Bistro Metrovia belonged to the urbane/urban wannabe type of local restaurant. Their NO SHOES, NO SHIRT, NO SERVICE sign went on to specify which designer labels were *de rigeur* wear for patrons who even *hoped* to be seated. But no promises were made. Donna was one of the privileged people who'd established Bistro Metrovia *bona fides* ages ago, indicating Godzilla-sized clout. Her table was always ready.

Oh yes, Helen Norris was there within the fifteen minutes Donna decreed. Donna herself showed up a good thirty minutes later because she could.

Within the elegantly chilling atmosphere of Bistro Metrovia, Helen's hysterics shriveled into mousey peepings. Donna smiled while her friend once more recounted the tale of Nathaniel's grandfather's irate e-mail. No matter how upset Helen was, she'd sooner open a vein or a charge account at Wal-Mart than make a scene in *this* establishment.

"—and he says he's going to take *action*, Donna," Helen whispered, nervously shredding her ciabatta roll to crumbs while she spoke.

"That's a pretty empty threat unless he said *legal* action," Donna replied. "And even then, your family's got a good lawyer."

"*My* family?" Helen's eyes widened in distressed surprise.

Donna sighed more mightily than necessary, just to make sure the message got across that Helen's behavior was coming dangerously close to annoying her. Much of the power in Donna's hands came from her subtle mastery of bullying-through-implied-but-unspecified menace. "Yes, *your* family, Helen. When you were *entrusted* with the leadership of this crusade, you accepted the responsibility for handling every aspect of it like an adult. I wanted to do it myself, but as I explained to you in *great detail*—" (Behold another subtle barb, shot from the Master's bow, reminding Helen that Donna had already invested a vast amount of her much-more-valuable-than-yours time bringing her minion up to speed.) "—my schedule simply does not allow me to take on even *one* more commitment. It broke my heart, really it did, but then I asked myself 'Who is the only person I know who comes *marginally* close to equaling my devotion to the welfare of The Children?' " (Yes, Donna *did* have the oratorical ability to speak in audible upper case letters.) "That's why I called you." She scowled at Helen, although her latest round of Botox injections fought the effort every dermal micromillimeter of the way. "Now it seems that I was wrong."

Helen turned pale, which was a neat trick considering all the hours she spent getting broiled to a turn at the local Tan-a-Lot parlor. "I—I certainly hope you're not questioning my dedication to our children's best interests. You and I have worked together on enough committees—"

Donna waved away any attempts to invoke the Sisterhood of Robert's Rules of Order. "Helen, darling, you know that you're like a *sister* to me—" (Donna's birth sisters hadn't spoken to her in years, not since she'd pulled off an absolutely brilliant outflanking maneuver when their grandmother passed away and all of those valuable antiques were just *lying* there.) "—but if I'd thought you were going to do such—such a *half-assed* job on this, dropping the ball the instant you're asked to do some trivial follow-up work, I would have gotten somebody *capable*. You know I'm only saying this because I love you, don't you, dear?"

And there it was, the Love bomb. Donna didn't drop it often, but when she did it could only mean that she was about to flay the hide off of her chosen Target and send them a bill for a Therapeutic Exfoliation treatment afterwards. No matter how heavily laden with offense, churlishness, outright bitchery or classic schoolyard snottiness Donna's words might be, anyone who called her on it was promptly slapped with a wounded, "But I'm only telling you this because I *love* you!" And then she'd be off in a whirlwind of phone calls, e-mails and text messages, letting all the world know what an unappreciative, cruel and unfair person Target A was, and how anyone who would ever want to associate with Target A after this was probably just as bad.

It was astonishing how well this tactic worked in the hothouse-cum-loony bin of suburbia, especially when there was nothing good on TV.

Helen had viewed the blast crater of more than one of Donna's unlucky Targets and she wasn't stupid. "Oh yes, of course, absolutely, and I can't tell you how much I appreciate the way you believed in me and trusted me to do a good job and—"

"But—?" Donna knew that one of those nasty little interjections was en route and wanted Helen to get to it in a hurry. Lunch time was almost over and she had a hot date with a seaweed body wrap at 1:30.

"But this isn't just about me. If it were, I'd be right out there, facing up to little Nathaniel's grandfather no matter what!" She lowered her head and sighed. "It's my husband."

"*What's* your husband?" Donna asked, checking her watch.

"The reason why I can't—I can't continue being solely responsible for the fallout from this whole mess."

Donna momentarily debated whether or not to chastise Helen for referring to anything regarding The Children as a "mess," then decided it would be a wasted effort. Her underling's spine was already reduced to the consistency of (ugh!) white bread with the crusts cut off. To hammer at it any more would just be overkill.

"I'm so sorry, Helen, but you'll have to explain this to me just an *eensy* bit better. You don't mean to say that your husband . . . *controls* you? This *is* the twenty-first century."

Ah, another masterstroke! There wasn't a single woman of Donna's acquaintance who didn't claim, loudly and publicly, to be Liberated. Which in their social context meant they were happy to make their husbands set them up in business running darling little giftware or fashion boutiques, but actually *campaign* to get equal pay or to retain reproductive freedom? With *Feminists*? Too loud, too scary, and besides, who'd stay home and run the boutique?

"It is! He doesn't! I'm not—!" Helen's eyes began to dart wildly about Bistro Metrovia, as if seeking a bolt-hole among the potted plants and Chihuly glass sculptures. But there was no escape to be had, and so she declared, "My God, Donna, do I have to say it? You know as well as I do that Larry is—is—" She clapped her hands to her face, shuddered massively, and in a pathetic, broken voice exclaimed: "—*an investment counselor!*"

So much for Bistro Metrovia's vaunted scene-discouraging power. Some parts of the human condition simply happened to contain too much visceral horror to be suppressed by the possibility of incurring a maître-d's cultivated sneer. (Although ever since the stock market's recent shenanigans, with people's investments and retirement funds faring about as well as squirrels trying to cross a NASCAR track, the aforementioned sneer well might have been invoked less by Helen's outburst than by the revelation that her husband did . . . *such* things for a living. *Sic transit gloria* Wall Street Journal *mundi*.)

Donna pursed her lips and regarded the top of her crony's bent head with mild distaste. People were *looking*. Helen had effectively banned herself from Bistro Metrovia with such ill-considered and immoderate behavior, but Donna would see herself in Hell or an all-you-can-eat buffet line (same difference) if she let this dismal wimp take her down with her.

She summoned the waiter and, in a voice that was at once refined and unquestionably audible to every other person in the restaurant, ordered the most expensive bottle of wine on the menu. It didn't matter that she wasn't going to drink a drop of it. What counted was the subtle reminder of her position of steadfast economic security. She couldn't have distanced herself further from Helen and her [*shudder!*] investment counselor husband if she'd used a gold-plated ten-foot pole. Only then did she address her dining companion.

"I do know . . . *that* about Larry, dear. There's no need to attract attention. So I take it that little Nathaniel's grandpa is one of your husband's biggest clients and he's threatened to take his business elsewhere? Is that what you meant when you said he was going to 'take action'?"

Helen nodded without looking up.

"Well, my goodness, why didn't you *say* it was about money from the start? You just stick to your guns and I promise you, I will do everything in my power to help—from behind the throne, of course. If I joined you on the front lines, it would look like you couldn't handle this on your own, and we don't want people thinking *that*, do we?"

Helen shook her head a little hesitantly.

"*Good* girl. *Well* done." Donna said. She wasn't talking about Helen. "Now you just hold your ground and don't let anyone, make you give up even one inch. I'll be right behind you all the way, don't you worry."

Donna's promises of support—spiritual and material both—were not empty ones. She relished a good fight in the holy cause of Getting Her Own Way almost as much as she loved whipping the hired help (in this case Helen) back into line. She would put her family's lawyer on the case, with the strict injunction that under no circumstances was Nathaniel's grandfather to have even the ghost of a suggestion of a rumor of a hint that she was behind it. She was fairly sure that somewhere in the eternally resectioned bowels of the Law there had to be *something* smelly enough to discourage the irate Corbett grand-*pater familias* from taking out his fury on Helen's household with the Big Mallet of Financial Clout. By this means, Donna Vincenzo would be able to help her obedient minion and continue to keep herself in Burgoyne Corbett's good-if-unwitting graces.

And if it didn't work out well for Helen and Larry after all—

Oh, well! *C'est la* PTA!

Overcome by a surge of kickass jubilation, Donna had the waiter fill her wine glass to the brim, less the mandatory space needed for a theatrical sniff-swirl-sip-and-showboat ("Ah, yes, this has a ripe, deliquescent nose reminiscent of all of those succulent burgundies we sampled on our fifth visit to the Loire Valley. Don't you agree that *châteaux* are the only way to endure France?") and drank fully half of it. Damn the calories, *half!*

Then she went home and jogged her sins away before making that pledged call to her lawyer.

Per Donna's request, the loyal attorney did not bother her with anything except results, which came with remarkable swiftness. Only a fortnight of billable hours had passed by the time the call came, assuring Donna that there would be no more threats of material sanctions leveled against Helen's family. Donna went to sleep that night wrapped in a snuggly cocoon of satisfaction and, if she could not lay claim to the sleep of the Just, she could at least enjoy the slumber of the Self-Justified.

The next morning, as she was conquering a new Pilates routine, the doorbell began to chime. She tried to ignore it—her Me-Time was sacred, as was her Me Everything

Else—but the caller just would not give up and go away. Donna's devotion to Pilates was that of acolyte rather than mundane practitioner, so imagine if you will the effects of a determined doorbell ringer (and a sufficiently disruptive doorbell) at a Papal High Mass. Donna turned off the CD, flung down her resistance band, and stalked to the door, ready to flash-fry whoever was on the other side.

"What do *you* want?" she shouted as she flung wide the portal. She had no fear that her impudent caller might be some sort of malefactor, intent on a home invasion. Her house was part of a planned community whose plans included a security system so efficient and detail-oriented that in the summertime, the mosquitoes needed passports to get in. Thus, anyone calling at the Vincenzo domicile was either a neighbor or on the family's Approved list.

The man standing on Donna's doormat was neither. "Where I come from, *madame*, the proper greeting to offer a caller—even an uninvited one—is 'Good morning.' " He spoke in a deep, melodious voice, spiced with a slight accent that Donna was unable to place more specifically than the *original* Borscht Belt.

Donna was not a dull-witted person. She didn't require a formal introduction nor even a few more salient hints as to the identity of the silver-haired gentleman. From the moment she'd laid eyes on him, her brain went on Unidentified Individual Alert and leaped into processing all incoming visual, aural, and even nasal data. (Incomplete information, true, but she wasn't about to touch *or* taste the man!) The long face, so reminiscent of a hunting hound, the slightly pointed ears, the exceptionally white and likewise pointed teeth, the shaggy silver hair that was downright peltlike, the yellow eyes and the faint (though possibly imagined) aroma of kibble clinging to her caller were all set in place like an epic, elaborate arrangement of dominoes. The accent was merely the clincher, the finger tap that sent all of those snippets of evidence tumbling down in a floor pattern that spelled WEREWOLF.

"*Eeeeeeee!*"

Donna shrieked and slammed the door. And really, what other sort of reaction might a recognized member of *Lycanthropus Erectus* expect, under the circumstances? She raced through the house to the dining room where she dove into the drawer holding her wedding silver and yanked out a steak knife. Then she grabbed a fork, just to be on the safe side, and returned to the front door.

The man was halfway down the tapestry brick walkway when she hailed him. He raised one frosty eyebrow, surprised and intrigued, before coming back. "I beg your pardon, *madame*," he said with a shallow bow. "I did not expect you to open your door to me a second time. I admire your bravery and"—he noticed the improvised silver cross that Donna held up between them, steak knife transversing fork, and smothered a laugh— "prudence."

"You're not afraid of the cross?" Donna looked cheated.

"That would be the other team."

"Or silver?"

"Only when my wife expects me to pay for it. I will not lie to you: A silver bullet is another matter, when I am in my wolf form." He smirked. "In this form as well, if your aim is good. The same may be said for that knife you're holding. But really, *madame*, it's not necessary. Your life is in no danger from me."

"Oh, I know *that*," Donna said, with a haughty toss of her head. She lowered the cutlery. "You're here because of that business with your grandson. You're probably going to argue that he should be allowed to attend kindergarten with the normal children because he's no danger to anyone except on nights when the moon is full. It would hardly make your case if you tried to rip my throat out. On the other hand, I don't want you just biting me, either."

"Indeed," the older man replied. He bowed a second time and added: "Teodor Barbu, at your service. May I come in?" He stared intently into her eyes.

"Stop that!" Donna snapped. "If you think you can put some kind of a spell on me—"

"*Madame*, you are confusing werewolves with vampires, Mesmerists, witches, or possibly Jedi knights. If I hold your gaze, it is because that is how my kindred initiate a challenge. You are a worthy opponent, but I have established pack dominance many times in my life. I admit that this will be the first time I attempt to do so with words rather than fangs. One must move with the times. *May* I come in?"

Donna was reluctant to allow Mr. Barbu across her threshold, but she reasoned it would be better to get through this awkward interview in private. "I don't know why you're wasting your time, coming to see me," she said as she ushered him into the living room. "I did support the movement to eject—to provide your grandson with a more suitable learning environment for his needs, but I mustn't take credit for initiating it. That would be Helen—"

"Yes." Mr. Barbu was curt. "I have spoken with her. I should have done that from the start, but—I am an old man with old-fashioned ways. In my day, if you wanted to bring the wife into line, you went to the husband."

Donna was taken aback. "*You're* the one who threatened Larry?"

"*Madame*, even a man who becomes a wolf when the moon is full and bright may also have a diversified and lucrative portfolio."

"And I suppose Helen sent you here?" Donna asked dryly. He nodded. "I told her to keep me out of this. Just wait until I get through with that useless, treacherous, cowardly—"

"*Madame*, do not condemn your friend. I could see she was no leader, and so I cajoled her into revealing whose hand it was that pulled her strings."

"You *cajoled* her?"

He smiled and spread his hands. "I said I'd devour her shih tzu if she didn't talk. It is practically the same thing."

Donna resigned herself to hearing him out over a pot of herbal tea and a plate of sliced excellent-sources-of-roughage-potassium-and-antioxidants (i.e. fruit). She was fascinated and aghast to see how he—pardon the expression or not—wolfed down every last morsel on the platter, including a pomegranate, rind and all.

"You've certainly got a healthy appetite for a man of your age," she remarked. "Your grandson is very proud of your war record. Even if you were only a pup—*boy* at the time, that would still put you in your eighties."

"The appetite goes with my heritage, *madame*, as does my lusty health. Plenty of fresh, woodland air, a high-protein diet, an intense, regular exercise regime, maintaining the ability to outdistance one's pursuers, all these are the keys to my longevity." He sized her up from top to toe and added: "You too look as if you like to keep fit."

" '*Like* to—?' " Donna echoed, then laughed. "Try *live* to! I don't care how far the rest of this country slides into a super-sized bucket of lard, I'm not going."

"Your devotion to good health is admirable, *madame*."

"Oh, please. If I could show you photos of my husband's two exes, you'd understand. *On* went the wedding ring and *off* went the gym membership. He's rich enough to afford two sets of alimony and child support payments, but I'll be damned if I give him any excuse to make it three. I'm not about to eat table scraps when I can own the kitchen."

"A pity. You would look even lovelier with a little more meat on your bones. A little fat never hurt anyone." Mr. Barbu licked his lips discreetly.

"Fat equals failure." Donna was adamant. "Even my little Gilda knows that, and she's only five years old."

"A delightful age," Mr. Barbu agreed. "But also—such a tender one. The hurts a young child receives are never forgotten. My Nathaniel has taken his banishment to heart. If only you could hear how piteously he asks his parents why he can't return to his former school! He believes it's because of something he's done wrong, poor innocent."

"Didn't his mother and father explain that his exclu—educational upgrade is a needful *preventative* measure?" Donna clucked her tongue. "Sloppy parenting."

"Preventative? What is being prevented?"

"Turning other children into werewolves, of course! We've all seen the movies. If a vampire bites you, you become a vampire, if a werewolf bites you, you become a werewolf, and some children bite *anything*."

"And you believe that my Nathaniel—?" Mr. Barbu was at a temporary loss for words. "*Madame*, if you live the rest of your life according to what your American movies teach you, then you have my sincere compassion. A werewolf's bite is like a knife. In the hands of a madman, it kills; in the hands of a doctor, it heals. Its transforming magic has been called a curse, but when you learn to *control* a curse, to make its magic serve *you*, then it can become a blessing. Oh, there are as many different ways of looking at a werewolf's bite as there are leaves on an oak, but one thing holds true for all—" He raised one finger, leaned forward, and bellowed in Donna's face: "To *give* a werewolf's bite you must first *be* a werewolf, and that my Nathaniel is *not!*"

Donna recoiled. "But-but-but he's your *grandson!*" she protested.

"Lycanthropy is not genetic," Mr. Barbu said in a somewhat calmer voice. "Not like that whatever-it's-called Ukrainian curse, the one that makes you turn into a ferret on Saint Vaclav's Day. *Madame*, you are a woman of great authority in this town. When the next full moon rises, come and see for yourself—under whatever conditions you dictate!—that what I've told you is true, that my grandson is *not* a werewolf. And once you have witnessed this, I beg of you, *use* that authority to restore a small child's happiness and to right the great wrong you have done to him."

It was a very good speech. Unfortunately, if it had been a *successful* speech, it would have stopped before bringing up the thorny-though-accurate juxtaposition of *you* and *great* wrong, two concepts that just plain did not coexist in Donna's universe.

"My goodness!" she chirped. "I'd really be doing a great wrong if I didn't help you out after all that, Mr. Barbu, but—well, it's just not possible. Helen and the rest of us went to an awful lot of trouble, doing what we thought was best for *all* of The Children, so if any of us says that a mistake was made, it would entirely destroy our credibility the next time we need to protect them. Don't you *worry* about protecting The Children, Mr. Barbu?"

"I do." The older man slapped his knees and stood up slowly. "I worry that no one can protect them from stepping into a large, steaming pile of whatever it was you just said."

"What?"

"Never mind. *Madame*, I see you are resolved to remain unswayed by reason. You see yourself as a woman of conviction, steadfast in your beliefs. I must respect that. May your devotion be suitably rewarded. Farewell." Before Donna could react, he seized her hand, raised it to his lips, and gave it a courtly kiss.

"Eep!" She yanked her hand away in horror. "You bit me! You horrible monster, you *bit* me!"

"You are quite mistaken," Mr. Barbu said evenly. "Use your eyes. Has blood been drawn? Is the skin broken?"

Donna studied her hand carefully. "Nnnno . . . But I felt something."

"At most it was the glancing touch of my eyetooth across your knuckles."

Donna giggled nervously, embarrassed by her unaccustomed flare of hysteria. "I guess that doesn't count as a bite."

Mr. Barbu placed one hand over his heart and bowed. "By my adored grandson's life, I swear what I have done has no power to turn you into a monster such as I."

A full moon hung ripe and radiant in the autumn sky, gazing down in distant serenity at the hulking, shaggy-haired, shambling creature making its way up the crazy-paved path of the slumbering house. Its jaws champed mindlessly, its eyes blazed with bestial frenzy, and its brain throbbed with one thought and one thought alone: *The hunger . . . feed . . . the hunger . . . feed . . .*

It threw back its head and the night was pierced by a long, heart-sickening howl.

Teodor Barbu stuck his long, gray-furred snout out of the bedroom window and peered down at the midnight caller. "Hey! Stop all that racket. Don't you have a den to go to? Some of us are trying to sleep."

"Fiend!" the creature on his doorstep bayed. "What have you done to me?" It raised one trembling fist and shook it at the grinning wolf in the window. A fried chicken drumstick dripping with oil glistened in the moonlight for an instant before Donna Vincenzo stuffed it into her mouth and devoured it down to the bone. More crispy chicken parts awaited similar fates in the cardboard bucket she clutched to her chest. The fanny pack that once held her pedometer and water bottle now bulged with cheeseburgers. Her designer running shoes reeked of french fries. "You *swore*—!"

"—that you would not become a monster such as I." The gray wolf's tongue lolled in a jolly manner. "I have kept that promise. The delicate touch of my tooth to your skin was only enough to let you experience one tiny aspect of the lycanthrope's existence: Our ravenous hunger. Do you like it?"

"It's terrible!" Donna wailed. She dug a squashed brownie out of her jacket pocket and ate it in one bite, tears streaming down her cheeks. "Please . . . please make it stop! Oh my God, I can feel the cellulite growing, spreading, taking over every inch of my butt! Help me or kill me, but for the love of God, *don't let me get fat!*"

"Poor woman, you break my heart. Be comforted: What I have done, I have the power to undo . . . as do you. For every curse there is a cure, for every cure, a price." The wolf rested his chin on the windowsill. "I think you already know mine."

Without another word—but with virtually nonstop chewing—Donna Vincenzo took out her cell phone and keyed in a number. "Hello, Helen? (*om, nom, nom*) Yes, I know how (*om, nom, nom*) late it is but this (*nom*) is an emergency. Yes, I know I'm (*ommity-nommity nom*) eating, so would you shut up and listen? We were—I was (*om, nom, nom*) wrong about little (*Nom!*)thaniel Corbett and we've got to make it right as soon as possible or—" The rest of the conversation was overwhelmed by the sound of a host of cheeseburgers meeting their doom.

Teodor Barbu howled with laughter.

Linda Donahue, an Air Force brat, spent much of her childhood traveling. Having earned a pilot's certification and a SCUBA certification, she has been, at one time or another, a threat by land, air or sea. For 18 years she taught computer science and mathematics. Now when not writing, she teaches tai chi and belly dance. Linda has published about twenty stories and has co-authored a piece with Mike Resnick for *Future Americas*. In recent publications she has another story involving wolves in *Sword & Sorceress 23*. She and her husband live in Texas and keep rabbits, sugar gliders, and a cat for pets. *www.LindaLDonahue.com*

Prowling for Love

Linda L. Donahue

Marta stared at the calendar. Saturday's full moon fell smack in the middle of Purrfection. So much for her plans. But better another lonely year than go wolf-mode during the convention.

For Marta, the days before and after a full moon were full enough. Sometimes, *two* days before she'd grow a muzzle or big ears. And no matter the moon's phase, PMS triggered hair in places she didn't want it and long nails, which was convenient as she used them to scratch those itchy, hairy spots.

Her keen sense of smell could track a pizza delivery car four blocks away and knew how many pieces of pepperoni were on each slice. But could she track down a good man? No. Unfortunately, delicious and good weren't the same thing. Not that she ever ate people.

A member of Maulaholics Anonymous, Marta ate strictly werewolf-kosher . . . meaning she got her food like normal people, calling for takeout. And no, delivery boys weren't on the menu. Not that backsliding members of MA didn't occasionally snarf one down.

Being a werewolf entailed more than untangling matted fur, eliminating wolf breath, replacing shredded furniture, and unsightly posture. It meant no more romantic strolls under the full moon, as if dating wasn't hard enough at thirty-two.

Not that Marta hadn't tried everything. Speed dating, wine socials, online services, personal ads and set-ups by well-meaning friends had all proven disastrous. Purrfection was her last shot at finding someone to grow old with, someone who wouldn't mind losing his hair and teeth while she grew extra. If any man could accept her alternative life-style and possibly embrace it, he'd belong to furry fandom. He'd be at the convention while she sat home combing out her coat and flossing.

The whole "Granny, what big teeth you have" should really have been "Wow, Granny, you've got a *lot* of teeth," because flossing after every meal took an hour . . . two if she ordered stringy, cabrito burritos.

Marta glared at the calendar. "Fine. Be full. I'm still going!"

She was, after all, prepaid. Since she couldn't change the moon, she decided to disguise her appearance. This way she'd know up front who dug wolves.

Her wolf head rested on the bed. The costume hung on her, obscuring what few feminine curves she possessed. Marta cinched the fursuit, as furries called it, with a rhinestone-studded belt and added dangling earrings. She glued on false eyelashes—twelve sets—and painted the gloves' nails a bright red.

Shades of werewolf slasher films, claws dripping with blood, flashed through her thoughts. Marta hit the nails with polish remover and pulled out a bottle of demure pink.

Finally, to ensure everyone knew she was female, she doused herself with perfume.

With the head on, her eyes watered from the intense rose-scented cloud. Coughing, Marta peeled off the fur-suit and showered again. Yet the perfume had permeated the fake fur fibers enough to overwhelm her sinuses.

While she couldn't track a pizza delivery car now, neither would she inadvertently stalk anyone at the convention. It was a simple fact of life; some people smelled more like food than others. Vegetarians mostly.

So she wouldn't accidentally act on any inappropriate urges, and to keep the conventiongoers in ignorant—and living—bliss, Marta stuffed herself with nine Arby's sandwiches. Few things gave away werewolfism like a bloody feeding frenzy.

Once outside the hotel she put on the head. Instantly her peripheral vision vanished. She only saw straight ahead, like looking in a never-ending tunnel. But it was going to be worth all the trouble. That, she decided, would be her mantra for the weekend. Come what may . . . it would all be worth it.

Surely among the thousand plus people attending Pur-rfection she'd find Mr. Right. The werewolf who turned her was *not* Mr. Right. He was a real animal 24/7. Actually, he was less of a jerk *during* the full moon.

"There's ear tags if you'd prefer," said the registration guy, while Marta struggled in vain to pull the badge's lanyard around her big wolf head. "Most people take off their heads. Or maybe you'd rather have a dog tag and collar. There's a dealer selling—"

"Why would I want a dog tag?" Marta stiffened. Was he really calling her a *dog*?

"Aren't you a dog person?"

Remembering the connotations weren't the same *here*, Marta relaxed. Before becoming a werewolf, she liked dogs and cats equally. Now, neither liked her. Dogs actively disliked her. Perhaps because they knew werewolves were superior. Even though it was an idle prejudice, she felt superior. Dogs were *domesticated*. Wolves were wild and free.

Marta burped, tasting Arby's sandwiches. Okay, maybe she'd been a tad domesticated too.

Marta perched her paws on her hips. "I'm a wolf."

"No need to get all huffy and puffy and blow my table down." He grinned. "Your outfit confused me. Wild animals don't usually dress up . . . unless they're a particular character like Yogi Bear. So, is it head off or ear tag?"

Marta's face felt human. Then again, so did a werewolf face. She hardly noticed the transformation unless she passed a mirror. Or somebody screamed.

Positive she was still human, or mostly human, Marta removed her head. She plucked off the earrings, removed the rhinestone belt, but left on the eyelashes.

Handing the items to the registration guy, she said, "Give these to a lady dog person, okay?"

"That's really nice. Here." He handed her another badge. "It's for the dog groomer's show. The hotel double-booked conventions and gave us a few extra passes to hand out."

"Thanks, but I'm here for this." To say she was here for love would only sound sad.

"They put on a great show. If you think we have a wild parade, you should see theirs."

"They dress up the dogs?" Of course they did. Dogs had as many Halloween costumes as kids. "No thanks."

Remembering she hadn't bothered with makeup, she put on her badge then head. Why doll up when she was wearing a wolf head, then later would *have* a wolf's head? She hadn't even bothered with clothes, making her wish the fursuit wasn't so scratchy inside.

Marta waded into the crowd wearing animal prints or T-shirts with animals on them. Several people carried stuffed toys—plushies, furries called them. And dozens of fursuits prowled the hall, making the convention look like a job fair for muppets.

As she squeezed between a purple squirrel and a pink cat, she reminded herself she wanted weird. Really, *really* weird. Normal people didn't date werewolves. Part of her blamed Hollywood for giving werewolves a bad rap, but if she hadn't dated that "wolf" she'd still be normal. So maybe there was some wisdom to the whole "werewolves are dangerous" thinking.

A blue bear pawed her arm and a husky voice asked, "You going to the late-night yiff?"

"I don't know." She wasn't sure she was up for a mascot orgy where everyone scritched and rubbed each other. Then again, it'd be the perfect place to meet a guy with a fur fetish.

"You *are* over twenty-one?" the bear said.

"Reasonably so," Marta answered. Thirty-two and never married. No wonder she'd dated that wolf.

What if *he* was here on the prowl? Her fists curled. If she saw him, she'd tear out his lying throat. The only one . . . really! To make matters worse, when she found out, he tried to pull the old "she was his alpha female and the others were just part of the pack" drivel. Did he think she was a moron? Or a Mormon maybe?

"Sorry to bother you," the bear said, ambling away in a hurry, heading for a buxom woman carrying a teddy bear.

Marta sighed. She'd just scared off a guy who was probably weirder than she was. Needing a plan, she headed through her tunnel vision toward a padded bench, bumping into four people along the way. Sitting was uncomfortable, as the costume chaffed her bottom, but it was an improvement over banging through the crowd like a pinball.

Marta flipped through the program. The convention had a Fursuiter Headless Lounge . . . but that could be risky. The schedule listed an evening Parade followed by a fursuiter dance, which could be promising. For now, panels were the only choice. Animal Magnetism had potential. Woodland Games caught her eye; then again, she might not be ready for whatever those were. Furry Secondlife sounded perfect. Then she spotted Animal Totems and Therianthropy.

Maybe before meeting someone, she should try learning more about her "condition." She'd only been a werewolf for eight months.

She made her way to the Sycamore room, managing with only a few collisions. Maybe her keen sense of smell could have told her where people stood if her costume didn't reek of roses.

Marta slipped into the back, feeling a bit like Jane Goodall watching a new breed of animal. Furry heads nodded like life-sized bobbleheads, agreeing with whatever a panelist had last said. The humans in the audience looked out of place sitting between fursuiters. Elaborate face painting "morphed" the panelists' features into animal ones.

"We are all animals beneath our human masks," said one panelist wearing monkey makeup.

"Some of us more than others," Marta mumbled.

Just then, a guy in a staff T-shirt led a white rabbit to a chair up front and helped him sit.

Marta hummed. "I should've brought a seeing-eye human."

An elbow nudged her. "Oi! That's a good one." The man had a sexy Australian accent.

Marta turned sideways hoping for a handsome Aussie with a dazzling smile. Instead she stared into the dark, unfathomable eyes of a red kangaroo.

"G'day, miss. You seem a right smart sheila. What say we hop on outta here?"

Another panelist squawked, then said, "Before you can transform your soul, freeing your wild spirit, you must know your totem animal."

"Yeah," Marta said quietly, "let's go."

The kangaroo hopped into the hallway, leading the way. "I hear they got a fabulous headless lounge, if you're game to go topless—"

Marta's throat tickled. She ran her tongue across her lip and felt the new hair which had sprouted. "I'm not that kind of girl." She hoped that sounded funny. Certain it was lame, she added, "At least not on a first date."

Marta groaned. First she'd scared the bear and now she was going to shoo the roo.

Instead of running, or hopping away, Big Red Roo said, "All right! First date, eh? Guess we oughta exchange names." He thrust out a furry paw. "Name's Bink, but the girls all call me Binky."

Alarms rang in Marta's head. She shook his hand stiffly. "I'm Marta. The girls, huh? You get around?"

"Naw. I coach girls' football, ages nine to twelve. Sorry, I mean soccer. Still getting the hang on what you Yanks call things."

"And the kids call you Binky?"

"Sometimes I wear the suit and play mascot. They seem to like it and, to be honest, there's days when I don't have anything to wear."

"Not much for doing laundry?" Marta joked, but she knew exactly how he felt.

"So, love," Bink said, "how's a show sound for our *first date?*"

Marta laughed nervously. "Who's going to let us in a show dressed like this . . . and I'm not dressed for any-place else." Not dressed at all, actually.

"I was thinking we might catch the Wild Wild Westies before the dance, if you don't mind being a cheap date."

"The Wild Wild Westies?"

"You'll love 'em. A bunch of girls dress up as saloon-gal westies. They do the most amazing cancan."

"I wouldn't miss it." Seeing that Bink offered an arm, Marta looped her nail-painted paw inside the crook of his furry red elbow.

"The courtyard here is real nice, too," Bink said, lead-ing her toward a glass door. "Not as hot and stuffy as inside and it's a shortcut to the main ballroom."

"Sounds lovely." The fursuit felt hot. Much hotter. Much, much hotter. *Crap.* The suit was suffocatingly hot, yet Marta wasn't sweating. She panted. *Just perfect.*

The pale moon against the deepening sky mocked her. She hated it when the full-enough moon rose in daylight. No wonder she felt faint from the heat generated by fur in fur. At least the costume wasn't scratchy anymore.

As she and Bink strolled through the courtyard, she glimpsed her reflection in the hotel's glassed walls. She walked hunched over, with her head stuck out. *Wolf posture. That's so attractive.* At least she walked upright.

"You've got a great animal walk," Bink said, hopping beside her. "I wager you win a prize in the Parade."

"I see you get into your animal character too."

Bink shrugged. "That's the whole point, right?"

The courtyard led to another entrance. People crowded the hall. No fursuits, just people wearing clothing with dog motifs.

Marta squeezed Bink's arm. "We're at the dog show!"

"Just cutting through. You don't have anything against dogs, do you?"

"It's more the other way around." Marta swung her head erratically, searching for a pack of angry dogs.

"If a dog liked you, you'd have nothing against it, right?" Bink asked.

Marta stammered a moment before asking, "Do you have a dog?"

"Hey!" someone shouted. "That's a great dog outfit." The voice belonged to a short man with excessively groomed hair. "Would you mind walking through the showroom? People will go wild." The man looked at Bink. "You, too. Who doesn't love kangaroos, right?" He grabbed Marta's and Bink's arms and dragged them toward open doors.

Marta started to lecture the man on the rules of etiquette when approaching a person in a fursuit, but her straight-on, tunnel vision locked on the room filled with dogs, mostly standard poodles.

She dug in her heels but her wolf feet had poor traction and she slid across the threshold.

Not helping matters, Bink said, "Relax, Marta. These dogs are used to strangers."

Every poofy-cut canine reared its head and pinned its ears, in direct contrast to the smiles and applause the costumes garnered from the audience and groomers. Low growls rose from the throats of dogs that should've been ashamed of their prissy appearance.

What self-respecting poodle let someone cut its fuzz into stripes then dye its coat orange and black? Tiger or not, it was still a dog groomed to look like a cat. One poor animal's coat had diamonds dyed in a jester's motley pattern. The jingle bell hat just compounded the insult.

Every dressed and dyed pooch had the nerve to growl at Marta. She hunched over, nearly dropping to all fours, wishing werewolves could communicate—*really* communicate—with dogs. Yet being in werewolf-mode while wearing a ridiculous wolf costume, she lacked the moral high ground to make much commentary.

"Let's just go, Bink, okay?" She tightened her hold on his arm.

Gently, Bink extracted himself from Marta's death grip and strode deeper into the overgroomed pack. He turned in a slow circle and the dogs quieted. "You just gotta stare 'em down. Let 'em know who's boss. Come on, Marta. Give it a chance."

A chance. That was why she'd come here. She repeated her mantra . . . doubting the outcome of this scenario was really going to be worth it.

Marta tiptoed up to Bink. Though the dogs couldn't see her face, she felt them staring into her mask's eyelash-rimmed eyes.

Dogs bared their polished white teeth and growled. Marta bared hers in response, while swallowing the rising snarl.

The tiger and jester poodles, each at least four feet tall, jumped from their grooming tables, landing on painted toenails. More poodles joined in—a fairy, a dragon, a harem dancer, a ballerina, and a quartet of schnauzers dressed up like the Village People. No wonder these dogs were in a pissy mood.

Bink shouted, "Sit!"

A few groomers shouted versions of "Don't mess up its cut!" and "Tutu, you come back here!" All the dogs had names like Tutu, Fruball, Fluff-Fluff and Baby.

The rest of the groomers screamed and waved frantically.

Marta turned . . . and faced more dogs.

She'd never seen them creeping behind her in her blind spot—although spot was too small a word for it.

A poodle wearing a tutu jumped Marta and bit her arm.

Between fake fur and her own fur, the bite didn't break skin, even though standard poodles had needlelike teeth. But, as Marta learned, poodles clamped down hard—sort of like snapping turtles.

While she shook her arm, the poodle prince attacked her calf. If someone was recording this, no doubt it'd air on YouTube later that night.

Another pair, one with a halo and angel wings, the other in devil horns, knocked Marta onto her back. The Village People schnauzers—which couldn't squeeze between the four large poodles—paced, sat and reared in sync, the routine scarily similar to YMCA.

Then devil dog grabbed Marta's mask by an ear and shook it, tugging and yanking upward. All strains of the addictive song fled her thoughts.

She tried to grab the mask, but with ballerina poodle pulling on one arm and angel dog latched onto the other, all she could do was flop like a giant chew toy. At least her costume didn't squeak.

Bink tried to wade through the dogs, but the poodle pack jumped around him, leaping over his kangaroo tail like circus performers. Maybe it only looked that way because one of the poodles resembled a berserk clown. Finally, Bink backed off.

Devil dog yanked the mask from Marta's head.

Marta snarled at the dogs.

The groomers who'd been screaming frantically now screamed like sorority girls in a horror movie. People ran in all directions. A few dogs yelped and backed off. But not the determined ones that had Marta pinned down.

She growled and snapped, trying not to bite them, not wanting to escalate matters . . . not on a first date. *Oh, dear God, what must Bink think?* Marta tilted her head just enough to see Bink's big kangaroo feet some twelve feet away. At least he hadn't run.

She looked up and saw him tucking his roo head under his arms. A dog head poked from out of his costume. He barked and snapped at the poodles until they all backed off.

Forsaking his hop, he loped over doglike and extended a hand. "Sorry 'bout their behavior. I had no idea you were really a wolf in there. Just thought you were some hot sheila afraid of dogs . . . and well, you can see I need a girl who likes dogs." When he grinned, his tongue flopped out.

Marta met his puppy-dog gaze. "You're a weredog?"

"Dingo, actually." He flashed his canines proudly.

"You thought I was hot?"

"Sure thing. You've got a right sexy voice. Guess I'll have to wait until tomorrow to see the rest of your package."

"Tomorrow? You aren't put off by me being a wolf?"

Bink laughed, a bit like a hyena. "I'm no speciesist, love. Besides, I figure our kind's distant kin and we gotta stick together."

As they headed for the exit, the fancy-cut dogs crowded together, staying just out of snapping range—her snapping range.

"Maybe we should put our masks back on," Marta suggested.

"Yeah. Sorry 'bout the tears in your outfit. Guess that means the show's off."

"You're not getting out of our date that easily. Believe it or not, I've had worst first dates."

"You're my kind of gal. Maybe afterwards we can hit a drive-thru? I don't know 'bout you, but I'm famished."

"How about instead we go to my place and I'll *not* cook us something to eat. I make an excellent steak tartar."

"Sounds like a plan."

"So," Marta asked, "why a kangaroo?"

" 'Cause you can find kangaroo costumes most anywhere, whereas there's not much call for dingo mascots."

"Oh." Marta glanced at the big kangaroo feet. "I was hoping there might be another reason."

"What's that? You wishing I was a wereroo?"

Marta grinned. "Wouldn't it be a Down Under-Roo?"

"I never met a funny wolf before. No offense, but your kind doesn't usually have much of a sense of humor. You're not disappointed, are you?"

A giant wereroo might've been a little too weird, even given her situation. Besides, kangaroos were vegetarians. "It depends. I was thinking about your costume's big feet . . . and wondering if it was true about big feet—"

"Oh, I've got big feet all right. Size fourteen here in the States. That's the other reason I picked the roo."

As they walked into the Wild Wild Westie show, Marta rethought her whole position on dogs. After all, dingos were wild dogs and dogs were loyal, right?

Robert Anson Hoyt has been writing since he was first able to hold a pencil, often being assisted in this endeavor by his varying, (though consistently large) number of cats. He has sold two stories to DAW anthologies, *Better Off Undead* and *Fate Fantastic*, and currently has a novel under consideration by a major publishing house. He is not a werewolf, but would be willing to consider it if his cats were not certain to kill him.

Lighter Than Were

Robert Hoyt

I checked the seals on either end of the fluorescent light as I leaned back comfortably in a used office chair, reveling in the cold, musty scent so pervasive in storerooms everywhere. There are unexpected advantages to being a mall technician. One of them is that not only do people not give you a second glance, but most will go out of their way to avoid giving you a first one. When you have a tendency to grow hair unexpectedly in exotic areas depending on the time of month, any job with a certain acknowledged amount of privacy is instantly an advantage.

Admittedly, it was more comfortable now, than it had been. A hundred years ago, I would likely have been running through the forest for my life, pursued by villagers armed with silver-tipped arrows and a lack of patience with disappearing livestock; whereas today I was the executive engineer at an anonymous mall, and my only major worry was what excuse to make for my suspiciously timed sick days.

I picked up the needle-nose pliers from the toolbox and made a little tweak on the connecting wire of what would look, to anyone else, exactly like a normal fluorescent light. I glanced nervously at the door of the supply room as someone walked by. Of course, no one knew about my little invention, but all the same it made me skittish. According to my watch, a rather exclusive model which showed a little pictograph of the current phase of the moon in the top right hand corner, the pet store two floors down should have been opening now, which meant that Leroy would be calling any second.

Leroy was the manager of a fairly upscale groomer called the Pet Parlor, and he had always been very kind about helping me when I came up with a prototype for something. But this was perhaps my most important design yet, and Leroy had outdone himself in offering me a back room in the Parlor where I could test it. My skin was getting itchy, which was a sure sign I had too much wereglobin built up in my bloodstream as it was, and I was beginning to wonder if I would end up barking mad, when finally the phone rang.

I picked it up quickly, but tried to sound normal, just in case it wasn't Leroy. I had learned a long time ago to be guarded about answering phones, and had fallen back on the old tradition of sounding generic or bored. It didn't do to ask some poor non-were if he'd gotten rid of the fleas he got last month mating. If I had the ability for that sort of thing, I could have been a novelist, which, like maintenance, was not a bad profession for the naturally reclusive.

One had to wonder about Stephen "King."

"Maintenance department. Harry Silverbane speaking,"

"Good morning, Harry. Don't worry, it's me. Sorry, wereglobin had me feeling dog tired this morning, so I ran a little late."

I chuckled. "Morning, Leroy. Hold on a sec." I moved to hold my hand over the doorknob.

"All right, I can talk. Can I come down to install the moonlight tube in the back room? It's making me nervous bringing this thing into work at all, and I want to test it out as soon as possible. I have to know if it works."

"Actually, that's going to be a bit of a problem." He coughed on the other end of the line, and then, when he spoke again, was a great deal quieter, "I don't like talking about this on the phone. Can you see me downstairs in about five minutes? I'll tell the staff I'm double-checking our upkeep status."

I swore inside my head, and grimaced. It couldn't ever be simple or easy, could it? But Leroy was a practical business owner, and if he was concerned, there was a reason.

"All right," I said, frowning, "but I'm not happy about it."

"Believe me, neither am I," Leroy said, and hung up.

I looked around the room for a place to store the moonlight tube while I met Leroy, lest it get broken by someone waltzing in here. That was the last thing I needed.

The tube rack. That was the obvious answer. We tended to keep an extra box or two around in case the glass from a tube we took out broke. I hastily piled it on top of the pile, hiding it in plain sight. Mainly, I wanted to keep it off the floor and minimize chances of it breaking.

As I was leaving, the phone rang again. I hastily picked it up.

"Maintenance department. Harry Silverbane speaking," I said.

"Hi." A soft voice which brought to mind a twenty-something blonde and hinted at the sort of perfume that made men weak at the knees said, "Could you send someone around to Sherri Soda's? We've had a bit of an accident in the men's shirts and I was hoping we could clean it up before someone hurts himself."

I picked up a legal pad to write a note to any of the interchangeable maintenance workers who stored a tool belt here.

"I'll get someone right on it," I lied, scribbling down the note. Then I tacked it on the board, and hurried out the door.

As it turned out, Leroy had a very good reason for not having the tube installed today. Leroy—a well-built man with black hair and a jovial face—was a good friend, and when I had told him about the moonlight tube, which I hoped we could use to burn off wereglobin while the amounts were small enough, to prevent a change at the wrong time, he had set aside a back room specifically for the purpose. Unfortunately, like many business owners, he had investors who helped keep things afloat in return for a share of the profits, and one of those investors was coming to look things over, meaning the last thing Leroy wanted to do was draw attention to the room which had been recently wolf—and soundproofed at some expense. The second to last thing he wanted to do was fiddle with the lights for no apparent reason. Leroy wanted things to look well-oiled, smooth, and seamless.

"Murphy's law, I'm afraid. They had to pick today of all days to come by." he said, sipping what was billed as a "Moonlight Mocha" by the somewhat romantically minded coffee shop owner next door. He glanced as his watch. "In fact, I have to run in a minute."

He must have noticed me shifting nervously in my seat. He lowered his voice and leaned forward, "Harry, how long has it been since you burned wereglobin out of your system?"

I thought about it for a moment, and sighed, "Probably about two months."

He winced, and jerked his head to the side, "How did you even manage that? Shouldn't have been more then a month."

I shook my head. "Mall air conditioning system went haywire last month over the full moon. Thank Dog it happened close enough to summer that I could avoid being out at night, so I didn't have to abandon my post in the middle of a crisis. No moon, no reaction."

He looked up in the direction of his Parlor, and back down at his watch again. Then his clear blue eyes bored into me.

"You know that was a stupid idea. There's enough wereglobin in your system right now, I imagine that if you put silver near enough to you to bond, you'd be dead before we could say 'contact dermatitis.' You're a brilliant engineer, but you aren't going to help anyone if you're dead. Try to burn off tonight, you got me? Take a sick day if you have to." He took a final look at the watch, "I gotta go. Meet me tomorrow with the bulb. I'll call you, same as usual. And hey," he said, pointing at me as he stood up to leave, "I mean it about burning some off. I'd hate for the next thing to send along in the howl to be your obituary." And he hurried off.

It was an otherwise uneventful day. The worst little adventure was cleaning up after a kid in the obligatory slushy stand who took the dare of a friend to drink four extra large slushies in quick succession. I made the decision to leave my bulb alone. With this much wereglobin in my system, it was just best if I didn't do anything to aggravate my anxiety, in case I grew a spontaneous and sudden beard. In any case, the bulb was probably safer stored away than it would be if I took it home and were tempted to tweak it, especially while I was this wound up.

I made my excuses, and handed things over to the night shift at the earliest possible moment. The moment I got home, I started undressing, as much as anything because of the strange feeling that my clothing was beginning to have. I considered going to my "kennel," as we typically called it.

It was a fairly typical appointment for an older were's house to have some room where you could turn in without damaging anything, while the younger generation tended to have a cavalier attitude, and could be counted on to do it very nearly in public. This tended to be the most common explanation for why you occasionally saw a mysteriously orphaned article of clothing on a sidewalk in the city or suburb. Someone had lost track of time and shifted unexpectedly.

While I did have a room of this type, I was uncertain about using it. I could only afford to if . . .

I went to the kitchen and checked the calendar. It did not look pretty. I had about three of my sick days left, and more than three full moons coming over the course of winter.

Although I understood Leroy's concern, and knew he was right about the danger, especially with this much wereglobin in my bloodstream. If I transformed, I could still be in the process of burning it by tomorrow evening.

Wereglobin worked like gasoline, and once moonlight started metabolizing it, you were stuck for as long as it took to process everything. Usually, you metabolized it as much as possible with moonlight, but most people still had between six to eight hours left by the full moon, unless they used a metabolism enhancer like the moon bulb.

Unfortunately, that had served as an evolutionary advantage when humans and weres alike were nocturnal and moonlight exposure was guaranteed. Now it meant my blood composition got downright inconvenient when I spent most of my time indoors.

Which meant that I couldn't afford to risk changing. I was almost out of sick days, and for all I knew I'd be out for sixteen hours. That, and I absolutely had to get that bulb installed tomorrow.

So instead, I took two aspirin, and ate a raw steak out of the fridge. Protein tended to help calm things down. It took an enormous amount of protein to transform between a human and a wolf, just to repair damage wreaked by bone rearrangement and muscle realignment. If you sated your cravings, it helped deal with most of the nervousness.

At around nine o'clock, I crawled into bed, exhausted. It was going to be a restless night for certain.

And at nine-fifteen, give or take, it finally got unbearable, and I crawled out of bed and curled up in the corner of the room on top of my blankets.

When I dragged into work the next day, the place was far more exciting than usual. There was a gaggle of security guards crowding a very embarrassed looking young man. He was standing in the circle of rent-a-cops wrapped in a blanket.

I tapped a rubbernecker on the shoulder.

"What happened?" I asked, fearing the worst.

The guy turned around, laughing softly.

"Guess he lost a bet. Get this. Kid sends the security guards on a chase after some big dog he brought into the mall as a distraction, then runs out through the middle of the mall in his birthday suit, screaming at the top of his lungs."

My blood ran cold. Without bothering to make an excuse, I ran up to the maintenance closet. Sure enough, the box in which I had put the moonlight bulb was missing.

At that moment, I heard the door open behind me, and one of the junior maintenance workers came in, apparently looking for something in the toolbox.

"Oh, hi, Mr. Silverbane," he said quietly as he walked to the desk.

I cleared my throat and tried to suppress my nervousness. The last thing I needed to do was make this situation any hairier.

"Derrick, did you find out who did the maintenance job I posted on the board yesterday?"

The kid looked up with a slightly scared expression.

"I did that job, Mr. Silverbane. Someone had evidently been swinging one of the studded belts around and had broken a fluorescent light. I got to it as soon as I saw the note. You know how clothing stores are about lighting." He paused, and bit his lower lip nervously. I realized that I had been standing there with my mouth open, and the fact that I was shaking and sweating probably didn't make me look any more sane. It didn't help that I was plagued with guilt. The poor kid out there had probably just been a college student going in to buy a set of dog tags, which turned out to be quite literally useful, since they were loose enough they wouldn't strangle you when you changed, and stopped the younger generation from being dragged off to a kennel during a night of roaming. And he had unexpectedly become a victim of the moonlight. I had to see Leroy.

Derrick broke into my thoughts. "Is, um, something wrong? I didn't take too long getting there, did I?"

I nodded at him, in what I hoped was a reassuring manner.

"No, no, nothing is wrong. Would you excuse me a moment?"

At which point, I ran downstairs as fast as my legs would allow me to.

I found Leroy standing at the entrance to the pet shop when I got down. He didn't even chew me out for not waiting for the call. He just took me by the shoulder, and with uncanny smoothness led me towards the office.

"Ah, sir, I knew you would be worried about Fifi. Right this way, please. I'll take you to"—and as the office door closed, he changed direction completely, without even pausing—"we have a problem."

"I noticed." I said, gritting my teeth to stop from shaking.

"You can thank your lucky star, which in this case I would say is Sirius, that Frank, from security, is one of us. He's going to see about fixing up the security tapes, and trust me, that implies no small amount of danger on all of our respective parts. And before you ask, he was already talked to by one of our people down at the police station, and the kid'll probably just get a bit of steak and they'll call his parents to pick him up before he's even thinking like a human again. May I ask how on earth you lost the bulb? And"—he said, barely looking up—"why you're still hopped up like a Chihuahua on a barbeque grill?" he asked. And then his expression froze.

"I suppose I should have guessed from the fact that you showed up. You skipped last night, didn't you?"

I just nodded, and then added, "I lost the bulb because I didn't want to take the bulb home while I was feeling so nervous." I was starting to get hot, and my skin was itching like the blazes.

"Very sagacious of you," he said, quietly. Then, after thinking for a moment he added, "Then you can't go remove the bulb. If you did, you'd turn almost instantly. And, it occurs to me that the kid probably went roaming at least on the half and full moons, knowing kids, whereas you have nearly two full moons to burn off. We need an excuse for getting it out of there."

"We can't destroy it," I said. "A lot of the plans never got written down, in case anyone started looking for the maker."

He swore under his breath.

We needed to get that bulb out of there, and do it in a way that wouldn't attract too much attention.

And then a thought occurred to me. Maybe because I was so racked with wereglobin, I found my mind going at right angles to the way normal humans usually did.

It was fairly obvious, of course, that a non-were would have to change the light bulb. The trick, however, was giving a good reason why they would change it.

"I have an idea." I said, and picked up Leroy's phone.

"Derrick, maintenance department." A voice said on the other side.

I smiled.

"I'm not quite sure I follow you." Leroy said, as we walked along the corridor to Sherri Soda's.

"Look, just trust me here," I said, jittery with excitement, "The kid who changed the bulb is still learning the ropes, so I told him that the bulb he installed in the clothing shop was actually supposed to go to the Pet Parlor."

Leroy nearly dropped his jaw on the floor.

"Are you crazy? How can you tell him that?" he said in a frantic whisper, "Look, I've hosted your experiments more than my share of times, and I don't mind. But it's another thing entirely to stick me with a device I've never seen, in the public view, of all things. Did you even give him a decent explanation, or is he going to spend a bunch of time poking around to find out why?"

I smiled coyly. "He provided his own explanation. Figured that that 'weird tinge' of light might help to calm the dogs."

Leroy gulped. "If I understand your explanations correctly, he's too close to the truth for my taste."

I wheeled on him unexpectedly.

"Leroy? You are the absolutely most firm-minded businessman whom I've ever talked to. And I've just had a brilliant idea for field testing my moonlight bulb, without risking any more public exposure." And now my smile grew, "And not only that, but if you play your cards right, then I think you might get a ton of profit."

And then I succumbed to the urge and scratched at my ever-more-itchy skin.

"But first," I added, "I'm going to be your guinea wolf."

About a month later, I strolled into the Pet Parlor. I had heard on the howl, which these days was available in podcast for those who didn't want to sit in their backyard listening all night, that the keywords for the spa service today would be a pet name associated with mythology, and two words beginning with r. Changing the passwords on a regular basis and communicating on the howl made sure all the werewolves in town knew that Leroy had an answer to "that time of the month," and that anyone who thought something was suspicious would be kept guessing.

That, and it provided endless entertainment as people came up with something that fit to say to the receptionist.

I walked up to the counter.

"I'm here to see poor little Pegasus. You know how Romanian cats hate to get rinsed."

The receptionist, who so far believed that this was part of some form of promotional giveaway, nodded and pointed her finger.

"Just down the hall and to the left."

I stepped into the room, and saw Leroy standing in front of a Chinese screen. He turned around and grinned.

"Harry! Nice to see you. I think you'll be pleased to know that business is booming. In fact, the profit has been so good, pretty soon we'll need to hire a dishonest accountant to steal some cash, so we look a bit more even. We must have gotten half the werewolves in this town so far, and still more are on the way." He grinned.

"Glad to hear it. Besides, the credit has to go to you. There's no way I would have thought of calling it a 'Werewash.' That was inspired. I was laughing for the rest of the night when I got back to human form and translated that." I finished unbuttoning my shirt, and put it on a hanger.

"Thought it sounded better then 'wereglobin metabolizing treatment.' I have people requesting personal 'moonlights', but . . . " Leroy's eyes darted towards the door, and he lowered his voice as I undid my pants. "Between you and me, I wouldn't mind if it took awhile. I don't suppose that somewhere in the course of development, by the by, you could maybe ensure that they aren't so durable?"

"I thought you said you had too much money as it was?" I stepped on my socks to get them off and started rolling them into a ball.

He sighed, for a moment, and then came back in the voice of a businessman doing what he does best.

"I'm positive that we'll just have to grin and bear it."

I chuckled. "I'll see what I can do," I said, climbing into the kennel.

"Excellent!" he said, smiling to himself. And then he remembered what was going on. "I'll, er, just turn on the lights and give you some privacy, then, shall I?"

I merely nodded.

And then I remembered the receptionist.

"By the way, the receptionist isn't a were, is she?" I asked.

Leroy turned around grimacing and shook his head.

"No. We're kind of hard to find. I'm hoping we'll get a customer who wants work."

"You'd better get hopping on that." I laughed. "I'd like to see this place go to the dogs!"

Steven Piziks has greatly enjoyed the migration from chicks in chainmail to supernaturals in suburbia, and "Enforcement Claws" is set in the same subdivision as his story "Witch Warrior" in *Witch Way to the Mall*. He lives in a perfectly normal subdivision of his own in southeastern Michigan. Hit his very strange web page at *http://www.sff.net/people/spiziks* or *http://spiziks.livejournal.com* .

Enforcement Claws

Steven Piziks

"I'm sorry, Mrs. Cassidy, but you simply can't grow wolfsbane in your front yard. The Homeowners Association regulations are quite clear." My fingers grew white around the edges of my clipboard, but I managed to keep my voice level. The poisonous smell of that horrible little plant rubbed at the inside of my nose like a cheese grater, and I instinctively shied away from the shiny green leaves that surrounded the Cassidy front porch.

"It's not wolfsbane, Ms. LaMond," Felicity Cassidy huffed. "It's poison oak. And witches are allowed to have it. For potions."

"Witches?" I flipped through the forms on my clipboard, but more to cover my surprise than actually check anything. "I'm sorry, I don't understand—this is a zombie household."

"We prefer the term 'recently revived,'" Mrs. Cassidy sniffed. The pastel coloring of her carefully tailored pantsuit couldn't hide the pallor of her skin, and the padding rather failed to disguise the emaciated build of her body.

It looked as if a florist had exploded all over a toast rack. "Using the word *zombie* shows you're clearly prejudiced against me, and I'm going to register a complaint."

I sighed. "In any case, Mrs. Cassidy, zom—the recently revived are not authorized to have poison oak *or* wolfsbane."

Now Mrs. Cassidy sighed. "Listen," she murmured, leaning forward, "actually it's that my daughter Zoe recently announced she's a witch. She's been babysitting the McCrae kids ever since William McCrae had that fight with Baba Yaga and won, remember? I think Zoe has a little crush on him, to tell the truth. Anyway, now Zoe says she's a witch, and we're trying to be supportive. That's why we planted all this."

I gaped, then caught myself and forced my expression into something more neutral, even though a creepy feeling oozed through my stomach worse than that time I tried Alpo on a dare. Zoe claimed to be a zombie witch. The Cassidys were mixing phyla!

I struggled to keep the disgust off my face. Now, it may be true that modern times bring modern ideas, even to those of us with a supernatural bent. When I was girl, I didn't know it would one day be possible to get WiFi in a mausoleum, keep track of your friends on web sites like Flitter, and send voodoo curses by text message. And I definitely didn't know it would one day be possible for people with a little extra zing to their makeup to band together and form gated communities where everyone could live—or unlive—without worrying about torches, pitchforks, and reality TV producers.

For the most part, this modern world is a better place. My son Colin, for example, doesn't worry about getting peppered with silver buckshot every month. But you still have to draw the line somewhere, and the Homeowners Association agrees. Mixed phyla are just . . . wrong. Can you imagine a zombie witch? Who would she marry? What would you call the children? Would she be undead or some kind of un-undead? And here was Felicity Cassidy, standing on her own front porch and telling me she was trying to be *supportive* of this! Wake up and smell the formaldehyde, woman!

Under normal circumstances, I would say that Zoe wasn't *my* daughter, and it wasn't my place to comment. Keep your nose in your own pack, as my mother always said. Unfortunately, these goings-on clearly violated HOA regulations, and as Chair of the Homeowners Association, it was my duty to handle it.

I tried to start off diplomatically. "Zoe's babysitting now? Didn't you just raise her?"

Mrs. Cassidy put a hand to her heart. It hadn't beat for twenty years, so I don't know why she bothered. "It certainly seems that way. Children. You chant runes over them, raise them, teach them to lurch, and suddenly they're little adults with jobs and a hearse license and demanding their own morticians."

My cell phone chittered and I glanced at the readout. It was just Ann Viani, the assistant chair of the HOA texting me: RU AT CASSIDY? I flicked back a hasty Y in response and simultaneously realized my teeth were getting sharp. It was later than I thought. A little pang went through me, followed by a tinge of red anger. Not good—I was trying to be delicate with Mrs. Cassidy.

"Be that as it may," I said to her, snapping my phone shut, "you can't have wolfsbane on your front lawn. As the alpha—I mean, *chair*—of the Homeowners Association, I'm required to inform you that you have five days to remove it. If you don't, the HOA will hire pixie gardeners to remove it at your expense."

Then I leaned forward. "And just between us, you should have a word with your daughter about her . . . predilections. We can't mix phyla here, you know that. Next thing you know, we'll have members trying to bring in mortals."

Mrs. Cassidy's nostrils flared. "Xavier Killfoil brings in mortals all the time!"

"He imports them from Canada for snacking," I pointed out. "Well within regulations. I'm sorry, but the wolfsbane has to go, and Zoe will have to give up the . . . other business. If you can't bring her into line, your family will have to leave. You have the right to protest before the Association, of course, but a hearing isn't likely to go in your favor."

At this, Mrs. Cassidy dropped all pretense of friendliness. "Bring on the pixie gardeners then! Zoe can put an antifairy circle around the house. She's getting very good at repelling."

"I'm sure she is," I said tartly, "especially if she's between morticians, but an anti-fairy spell would constitute another HOA violation. You *did* sign the agreement before you moved in, you know." I added, not unkindly, "I'm afraid we've no choice. The regulation protects the were-children. Those berries are doubly poisonous to shapeshifters, you know."

"Only to ones foolish enough to eat them," she snapped, "or those who don't parent their children properly."

The angry tinge blew into scarlet rage. My nails lengthened into black claws and red-brown fur sprouted from the backs of my hands and arms. Without pausing to think, I grabbed Mrs. Cassidy by the throat and lifted her off the porch. Her flip-flops dropped off her long, bony feet. She clutched at my hand but was unable to break my grip. Fortunately for her, the recently revived don't breathe.

"You will remove the wolfsbane from your front lawn," I snarled, "or I will remove the head from your shoulders. See if your mortician can repair *that.*"

With those words, I dropped her on the front porch, stalked to my little red Chrysler Fortwo, and zipped away. Thanks to my little half-transformation, my head now brushed the roof, my knees bumped the steering wheel, and do you have any idea how hard it is to drive a stick with three-inch nails? I should have stayed where I was and taken a moment to get myself back under control, but I could hardly sit in Mrs. Cassidy's driveway after I'd attacked her. I was also having the strongest urge to pee all over her sidewalk—and I'm not even male, for god's sake.

I drove through the streets of Hidden Oaks Veneficus Community, breathing deeply and regaining my composure. My claws retreated and I shrank a little, but I couldn't get rid of the body hair. The sun was setting in a clear blue sky above the lush oak trees that lined the sidewalks, and I could feel the moon rising. In an hour, I would be fully lupine. Really! I should have put Mrs. Cassidy off until tomorrow.

I pulled into my own driveway. The house was a Luna model, with plenty of skylights for observing the moon and space in the basement for puppy cages near the washing machine. Adult werewolves are a bit ill-tempered during that time of the month, but we can control our little urges with some effort. Puppies, however, will be puppies, and you can't blame them for trying to disembowel their playmates for those three nights when the moon is full.

I went inside, dropped my clipboard on the foyer table—

—and came to a dead stop. My sixteen-year-old son Colin was sitting on the living room sofa. I rushed over to him.

"Honey, what's *wrong?*" I said, pulling him into my arms.

He struggled out of my motherly embrace with little more than a look of unease, which only made me more upset. His night-black hair, a gift from his father, was tousled and fluffed, and his nails were already lengthening into claws. His ears came to faint points, and his blue eyes were tinged with red. He always looks so handsome during this phase.

"What makes you think something's wrong?" he demanded.

I ticked off points on my fingers. "No iPod, no cell phone, no video games, the TV is off, and you didn't snarl at me when I hugged you just now. Darling, what's the matter?" I smoothed his hair and flinched inwardly when he failed to bat my hand away. "Oh dear—it's a bitch, isn't it? Who is she? Are you afraid to tell me her pedigree? You know that's not important to me. I mean, it would be *nice* if you found someone who could trace her line back to Walachia like we can, but a second-generation bitch has a certain appeal. As long as she makes you happy."

He looked at me for a long, silent moment. I could feel the moon's pull strengthen with every passing second, and the urge to change grew worse. Colin is long past cage age, but still, I often feel nostalgia for all those times I had to wrestle him in and slam the door before he could escape. He fought and bit, of course, and when he was nine he left me a long scar down the inside of my forearm. I have to admit I was insufferable and showed it off for weeks at soccer games until Bitsy Baneshee said she would positively scream if I rolled up my sleeve one more time. A serious threat coming from her, so I stopped.

"It's not a bitch," Colin said at last. The words came out a little slurred around his lengthening teeth. "It's something else."

I glanced at my watch, which had a lunameter set into the dial. Sixteen minutes before full moonrise. My legs were itching under my pantyhose. "Honey, I want to hear it, I do, but will we have time to discuss it now?"

He took a deep breath beside me on the couch. "Mom, I have something important to tell you."

There are certain phrases that never fail to strike terror into a mother's heart. *Uh oh* is one of them. *I told my teacher you could* is another. But nothing beats *I have something important to tell you* to bring out the icy sweat of fear.

"What is it, Colin?" I asked, keeping my voice level with great effort.

"Maybe I should just show you." And he began to change. Black fur grew from his body as it always did, but then . . . then . . .

His face didn't grow that long, boyish muzzle I knew so well. Instead, his nose shrank into a horrifying little button. Small ears poked out of the top of his head. Then his entire body dwindled away and vanished. A lump struggled around inside the pile of his clothes for a moment, and out of them emerged . . . it was . . .

. . . a large black cat.

I'm afraid I reacted very badly. I snarled at it and lunged. Suddenly the cat was half again its normal size. Startled, the lupine part of my brain hesitated, and the cat took advantage of the moment to leap off the sofa and flee down the hall into Colin's bedroom. After a second, the human part of my brain regained control, and I realized I'd been tricked. It's just not fair that cats can puff up like that, and it's equally not fair that we lupines and our canine cousins seem hard-wired to fall for it.

I sat on the sofa, stunned at what I had just seen. Colin had become a cat. Outrageous! Oh, I knew intellectually that weres *can* become other creatures, and I know it *happens* in a certain percentage of the population. Some weres secretly enjoy dressing in the underfur of other animals. My own uncle Hubert was once caught with the entire skin of an anaconda. Everyone pretends they don't know a thing about it, even though you can still smell the scales on hot summer days. But seeing it in my own home . . .

I pulled myself together and checked my watch. Ten minutes before moonrise. I had no idea what I was going to say or do, but I couldn't let this ride. I hurried down the hall to Colin's room. The door was open, and I found him sitting on his bed in human form, thank god, with a blanket wrapped around him. His fur hadn't completely gone away, though, and his eyes had become an ugly shade of green with a nasty slit up the middle. Cat's eyes. I wanted to bite something in half and feel the blood run down my chin. My own arms were growing hairier by the moment.

"Honey," I said, "let's talk about this."

"I don't know what there is to talk about," he said defiantly. "This is who I am. I've felt feline my whole life."

Oh, god. "This is because I drove your father away, isn't it? After I caught him with that bitch in heat. You didn't have a proper alpha male around to—"

"No, Mom. I was like this even before the thing with Dad."

Something occurred to me. "This explains why that trial subscription to *Cat Fancier* showed up last year. It wasn't a mistake, was it? *Was it?*" A growl was invading my voice.

"No."

"And those catnip leaves I found in your closet?"

He flushed. "Don't ask, Mom."

The situation was rapidly slipping away from me, and I desperately tried to get a handle on it. "Listen, sweetie, everyone thinks about other shapes sometimes, especially during adolescence. When I was your age, I wondered what it might be like to be a coatimundi. Your aunt Bernice once had a fixation with horses. And the less said about Uncle Hubert, the better."

"Scales," Colin said. "Yeah."

"So this is just a phase. You see? It'll pass."

He shook his head. "It's not a phase, Mom. I've been a feline—"

"Don't you dare say that word!"

"—as long as I can remember. I run down alleys and yowl at the moon. I climb trees and sharpen my claws. Mom, I hunt *mice*."

"My puppy!" Tears filled my eyes. "And all this time I thought you were out with your pack friends on full moon nights." My whole world was crashing in on me. My son, my only child, was a felinathrope. A *purry*.

And I changed. Destroyed a perfectly good dress, not to mention a new set of pantyhose, though that didn't really register until much later. The next several hours were a bit of a blur, I'm afraid. I haven't lost myself to fury like that in over twen—well, in several years. When I came to myself, I was curled up on the front porch, completely naked. The sun was just coming up, and I was smeared with blood.

Horror struck me cold. Hidden Oaks Veneficus Community was set up as a suburb where folk with a supernatural bent could live freely, but there are rules. These rules exist partly so we can all coexist, but mostly so we can live without invoking the wrath of various law enforcement agencies. High up on the list of don'ts is "Thou shalt not munch thy neighbor's wife." Violators meet quick and merciless consequences. Vampires are dragged kicking and screaming into the sunlight. Witches are burned at their own broomsticks. Zombies are magically paralyzed and donated to the university medical school for dissection. And werewolves . . . werewolves are trapped in lupine form, spayed or neutered, and sent to the pound.

Frantic, I sniffed myself all over. The fresh, coppery smell made my mouth run with saliva, but even my currently weak nose could tell the blood wasn't human. It was all feline. I had another sick moment before I realized that none of it smelled even remotely like Colin. I felt a little sorry for all those cats whose paths had crossed mine last night, but what kind of fool lets the cat out on a full moon night in a suburb with werewolves living in it?

A misty form glided down the sidewalk. Mr. Gorbinski was out for his usual bit of morning exercise after a night of haunting, and here I was, naked and bloody, on my own front porch. I fumbled for the door, my hands still clumsy after spending the night as paws. Mr. Gorbinski glided closer, his ghostly Walkman plugged into his ears. Poor man, stuck jogging to Wham! for eternity, though right then I was more worried he might see me. I finally got the door open and stumbled into the house.

Colin was sitting on the couch, calm as a ticking time bomb. *He* was fully dressed, his hair perfectly combed. I wondered if he'd licked it into place before changing, and the idea made me want to gnash my teeth. I snatched up a fleecy throw to wrap around myself.

"I can smell the blood," he said. "You better not have killed anyone I know."

"Anyone you know?" I squeaked. "How many of you are there?"

"You'd be surprised, Mom. There are Internet chat sites for just about everything."

"I'm going to shower," I said, sweeping past him with all the dignity I could muster. This wasn't easy in a fluffy throw with a pink unicorn on it. "Then we'll talk some more."

I felt more human with the cat blood rinsed off and a fresh set of clothes on. The warm morning sun promised a fine summer day. I found Colin in the breakfast nook eating a bowl of cereal.

Oh. Oh no.

It wasn't cereal. He was drinking a bowl of cream with delicate little tongue sips, just like—

"Stop that!" I said, pulling the bowl away from him. "Don't flaunt yourself."

"I'm not in public," he said. "And even if I were, so what? This is who I *am*, Mom. WTF says—"

"WTF?" I sat down at the table, already feeling like I was losing control of the conversation again.

"Wear the Fur," he said. "They said we should be proud of our shapes, whatever they are. Lots of weres want to be something besides wolves, Mom. Maybe you should join PFLAG."

"PFLAG," I said weakly.

"Purries, Furries, Lycanthropes, And their Guardians. They have some really good support resources. Don't you ever surf the Internet?"

"Apparently not the same parts you do."

He touched my hand. "It's okay, Mom. Look, I'm sorry I upset you, but I'm glad you're taking this so well."

"Am I?" I said. "I don't feel like I am."

"You didn't try to kill me—not seriously, anyway—or throw me out of the house. Kenny Biddlemeyer's parents caught him changing into a platypus, and they sent him away to taxidermy school."

I was shocked. "Taxidermy school? I thought he was going to a hunting camp."

"That's what they *told* everyone. Taxidermy school freaked Kenny out so much, he can't even change completely into a wolf anymore, let alone his TS. When the full moon comes, he just gets a bad case of hypertrichosis and has to hide in the basement until sunrise."

"That's dreadful! Wait—his TS?"

"True Shape, Mom. Get with it!"

"I'm trying, honey, but you aren't making it easy." I felt my voice rising. I thought I could handle this, but I couldn't. The more I thought about my son turning into a . . . a *cat*, the more my stomach felt like I'd eaten something from a bad Dumpster. Every time I looked at him, I only saw slitted eyes and a disgusting rough tongue. I couldn't have it here in my house. I couldn't! He would have to change his ways or . . . or . . . well, I wasn't sure what, but it would be *something* harsh. "Colin," I said, my voice rising, "I'm afraid . . ." I trailed off.

He looked at me with those horrible cat eyes. "What, Mom?"

I began again, with more strength. "Colin, I'm afraid I—"

The doorbell rang. Feeling both annoyed and relieved, I jumped up to answer it. Ann Viani stood on my front porch. She was a small woman, fine-boned and blonde. She was also a werewolf and the assistant chair of the HOA committee. All the HOA committee members are werewolves, actually. We're the only ones in the community who are willing to work in groups, once the issue of alpha is settled, and I had done that with the accepted paw-to-paw combat years ago. Colin says I *pwned* Ann, whatever that means, and she was happy being beta to my alpha now.

I caught a whiff of Ann's lilac soap as I peered outside. Most of us wolves take a long shower after a night of prowling that also often involved rolling in things that would, in polite company, be described as fertilizer. It's one of those lupine things that we all know but rarely discuss. My own preference is for tangerine body wash. Normally I would have invited her in, but I didn't feel up to butt-sniffing right then. I put on a little smile instead. "Ann! What can I do for you?"

"Greta," she said stiffly. "I'm afraid I have this for you." She handed me a folded sheet of paper. "You are in violation of your homeowner's agreement. You have five days to right the matter or leave Hidden Oaks."

My mouth fell open. "In *violation?*" My voice squeaked in outrage and I crumpled the paper in my hand. "I *wrote* the violations list, Ann. I'm not in violation of anything."

"Oh? Then do you deny mixing phyla by harboring a . . . " here she paused, as if the forthcoming words were dead skunks on a highway, "a . . . multiply-shaped were in your home?"

My stomach went cold. With everything that had happened, I hadn't even considered this. My son was mixing phyla. Ann was right—I was in clear violation of the HOA.

"I have an eyewitnesses report that a cat leaped over your fence last night and changed into a human in your backyard before going inside," Ann continued. "The human's description exactly matches your son Colin." She sniffed delicately and lowered her voice exactly the way I'd done for Mrs. Cassidy yesterday. "And I'm afraid I myself can smell cat fur."

I still couldn't do anything but stare at her, the paper still a crumpled ball in my hand.

"The sheet I gave you is a notice of formal complaint," she said. "You have the right to appear before the Association, of course, but really—you have to know that we can't allow mixing of phyla here. Next thing you know, we'll have members trying to bring in mortals."

I continued to stare at her.

"Don't you have anything to say?" Ann demanded. "I'll have to take over as alpha of the HOA if you leave."

At last I came to myself and glanced into the dining room, where Colin still sat at the table, the empty bowl in front of him. He could hear every word. "Of course," I said hoarsely, and automatically lifted my chin, baring my throat. "I'll take care of the problem. I'm . . . sorry."

"These things happen," Ann said in a tone exactly like the one I had used with Mrs. Cassidy. "See you at the HOA meeting tonight." And she left.

Colin didn't say a word when I sat down at the table again. He didn't even look at me. Instead, he set his bowl in the kitchen sink, went into his room, and shut the door. A moment later, I smelled catnip.

I couldn't stay in the house. Outside, my feet took me on a meandering path around the subdivision, along the shady sidewalks, past the security gates where the golems Greg and Gertrude stood guard, and through the little park in the middle—no signs about cleaning up after your dog here, thank you. The diurnal inhabitants were out and about. Children played tag in the yard and in the treetops. Adults waved to me. Which one of them had reported Colin? I tried not to slink as I passed by.

Eventually I found myself in front of Felicity Cassidy's house. The wolfsbane still lined her front porch, and the stinging scent crinkled my nose. I knew why my feet had brought me here, but I still didn't want to go through with it. Finally, I straightened my shoulders, forced my traitorous feet up to her door, and rang the bell. She opened the door a moment later in a cloud of formaldehyde and ethanol, her thin face set harder than rigor mortis.

"What do you want?" she demanded.

"I came to apologize," I said, getting the words out quickly, to get it over with. "It was close to moonrise yesterday, which always puts me in a temper, and I should have waited until . . . well, in any case, I'm sorry."

"Fine," she said shortly. "Accepted."

She started to close the door, but I said quickly, "How do you handle it?"

Mrs. Cassidy blinked at me. "Handle what?"

"Zoe's situation," I said miserably. "How do you handle it? You seem so calm about the whole thing, and I . . . I'm not."

Light dawned on her face. "So it's you who has a purry in the house."

"Don't call him that!" I flared.

"If the shoe fits," she said with a shrug. "There *have* been rumors, you know."

The surprise drove the anger away like a lion startling off a cat. "Rumors?"

"You'd better come in."

A bit later, Mrs. Cassidy was serving me tea in her bright, cheery kitchen, though after a look at my face, she reached into a cabinet and added a dash of something from a brown bottle to my cup. I'd already been up all night, but the contents of a housewife's hidden brown bottle are guaranteed good for the nerves, even in a kitchen for the recently revived.

"There have been rumors around for quite a while," Mrs. Cassidy said, sitting down next to me. "But no one knew for sure."

I drank, and the tea burned from more than just heat. "I'm not handling it well, Mrs. Cassidy. I thought I could take it, but I feel like I'm falling apart."

She shook her head. "If you're going to fall apart in my kitchen—and that's not something a zombie says lightly—I think you'd better call me Felicity, even if we do come from different phyla."

"I thought you preferred the term—"

"Never mind that. The point is, this sort of thing is never quite the secret everyone thinks."

"Except from me, apparently," I said, with an unexpected bark of laughter.

"Look, I'd be lying if I said Zoe didn't shock me. I'll never forget the day I found a book of transmography under her headstone. But in the end, I realized she's still my daughter, and we'll have to work things out somehow."

"I don't want to lose my house," I howled. "And what will the rest of my family pack say?"

"You'll think of something. You're a strong alpha bitch. That's not the real issue, and you know it." Felicity touched my hand with hers. It was cold and waxy, which was nice—I didn't have to control the urge to nibble. "Listen, dear, you need to think of it this way: your son hasn't changed a bit. You just know more about him."

Her words stayed with me all the way home. I was so deep in thought that I was practically at my doorstep before I saw it. Someone had scrawled PURRY in sloppy red letters on my garage door. Below it, the vandal had superglued a poster of a cartoon cat moaning about how he hated Mondays. And when I got to the front porch, I found taped to the door a notice that our "recent unauthorized redecoration" had combined with my son's "special predilections" to create a "severe, negative impact on surrounding property values." In light of this new situation, my previous five-day warning was rescinded, and Colin and I were to vacate our house within twenty-four hours or face "surgical consequences, as laid out in the enforcement clause of the HOA Contract." A postscript informed me that I had been impeached as HOA chair. The notice smelled of lilacs.

And then I knew what was going on.

I tore down the notice and ran inside the house, calling for Colin. He was nowhere to be found. Frantic, I dialed his cell phone. He answered on the third ring.

"Where are you?" I demanded, loving the relief that swept over me. "Are you all right?"

"I'm fine, Mom. What's going on?"

"Someone just—never mind. What is that noise in the background? It sounds like—"

"I'm playing horseshoes over at Aunt Bernice's house. Are you okay? You sound upset."

"Oh god—Colin, have you told her about . . . you?"

"Long time ago, Mom. She doesn't care."

I put a hand to my forehead. "Did everyone know except me?"

Thoughtful pause. I heard another clank in the background and a cheer from my sister Bernice. She must have scored a ringer. "Not *everyone*. But Uncle Hubert thinks it's hilarious."

I blew out a long, heavy sigh. How could I have missed this in my own son? Sometimes I could be so blind. It's not as if it didn't run in the family. "Honey, I need you to answer me straight. How do you feel when you change into a cat? Be honest, and don't mince words just because I'm your mother."

"Honestly?" He paused, and for a moment I thought the cell phone had dropped the call. "Mom, the first time I changed into a cat, I felt like I'd been dead all my life and only just then started to live."

I stared down at the eviction notice and my earlier relief turned to anger. This was a violation. This was my house, my territory, my *son*. Colin had found happiness, and if he was happy, I was happy. No one was going to force me to move out on account of happiness.

"Colin," I said firmly, "put Bernice on the phone. But tell her to grab her address book first. We have some calls to make."

Ann Viani, new chair of the Homeowners Association, banged the gavel. "This meeting of the Homeowners Association will come to order."

The meeting room in the commons was crowded and damp. The HOA always meets in the generously-sized basement to accommodate those with allergies to sunlight. Witches, vampires, ghouls, zombies, and weres all in a single place, trying to hammer out common living arrangements. Who would have ever thought? Colin sat next to me with absolute calm. He had always had a sort of regal charm about him, even as a child. Now I knew why. I actually envied him right then. On my other side sat Felicity Cassidy with her daughter Zoe.

"The first item on the agenda is—" Ann continued.

"Mine," I said, standing up.

Ann gave me a frosty look. "I'm afraid you're low on the list, Mrs. LaMond."

A low mutter went through the room. A member of my own phylum addressing me by my last name was a grave insult. I ignored this.

"No one cares about the sprinkler systems, Ann," I said. "Or the golem maintenance fees. We all know why everyone's here, so let's stop wasting time and get this out in the open." Every eye in the room was on me, and I plowed on before Ann could object. There was enough alpha bitch left in me to stop her from interrupting. "We started this community so we could all have a safe place to raise our offspring. We fled fear and prejudice. But it turns out we brought both with us. My son Colin feels the need for a different shape than other weres. So what? It doesn't hurt anyone. Felicity Cassidy's daughter Zoe has a talent for witchcraft. So what? She's good at repellent magicks. We've suffered prejudice at the hands of humans for centuries. How can we allow it to continue among ourselves?"

I saw some nods of agreement among the other home-owners, and an equal number of headshakes. Still, I was encouraged.

"That doesn't matter," Ann said from the podium at the front of the room. "You signed the HOA agreement, and you're in violation. You and Felicity Cassidy both. The graffiti on your garage has confirmed it—and already lowered property values in the neighborhood."

I let a little of the lupine out. "That was *you*," I snarled. "You claimed to be that 'eyewitness,' but it was just a guess based on the faint smell of cat fur in my house. You painted the graffiti on my garage and put up the notice to force my paw."

"And how do you know that?"

"You should rinse better, Ms. Viani. I smelled the lilac soap. Now you're chair, just like you've always wanted. Alpha of the Association." I advanced on her. "An HOA ho."

"How dare you!" Ann shrieked. Her fangs grew and her nails lengthened into claws.

"I wouldn't," I said. "I have friends."

With that, my sister Bernice burst into the shape of a Clydesdale mare. Uncle Hubert hissed and became the biggest anaconda the world had ever seen. And my son Colin shifted shape into an enormous, sleek black panther twice the size of any wolf. I stood proudly beside him, one hand on his shoulder.

The other homeowners scrambled out of the seating area to get their backs to a wall. Most of the vampires changed shape as well, but really—bats? Who cares? Felicity and Zoe rose to stand beside me. Ann stayed at the podium.

"I think it's high time we amended the HOA agreement," I said. "Does anyone care to second the motion?"

A snarl, a whinny, and a hiss thundered through the room.

"Objections?" I asked archly.

"Just one." Ann reached into her pocket and pulled out an ugly-looking pistol. "A silver-plated one. The HOA hasn't been amended yet, LaMond, and I'm still within rights to destroy you. Only filthy people mix their phyla!"

We all recoiled by reflex. Silver was worse than wolfsbane. Uncle Hubert flickered his tongue and Bernice stamped a hoof the size of a dinner plate. I started to step in front of Colin, not sure what I was going to do, but certain I wasn't going to let Ann shoot him. The room had gone deadly silent. Several other residents could have interfered, but this had become a pack matter, and I could tell they weren't certain if they should get involved, so they simply waited to see how this would play out.

Colin abruptly swirled back into his human form. "Wait a minute," he said. "Ann Viani. I just realized—you hang out on the WTF boards as 'Aviani,' don't you?"

Ann went pale and the pistol wavered slightly. "I don't know what you're talking about."

"Sure you do. You post in the Feathered Friend Forum all the time."

"Certainly not! I would never—"

"You're wearing feathered underwear right now," Colin said. "I can tell. Cats are especially sensitive to that scent."

"Ann!" I said. "Lashing out against your own kind. What is it the psychologists say? The ones who object the loudest are the likeliest to—"

Ann pulled the trigger. Before the gun went off, however, Zoe Cassidy made a sharp gesture, and Ann flew backward. The pistol fired, the silver bullet flew wild, and the report nearly deafened me. Ann slammed against the basement wall and hung there for a moment, held by Zoe's repelling spell. Then she went limp and slumped to the ground.

Uncle Hubert resumed human shape, strolled over, and peered down her blouse. "Ah! Feathered bra. From Ursula's Undercover Undergarments, if I'm not mistaken. Good brand."

Ann tried to groan, but it sounded suspiciously like a squawk.

The meeting eventually came back to order. The HOA agreement was not amended—it was abolished outright. Ann has disappeared, and her house is up for sale, but WTF rumor has it that she's been sighted stroking a cockatoo in Waco, Texas. With the HOA disbanded, I have to find another organization to lead. PFLAG should do nicely. I've gotten used to the smell of catnip, and the idea of one day entertaining a grandkitten or two does have its charm.

But I've told Colin I draw the line at emptying a litter box.

Selina Rosen's short fiction has appeared in several magazines and anthologies including *Sword and Sorceress 16*, *Such a Pretty Face*, *Distant Journeys*, Marion Zimmer Bradley's Fantasy Magazine, *Tooth and Claw*, *Turn the Other Chick*, *Anthology at the End of the Universe*, and *Thieves World*. Some of her fourteen published novels include *Queen of Denial*, the *Chains* trilogy, *Strange Robby*, *The Host* trilogy, *Fire & Ice*, *Hammer Town*, and *Reruns*. *Bad Lands*, a gonzo-mystery novel co-written with Laura J. Underwood was released in 2007 by Five Star Mystery, and *Sword Masters*, Selina's first full-length epic fantasy novel was released in February of 2008 from Dragon Moon Publishing in Canada.

Where-Wolf

Selina Rosen

Kevin wished he hadn't signed up now.

It had seemed like such a good idea at the time, and after all it was such a worthy cause.

Now he'd been sitting here staring at a wall for three hours and it just seemed meaningless and stupid. He still had two hours to go. This was boring! No, boring wasn't a true depiction of just how dull this was, and he'd make up a word in a few moments that would describe it suitably. After all he had the time.

The most exciting part of the evening had been when he'd answered a prank call. In fact, in the month that he had been doing this, that had been the only time he hadn't damn near gone to sleep on his watch.

A suicide hotline in an upper middle class suburb where the most tragic thing the kids in his school ever seemed to go through was that Daddy bought them the wrong color car for their sweet sixteen was absurd. But the PTA didn't want to be caught sleeping at the wheel. With the rise in teen suicide nationwide, they thought a teen suicide hot line was in order. It didn't matter that there had been like two suicides in the entire history of the town or that neither of those had been teenagers.

And why was he really here? Well, it was a really mature reason. Yes, Kevin had volunteered to answer the teen suicide hot line two nights a week to impress a girl.

It hadn't worked of course because it turned out that Vicky was assigned to Tuesday and Thursday nights because she had cheerleading on the weekends.

Of course Kevin had no extracurricular activities so now here he sat every Friday and Saturday night—not saving anyone—and Vicky was dating Mr. Captain of the Football Team Himself, Brad Johnson, the make-out king of Blue Springs High.

Vicky had no idea Kevin was even alive and now his weekends were filled with this bullshit so that any hope of getting a social life was impossible.

He had wanted to quit after the first night when he'd realized that not only would he not be working with Vicky but he'd be working alone. On that night the phone hadn't even rung once, and Vicky had gone out with Brad for the first time. When he complained to his parents his father had given him the timeless "learn responsibility" lecture. He had signed up for the project and therefore he would see it through to the end unless he wanted to give up his driving privileges.

So here he sat for the fourth Friday in a row, wondering if he needed driving privileges at all if this was the only place he could go.

He didn't really see how being bored out of his skull was building his character. He supposed this was one of those things he'd look back on when he was older and be glad he'd done. One of those things he'd only really understand when he had kids of his own . . . and then he'd know.

He played at doing his homework, brooded about having no social life, and wondered just what he would do if someone did actually call with a gun to their head just seconds from pulling the trigger.

Wasn't it kind of stupid to put someone's life in the hands of a seventeen-year-old kid? A kid whose greatest worries were whether he was going to break out the night of the spring dance, if he was ever going to get laid, and if playing with yourself could really make you go blind.

Yes, Kevin could see a lot of flaws in this program. He could make a list starting with the number being printed wrong in the phone book and ending with the fact that the hot line kept hours. The hot line was open six nights a week from 6:00 P.M. to 12:00 A.M. Kevin supposed depression and death took a holiday the rest of the time.

Who would be inconsiderate enough to off themselves on Sunday or between the hours of 12:00 A.M. to 6:00 P.M.?

The people of Blue Springs were not known for their heightened insight. Driving cars that got two miles to the gallon and living in houses so big their kids got lost in them and they had to send out search parties, yes—actual insight, no.

Only two more hours and he could go home and do nothing there and everyone would just have to wait till tomorrow night to kill themselves.

They kept telling him that they were going to get some other poor shlep in here to help him. But help him do what? Kevin could sit on his own ass; he didn't need help doing that. Of course he didn't try to discourage them when they said they were trying to get someone to help him because at least then he would have someone to talk to. At least it wouldn't be so unbelievably snordulling . . .

There. He had done it. He had created a word which accurately explained how boring this job was. "Snordulling" it was sort of a cross between snore, dull with the—ing off boring thrown in for good measure.

"Damn snordulling job," Kevin said with an extravagant yawn.

The phone rang.

At first Kevin just stared at it. It rang again and he quickly picked it up trying to remember what he was supposed to say.

"Hello, suicide hot line."

Just in case it was for real this time he went over what they had told him in the quickie seminar they had given him and grabbed the list that lay ready by the phone and went over it quickly.

Keep them talking.

Try to get their name.

Sound genuinely concerned.

Try to find out where they were.

There was no answer and Kevin thought he had another crank caller. "Hello, suicide hot line. Can I help you?" This time he didn't sound at all genuinely concerned. This time he just sounded pissed off because he wasn't in the mood to be screwed with.

There was still no answer so he said, "Hello, suicide hot line. Have a nice day." He started to slam the receiver down.

"I'm an animal. I don't deserve to live." The voice was young, male, and more than a little unsure—choked like he'd been crying.

Panic welled up inside of Kevin as he pulled the receiver back to his ear. God help him, this call was for real.

"What's wrong?" Kevin asked. He hoped he sounded concerned and not scared out of his wits, which is what he was.

"What isn't wrong?" There was anguish and hopelessness in that voice. If the guy was just another crank caller he was a hell of an actor. It was a hell of a lot more than Kevin had bargained for and way more than he was prepared for.

"Wha . . . Why do you want to kill yourself?" Damn. He couldn't pull this off. Where were adults when you needed them? They were always there right outside the bathroom door when you didn't want them to be, but where were they when you really needed them?

"I'm an animal, man. I don't deserve to live." The voice broke in a jerking cry.

Kevin drew in a deep breath. He couldn't afford to lose it. "Ah, now come on, no one's that bad. Why would you think that?"

"Man. Don't you get it?" the tormented voice asked. "No, man, you don't get it. No one understands. I don't even know why I called. I know what has to be done."

"No! No, man, don't hang up," Kevin pleaded. "I want to understand. Please just don't hang up." If his first caller wound up offing himself, he was just never going to hear the end of it. He looked at the list again.

There was a long silence and for one horrible moment Kevin thought the caller had hung up.

"No. You can't understand, how could you?"

Kevin sighed with relief. "Let me try. Please."

"In thirty minutes the moon will hit its zenith. No one can help me then."

Kevin decided the man was on drugs. "My name is Kevin. What's yours?" he asked, referring to the list.

Once again there was a long, silence-filled pause, and Kevin got a sick feeling in his stomach. He decided that he liked this job better when it was snordulling.

"Jack." For the moment he sounded calm.

Kevin tried to phrase his next sentence as tactfully as possible. "You know Jack, sometimes drugs can make us think really strange things . . . "

"Dude, I'm not on drugs!" Jack screamed in anger. "Hell, that wouldn't be any problem at all. Listen to me and listen good, man. I *am* an animal. Hell, I don't know what I might do."

"What are you trying to say, Jack? I want to understand. I really do."

"My parents don't understand," Jack said in a choked voice.

"Parents never do," Kevin said and relaxed a little as he realized. *That's the psychology behind having us answer the phone that we might better understand a kid's problems than some old guy.* "Parents get some real goofy ideas. I want to be hanging out with my friends but my dad insists I sit here on this hot line. We all have problems."

Jack laughed bitterly. "Ah come on, Kevin. What kindah problems you got? Dating? Pimples? Big deal! I turn into an animal. People just don't understand that. You forget to put your socks in the hamper and don't put the lid back on the toothpaste, maybe you forget to put the toilet seat down and your old lady falls in. So in the middle of the night she comes up screaming and wakes the whole house. Dude . . . I tear up the furniture, wet the carpet, and last time I ate the cat. I ate the family pet. And I liked the cat! I'm worried about my sister. After all, I can't stand my little sister."

Kevin's temporary calm was shattered. This guy wasn't playing with a full deck or it really was just another crank call—and what was more likely? "If this is some sort of joke, I don't think it's very funny."

"Do I sound like I'm having fun? You jerk!" Jack said hotly. "My father gave me a gun and locked me in my room. Does that sound like a field trip to you?"

"He did what?" Kevin gasped in horror.

"He's scared." Jack's anger seemed to leave him. "I don't blame him. Hell, I scare myself. I don't think I'd hurt anyone. But . . . I just can't be sure."

"You won't hurt anyone, Jack," Kevin said insistently. It was no wonder this poor kid was nuts. His parents were probably religious zealots who had the guy convinced he was possessed or some damn thing because he touched himself. "You sound like a pretty together guy to me." Kevin almost couldn't believe he had said that.

"I can't help it," Jack's voice had a bitter edge to it. "It's not fair. Just because I grow fur and fangs, and mutilate small animals doesn't mean I'm not a good person."

"Of course not, your dad can't make you kill yourself. He's sick and he's talked you into believing that you're something less than human."

"Not less than. I'm more than human. Don't you get it man? I'm a werewolf. There's a silver bullet in this gun, and I've got to use it," Jack said.

"Jack, listen to me. There is no such thing as a were-wolf. I don't know why you believe this, but you are not a werewolf."

Jack laughed heartily, and then said in a dark voice. "Tell that to my hands, Kevin. My hands which are even now turning to claws. Tell it to the fur starting to grow on my back. I don't want to die, Kevin. But I don't want to kill, either, and I feel like I will. I feel it even now, the need to kill, to destroy, to feed."

Kevin decided to try a new approach. "So you're a werewolf, big deal. That doesn't mean you're necessarily going to go around ripping people's throats out."

"Man, you don't know that," but Jack's voice held hope for the first time.

"Yes, I do." Kevin felt that he was making progress. "You don't sound dangerous to me. Don't listen to your father. What does he know about werewolves anyway? If you really are a werewolf . . . Well that's a rare commodity and I don't think anyone is going to bitch about a few missing cats."

"You really think so?" Jack asked.

"Hey, if you haven't eaten anyone yet I don't think you're likely to," Kevin said. He was doing it. He was talking this guy out of suicide.

"I still won't have any friends. You know I won't, not once people find out what I am. No one will like me." Jack said, lapsing back into depression.

"Hey, man, I'll be your friend. I think it would be cool to have a werewolf for a friend," Kevin said. "I'll be done here in an hour and a half. I could meet you at the Dairy Drive; we could have a shake, my treat."

"But by then I'll be a werewolf," Jack reminded him.

"Then I'll get you a burger extra rare. I trust you, man."

"I . . . I think I can get out of my room. OK, I'll meet you. I hope you won't regret this."

Kevin felt like a hero. He couldn't wait to tell his mom and dad. He couldn't wait to tell Vicky at the weekly suicide club meeting.

He swung into the Dairy Drive parking lot. He parked away from the drive-in itself and away from the action, just as he had promised Jack that he would, and waited. He was very anxious to meet this boy who thought he was a wolf. This would be one to tell his grandkids.

He didn't have to wait long. A red Mustang that he knew only too well pulled in beside him. "Jack" turned out to be none other than Brad Johnson.

Before Kevin had time to kick himself for falling for such an obvious gag, Brad was in his car with him.

"Real funny, Brad, you're a riot. Well, if you've had your laugh, I really need to get home," Kevin said hotly.

"You said you would be my friend." Brad's voice sounded funny.

"You got me. OK already, Brad. So have a good laugh and quit screwing with me."

"I meant what I said, Kevin. I won't have any friends, not when they find out what I am and how long can I hide it? You have to help me . . . "

"You're a werewolf? Come on, Brad. The joke has gone on long enough, give it a rest." If Brad wasn't three times his size he would have kicked him out of the car already.

"Damn it all, Kevin. Not now, oh God, not now." He let out a horrible crying, growling sound. "My God! I'm changing! Run, Kevin! Run!"

Kevin folded his arms across his chest. "Yeah, yeah, real good, I get up and run screaming across the parking lot for God and everyone else to see, you drive my car in the lake, and I don't get laid till I'm thirty. No thanks."

Brad turned to him. His face was covered with hair and his eyes glowed, but it wasn't till he growled, revealing a mouth full of slobbering yellow fangs that Kevin realized that it wasn't just some stupid prank. By then it was too late. The fur-covered body pounced on him. Fangs bit into his shoulder. He screamed and tried to beat the wolf off of him. Then the fangs were closing in on his throat. In a few seconds those horrible teeth would bite in and he would be dead, all because he had talked this thing out of committing suicide.

The phone rang.

Kevin shook himself awake. He looked around the room. He wiped the sweat from his forehead. "God! All just a dream." The phone rang again and Kevin quickly answered it. "Hello, suicide hot line."

"I'm an animal. I don't deserve to live!"

"Listen wise ass, do us all a favor and kill yourself!" Kevin yelled and slammed down the receiver. He looked at the phone in horror, "My God, what have I done?" The phone rang again and he picked it up quickly. "Hello, suicide hot line."

"Hey, bud," it was the same guy.

"Listen I'm sorry . . . "

"No, I get it. You're right. Suicide is stupid. Thanks."

As the caller was hanging up, Kevin swore he heard a low, lonely howl.

David D. Levine is a lifelong SF reader whose midlife crisis was to take a sabbatical from his high-tech job to attend Clarion West in 2000. It seems to have worked. He made his first professional sale in 2001, won the Writers of the Future Contest in 2002, was nominated for the John W. Campbell award in 2003, was nominated for the Hugo Award and the Campbell again in 2004, and won a Hugo in 2006 (Best Short Story, for "Tk'Tk'Tk"). A collection of his short stories, *Space Magic*, is available from Wheatland Press (*http://www.wheatlandpress.-com*). He lives in Portland, Oregon with his wife, Kate Yule, with whom he edits the fanzine Bento, and their website is at *http://www.BentoPress.com.* David's story in this volume, "Overnight Moon," revisits characters introduced in the story "Midnight at the Center Court" in Esther Friesner's earlier anthology *Witch Way to the Mall.*

Overnight Moon

David D. Levine

" . . . so get some Comet, and vomit, today!"

Julian held his ears and winced as the bus jounced along the last stretch of road before camp. The Flickers, squeaky little third-grade girls, had been shrieking the Comet song over and over for the last twenty minutes, and he was just about ready to lose it.

He wished he could cast Angerona's Silence on them.

Liz, Julian's best friend, snoozed beside him in the window seat; she could sleep through anything. A wiry freckled redhead, Liz was a twelve-year-old sports nut, as unlike the pale bookish Julian as could be, yet the two of them shared an inexplicable kinship that had only deepened in the last year.

Outside the windows houses went by, big new ones in the same three earth tones over and over. Julian's parents had gone to Camp Acadia as kids, and it had all been farms around here back then. But now it was 1975, and there was a housing development just across the road from the archery field. Julian didn't mind; he was fundamentally a city boy.

The bus swerved into the camp's driveway, making the Flickers screech with glee, and Julian had to let go of his ears to keep his humongous pack from crashing into the aisle. He knew he'd brought too much stuff, but this was going to be his only overnight all summer and he wanted it to be perfect. Jacket in case it rained. Canteen in case he got thirsty. Marshmallows, graham crackers, and Hershey's chocolate, in case no one else had thought to bring them for s'mores. And sleeping bag, in case anyone actually went to sleep.

Hey, it could happen.

The bus squealed to a halt and all the kids tumbled out, shrieking and chattering as they headed down to the lake. Julian stumbled under the weight of his pack, lagging behind even the little Flickers and Blue Jays. All the girls' units were named after birds; the boys' units had tough names like Apaches, Bears, and Scouts. Liz was a Duck, and thought her unit name was bogus; that was one of the things Julian liked about her.

Julian himself was a Cougar. The Cougars were the only unit for seventh- and eighth-grade boys—next year he'd be too old for day camp.

Liz, who had nothing more than a sleeping bag and a little blue duffel with a change of clothes, paused and looked over her shoulder at Julian. "C'mon, slowpoke! You're holdin' up the flag ceremony!"

Grimly Julian hefted his pack higher on his back . . . but the shift in weight made him fall over backwards, crashing to earth like an overturned turtle. Liz snickered and turned away, but at least no one else had seen him.

Bruised, embarrassed, and intensely annoyed, Julian struggled to right himself. Panting hard, he managed to roll to his hands and knees, but returning to a standing position was too much to ask. Finally he peered all around, then centered himself and muttered the syllables of Cratus's Vigor.

Julian's limbs tingled with an electric feeling as the spell took effect. He got his feet under him, hoisted himself vertical, then jogged down toward the lakeshore.

He wasn't supposed to use magic around lay people. But Cratus's Vigor was only a God spell, so it barely counted. All the really cool spells, like flight and invisibility, were Goddess spells, off limits to Julian because of his gender—not that he hadn't studied them, and even practiced a few in private. Cratus's Vigor was such a lame little spell that no one here would notice the effect, and by the time he got home his mother wouldn't know either. He hoped.

Still, the pack jouncing against his butt felt like a reprimand.

After the Pledge of Allegiance came the usual announcements. While the adults droned on and on, Jim Wisnewski, one of the other Cougars, leaned over to Julian. Wisnewski was a fat, blond, freckled kid with a pouty lower lip, but he was all right. "Hey, didja see *Happy Days* last night?"

"Nah. My mom wanted to watch *Good Times*, and she says it's her TV."

"Bummer. It was a rerun of the Christmas one, where Fonzie comes over."

But while Wisnewski proceeded to recap the highlights of the episode, Julian was distracted by the sight of Cindy Harrison, sitting with the rest of the Cardinals two benches ahead of him. He hadn't thought about her when he'd cast Cratus's Vigor on himself.

Harrison was the only other kid at Camp Acadia who was in the Craft—her mother was the treasurer of Julian's coven and her father was a werewolf. Julian's age, but a good six inches taller and beginning to "develop" in the chest area, she was smart, punctual, diligent, tidy . . . in other words, a total suck-up. Julian worried that she'd notice he'd used the spell and narc on him to his mother.

Eventually the announcements wound up, and all the units grouped up around their counselors for the first activity of the day. Julian's counselor, Todd, was a lanky guy whose brown hair and beard puffed out around his head like dandelion fluff. "Hey, guys!" he said, all bouncy and smiles.

"Hey," the Cougars said. They were thirteen and fourteen, too cool for enthusiasm.

Todd checked his clipboard. "How do you guys feel about . . . swimming!"

Julian groaned. The pool was always hideously cold first thing in the morning.

First, though, the Cougars hauled their stuff to the campout area at the far end of the lake. They'd be sharing the space with the Bulls, Cardinals, and Ducks tonight, roasting hot dogs and telling ghost stories around the fire pit. Even though they were in the middle of suburbia, not the deep dark woods, Julian still loved it. An overnight was Julian's chance to forget the grimoires and crucibles and herbs, and just be a *kid* for one night of the year.

Julian heaved his pack onto the pile in the gazebo, then trooped with the other Cougars and the Cardinals down to the swimming lagoon. He stripped down and put on his swim trunks as quick as he could, then stood shivering on the sand with his towel wrapped around his skinny shoulders. He almost envied Wisnewski his blubber.

The girls took longer to get ready. They always did, and they always emerged from the changing room in a group, chattering among themselves like the birds their units were named for. Julian wondered what they did in there. The boys hardly ever talked in the change room, or the bathroom—they just got in, did their business, and got out.

The pool itself was as cold as he'd feared. But even as they paddled around, practicing their kicks and breathing, Julian kept an eye on Harrison. He was still concerned she might be able to sniff out his illicit use of magic. Once, as they were both clambering out of the pool side by side, she noticed him watching her. She glared, covered her chest with her arms, and turned away.

Huh? She'd never been so twitchy before.

Girls were weird.

Later that day, at a softball game, Julian found himself sitting in the grass next to Liz while they awaited their turns at bat. He pulled up a grass stalk and began pulling it apart, stripping away layer after layer. "I don't understand girls," he said. "Harrison and I used to hang out together all the time, but lately she's gotten all weird."

Liz peered over her glasses at him. The thick black plastic frames were taped in two places, victims of many a sporting accident, and her white baseball cap was dirt-stained from her last slide into home plate. "You're asking *me?*" She shrugged. "Everything changes when they start to, you know . . . " She gestured with both hands at her chest. "I'm not really looking forward to it myself. I wish I could just wave a wand and avoid it, you know?" She gave him a significant look.

Julian wadded his mangled grass stalk into a ball. "You know I can't do anything like that."

Liz was the only lay person who knew anything about Julian's life in the Craft. He'd been forced to involve her in a major spell last fall—it was that or let the forces of darkness take over the Alewife Bay Mall—but since then he'd told her as little as he could. Most of the time she seemed content with that.

After the softball game, the overnighters convened in the campout area, where Julian and Wisnewski spent the rest of the afternoon setting up the tent they'd be sharing. Pretty soon it was time to gather together for the flag-lowering ceremony. Then everyone else trudged off to the buses, leaving the Cougars, Cardinals, Ducks, and Bulls behind. Julian grinned and waved as the buses pulled away, trailing rooster tails of dust. They had the whole camp to themselves until tomorrow morning!

While the counselors got the fire going, the kids ran around in the woods behind the campout area, looking for long straight sticks. Julian found a great one right by the fence that marked the boundary of the camp.

As he bent down to pick it up, suddenly a huge dog started barking like mad on the other side of the fence. Heart hammering, Julian jumped back, clutching the little stick to his chest as though it would help. He couldn't see the baying hound, but the rattle of the fence as its body struck again and again told him it was a big one. "Nice doggy," he said as he backed away.

The fire was going strong when he got back to the campout area. Julian stood in line, got a hot dog, and threaded it onto the end of his stick. Then he joined the mob jockeying for position around the fire. The orange and yellow flames licked delicately at Julian's hot dog, mirroring the banded colors of the sky above.

"Not like that!" Liz said. "You have to hold 'em near the coals." She had a forked stick with two hot dogs on it, and she rotated it slowly near the bottom of the fire. "If you hold 'em in the flames they just burn on the outside."

"I *like* 'em burnt on the outside," Julian said, still holding his stick high.

"Yuck!" said Harrison, and all the other Cardinals followed suit: "Eew!" "Gross!" "Grody!" Julian tried not to react, but as soon as his hot dog was reasonably done he backed away from the fire and headed off to the lakeshore to eat by himself. He wasn't going to let those girls ruin his overnight.

Despite the importance of the sun and moon cycles to his Craft work, Julian rarely got to enjoy the sunset. Munching his hot dog, he watched the sun shimmer, seeming to melt as it slid down the sky toward the horizon. Behind him, he knew, the full moon would be rising, lost among the trees.

Then he heard a retching sound.

Julian turned and saw Harrison running, doubled over, away from the fire. The other Cardinals started to follow, but she shouted something and they all turned back, chatting among themselves as though nothing had happened. Harrison continued on, vanishing into the woods.

What the heck?

Julian hurried up the sand to the fire pit. As soon as he reached the point where Harrison had shouted, his suspicion was confirmed: she'd used Peitho's Command to turn the others back. That spell was such a strong one that even Julian couldn't fail to recognize it.

Harrison the narc, using such a powerful spell on lay people? If her mother found out, she'd kill her.

Then, in the distance, a dog barked.

It was the same deep-throated *woof* he'd heard earlier, only even angrier.

Harrison's father was a werewolf . . .

Julian set off at a run toward the sound, sand and then dirt thudding beneath his feet.

A minute later, he heard pounding feet behind him. He looked over his shoulder and saw Liz. "Whoa!" he said, stumbling to a halt in a stand of pines.

Liz stopped neatly beside him. "You *never* run. What's up?"

"Witchy stuff," he gasped, winded, hands on knees. She was right . . . he didn't run much. "You'd better stay out of it."

Liz just planted her hands on her hips and glared at him.

The dog was really going insane. Someone yelled at it, but it just kept barking.

If Julian was right about what was happening, there wasn't much time to spare and he could use Liz's help. "Okay, but you've gotta keep quiet about it."

"You know me." She made a zip-my-lip-lock-it-and-throw-away-the-key gesture.

"Okay. You go that way," Julian said, pointing down the length of the fence. "I'll go this way. If you see anything, don't go near it, just yell for me."

"What am I looking for?"

Julian swallowed. "A wolf."

Liz shot him a look. "There aren't any wolves around here."

"Not usually. Look, just do it, okay?"

"Shouldn't we get a counselor?"

"Witchy stuff."

"Got it." She took off down the fence.

Julian moved off at an angle from the direction he'd sent Liz, picking his way through the trees. Between the remaining skyglow and the rising full moon there was still some light, but it was getting harder to see.

The dog began to quiet down a little. Maybe the wolf—Harrison—was moving out of its smell range.

If it *was* Harrison. If she *was* a wolf.

He almost hoped he was wrong. If he was right, he might be putting himself and Liz into serious danger. But he was the only person for miles who'd have the slightest chance of defusing the situation . . .

"Julian!" It was Liz.

She sounded freaked out.

Julian ran toward the voice. "Don't antagonize it!" he shouted. He *really* wished his mother had let him learn a few of the more powerful Goddess spells.

He just about ran past Liz, but she called his name and he managed to stop himself without running into a tree. Liz was standing in a small clearing, but there was no sign of the wolf. "Where is it?" He peered all around into the rapidly deepening night.

"I'm right here, lame-o."

Julian looked down. Harrison was curled up on the ground at Liz's feet with her arms wrapped around her stomach. Her voice was wavery and muffled, but she was still wearing her clothes, still had hands and feet and head in all the usual human places.

Oh, thank the Goddess. He'd been all wrong. Julian breathed a sigh of relief.

But when he bent down and saw her face . . .

Harrison didn't have a wolf's shape, but her face and her hands were all covered with bristly hair, silvery in the moonlight. Her nose had turned small and dark and shiny.

She smelled like a wet dog.

Julian resisted the urge to pet her. "Are you all right?" He realized how stupid the question was as soon as he'd asked it.

Harrison glared up at him, her eyes shining like a cat's. "Of *course* I'm all right! I've got cramps like you wouldn't believe, I ache all over, and I'm covered with hair! Everything's *fine!*"

"But you're not going to run around tearing people's throats out?"

"Only yours," she growled. Her voice, Julian realized, was now deeper than his. "If you don't help me!"

"Okay, what can I do?"

"Well, I can't go back to my tent looking like *this!*" Then she grunted and curled tighter around her belly, obviously in pain.

Julian sat on the ground. "Are you going to . . . transform any further?"

"I don't know!" Harrison's voice quavered and Julian realized that, behind her bluster, she was terrified. "I . . . this has never happened to me before. Dad said . . . he just hoped I'd avoid it. It'll go away when the moon sets, but . . ."

Liz squatted down behind Harrison and stroked her shoulder. "It'll be all right."

"I don't see how. I can't hide out here all night. Bed check's at ten."

Julian checked his watch, then looked up. It was about 9:15 and the moon was just clearing the trees to the east. It wouldn't set until 7:00 tomorrow morning. "The moon's well up, so maybe this is all the transforming you're going to do for now. You could use Aphrodite's Glamour to give yourself the illusion of your normal appearance."

"I don't think I can cast a spell"—she gasped and clutched her stomach again—"like this."

Julian stood up, brushing pine needles from his knees. "I'll have to cast it on you, then."

"But that's a Goddess spell!"

"I've been studying it anyway." But as he ran through the spell in his mind, he realized it wouldn't work. "No, wait. You can't cast a glamour on a supernatural creature."

Liz shook her head. "Even if you can make her look like herself, she's not going anywhere in this shape."

"Well, *someone* has to be in my bed at ten!"

Then Julian had an idea. "Someone will."

Harrison looked up. "What?"

"I'll cast Aphrodite's Glamour on *myself* . . . make *me* look like you."

"What about *you*?"

"I . . . I'll think of something. But we need to hurry . . . that Peitho's Command you used will be wearing off soon, and then you'll be missed. We all will."

"Yeah, but—" Harrison cut off with a grunt, her face clenching in pain.

Liz looked from Harrison to Julian, her eyes white in the deepening dark. "Maybe we should get a doctor."

"No!" Harrison groaned.

Julian bent down and laid a hand on Harrison's shoulder. The warm fur trembling under the fabric of her shirt felt like a pillow full of puppies. "You're sure?"

She just nodded, her furry forehead scraping against the hard earth.

"Okay." He moved a little way away and started clearing a patch of ground for the spell. "We need two candles, salt, water . . . and some of your hair."

"Take it all," Harrison said, her words muffled.

Liz stood up. "We've got candles in my tent, and I can get some salt from the picnic table."

Julian glanced around. It was really starting to get dark fast. "Bring a couple of flashlights too. And a glass of water."

"Will bug juice do?"

"No. It has to be pure clear water, in a glass you can see through. And hurry."

"Right." Liz took off through the woods. Julian was worried that she'd bash into a tree, but she seemed confident and light on her feet.

Julian tried to keep Harrison's spirits up by describing his plan as he prepared the spell. First he raised his pocketknife in the four cardinal directions, invoking the God and Goddess and blessing the area. "I'll go back to camp as you, then tell everyone I've got a stomachache and I'm going to bed early." He scratched a pentacle in the dirt with a stick, keeping the lines as straight as he could. "Then I'll put some clothes or something in your bedroll, sneak out of your tent, and come back to camp as me." He breathed on his knife blade and cleaned it with the tail of his shirt, carefully inspecting the reflection of the moon in the blade's shiny surface. "When the moon sets, you sneak into your tent, then come out in the morning and say you're okay. Nothing to it."

Harrison raised herself on one elbow. Her expression was hard to read, what with the hair all over her face and all. "That's your plan?"

"Yeah."

She sank back to the ground and covered her face with her hands. "We are *so* doomed."

"Don't be such a worrywart." But Julian was deeply concerned. He'd never performed Aphrodite's Glamour for real before; it would have to work perfectly the first time, using improvised equipment, with a supernatural creature as the objective and lay people as the target. And there was a lot of sneaking in and out of tents involved . . .

Julian's cycle of apprehension was broken by a brief spike of panic when he saw a flashlight beam probing through the trees toward them. But it was just Liz. "Here's the stuff. How's Cindy?"

"No worse," Harrison muttered from the ground. "But if this doesn't work, I'm dead."

"It'll work." It had better work. "Give me the cup."

Julian set the plastic cup in the center of the pentacle and filled it with water from Liz's canteen, adding a pinch of salt with a blessing to the Goddess. Then, chanting the words of the spell, he cut a snippet of hair from Harrison's head and one from his own, tying each around one of the two candles. Finally he stuck the candles in the dirt on either side of the cup. "Okay, here we go."

He swallowed and lit the two candles, trying hard not to drop a syllable of the incantation or burn himself with the bent little paper match. Then he opened his pocket-knife and, using the blade as a mirror, reflected the light of Harrison's candle through the cup and onto the flame of his own. As the incantation reached its climax, he held the image of Harrison as she'd looked this afternoon in his mind, licked his fingers, and pinched out his candle.

A dim flickering ghost of a flame remained on the dead black wick, exactly matching the trembling motion of the remaining candle's flame.

Liz's eyes widened at the eerie sight, but Julian cautioned her with a finger to his lips. Then he picked up the cup, said another blessing to the Goddess, and drank the water down.

It tasted of salt and nothing more.

"Whoa," said Liz.

"Did it work?" Harrison muttered from where she lay outside the charmed circle.

"Yeah. It's amazing." Liz walked all around Julian, shining her flashlight at him and peering hard. "He looks totally like you."

Julian felt no different. He tried to inspect himself with his knife blade, but the little reflected sliver of face looked the same as ever to him. "How's the voice?" he asked aloud. He sounded like himself too.

"Whoa," Liz said again. "Freaky. You sound just like her."

Harrison lifted her head and stared at him, eyes shining in the light of Liz's flashlight, for a long time. "Maybe this *will* work," she admitted at last.

Liz was staring at Julian too. "So, how long are you stuck like this?"

"The spell lasts about a day, but I can turn it on and off." He closed his eyes and thought a brief incantation.

Liz actually clapped her hands with glee. "You're you again! Cool!"

Julian leveled a finger at her. "This is no game, Liz! And remember, you can't tell anyone. Not even your parents. Not even your best girlfriend."

Liz looked abashed. "Sorry."

Harrison lay back down. "You'd better head back to camp."

"Are you sure you'll be okay here?"

"I'm feeling a little better. Just leave me that canteen and one of the flashlights."

Julian took off his jacket, rolled it up, and slipped it under Harrison's head. "Liz and I will try to come out here and check up on you." Liz nodded.

"I'll be fine. Just go."

"Okay." Again he thought the incantation.

Harrison gave him a little smile, the first one he'd seen on her fuzzy face. "You don't look half bad as me, if I do say so myself."

"Thanks . . . I think." Julian and Liz headed back toward camp.

"Break a leg, sis," Harrison called after them.

They picked their way cautiously through the woods. The full moon gave a cold, clear light but there wasn't really very much of it, and they only had one flashlight between the two of them. But then Liz stopped, staring at Julian.

"What's wrong?"

"This is too weird," she said. "You look just like Cindy, but you still walk like Julian."

"Huh?" Suddenly Julian realized that this might be harder than he thought. "What's the difference?"

"I'm not sure. Lemme watch you a minute." Liz hung back with the flashlight and watched Julian walk back and forth. "I dunno . . . " she said after a bit. "She walks . . . smoother than you. Try taking shorter steps." He did. "Don't slouch." He put his shoulders back. It felt horribly weird and awkward. "Better. Try swiveling your hips a little?" But when he did that, she just made a face.

"Not like that." He tried again, a couple of different ways, but finally she shook her head. "Forget it—you were better off before."

"Whatever." Julian rubbed his arms. Leaving his jacket with Harrison had been the right thing to do, but the night was getting cold.

"Maybe no one will notice."

They hurried back to camp, where most of the kids were sitting in a circle around the embers of the fire. Todd was holding a flashlight under his chin. "But when she turned around . . . hanging on the passenger door handle . . . she saw . . . *a HOOK!*"

As all the kids screamed, Julian and Liz took advantage of the chaos to slip into the circle and seat themselves on a log. "Hey, Cindy," one of the Cardinals said. It was Sager, one of the girls Harrison was sharing a tent with.

"Hey, Sager."

Sager gave Julian a funny look, and Liz elbowed him hard in the ribs. "Melissa!" she hissed in his ear.

"Huh?" he whispered back.

"If you call her Sager she'll think you don't like her."

Oh. Guys called everyone by last name all the time. This was going to take some getting used to. "Uh, hey, Melissa."

Sager looked somewhat mollified, but not completely. "Where've you been, anyway?"

"I was in the KYBO." KYBO was the stupid official camp name for the toilets. It stood for Keep Your Bowels Open. Julian hated it. "My guts are all in an uproar." He stood up and yawned theatrically. "I think I'll hit the sack early."

"Okay," said Sager. Melissa. Whatever. She stood up, and so did Gensler and Piaskoski, the other two girls in

Harrison's tent. They followed him as he headed toward his tent.

"Where you going?" said Gensler . . . no, Barbara.

Julian swallowed. "To bed?"

"Our tent's that way."

"Oh. Yeah, right." He turned around, only half faking disorientation. "Sorry, I'm . . . I'm not feeling too good."

Piaskoski—what was her first name?—moved up close to Julian and winked. "Yeah, me too." The others giggled.

"Great plan," Melissa whispered to him. "Now we can get straight to the important part of the evening. Gossip!"

This wasn't going at all the way he'd hoped it would. He shot a desperate look at Liz. *Cover for me*, he mouthed. She gave him a thumbs-up and dashed away toward Julian's tent.

He hoped she had a better plan than he did.

The three Cardinals fluttered around Julian as they made their way to their four-person tent, trading rumors about first names he didn't recognize . . . they might be other campers, or TV stars, or high school students, or imaginary friends. He kept quiet, hoping they'd take his silence for stomach distress. At least he managed to figure out that Piaskoski's first name was Patricia.

After the communal brushing of teeth—the chattering barely slowed down—Julian had a moment of panic when it came time to undress for bed. But all the girls wriggled into their sleeping bags fully clothed and thrashed around, emerging in frilly little nightgowns like butterflies breaking out of their chrysalises. Julian found Harrison's nightgown in her duffel and followed suit, but simply stuffed the nightgown into the bottom of the sleeping bag and changed his mental image of himself-as-Harrison to include it. He hoped he hadn't imagined it backwards or something. But when he emerged, no one commented on his appearance so he must have gotten the illusion more or less right.

They spent the next hour talking about who had a crush on whom, whose hair was the most atrocious, and which Hudson Brother was the most kissable. Bed check came and went. Julian crawled into his sleeping bag, continuing to feign illness, but even if the other girls would leave him alone—which they wouldn't, they kept pestering him for his opinion on whether Donny Osmond was cuter than Jan-Michael Vincent—he couldn't possibly sneak out as long as they were awake. And even if Liz had managed to find some way to get him past his own bed check, if he wasn't back in his own bed by morning someone was sure to notice.

Finally one other factor rose to the forefront of his attention: he desperately needed to pee. Even if he couldn't use it as an excuse to sneak away, he had to do something about it. He slithered out of his sleeping bag as quietly as he could.

"Where you going, sickie girl?" said Patricia.

"To the KYBO."

All three girls stood up in unison, slipping on shoes and jackets.

"Don't worry about me," Julian protested. "I can find my way there by myself."

"Ha ha," said Melissa. Without further comment, they all followed him out the tent flap. Fortunately the girls' KYBO was right next to the boys', so he didn't have to embarrass himself by asking directions.

Julian could barely hold it until he got the stall door closed. He breathed out a sigh as he relieved himself.

"What the hell are you doing over there, Cindy?" came Barbara's voice from the next stall. "Sounds like rain on the roof!"

"And your feet are pointing the wrong way!" That was Melissa, on the other side. There was about a nine-inch gap at the bottom of the wall.

Oh shit. He was peeing standing up. "Uh . . . I'm pouring out my canteen." He tried to stem the flow, but it was incredibly difficult once he'd started.

"Huh?"

"I . . . I think it was the bug juice in there that made me sick."

"Bug juice, huh?" Barbara giggled. "Boones Farm Strawberry Bug Juice, maybe?"

All three of the other girls tittered. "Ha ha," said Julian.

Finally he finished his business and zipped up. At the last minute before opening the stall door, he remembered what he'd told them and added an empty canteen to his illusion.

Back in the girls' tent, Julian stole a glance at his watch. It was after midnight and the chatter showed no sign of slowing down. It was all about hair and clothes and fingernail polish now, meaningless and totally boring; Julian, still feigning illness in his sleeping bag, was having trouble keeping his eyes open. He had to do something soon, because if he fell asleep here there'd be serious problems in the morning.

"Wanna hear a scary story?" he said, sitting up in his sleeping bag.

"Okay . . ."

"First you have to turn off your flashlights."

In the dark, he told them a story—all true, he swore, it had happened to his cousin, though he was making it up as he went along—about a boy and a girl who went camping at an isolated lake way out in the country. He played up the darkness, the eerie waving branches, the spooky wind in the trees.

He was hoping to terrify the Cardinals to the point that they'd crawl into their sleeping bags and pull the covers over their heads until dawn. If that didn't work, he'd just sneak out of the tent in the dark.

It wasn't much of a plan, but it was the best he had been able to come up with.

"And then she heard a noise outside the tent," he said, pitching his voice low and ghastly like Doctor Cadaverino on *Nightmare Theatre*. "A horrible, slithering footstep. Thump-*kssshhhh*. Thump-*kssshhhh*. Thump-*kssshhhh*."

The girls just giggled at that. This wasn't working at all.

And then they heard a noise outside the tent.

It wasn't a horrible slithering footstep.

It was the howl of a wolf, not far off.

All sound and movement inside the tent ceased.

"Did you hear that?" said Barbara.

Patricia said "There aren't any wolves around here . . . " but she just sounded as though she was trying to convince herself.

"Hush!" Julian said.

They listened intently, straining the silence with their ears.

Then the howl came again: "*Awooooooo . . .* "

It was much closer this time.

Patricia let out a strangled little shriek.

"Be quiet!" Julian whispered. "Or it'll hear you!"

The darkness vibrated with tension as the silence went on and on. Every cricket's chirp, every frog's croak, every branch's creak struck their ears like thunder.

Then came a snuffling of breath against the ground.

A slow, steady pad of feet on fallen leaves.

A low, tentative growl.

And then, just outside the tent flap: *"AWOOOOOO!"*

Even Julian screamed, his voice lost in the general cacophony.

Everyone sat trembling in the dark. Then came a voice, a low growl almost unrecognizable as words: *"Cinndy Harrrrissssonnnn . . ."*

Julian didn't react until someone poked him in the shoulder. "Y-yes?"

"Come ooouuuuut . . ."

Julian stared into the darkness. What the hell was going on?

"Cinnndy . . . come oooouuuuutttt . . ."

Someone whimpered. Maybe it was Julian.

"Sennnnd Cinnndy Harrrrrissson ouuuut . . . or I will EAT YOU ALL!"

Again the tent exploded in screams. Hands grabbed at Julian's clothes, some pushing him toward the tent flap, others hauling him back. A fierce whispered argument ensued about what to do.

"Sennnnd herrrr oooouuuuttt . . . NOW!"

And then Julian recognized the voice.

"I will go," he said. "I will sacrifice myself for the sake of the Cardinals!"

And before anyone could stop him, he dashed out the tent flap.

Furry hands grabbed him and hustled him away into the woods.

"Tree on your left . . ." Harrison whispered in the moonlit dark. "Don't step in the ditch . . ."

Werewolves had very good night vision.

They didn't stop until they got to the little clearing where they'd left Harrison earlier. Liz was waiting there.

"What the heck do you think you were doing back there?" Julian demanded of Harrison. "Someone could have seen you!"

"After listening to you for an hour, I had to do *something*!" Werewolves had very good hearing, too. "You make a totally pathetic girl! You've ruined my reputation forever!"

"Sorry." Julian sighed. "Thanks for the save, though."

"Well, it was your stupid ghost story that gave me the idea."

Julian grinned at the backhanded compliment, then turned to Liz. "I hope you did better than I did."

"I told everyone you'd gone to bed early with a stomachache," Liz said, "and stuffed your big ol' pack into your sleeping bag. Your counselor didn't notice the difference. Neither did Wisnewski. He's snoring away next to it right now."

"Thanks." Julian let out a breath he hadn't known he was holding. "So what do we do now?"

"I've got it all figured out," said Harrison. "We wait out here until after moonset, then we come back to camp all chipper, and say it was just a gag the three of us cooked up. We might get in trouble, but after all that, anyone who says they saw a werewolf will just get laughed at."

They all walked down to the lakeshore and sat on a log side by side, watching the moon as it crept down the sky. Eventually, as the dawn began to brighten behind them, the moon slipped below the horizon and Harrison gave a little gasp. When Julian turned to her she had returned to normal.

"You should probably change too," Liz said.

Julian realized he was still wearing Harrison's face. He thought the incantation and returned to his own form.

"That's much better," Harrison said.

"Oh hey," said Liz, "I almost forgot." She reached into the pocket of her jacket and pulled out three napkin-wrapped packages. "You guys were, um, kind of busy, so I saved some for you."

Julian unwrapped his package. It smelled of chocolate . . . and marshmallow . . . and graham crackers. "S'mores!"

They dug into the sweet gooey goodness as the sun rose, casting their shadows across the surface of the lake.

Dave Freer is a former Ichthyologist/Fisheries Scientist turned sf/fantasy writer. He now has ten books in print (the latest being *A Slow Train To Arcturus*) a number of which are co-authored with Mercedes Lackey and/or Eric Flint. He is also the author of about twenty other short stories, and a teens novel. He lives in Zululand, South Africa. He hasn't howled at the moon for days and utterly denies knowing any short, tattooed private detectives.

Wolfy Ladies

Dave Freer

"Yes. A werewolf in an advertising agency... That's me," Scarlett said, crossing her long slim legs. She was wearing a skirt. Or at least quite a broad belt. The top was low-cut enough for most men not to notice the choker she wore. A beautiful piece—Irish at a guess, a golden eagle in flight, each feather perfect, with ruby-chip eyes. The rubies matched her lipstick. "I was told you were quite used to that sort of thing."

"A very appropriate profession, I would say," I said calmly. I was a little low on silver bullets right now. Actually I was low on silver of any sort, being down to copper, which is why I had taken on this job. I'm a private investigator. Nature dealt my genes a couple of odd hands. I'm a dwarf. Not the beard-axe-and-gold-obsession kind from fantasy, but the kind with achondroplasia. It meant that I investigated all the weird to paranormal cases. There are a lot more of them than you'd think. It's bias, but then I have my own biases. I don't like working for women or even cases involving women. I can repress men . . . But I've been around a long time and learned to cope with them. 'Cause genetics dealt me another odd card, in that I have abnormal telomeres. I'm not a microbiologist, but it means that I'm still not dead, and I should have been, a long time back. People keep trying to change that, but I'm better at avoiding death than dealing with women.

You could say the same about the man Scarlett wanted me to find. Fintan mac Bóchra. Supposed to have married one of Noah's granddaughters. Shape-shifter and symbolic magician extraordinaire. Wise man to Irish kings. Clever with anything except money or women. Oh, and he's a master of sartorial elegance. He wears an old robe and he doesn't like hairbrushes. Just her type. "So what's the interest in Fin, Ms.? Romantic?"

She waved a langorous hand at me, the inch-long red nails perfectly manicured. "Oh please! His potions. I'm only a wolf at full moon, sweetie, and Fintan being missing is playing havoc with my social life and my love life, not to mention the chance of my being charged for murder, animal cruelty and occasional casual sex with Alsatians. Do you know how embarrassing and demeaning that is? But when a bitch-wolf is in heat and the nearest male wolf is in some wildlife refuge a thousand miles away . . . a girl has to do what she's got to do."

Too much information already! My mind insisted on illustrating the scene for me. "You could, er, go on holiday . . . " my voice trailed off. She wasn't the camping-hiking kind.

She sniffed. "Wildlife reserves. Huh. I tried visiting one of those dumps at the right time of year—and you thought PMS was a problem! Darling, they're just *so* primitive. I don't DO the countryside, unless it comes with a luxury spa, Jacuzzi and heated towel rails. And I haven't heard any complaints from the Alsatians. I mean, they should be so lucky."

They should. The rest of the time she was the original Coco Chanel girl from the tips of her Manolo Blahniks to her hair extensions. Anyway, I gather Alsatians aren't proud. You pick up that sort of information in my line of work. Actually, I could find her a couple of were-wolves. This 'burg had a few. "Anyway, Ms. Ralph . . . "

"Scarlett, Mr. Bolg."

Huh. Did she think I was going to fall for that one? "Oh, call me Eochaid"? I wasn't born yesterday, or even the day before. Back where I come from we still know that giving someone your real name is a bad idea. Okay, there are some things to be said for the twenty-first century. Being four foot six high and tattooed from head to foot (it's a cultural thing. Which means you don't ask and I won't tell too many lies) no longer means I can only work in a circus. A chopped Harley and a leather jacket and the world is my snot-flavored bivalve. But people forget things that were hard-learned. Look at Fintan. Smart as a whip, but he'd ended up doing time as a salmon and a hawk, and an eagle, and two out of three times had been because of women. Not me. I still got the scars from the first time. I ignored the bait. "So, Scarlett, when did you last see Fintan?"

She looked at me through her sooty false eyelashes. "I'm paying you to find him, Mr Bolg, not to suffer the inquisition. I saw him when I got my last fix, of course. I've given you the names of a couple of other girl-wolves. Check them out. If anyone asks how you knew . . . You can say you come from me."

She loved saying that bit about the fix, naturally. It would amuse her perverse sense of humor. And it had

the merit of being true. The potions Fin sold would fix
her body form, at least for a while. Humans have this
idea that shape-shifting is wonderous, and to be sure it
is, at a board meeting, or when the other side is winning.
It's just not a good trait when it happens inconveniently.
Times have changed, and if you're going to live among
the rest of society, well, controlling the shifts helps. Fintan's potions were a blessing to the average suburban
shape-shifter. That's why they tended to gravitate close
to here. To be near the supplier. Word got around among
the undead and inhumans too. Fin was a master at it
himself. He could even split himself in two. Which was
very clever, except that you had to get them back
together to have Fintan.

I took my leave of her, and took the bike grumbling
through town to one of my informants. I could have
followed her "leads" but . . . that's not how I work. I've
become cautious over the years, and not just with
women.

"Cost you a pigeon up front," he growled before I even
started to speak. I've got a message for the architects in
this town: When you do fake Gothic, to add a bit of
character to your mall, the big trick to remember is to
put the gargoyles at a height, and in a place, where they
can catch their own pigeons. Sooner or later all gargoyles
become animate, even concrete ones. It's symbolic
magic, see. Same with the garden gnomes, only the gargoyles are less bad-tempered.

Anyway, Larry sees everything around here. Except
pigeons. They sit on a sill about four feet above him, and
his arms are only three foot long and he doesn't jump
well. I had one ready in my bag, so I gave it to him,
ignoring its squawks of outrage. Contrary to rumor, Gargoyles don't eat them. Just hold them down and pay the

pigeons back. I'll spare you the details, but I reckon the pigeons would rather be eaten. I waited patiently. There is no other way with gargoyles. Eventually he gave a stony sigh of satisfaction and asked, "So whatcha want, Blue-boy?"

It's the tattoos. From a distance I am blue. "Fintan."

"Ain't seen him in coupla months. He useta regularly get chucked out for loitering before that."

"That's a pretty poor return for a pigeon. I got pecked catching that one."

"Thass the breaks, Blue-boy." He gave a rumble that might have been gargoyle stomach noises, or maybe a laugh. "But ask me another. I needed that pigeon."

"Werewolves. You seen any lately? Changed ones, that is."

"Funny you should ask. You don't see them with the fur out much, but lately . . . full moon and there's a pack running. I saw them over on that vacant lot by Campher's. In between the used cars they got parked there. Hunting hobos, most likely."

Now if there is anything that is just unnatural it is weres hunting hobos. Werewolves are not your equal opportunity biter. They have a tradition to stick to: their nearest and dearest (if they don't happen to be wolves themselves), and then soft white throats. They weren't going to find many of their normal diet items among the clapped-out special bargains on the lot. "Anyone you recognized?"

"Coulda have been, " he said, coughing meaningfully.

"What about an IOU?" I asked, already knowing the answer.

"Paper is no substitute for a pigeon," was his gruff reply.

And he wouldn't take plastic or Kentucky either, I knew.

So I had a choice—go pigeon hunting or try to read between the lines. It had to be someone I would know. That rounded it down nicely to half the town. And someone that didn't fit the bill of "ordinary human." That was down to about five percent, then. Only problem was that even I didn't always know when they weren't ordinary, which left me back where I had started. I was going to have to try arcane means. I hate the yellow pages, and if I'd been any good as a magic worker, I wouldn't have been working in the private investigations line. OK, so most of my work is with the undead—but ask any PI: that's normal. Right now it was the phone book or following her leads . . . So I went back to my place, and faced up to it. Now, I'd like to say that I live in palatial splendor, but I haven't done that for a couple of thousand years. If I had a ratty office it would go with the image, but I work from home. I spent my pension money from the freak show on buying property back when it was both reasonable and a good investment. I've got a white picket fence and so far I have managed to resist putting the skulls of my enemies on the spikes. I've grown some sweet peas on the trellis, though, which is nearly as good.

It took me awhile to get the divination paraphernalia out of the attic. It was one of Fintan's experiments . . . which meant that it was brilliant, expensive, and dangerous. He liked high-end symbolic magic . . . In the old days it was just a quick appeal to the Gods, a slash of the athame and a spill of entrails, but there are bylaws about that kind of thing now. I don't always operate strictly inside the law, but divination didn't work too well anyway. Not that fuzzy logic, electronic inertial dithering, and a CD of Gregorian chants played backwards can't mess me around badly, but once I've hooked up the laptop to the mechanical dart-thrower, there is no way out of the spell that isn't terminal. I switched on the fan, put the telephone book in the pentacle and took cover, hoping the neighbors wouldn't complain about the wailing again. Last time the dart ended up in the attending officer's forehead. I got off on self-defense, seeing that it had worked, and it turned out that he was the murder perp I was looking for.

The dart ripped through my earlobe, ricochetted off the shoulder of a small marble bust of Beethoven on the piano, and severed the electric cable to the hanging light in a shower of sparks and cascading light-fitting. In the sudden darkness and silence I heard the solid thunk of the dart hitting paper. PIs like me, with experience of the arcane, always put a flashlight in their pockets before doing this sort of experiment. Some of them probably remember to check the batteries first too. I found and lit one of the black candles without breaking too much more or setting fire to anything. I crunched across the glass to the telephone directory.

The dart had spiked through a bunch of oyster-folded and half-torn pages, in a sort of phone-book origami of a wolf's-head.

I went and tried the earth leakage switch on the mains. It must have been my lucky day, because the rest of the lights, the chants and the fan came on again. By the time I had the CD player turned off, the breeze from the fan had ripped several of the dart-stabbed pages. Oh yeah. Divination and the occult, at its best!

I sat and made a list—as best I could—from the ripped pages. Some of it was so obvious . . . natural professions for werewolves, occupations where the wolfish side was bound to help, like repossession and dog-catching. Or ones that could be really useful . . . like Marie's Manicure and Beauty Salon. The last page was really shredded . . . something that began with an A. I decided that a manicurist was safer than a repo man. Shows how wrong you can be. Oddly—none of them were names from Scarlett's list. And yet part of the search parameters had been "Fintan" and "werewolf."

I kicked the bike onto its stand, just in time to hear a shriek of mortal agony from inside the salon. Once I would have kicked the door in and entered swinging a sword around. Now . . . I just loosened the Glock in its holster and peered in at a window. Someone peered right back at me. Opened the door. She was one of those leggy women who always make me feel even shorter. "Get out of here before I call the cops."

"I thought you might need me to call them for you," I said as I heard another choked-off scream.

She snorted. "That's just Candace. She's such a baby. No real woman yells. So what are you here for, Blueboy? Nails, feet or legs?"

"Uh. I just wanted to talk to about . . . "

"Honey, I only talk to customers."

I took a deep breath. I had said "and expenses" when I took the job. "Well, I'll have be a customer then. I need to ask you a few questions."

"I need to ask you a few too," she said, leading me inside. "What's it to be? Toenails, fingernails or wax?"

"My ears could use a bit of a clean-out. I guess. Wax, eh?"

She looked me up and down. "Bikini wax?"

"Whatever you want to wear is fine by me. I mean they have topless carwashes."

The little silver salmon between her breasts jiggled. "Full Brazilian or French?" she asked.

I shook my head. "I stopped at Starbucks on the way over. American, but pretty good."

"American it is," she said, seeming a little disappointed, but I drink too much coffee anyway. "There's a changing room over there. Get your kit off."

I was beginning to wonder if I'd stumbled onto a vice ring. Yeah well. I wish I had. What that woman did with HOT WAX!? And werewolves are unnaturally strong. It did get the wax to blow itself out of my ears.

Finally I got a chance to ask: "Fintan?"

She might have paused, briefly. "Suntan? You could use one."

"No . . . Fiaaaaaaaargh!"

"You're a baby. Just like most men."

It was not one of the easiest interviews I've conducted. If she knew anything she wasn't saying. But she took a call on her mobile while she was torturing me . . . Now, I wouldn't be in my profession if I had any qualms about listening in. My torturer was very circumspect. The person on the other end of the line wasn't. They were shouting. " . . . Time of month . . . " I tried to stop listening. It was like not thinking of pink elephants.

"Calm down, Bertrade," said Marie, turning away from me. "We can reach some arrangement with . . . "

" . . . hair on the backs of my hands, Marie!"

"I'll call you in few minutes, Bertrade. I'm just dealing with a client," said Marie snapping the mobile closed.

Months are based on the lunar cycle. The moon would be full soon, with a certain effect on werewolves . . . . hair spreading down onto their hands ... And Bertade was one of the names Scarlett gave me. I was going to have to stake out this place.

"You know," she said casually, while adding to the agony on the plastic—I'd better get these expenses paid or my credit card might just explode, "I can recommend a good tanning place. Tan Studio. Get you a discount if I book you in."

Now, I was just about to tell her I'd rather be dunked in an outhouse, when it occurred to me that "Tan Studio" was on my list too. And ... "Those are the places with the ultraviolet lights, right?"

"If you mean sunbeds, yes."

"Are they open at night?" I asked artlessly. "I've got a busy schedule."

"Oh yes. Mind you, evenings are their busiest times."

"I'd better try it, I suppose. Improve my looks a bit."

"Have you ever considered botox?" she asked, as she dialed. "Tonight, Mr. Bolg?"

"I'm busy tonight. Tomorrow."

"They're always quite booked up for f ... Friday nights."

For full moon? I thought, but said nothing.

She had a hard time with the Tan Studio. And annoyingly the person on the other end had one of those murmuring voices. So I was left listening to "well, what about 10 to 11?"

She smiled toothily at me. Good teeth, all the better to bite you with, I thought. "They'll squeeze you in on the late session." She handed me a card with the address. I got on my bike and out of there, before she could talk me into Botox. I found a nice quiet parking lot, not overlooked by any gargoyles and gave one of my connections up at City Hall a call on the mobile. He owed me. He was always eager to oblige.

"NO! No! No! No! What is it about that that you don't understand, Bolg?"

"I'll be there in about ten minutes."

"Just leave me alone."

"Sure. I'll drop by some other time and post some photographs on the notice board in the hall. Dwarf porn is one thing, piano porn another . . . but together?"

He sighed. "I'll meet you on the back fire escape. What do you need this time?"

"A password, and access to a computer on the LAN. Need to look a few things up."

"No fires? No screaming women?"

"Would I do something like that?"

"Yes," he said bitterly. "You usually do," and cut the connection. But he was waiting for me.

I spent the afternoon doing a bit of research in the city records. Checking out the leasehold on Campher's used car lot. Henry came back into his office while I was busy. He spit coffee on the keyboard. "Damn you, Bolg. How did you know about that?"

"I didn't, but I do now. So fill in the gaps and save me having to do the legwork," I said, lighting one of my small cigars. "Otherwise we'll have to have a conflagration in the waste bins again."

"Put that damn thing out! It's a non-smoking area."

"Never mind smoking. It'll be on fire soon enough. You know, no smoke without fire . . . "

"Just put it out!"

"I wouldn't dream of smoking while you explain." I said stubbing it out in the potted plant. I have never liked begonias much anyway. I hoped that it stayed stubbed. They had a nasty habit of bursting into flames and singeing your eyebrows off.

"What the hell are you smoking?" he asked, sniffing suspiciously.

"They're herbal. All legal. Not tobacco—you can smoke them in public buildings until the bastards turn blue. Now . . . tell me about old Campher's lot . . . and the vacant lot next door."

"It's been earmarked for a . . . development. That's all I'm saying right now."

"Oh. And what's that got to do with hobos?" I said, taking a flyer.

He choked on his next mouthful of coffee. Sprayed the begonia this time. Coffee wouldn't revive it after its brush with my herbs. I live in fear that I'll have to smoke one of those things one day. But people are so scared of the smoke police that they tend to talk before I have to.

Henry scowled at me. I scowled right back. I'm good at that. He sighed. "There's a prior application by someone wanting to build a homeless shelter. Got as far as committee approval. Only we haven't been able to track the applicant down. The mayor set up a commission to see if a homeless shelter was called for."

"Let's guess," I said wryly. "Applicant is one Fintan mac Bóchra. And he paid everything in cash."

"You are just plain scary. The implication from the developers is that it must be drug money."

"I'll bet they claim that there is no need for a homeless shelter in this town." In a backhand way the accusations were quite accurate. It was drug money . . . even if antilycanthropics weren't exactly what they were thinking of. Weres did refer to it as "getting a fix." Someone was making very sure that there were no vagrants about . . .

The begonia burst into spectacular flames and I decided that it was time to leave. I left quietly while he was trying to empty the water cooler onto it.

Back at my place I had a shower. Then I put some gloves on and went to pick some herbs. Wonderful things, herbs. Good for flavoring food, and they have many medical uses too. Most of them are not illegal—monkshood, foxglove, hellebore, and bittersweet are not much use to someone wanting to get high, but they too have their purposes.

Just before dusk I set off to stake out the beauty parlor. I have an old Toyota for that. It attracts less attention than the Harley. And it's warmer if I should fall asleep, which does happen. I've got a mattress in the trunk—that I can reach by lifting up the back seat. It's got a neat little rust hole that I can see out of, and I fitted a camera in one of the reflectors. A rusty old Jap clunker rarely gets stolen. I get very peeved when some kid full of dope wakes me up.

I lay there watching, thinking and staying awake. The beauty parlour was open late. Mind you, to get customers in this economic climate, they had to cater to working women. One of them, I was not surprised to see, was Scarlett. Well, that appearance of hers must take a lot of upkeep. Unlike a lot of the customers, she was inside for a good long while. Hair and nails, I'd guess. I wasn't even going to think about what sort of waxing she'd go in for. I'd bet she never screamed.

It was a long night. Close to midnight I saw some grey shadows running past. Hairy grey shadows. Big . . . and with the occasional gleam of teeth. One of them stopped and sniffed at the car. Cleanliness is next to Godliness, and a bit of valerian and pepper added to your soap might stink, but it sure left the huge grey wolf sneezing after it broke my window. It didn't get to look in the trunk after that.

Then nothing happened for a long time. I only woke up when they were towing the vehicle off to the impound—but I was used to that. There are times and places when achondroplasia has been a pain in the butt. When I was growing up—or rather not growing up—there were ideas about me being a changeling, and suggestions that maybe drowning me would be a good idea. Fintan talked them out of it, and I still owe him for that. They had more respect for hairy salmon-and-eagle shape-shifting magicians back then. Now they're more worried about being politically correct instead. Picking on someone with dwarfism could lose them their job . . . Especially when I phrase it like "Oh so you're gonna tell the judge you didn't see me, 'cause I'm so small?" Look, there's nothing like a Glock, attitude and tattoos to make me the equal of any man—but life threw this at me without my asking for it, so I let others use their own prejudices in my favor.

"Hey look. We made a mistake, bud," said the tow-truck operator. "Didn't realize you was in there—saw the broken window. I can put you onto someone who can replace it real cheap."

"I drank too much and fell asleep rather than drive home," I said, with my best I-made-a-fool-of-myself smile. "I didn't even know some bastard had broken my window." It was a lot more believable than "I was hiding in the trunk when a werewolf did it."

He grinned back at me, showing a missing tooth. "I guess it's better than waking up in the morgue. No hard feelings, bud. Look, try Bernstone Parts. Tell him Fat Mike sent ya."

"I'll do that," I said. "Look, you know everyone in this game, right?"

He laughed, setting his paunch wobbling. "Pretty much."

"I got to find a repo man. Fellow called"—I checked my list—"Teodore Pansakov."

"Big Teddy. He don't like people to know where he lives."

"Hey, I am a threat! I haven't beaten up a repo man in, oh, maybe a week."

He snorted. "Big Teddy is the right place for you to catch up, then. He lives at the back of that used car lot on Main."

It was not a place that a "new development" was going to smile on. The barbed wire and chained metal gate had rustic charm—or maybe I mean rusty charm. The rust made it easier for the bolt cutters anyway. The yard felt undressed because it lacked a mangy Rottweiler to greet me. Generally speaking, werewolves have got what it takes to get ahead. But it looked like Teddy could be the exception. The gate had been locked, but the house door was open. Teddy was sleeping the sleep of the werewolf after a rough night, sprawled naked and hairy on the rumpled bed. There was a bit of blood in the greying stubble on his chin. One of the things that I'd found odd about my client's story was the part about the Alsatians. There were male werewolves around. But okay, maybe Alsatians bathed more often than this guy.

I looked around this cross between a tip and a house, and found a coffee machine, which looked like it could be the only working appliance in the place. I got it gurgling away, cleared myself a seat and waited. I've worked on werewolves before. They're very scent oriented. Shaking them awake is a sure way to get some new scars.

But the smell of coffee wakes them up . . . and gives you a lever.

Sure enough, his nostrils started twitching as the coffee machine worked away. Pretty soon the man opened one eye.

"Do you take sugar? Milk?"

"Three," he said dozily. "No milk."

About two seconds later he jerked awake. "What the hell are you doing here?" he growled.

"Getting you coffee," I said, pouring it. A cup of hot coffee is a good weapon in need.

He blinked as I spooned sugar into the cup. "I mean, what do you want?"

"Mac Bóchra," I said, stirring.

He laughed bitterly. "You and me both, mister. Why do you think I know where Fin is? I haven't seen him for three months now. And that's a problem, trust me."

I walked over, and handed him the cup. He drank a large mouthful that must have scalded all the way down. He looked at me. Sniffed. And looked truly afraid. Now, everyone is allowed their delusions of grandeur. But mine don't go as far as believing that a 6'8" repo man, weighing 300 pounds, was scared of my appearance. Anyway, it wasn't my appearance that worried him. It was my smell. I'd showered yesterday evening, with, it is true, valerian and pepper soap. People say valerian stinks. Cats love it. Wolves hate it. But that wasn't just dislike. It was fear. He was thinking about running. Strong emotion had its normal effect on a lycanthrope. He was going to have trouble holding that coffee if his hands went any further toward paws. I was between him and the way out. "Calm down. I'm no threat."

"What do you want?" he snarled. And I mean snarled.

"I told you. I've been hired to find Fintan."

"Who hired you?" he demanded; his teeth were growing as I watched.

"Scarlett Ralph."

That stopped the change right there. Saved his coffee. "Scarlett?"

I nodded. "Uptown wolf-girl who wears really short skirts."

He sat, and sipped his coffee, growing more human. "I thought she must be the one who had done it. We were talking about . . . challenging her."

"Only nobody really wants to?" I said. I could have used some of that coffee too, only I wasn't prepared to trust one of his cups.

He looked at the coffee. Said nothing. Eventually he looked me in the eye. "I'm sorry about the window."

"That was you, was it?"

"Yeah. I got a scent-swatch. Orders to find you and kill you. Eat you."

"Werewolves don't usually take orders too well."

"They do if they want their potion," said Big Teddy. "And I don't even like meat. I'm a vegetarian."

I just looked at him. "Except when I change. I can't help myself then," he admitted.

"Who gave the orders?"

"I don't know. I get notes, and they've always been careful about scent . . . they must be werewolves themselves. They've got contacts for the potion. Say it comes from out of town. It's expensive . . . I couldn't pay. I had to agree to some . . . work."

Out of town? Unless they'd moved Fintan, that was a lie. It did mean that the old fool was probably alive, maybe bespelled. If they got a scent-swatch . . . why?

From whom? I had some idea but it would mean sticking my head into a hornet's nest. Well. A tanning parlor. At full moon, near midnight. I got up to leave. "I'd give up on eating me. I'd disagree with you."

"Er," he looked thoroughly embarrassed. "We only bit the hobos, but we do eat . . . "

"Avoid hobos, and me. I'm argumentative. I disagree with anyone. You owe me a window."

The carefully shuttered Tan Studio was so not my kind of place. For starters most of the twenty people there—and a couple were men too, looked as if the Bahamas was a more likely place for them to be catching some ultraviolet. And some—with screens it's true—were catching more of a tan than they could get outside of Saint Tropez without being arrested. I felt quite naked myself. I'd had to turn in all my clothes—bar my shorts. The Glock was "safely" locked away. The luxurious white towelling gown dragged on the floor behind me. I was shown to my sunbed.

I went along with it all. Took the eyeshades. Passed on the iPod. Instead I tuned into the low burble of conversation. I've learned a lot in that way before.

" . . . bleaching. And then you suntan your bootie. When you bend over you must look like a target . . . " Well, this time I wasn't going to come by the sort of information most people considered valuable—and then the lights went off.

There were outraged and fearful howls, especially when someone outside threw back the shutters on the high windows, letting the baleful light of a full moon stream in. Towelling ripped as the convulsions of change racked them. I was too far from the windows, even if I wanted to run. But I bolted for the nearest corner. Most people would have been frightened witless, but I had seen Fintan transform. He was a master at it. He could do anything, even objects, although of course eagle and salmon were his favorites. So I was merely terrified.

And then huge, yellow-eyed and white-fanged in the moonlight, they came for me.

"Back off. The first one of you within three yards gets it," I said.

"Hrrrr. No gun. No silver bullets. They locked it away," snarled one.

"I want to talk to you about this bulge I had in my shorts," I said, holding the spray bottle up into the moonlight. "It's an atomizer with a mixture of monkshood—or as it is otherwise known, wolfsbane—with alcohol as a carrier. Mildly toxic to me. But it will kill all of you." I gave it a little squirt. "You should be able to smell that."

They obviously could. They frantically scrambled back, coughing and choking. "Now, I saw the mains box just next to the front desk. Go and nose the switch up, one of you. You wouldn't be here if you wanted to go hunting for soft white throats, and mine isn't soft or white."

There was a brief yelp. A spark must have bitten his nose, but the lights came on. So did the sunbeds. "Bed!" I said sternly to the pack. It worked better on the wolves, even the females, than it normally does for me. Great lupine shapes slunk up under the lights. The ultraviolet began to return them back to human form. "I don't imagine any of you know where Fintan mac Bóchra is. But I am willing to bet that you all came here via certain . . . wolfish connections. I want to know who they are."

It didn't take me long to figure it out, once I had those names. If they were very rich they could buy a fix. If not, they had two choices. A sunbed or doing dirty deeds. Suspicion had fallen on my employer, not surprisingly. And all the names she'd given me as leads were here in the room with me. If I'd gone straight to them . . .

I'd have found out nothing. But they'd have known that she was looking for Fintan herself.

I left them on the sunbeds, got my clothes and my gear, and headed south. Up Main.

To break into the beauty parlor.

Breaking into the lair of wolves is a chancy business. I hoped Fin would be alone. Of course he wasn't.

"Mr. Bolg!" The ruby eyes of the eagle around her throat looked kinder than she did.

"I thought I'd stop by and collect my check and my expenses claim, Ms. Ralph. And a cup of that Brazilian you offered me, Marie," I said. "Seeing as I've found Fintan."

"What are you talking about, Bolg?" asked the beautician, eyes narrow. The little articulated silver salmon between her breasts wriggling.

"Fintan is a shape-shifter. That's why he developed potions to control it. He's the oldest and wisest of the shape-shifters. I doubt if anyone could keep him prisoner."

"And so?" they said in unison, leaning over me.

"He's also a sucker for pretty women. And," I said, reaching up and snatching at their throats, ripping the gold eagle choker and the silver salmon free. "Great at symbolic magic," I said, ducking, squeezing the two together.

The jolt knocked me off my feet, which was just as well. It meant they missed me and fell over Fin.

He stood up. And dusted himself off, hairy and as scruffy as ever. "You took your time," he said mildly.

"I'm sorry, Scarlett. It's no deal. I've heard that some old friends from home had their hollow hill bulldozed. I need the place." He looked at her legs. At Marie's breasts. "But if you girls would care to join us for a drink . . . "

I rolled my eyes and took him by the elbow. "I'll send you the bill, Ms. Ralph. But lay off the hobos. Maybe you can find Fin and his friends alternate accommodations. But talk to me, not him."

Fintan sipped his rye. "The developer talked to her about advertising. She's a sharp one and checked out the lease. Got her sister Marie to take an option on them . . . Only they found out that I had an option on that vacant lot," he said, scratching absently. "So they came to see me. Got me drunk. Got me to show them what I could do. I bound myself into those two forms. Good thing you recognized them. And they, clever devils, never released more than half at a time."

I shook my head. "You never learn, do you?"

He shrugged. "Foxy ladies are a weakness of mine. They'd figured out, afterwards, that keeping me prisoner also gave them a powerful lever with the weres in this town. But I did tell her that you'd be ideal to convince the other werewolves they were also looking for me."

"They're wolfy ladies." I said and finished my drink.

Kevin Andrew Murphy lives in northern California, writes novels, short stories, essays, poems and so on, and loves a chance to play with mythology. His most recent short fiction is "The Tears of Nepthys" in *Busted Flush*, continuing the tale of Kevin's ace spirit medium, Cameo, in the second volume of George R.R. Martin's new Wild Cards trilogy, and "Tacos for Tezcatlipoca" in Esther Friesner's *Witch Way To The Mall*, a prequel to Bryce Pierponte's misadventures in "Frijoles for Fenris" in this volume.

Frijoles for Fenris

Kevin Andrew Murphy

"So what are you going to be for Halloween?"

That question took on a whole new meaning when you were a magician. Bryce knew how to turn himself into a jaguar, and could cast glamours for a dozen different guises, but dressing up in a costume? It seemed almost . . . quaint. "Uh, I don't know. A wicked magician maybe?"

"Wicked? Ooh, you mean like Crowley!" Stewie immediately started headbanging and air guitar, followed by reaching for an actual Stratocaster and, thankfully, a pair of headphones. *"Mister Crowley!"* he began wailing while bouncing up and down on his bed.

Bryce had not known what to expect when paired with his first college roommate, but one thing he had not expected was a music student and vintage metalhead. Stewie's side of the room was plastered with Iron Maiden and Metallica posters, which was fortunate because the few bits of discreet antique occult paraphernalia on Bryce's side of the room looked positively mundane in comparison. Stewie was also easy to distract, without even resorting to glamours.

He continued to headbang and wail. *"Mistaaah Crow-leeeeeyyyy!!!"*

"A bit of a prat," remarked a voice that jingled like an overwound music box.

Bryce raised an eyebrow and glanced under his bed.

A flash of teeth grinned back, a triple-toothed grin like a shark lurking in the shallows. This was not that surprising since Bryce's familiar, Matabor, was a genuine manticore cub—a manticore being a shark-toothed cross between a bat, a cat, a monkey and a giant scorpion. Since none of these were allowed as pets in the dorms (even if there wasn't a specific prohibition for bats) even beglamouring Matabor as one of the four wasn't going to cut it. Thankfully, Bryce had finally figured out how to weave a cloak of invisibility, or more accurately, the Shroud of Death.

The magical theory was simple: Mortals did not like to look at their own demise, and draped with a necromantic cobweb, Matabor became the *bête noire* people instinctively glanced away from and denied the existence of, a literal monster under Bryce's bed.

The practice was a little more difficult: Bryce had to contemplate his fears for his own mortality and spin them into tangible form. In an unhallowed graveyard. At midnight. During the dark of the moon. However, given that he had spent the past couple months passing himself off as a far older and more competent necromancer to a cabal of ancient magi who met in the back room of his hometown Denny's on alternate Fridays, skipping a meeting to sit on a tombstone and do macrame with his phobias was positively relaxing in comparison.

It was even more of a relief when he had left for college, leaving his new friends—meaning, for the most part, deadly rivals and backstabbing eldritch associates —behind. They had even given him going-away presents: a monkey's paw, a bottle imp, and a bag of magic beans.

Bryce knew better than to uncork the bottle or even touch the paw, and had locked them both in the bottom drawer of his desk. As for the *frijoles encantados*, until he ran into a dumb kid looking to unload a cow, he went for the hide-as-pretentiously-"magikal"-decorator-item approach: sitting on his bookshelf next to a Harry Potter action figure, glamoured up to look like a bag of Bertie Bott's Every Flavor Warner Brothers Feature Film Merchandising Tie-In Candy.

They were pretty odd as beans went even under the glamour. More like some sort of winged seed with the wings broken off, at least according to one of the botany professors after Bryce showed her a sketch. Maybe some species of giant ash? Bryce had been encouraged to bring in a specimen to put under the microscope (a bad idea) or to just plant one and see what grew (a worse one). But since his usual sources of arcane knowledge hadn't turned up anything more relevant than his high school production of *Into the Woods*, he was ready to try Wikipedia.

He flipped his laptop's window away from his exceedingly awkward and dangerous Freshman Composition essay topic (*What was the most interesting thing that happened to you this summer before college? {You know, apart from that time you used a fairy charm to wish for free ice cream for everyone, not expecting a gremlin monkey-wrench gang and an exploding ice cream truck?}*) and did a little web surfing. It turned out that ash nuts were also known as ash keys and had long associations with magic. While as for magic ash trees, the most famous would be the Norse world tree, Yggdrasil, whose roots extended into the misty Underworld of Niflheim, the realms of the gods and/or men (poets contradicted each other's mythological botanical geography), and finally Jotunheim, the literal home of the giants.

Bryce raised an eyebrow. A beanstalk, a world tree . . .

He glanced over at the bag of beans. They were no longer on the shelf.

"Damn," said Stewie, "these things are stale. They're still all sorts of different colors, but they all taste like the earwax flavor now."

"Those are mine!"

"Dude, I just ate a few. Don't have a cow."

Bryce retrieved the bag. "Leave my stuff alone, Jack."

"My name's Stewie."

Bryce shrugged. The usual was selling them to a dumb kid for a cow. The stories never mentioned having them sampled by your idiot college roommate.

Bryce grabbed his backpack and pulled out his formulary. He rechecked Master Seidel's notes on the Wicked Magicians Society and the amusing pastime of selling rubes cursed artifacts or alchemical formulae with insufficient product testing—Why drink a strange brew yourself when you can get some patsy to swig it for you?—but while there was a brief mention of magic beans, the general concept was that they were very old, fairly rare, and hijinks ensued when someone's mother tossed them out a window. No mention of what to expect when taken orally.

Bryce looked at the bag and the gaudy Bertie Bott's glamour. He should have just put them in a prescription bottle and labeled them SUPPOSITORIES.

Stewie, however, remained apparently unaffected. He went back to his guitar practice—this time with the headphones off and the amp on—bouncing around and occasionally waving the cornu, the apotropaic hand gesture appropriated by metalheads ages ago, making a Malmsteen concert probably the worst place to attempt the evil eye. But since he did not begin sprouting beanstalks from any orifice or turn into the Jolly Green Giant, eventually Bryce just went back to his essay, serenaded with Dio, Dokken, Mötley Crüe, and a smörgåsbord of Swedish death metal.

Then the music stopped. Bryce turned. Stewie still looked normal (relative to Stewie) but his logorrhea of mangled metal lyrics had slipped into spoken-word monologue. And while not quite "Fee Fi Fo Fum!" it was still pretty damned odd: "—made of what? Fish breath, bear nerves, bird spit, mountain goats, chicks' beards and the sound of little cat feet? That's freakin' weird."

Stewie stood staring at the wall, and Bryce looked: a concert poster for some Viking metal band called FENRIS, complete with a snarling wolf with a sword clenched in its teeth.

"Oh, mountain *roots*. That's even freakier. Mountains don't have roots. But I guess that's the point, huh?" Bryce had been on vision quests himself, but had never been around anyone else when they did. Or, for that matter, been around anyone stoned out of their skull, since knowing some of the wicked magicians, it was entirely possible the bag had been filled with "magic beans" in the Haight-Ashbury sense and Stewie was just trippin'. "Can't do anything about the chicks' beards, but the sound of cat feet? Oh yeah. I can cut that cord with my axe!"

Stewie did not have an axe in the literal sense, but in the figurative sense, certainly, and he picked it up and played a guitar lick that made the hair raise on the back of Bryce's neck. "Thing about sounds . . ." Stewie riffed. "Every sound has its opposite. Even cat feet. Play the opposite note, they both disappear. It's matter and anti-matter." Stewie played another lick. "All we need to do is find the right one." Stewie's fingers danced up and down the frets. "Play the one that makes it hum . . ." The opening chords of "Smoke on the Water" segued into a medley of "Cat Scratch Fever" and "Hell's Bells." "Play the lick that makes it howl . . ."

Bryce had read about musicians and their magical mystery tours. About Paganini and the Devil's fiddle. Orpheus in the Underworld. Tenacious D's *Tribute*, which was probably something Jack Black pulled out of his ass, but given what Bryce knew about magic now, made as much sense as anything, and could be explained by magical suppositories.

Stewie was playing a command performance for Fenris Wulf himself. Fenris, son of Loki, doom of Odin, the wolf whose release would kick off the Twilight of the Gods. But while the sound that came from Stewie's guitar didn't quite shake the nonexistent roots of the world's mountains, or cause fish to stop breathing, or make bearded ladies opt for electrolysis, it made Bryce's fingers and toes tingle in a way they didn't do except when he was turning into a jaguar. . . .

Stewie played and played until he sustained one last high wailing note, an electric howl everything the opposite of cat feet, until at last the string broke, the note fell silent, and Bryce's roommate fell back onto his bed. And something great and metaphysical and cosmic shifted.

Matabor came out from under Bryce's bed on not-quite-silent cat feet. "That made my paws itch," the maticore cub remarked, "but an impressive bit of magic all the same."

"Stewie's a magician?"

Matabor's round monkey eyes looked askance. "He's a musician."

Bryce nodded. There were separate metaphysical rules for idiots, madmen, children, and the musically inclined, and Stewie qualified as at least one. "What did he just do?"

Matabor switched his poisonous tail and surveyed Stewie's metaphorical axe, the broken string dangling portentously. "Sympathetic magic," Matabor pronounced. "The dwarves braided the ribbon Gleipnir out of six strands to chain the Great Wolf in Niflheim until the time of Ragnarok. Your roommate just broke one."

The sound of cat feet. The other five impossible things before breakfast were still intact, so Viking Doomsday was still a ways away—unless of course some kid, fool, or enterprising nutjob had already brought Fenris an Epilady or a recipe for bird's nest soup. "What do we do?"

"'We' do nothing." Matabor switched his tail. "Of course, were he *my* master, I'd advise him to ask Fenris for a boon. But he's not, so I shan't."

Bryce, however, was Stewie's roommate, and responsible for his current predicament, and could take a hint. Plus finding gods in a good mood was a rare occurrence, especially ones chained in the Underworld. Bryce leaned over Stewie. "Ask for a boon."

"A bun?" Stewie said in his sleep. "Sorry, Mr. Wolf. Cell phone. My roommate. Lemme get rid of him."

Stewie put a hand near his ear. "Hey, Bryce, buddy, kinda busy. Call you back?"

"Just ask the wolf for a favor. Anything."

"Oh, okay, natch." Stewie turned his head. "Yeah? Nah, he's not a dwarf. Sort of average. Said I should ask you for something, but you're still kind of tied up. But hey, if you can do it with that sword in your mouth, maybe there's something you can help me with. My concert scream's pretty wimpy, but I bet you could really show me how to howl. . . ."

There was a long silence, then Stewie bolted up, cocking his head like the Victrola dog, eyes closed, listening. At last he nodded. "Yeah . . . Yeah . . . I think I got it. Like this?"

He opened his mouth then, a note emerging, pure and echoing and growing louder, a primeval howl, becoming more perfect, more wolflike every second. Stewie's mouth did the same, his jaws and nose elongating into a snout, his ears rising to a pair of points, his hands knuckling up into a pair of clawed paws. Fur sprouted everywhere, shaggy and grey, and Stewie's clothes began to rip because they were now worn by a wolf. A big, bad, wolf.

The wolf looked at Bryce, and Bryce got the sense that while Stewie was still entranced by having eaten the seeds of Yggdrasil, his spirit was no longer viewing the Norse Underworld and was, in fact, looking at Bryce in the mundane present of a college dorm room. Or at least as mundane as it could be with a werewolf and an occasional wicked magician.

It was instinct, a spell Bryce had done a dozen times and was now like muscle-memory, and the werewolf was looking at a werejaguar. Then another twitch of another spell and the werewolf was looking at another werewolf.

Actually at a werejaguar beglamoured as a werewolf, but everyone's paws were making sound at the moment, so who was going to tell?

The werewolf cocked his head. *Bryce?*

Animal languages were something you had to work at as a shapeshifter, and so far Bryce had only really mastered cat. He tried to wag his tail rather than swish it. *Um, uh, yeah . . .*

Stewie ruffed and yipped. *Kewl! Let's go out and partayyyy!!!* The last ended in a bone-chilling howl, an echo of Fenris, and Bryce tried to look sheepish, or at least embarrassed-wolfish, rather than look like a werejaguar who knew his caterwaul would give up the jig.

Thankfully, even as a werewolf, Stewie was easy to fool. And he was too eager to jump out the window, despite the fact that their dorm room was on the third floor.

The huge wolf sprang to the ground, bounding off with hardly a glance behind. The jaguar leapt to follow, but cat pads were definitely making a sound and they smarted as Bryce tumbled across the lawn and rolled and then took off after Stewie, a werewolf in a Mötorhead T-shirt loping across campus. Like that wasn't going to attract attention.

Of course, it was a week before Halloween. And Stewie was headed for Greek Row.

A number of the frats and sororities were having parties early, and Bryce realized that Stewie had become a wolf in more than one sense of the word as he shifted upright and put one hand on a tree, blocking the path of a slutty barmaid, risque princess, and Little Red Riding Hood in bustier and fishnets. "Why hello, ladies. Where are you going this fine evening?"

The princess screamed, and Red Riding Hood jumped back, but the barmaid stepped forward. "Wow, that's an amazing costume. . . . Where did you get it?"

"Fenris."

"Is he that Icelandic guy in the theatre department?"

Stewie the werewolf shrugged. "Nah, I don't think so." He ogled the barmaid's assets, and she jiggled, flaunting her resemblance to the St. Pauli girl. "You look good enough to eat. . . ."

Bryce shifted upright behind the tree, coming over by Stewie and dropping his glamour entirely. He considered throwing another glamour to give Stewie back his human Seeming, but it would be hard without any props and ruined if Stewie shifted back to four legs.

Not that this was needed. The barmaid giggled coquettishly, Stewie slavered, and the princess and Candy Apple Red Riding Hood stepped closer to the jaws of death, or at least Stewie. Bryce wondered whether, if Stewie did eat any of them, it would be in horror movie or fairytale fashion, slow with carnage or all in one bite. He didn't really want to find out which.

A frat boy in traditional toga wandered up. "Hey, bro, can I have a word with you?"

"Oh, hey Marc," said the princess.

Marc Antony ignored her, and in fact everyone but Stewie. He locked eyes with the werewolf and his lip curled up in a snarl. *Bro, seriously, ixnay on the olfway . . .*

That was not quite the meaning, and the toga-clad frat boy was speaking Canid, not Pig Latin, but Bryce's only fluency was in Felid and he still got the gist.

Stewie cocked his head. *Huh?*

"Uh, Stewie," Bryce said. "Listen to the guy."

The frat shot Bryce a glance. *Brother wolf?*

Bryce didn't know how to wag his tail when he didn't have one so just nodded.

The frat made a low anxious puppy growl sound. *Is this his first full moon?*

Bryce nodded, and the frat boy took the initiative, grabbing Stewie by one extremely hairy clawed arm. "Bro, come back to the house. We've got a party."

Stewie whined. *But these bitches are hot!*

Bryce got Stewie's other arm. "Don't worry. We'll have fun."

It turned out that what modern werewolves did for the hunger of the full moon was have an all-you-can-eat-ribs night, including the actual ribs. It also turned out that Bryce had been a bit provincial in his thinking and had never considered that, instead of the local chapter of the Wicked Magicians Society, or some other witches' coven, conjurers circle, or thaumaturgists' kaffeeklatsch, the first supernatural organization he would encounter at college would be a fraternity of werewolves. Or that said fraternity would be pressing him and Stewie for membership.

Actually, Stewie was off the hook for the moment, having eaten his body weight in pork ribs and keg stands of beer, including a few slabs of baby backs all in one bite (partially answering Bryce's question of whether Stewie could swallow Little Red Riding Hood whole, fishnets and all) and was now sleeping it off on the couch. Bryce, on the other paw, was sober.

"Great Romulus and Remus!" swore Marc, the frat they'd met outside and chief recruiting officer for Gamma Rho Rho. "We shouldn't have any lone wolves! We are a brotherhood!"

Bryce held his tongue, not mentioning that he was pretty sure Romulus *slew* Remus, but then again, it was probably one of those unpleasant family scandals nobody talked about.

A particularly big werewolf loomed over Bryce and sniffed. "You smell like cat."

"Cat, it's what's for breakfast," said a skinny blond werewolf across the room.

"Meeeowww," said another werewolf mockingly. Bryce covered a laugh with a swig of beer. Given the intonation, that particular "meow" meant *I'm a fertile queen and want to have your kittens, you tomcat stud, you.*

"So," said the huge werewolf, "are you from another chapter or are you legacy members?"

Bryce could speak wolf-speak better than he could understand this. He cocked his head. *Come again?*

"He means," Marc translated, "were you bitten, or is lycanthropy something that runs in your family?"

Bryce considered the honest answer: neither. He was a magician who knew how to turn himself into a jaguar and how to throw a wolf glamour, and his roommate had tripped out on some seeds from Yggdrasil and been granted a boon by Fenris Wulf himself.

Neither story sounded like it would go over particularly well. Stewie they might actually be impressed with, but a jaguar priest of Tezcatlipoca? Not so much.

"Do I have to say?"

"It's nothing to be ashamed of," said a werewolf in a pink polo shirt with a popped collar. "Either is fine. Take pride in what you are!"

"Except being legacy is a lot cooler," said the blond werewolf.

"Shut up, Frank," snapped the one with the pink collar.

Frank snarled. "No, you shut up, Pinky. Listen. I've been changing since I was eight. They were bitten. I can tell from their accents. This guy's probably been shifting less than six months and he probably bit his roommate first week of school. And he reeks of some weird aftershave, which has to be why nobody sniffed him out and he smells like a cat."

Marc looked at him and sniffed. "What is that anyway?"

"Um, the Lesser Bath of Hebe." Bryce glanced around. "I think it contains civet musk." Actually, Bryce knew for certain that it contained civet since he'd compounded it himself.

"Why do you wear it?"

"It keeps me from getting zits." That, and other side benefits of a perpetual youth spell.

"We'll call you Kitty," said the huge werewolf, swatting Bryce on the back with a giant paw. "Call me Brutus. I head this chapter." There was a brief stare-down between him and Marc, but Marc looked away. "Good job, by the way, Marcus, finding these two," Brutus added softly.

"Thank you, sir," Marc mumbled, then glanced to Bryce. "Help you move in tomorrow?"

It wasn't exactly a request. "Uh, yeah, sure . . ."

Bryce considered his options. It turned out it was much easier to be a wicked magician than a good one. Wicked was just a matter of smiling and saying that you meant to do that whenever a spell went south. Or at least flying off in your chariot borne by griffins and letting someone else deal with the mess.

Good? That was about taking responsibility for your actions. Or at least trying to turn lemons into lemonade.

Not that Stewie being a Fenris-blessed werewolf was exactly a lemon, or that the bros at Gamma Rho Rho weren't a good support group, but Bryce had gotten him into the world of the supernatural, and he'd be a jerk to just ditch him. And there was a side benefit in that probably the best place to hide out from the local chapter of the Wicked Magician Society was as part of the local werewolf fraternity—if the bros didn't figure things out and eat him first.

Bryce wasn't about to use the bottle imp or the monkey's paw, since the first cost a soul and the second a life. But the bag of beans? Oh yeah.

After all, the best way to impersonate a werewolf was to actually be one, and there were plenty of magicians who had learned more than one alternate shape. Not taking this opportunity was simple laziness. That, or common sense.

Stewie was more than a bit addled about how he became a werewolf, but he had the most impressive howl that any of the bros at Gamma Rho Rho had ever heard, and he could shapeshift with the best of them, so he went with the flow, telling Bryce about the whacky dream he had about climbing around the roots of a giant tree and playing his axe for a big wolf.

Bryce took notes, and shortly after that, three magic beans.

They did taste like earwax. Or at least extremely stale magic ash nuts.

"So what happens now?" he asked Matabor.

"Do you have your offering for the god?" his familiar asked.

Bryce nodded. He had found an authentic recipe for bird's nest soup and hit the Asian shop at the local strip mall to get everything but the extremely expensive nest, not that this was an issue—he intended to boil the swallow-spit goodness right out of Gleipnir. And if helping to make Ragnarok come one third faster did not help his Wicked Magician street cred, nothing would.

"What are you going to make it in?" Matabor asked pointedly.

Crap. Bryce grabbed the bag of Asian groceries and rushed down the stairs of the Gamma Rho Rho house, trying to find the kitchen, but the place was an absolute maze of fancy woodwork and paneling, and he finally found himself in the garden looking at a squirrel. "I don't suppose you know where I could borrow a knife and a bowl?"

The squirrel paused, nibbling a nut. *Knife? Bowl? Sure!* It flicked its tail. *Follow me!*

Bryce ran after it, wondering for a second how, since his Canid was sub-par, he was suddenly speaking Rodent so well, but pretty soon he realized his spirit journey had begun. And the moment after that, he tripped and fell sprawling, Asian groceries bowling across a black-and-white-tiled floor. A floor tiled with patches of black and white ice.

You must pardon my threshold, a voice echoed in his mind. *Men call it the Pit of Stumbling. I mean to have it repaired properly, but my thrall never gets around to it and my maidservant does a half-assed job of everything, so ah well. So hard to get good help these days.* A woman stepped forward, dressed a lot like Glenn Close as Cruella de Vil, except that in addition to having her hair black on one side and white on the other, her face was the same way too, but opposite. The squirrel was perched on her white right hand. *Ratatosk here tells me you wish to borrow both my knife and my bowl? What possible need would you have for such things?*

"Um . . ." Bryce had saved time and was already prostrated at her feet. "Lady Hel?"

The Ruler of Niflheim nodded in assent. *Welcome to Sleet-Cold. Don't lick the floor.*

"Thank you." Bryce got to his feet. "I, um, have a recipe for bird's nest soup." The rest of the story spilled out of him: the Wicked Magicians Guild, the bag of beans, Stewie playing for Fenris, the glamours, and the trouble of being a werejaguar in a frat house full of werewolves.

Hel clapped her black hand and her white hand together in delight. *An ignoble task! A suitably wicked deed! Oh, I will happily lend my knife and bowl for such a feat. My brother's freedom depends upon it.* She looked serious then. *However, as much as it might aid my sibling and earn his gratitude and mine, I can not grant such a boon for free. A death goddess must keep up appearances. For everything you take from Hel, you must give something in return.* Her black-and-white visage turned to Matabor who had arrived sometime in the middle of Bryce's recitation and taken the form of a full-grown manticore. The Shroud of Death was perched atop his head, more a veil or kerchief than anything. *That is a pretty bit of weaving. May I see it?*

You did not say no to a goddess. Unless, of course, you were a familiar waiting for a cue from his master. But Bryce nodded, and Matabor bowed down before Hel, letting her take the web Bryce had knotted from his own fears.

Hel inspected it and smiled. *How charming. Fear of Mortality, yes?*

Bryce nodded, his heart pounding in his chest.

She gestured to a wall of glacial ice, beyond which Bryce could discern a dark shape. *My bed is Sickness. My bedcurtains I wove from Misery—Splendid Misery.* She weighed Bryce's Fear of Mortality in her black and white hands. *I could use this for a pillowcase.*

Bryce nodded again. "Yes, Lady Hel."

It is a bargain then. She smiled. *In return, I give you the loan of my knife and my bowl.*

They appeared, the bowl white as bone, the knife black as sin, on a table likely made of something improbable and awful with a dire name, and Bryce assumed the knife and bowl had names too, but he couldn't recall at the moment what they were. A moment later, he had both in his hands, along with a bag of frozen Asian groceries the squirrel had retrieved.

Lady Hel escorted Bryce and Matabor from her hall. They passed through the frozen mist, past a huge chained dog with a bloody neck and chest. *This is Garmr, my hound,* said the Mistress of Niflheim, obviously enjoying giving the grand tour of Her domain. She stroked the dog's ears with her black hand. *Garmr, my pet, tell my brother of our visit. . . .*

The dog began an eerie howl that echoed through the mist, and a moment later, another echoed in return, the howl of Fenris Wulf, the one he had taught Stewie.

Then came the vision quest as Iron Chef, with Bryce taking what little bit of slack Stewie's guitar solo had given the ribbon Gleipnir, soaking it in Hel's bowl, scraping it with Her knife, then moving it around until everything was drenched in chicken broth. But in the end, the ribbon was looser, Hel's bowl was filled with extremely expensive dwarf-forged Chinese soup, and Fenris Wulf howled in triumph. Bryce joined in, feeling himself shifting, learning the magic and form of the wolf while Hel retrieved Her knife and Her bowl.

She lifted them both aloft, bowl in her left hand, blade in her right. *I propose a toast to my brother's incipient freedom and the glorious death that awaits! Skål!*

It was a general rule of vision quests that when a god offered you a bowl of something to drink, you drank. And after Hel took Her share, She placed the dire dish on the ground between Bryce and Fenris Wulf, the upper half of a giant's skull, and they both began to lap it dry.

Somewhere along the line the apocalyptic bird's nest soup began to taste like cheap beer and instead of Hel's mental voice, Bryce heard Brutus: "Damn, Kitty, you can sure put it away. That's the third keg. You're the beer luge champion, but I'm cutting you off."

Bryce's stomach still felt like an empty pit. A wolfishly empty pit. And he was crouched on the floor in front of a cross between a beer bong and an ice swan, beer soaking into his fur.

He sighed then panted. The operation had been a success. He was now a werewolf as well as a werejaguar, and all it had cost was hastening Ragnarok another sixth. And his fears for his mortality. But having surrendered them, he wasn't worrying and fell blissfully asleep.

He awoke on a frozen black-and-white-tiled floor and looked up to see Hel polishing her cutlery. *Welcome back to Niflheim, boon-friend. I am pleased to see you again. Pleased, but not surprised.* She smiled a disturbing smile. *My bowl is Hunger. My blade is Starvation. And you are now one of my Helleder, my favored draugs.*

"I'm dead?"

Or undead. Whichever you fancy. She continued to smile. *The thread of your life is caught in my threshold, neither of Midgard nor of Niflheim. Yet the doors of Sleet-Cold are open to you whenever you choose, whichever way. Come freely, go safely, and leave some of the happiness you bring.* She chuckled. *You drank yourself until you came back to my hall. It's only fitting that I let you return to Midgard to drink others dry as well. And after all, you are favored by my brother.*

Bryce remembered something else he'd read in Master Seidel's formulary, under the section on Immortality: One of the ways to become a vampire was to be a dead werewolf.

He awoke back on the floor of the Gamma Rho Rho frat house, in a puddle of beer and ice, finding himself shifted back to human shape, but still sporting a pair of canines that would do any werewolf proud.

Or any vampire.

Bryce sighed. Curiouser and curiouser. Just when he thought his life, or unlife, couldn't get more complicated. He wondered if there were any vampire fraternities.

But at least this answered the question of what he was going to be for Halloween.

Sarah A. Hoyt has published over a hundred stories in magazines such as *Analog*, *Asimov's Science Fiction* and *Amazing Stories*, as well as a broad range of anthologies. Her latest novels are *Gentleman Takes A Chance*, in her Baen Urban Fantasy Series, *Heart and Soul* in her Bantam historical fantasy series and (as Sarah D'Almeida) *Dying by the Sword* in her Prime Crime Mystery series. Look for upcoming mystery *Dipped, Stripped, Dead* and science fiction *DarkShip Thieves*. Though she does get in a hairy mood, at times, when under deadline, Sarah Hoyt rejects all rumors that she might be a werewolf.

The Case of the
Driving Poodle

Sarah A. Hoyt

There are jobs you go out and look for. Jobs that come and find you. And jobs you find yourself in, without having the slightest idea how.

When I was twenty-two years old, I found myself—through no fault of my own—in one of these. As best I can explain it, sometime after my tenth application for a retail job had been rejected—as if a master's in classical history were not relevant for work in a shoe shop—I'd blindly sent out an application to work for a neighborhood firm: Nephilim Psychic Investigations. And against everyone's best judgement, the owner and sole proprietor had hired me.

He was an African-American man, of an age somewhere between thirty and fifty, fit without being particularly muscular and good-looking in an understated way, despite receding hair and the look of having been born to be dark-skinned and going about with a permanent pallor. Despite rejoicing in the name of Nephilim Kentucky Jones III—a name that *had* to be an indication of hereditary madness—he went by Ken Jones, which probably meant he had some grounding in reality.

Maybe. Having gone with him through cases that had ranged from a possessed grill which he had exorcized by reading it a selection of Romantic poetry to a case last week, in which he had repaired a witch's flying broom by dipping it in hot sauce, I will confess that I had to doubt his sanity. And yet his solutions seemed to work, so perhaps I should doubt the sanity of reality.

All the more so since Ken, who'd just picked me up in his tenth-hand Volvo with the hand-lettered "Nephilim Psychic Investigations" painted on the side, was looking cagey and had yet to tell me what exactly we were about to do, even as he took a route towards the suburbs. Howl Acres, to be exact, the newest and most ritzy subdivision inflicted on our fair city.

"Oh no," I said, when it became obvious where we were headed.

He gave me a look that might have been sympathy, but there was way too much calculation behind his gaze, as if he were doing some complex arithmetic behind his eyes. I remembered that our first investigation together—the possessed grill—had been in the suburbs and how much I'd hated it. And how much he probably knew I hated it. I thought I knew what was bothering him. He was afraid I'd throw a fit.

"It's okay," I said, as we drove through the summer evening, the Volvo merrily squeaking and backfiring into the serenity of manicured lawns, immaculate houses painted in earth tones, and families gathered on front lawns. "I think I can survive the suburbs for one more case."

He looked at me, an expression between surprise and a frown. "It's not that," he said. "It's . . . Look . . . " He pulled to the side of the road, in front of a house whose lawn was, mercifully, deserted, and took a deep breath, as though gathering his courage. "It's like this. We're about to go investigate a missing person's case."

"Missing persons?" I said. "But I thought we only did paranormal—"

He nodded, once. "This guy, Brent Barker, has been missing for three weeks," he said. "Wife and two small children. And his wife called me."

"Shouldn't she have called the police?" I asked.

He chewed on his lip.

I'd known Ken for almost a month now, and I'd seen him in all kinds of situations. I'd never seen him look like this. He appeared to be embarrassed and confused in equal measures. Or perhaps up to some complex calculation, as if there were a quadratic equation that absolutely needed to be resolved right now, in his head. But though I had been sort of an inverse wonder at advanced magic, I refused to believe that quadratic equations were paranormal.

"What?" I said. "Why didn't this woman call the police? Or did she? And are you sure that she has the slightest idea what we are or what we investigate? Or did she just look in the yellow pages under PI and got us?"

Ken put the car in park and pulled the parking break. He let out a breath with an explosive sound. "She didn't call the police because her husband is a well-known artist—at least a well-known local artist. He made that sculpture that's in the middle of the plaza at the end of Pythagoras Avenue."

Having seen the sculpture—which looked like an assemblage of bicycle parts rescued from a junkyard and soldered together willy-nilly—I understood that it might be important to the wife of the perpetrator to keep quiet about where he might be. Frankly, I was just surprised that he hadn't gone into the witness protection program.

Ken rubbed his nose. "The thing is . . . " he said. "That she called me, because she found my business card in her husband's wallet."

"Oh," I said. And then, as the salient fact hit me, "He disappeared without his wallet?"

Ken shrugged, which was hardly an answer, and I started wondering if our prospective client had, by any chance, killed her husband and buried him in the backyard. In which case, of course, it might be perfectly justified to call Nephilim Investigations. Anyone reading that name would think that of all the detectives in town—heck, in all possible towns—we were the most likely to miss the freshly dug grave in the backyard with the rose bush hastily planted in the center of it—even if it had a nice grave marker in front of it. At least, I'm sure that's what a stranger would think. I wasn't sure that was true.

"Yeah," Ken said and rubbed his nose again, managing to give off an impression of strong embarrassment. "That was part of what worried her. But . . . well, what you need to know is that her husband and I met in a support group."

"A support group?" I said. "Like . . . AA?"

"Yeah," he said, and looked away from me, managing to look about as transparent and truthful as a politician during campaign season. "Something like that."

So, something like that, but not AA.

Ken had told me that he used to be a computer programmer and had lost his job in the tech crash, but he'd never adequately explained why he'd chosen to leave the field behind entirely and to turn, instead, to psychic investigations. Of course, it was possible—probable—in fact that there was no adequate explanation for such a decision.

Or it was possible that Ken had some other problem that contributed to his inability to work a normal job—perhaps drugs, glue sniffing or . . . for all I knew, and considering what I'd seen in the last few weeks, perhaps black magic. Did Ken join a support group to break himself from a pesky tendency to perform human sacrifice? Or was his vice, perhaps, dancing naked in the moonlight?

I felt my cheeks heat at the thought of Ken naked anywhere—something to which, to be honest, I hadn't given much thought, despite having grown to like him very much.

In his turn, he gave me a startled look, his eyes widening in a way that made him seem like a cartoon. "What is it?" he said. "Do I have a blob of sunblock on my nose?"

"Sunblock?" I said.

"Yeah, I put some on just before we left. This summer sun is a killer."

I squinted at the faint sunset, quite unable to see it as a killer of any sort. Though the day had been warm, I doubted it had topped eighty. In fact, so far from looking homicidal, the sunshine didn't even look capable of menacing. And Ken—I ran an eye over his long-sleeved T-shirt and serviceable jeans—while not bad looking had never exactly impressed me as the sort to wear any sort of skin products, sunblock included.

Right. He and this woman's husband had probably met in a group for secret sunblock abusers.

I looked away, mumbling something noncommittal —because I would rather eat live, slimy toads than tell him that I'd been imagining him cavorting around naked. And screamed, trying to jump back as far as I could—which in fact meant I more or less ended up in Ken's lap.

At my window, bending low to look through it, and knocking on the glass right next to where my face had been was a slim blond woman of maybe thirty years of age.

Ken tried to push me off his lap without touching me, something that required more paranormal powers than even he possessed and that, in fact, involved his shrinking back against his car door like a Victorian maiden in distress.

My confused brain registered that he smelled like coconut sunblock even as he said, "Er . . . that is our client, I think."

"Oh," I said, and realizing that really, even in as small and odd a company as ours, it was very unusual to meet a client while sitting in your boss's lap, I threw myself in the general direction of the passenger seat. At the same time, Ken succeeded in opening his door and getting out.

Fortunately this led our client towards him, and left me able to open my door and compose myself, so that I looked—I thought—pretty normal by the time I walked around the car to stand beside Ken. Ken jumped a bit to the side, as if afraid I'd tackle him and sit on his lap by force. I wanted to reassure him that I very rarely did that to my acquaintances, much less to men I worked for, but he didn't give me time. He gestured towards me. "This is my assistant," he said. "Agnes Damon."

The woman nodded vaguely towards me, but it was clear that I was, at best, a distraction. She returned her gaze to Ken and said, in the tone of a woman interrupted in the middle of a heart-wrenching account, "And that's why I called you."

Now that I had time to look at her, without her face being pressed close to my window like a peering slasher in a horror movie, I thought she might be younger than thirty, but she looked stressed. Strained. Her oval face showed marks of sleeplessness in creases around the eyes and mouth, and her eyes were underlined by bruised half-moons.

"You say," Ken said, reaching in his back pocket and retrieving his small notebook and the pen he always kept there, "that your husband always disappears for about a week a month?"

She shook her head, then shrugged. "Not disappears, as such." She made a small, helpless gesture with her hands. "You see, he is an artist. He creates such lovely things, in metal and stone and—"

They both paused to look at me and I realized I'd snorted. Okay, fine. So I have opinions about art. At least, I'm quite willing to admit there is a lot about art I don't get. Like *Who invented this racket? And how come no one is giving me large amounts of cash for piles of rusting bicycle parts?* But this was neither the time nor the place. I cleared my throat. "Sorry, sinus."

Mrs. Barker nodded, because, after all, I was just decoration here, and Ken was the one she was talking to. She had started wringing her hands together again, one over the other. "I mean, the creative effort really takes it out of him, and with us having two small children, you know, sometimes he needs to isolate himself to think and . . . and to *create*."

I could hear the italics, clear as a bell in her voice, but I managed not to roll my eyes, which was good because Ken was writing rapidly in his little notebook. It looked like he'd just written *create*, underlining and all. "And when he does this creation," he said. "Where does he go? Or does he just travel around?"

"We have a cabin," she said. "Over in Walnut Grove."

Walnut Grove was not exactly a forest. It was in fact another suburb, just to the east of town, where the houses came with a minimum of two acres apiece.

"Is he perhaps there?" Ken asked. "Right now?"

She shook her head. "No, you see?" she said. "I've been there. That's where I found . . . " Her voice disappeared into a burbling of tears.

"You found?" Ken asked, his pencil poised over the page.

"His wallet and his *clothes,*" she said.

Oh, good, I thought. *It is definitely a support group for men who like to dance naked in the moonlight.*

Twenty minutes later, as we stopped in front of a small log cabin, at the end of a shaded lane, I asked Ken, "So, he was probably killed and is in a fresh grave somewhere under one of the trees here . . . " It had taken me a whole twenty minutes to stop myself from asking what exactly they danced to under the trees—waltz? Or was it a country dance? Swing your partner . . .

By the time we'd stopped at the cabin my tongue was raw from being bitten so hard.

Ken looked at me, and shook his head a little, then said, "It's possible, of course. A hunter, perhaps. But very few hunters have silver bullets these days. Particularly in the suburbs."

He got out of the car, and headed towards the house, forcing me to catch up with him. I managed to say, "Beg your pardon? Silver bullets?" just as he slipped the key into the door and opened it. "Do you know something I don't?"

"Obvious, isn't it?" he said, speaking as if from a great distance away. "I mean, she did say he disappeared a week a month, and when I pressed her for dates, it all became startlingly obvious."

"Not to me," I said, wondering if the man were in fact in the sort of league where he did quadratic equations in his head.

But he'd opened the door to the house and gone in. I don't know what I expected. Considering this was the creative hangout of an *artist*, I thought at the very least there would be a few paint pots strewn about, or perhaps a few rusted bicycle parts.

Instead, the house looked exactly like the type of place one expected Little Red Riding Hood to live in. It was very small, consisting of a great room with a huge fireplace and a couple of lived-in-looking sofas. At the far end there was a kitchenette and a sliding glass door looking out onto a large wooden deck and a profusion of trees.

Upstairs, and running about half the length of the great room, was a loft. A circular staircase led up to it, and I could see, through the railings at the top, a suggestion of a messed bed and a massive wardrobe.

Blinking, I realized the house smelled of dog, and that there were grey-brown hairs on one of the sofas and also that the back door had a large doggie door cut into it.

"He has a dog," I said.

"Possible," Ken said, sounding profound. "But it's far more likely to be a bitch."

"What?" I asked, sure that he must have seen something I'd missed, like perhaps a pink collar, or a food bowl marked "Trixiebelle."

I looked where I would expect the food bowls to be, in the kitchenette, and didn't see any. I traced my way back around the house, looking. Ken was kneeling down by the sofa and had extracted a magnifying glass, heaven knew from where, and was looking at the sofa.

I made sure my keen sense of observation wasn't missing anything, then came back to him. "Ken, there's no food bowl or doggie dish anywhere."

He looked up, as if he were trying to decide whether I was crazy or, perhaps, dangerously crazy. "I know," he said.

"But . . . " I said. "If he has a dog here . . . "

Of course, just as I said it, it occurred to me that perhaps the dog wasn't here all the time. After all, it must be pretty difficult to weld together rusting metal while keeping a dog out of trouble. "Oh, you mean the dog is with his wife?"

He opened his mouth, closed it, reached in between two sofa cushions and brought out a well-chewed rawhide bone, of the sort you buy in pet stores. He waved it up in front of my face. "Aha!" he said. And proceeded to sniff the doggie bone. I mean, really sniff it. As if . . . as if it were some spice whose fragrance he had to identify.

"Uh," I said. Apparently the recovery group was for men who danced naked in the moonlight and who liked to smell doggie saliva. Ooookay. All the reluctant respect I'd acquired for my boss over the last few weeks was fast vanishing, and I was starting to wonder whether I might not have dreamed up all the crazy stuff I'd seen while working for him. Perhaps it was some form of shared hallucination. Perhaps he was in fact so crazy that he managed to make me crazy on contact. Who had ever heard of a possessed grill? Let alone a broom that flew?

I took a step away from him. "I tell you what," I said. "I don't seem to be much use here. Perhaps I should go back to Howl Acres and find out if his wife knows about any activity in his account or . . ."

"To the car," he said, and sniffed as he went. I swear he did. Sniff, sniff, sniff, as if he were trying to trace the source of a burning smell. "It is exactly as I thought."

"Uh . . ." I said, wondering if doggie saliva had some hallucinogenic property. Ken's eyes looked to be the right size, and he wasn't foaming at the mouth or anything, but he still had that well-chewed bone in his hand and he looked, for all the world, as if he were hot on a . . . scent. "Maybe I should drive."

"Don't be ridiculous," he said, opening the door to the driver's side and climbing into the seat. "Get in. Come on. We don't have a minute to waste. You'd never be able to keep this car from stalling."

True as far as that went, I thought, being intimately acquainted with the Volvo's idiosyncrasies. I consoled myself with the thought that even if Ken drove erratically and even if he were stopped, police rarely did a breathalyzer test for dog spit.

I noted with alarm that he kept the doggie bone in his hand and that he sniffed it now and then and also that he kept his window rolled down and sniffed out the window, his nose twitching at the scent. Right. I slid down in my seat and closed my eyes. *There is no such thing as a drug made of canine saliva. There is no such things as a drug . . .*

The car wove sharply to the left and came to a stop, tires squealing. I opened my eyes, alarmed, to see Ken look at me and say, "Sorry," but he didn't look particularly sorry. What he did look, in fact, was all intent on sniffing the air.

Which was not nearly as disturbing as where we were stopped. I'd seen this place as we drove past it, on the way into Walnut Grove. It was one of those ramshackle buildings one sees sometimes, just outside towns. Made of unpainted wood, it could have been anything, from a club lodge to a diner. What it was, in fact, was advertised in a big sign by the roadside, which must glow neon at night, but which right now, in the fading glow of sunset, was just white with black plastic letters proclaiming WET DOG CAFÉ and underneath ALL NUDE DANCING.

I must have made a sound of distress—thinking I'd finally come to the source of Ken's secret life—because Ken looked at me, concerned. "I'm sorry," he said. "Sometimes, in the course of investigations, one has to go to less-than-savory places."

By that time, my keen sense of observation had helped me spot some posters by the entrance to the building and I'd realized that these showed definitely feminine bodies. So unless Ken had an entirely different form of secret life, this was *not* where he danced naked under the moonlight.

Which was just as well, as he was charging into it full throttle, and it was all I could do to catch up with him.

When I did, he was inside a dim little entrance area, which smelled, appropriately enough, like a wet dog. Facing him was a guy who would outweigh Ken at least three times—and that was just the weight of his hair. Not that he had long hair. Just a lot of it, on his head, face, arms, shoulders and legs. The T-shirt and shorts he was wearing seemed more like brief interruptions than like clothing, and looking at him one found the words *but rugs don't wear clothes* running through one's head.

Only, of course, rugs normally also didn't have eyes, and this man did. Little squinty black eyes that were giving Ken the glaring once-over, then turned to me, with just the same sort of unfriendly glare.

Now, I know I'm not a beauty queen, okay? But I'm also not the ugliest thing going. I have a face in the shape of face and what's more important, breasts in the shape of breasts. And very few men in our society look at a woman with that kind of glaring hostility.

"I don't know where you got that idea," he growled in Ken's direction. And in this case, it was definitely a growl, not a manner of expression. "I don't know any . . ."

Ken shook his head. "Brown-black. Possibly a wolf dog. I'm sure of it."

The man glared some more, a low throaty growl rising from between his lips, as his head kind of ducked into his neck, and I expected him to spring forward, growling. "You can't expect us to tell you that."

"Yes," he said. "Yes you can. Do you want me to lay the entire operation open?"

The man charged then. It was weird, because he jumped exactly like a dog would jump, white teeth snapping.

And Ken threw something over his head.

I saw it flash in the half-darkness, before realizing what it was—a necklace. Not a chain, just a necklace, about normal thickness for a necklace. Silver.

I expected the man to snap it with the force of his charge, but instead he jumped back, then slumped down, as if he'd lost all strength. Sweat sprang in his brow, so thick that it shone at the tip of his hair. He whined, a loud whine, and his hand went up, but it recoiled before touching the necklace. He slumped down, panting.

"Tell me," Ken said. "Who was it, and where is he?"

"It was consensual," he said. "He's been coming here forever. I mean, she is like . . . I mean . . ."

"I don't care," Ken said. "Tell me who she is and where she lives."

"T—Trixiebelle," the man said and stammered out an address a few blocks away.

I knew there was a Trixiebelle in the matter, but at this point I wasn't absolutely sure it was a dog.

"These things," Ken said. "Are always a matter of *cherchez la female*," he said.

"*Femme*, you mean," I said.

"Something like that."

We were back in the car, and driving fast amid the shaded lanes, stopping only now and then to look at street signs.

"So, he's with some woman?" I said, still confused.

He coughed. "You could say that." He had taken the silver necklace from around the manager's neck, and he looked ridiculously satisfied with himself. "If you had looked at the sofa with a magnifying glass, as I did, you'd have noticed some curly white hairs amid the others on the sofa."

"Oh?" I said, by now so confused that if he had announced to me this denoted the sofa's ability to fly I wouldn't have batted an eye.

He touched the side of his nose. "French poodle," he said. "You can tell by the smell."

From which I deduced that doggie spit had bouquets, but it left me still completely confused. "So, you followed the smell on the leather bone?" I said.

"Only till the café," he said, with a hand gesture in the general direction from which we'd come. "After that, she must have taken him in a car, you see, with the windows closed and the air on, so it was impossible to follow the scent."

"I see." In fact what I saw, clearly, in my mind's eye, was a French poodle driving a car, with a man hog-tied in the passenger seat. Possessed grills, flying brooms, living rugs and criminal poodles. I was going to need medication.

Ken pulled up in front of a house, still in Walnut Grove, but bigger than the one from which the artist was missing, with a large fenced yard.

He marched to the door and rang the doorbell. Waited a moment. Rang it again. Meanwhile my keen powers of observation told me that there was no car in the driveway.

"There is no one home," I told him. "No car. The French poodle must be out for a drive."

He nodded. "Yeah, I think so," he said.

He was going to need medication too, I thought, and wondered if they had some sort of company discount, or two for the price of one, particularly as, instead of returning to the car, Ken went galloping to the side of the house and around the fence, to where a sign read, BEWARE OF THE DOG!

"Ken!" I said.

He didn't answer. He was too busy applying shoulder to the gate, to break the lock. From inside a dog barked, whined and growled.

"I think the dog might be dangerous," I yelled just loud enough to be heard above the sound of the gate giving out. It fell in a cloud of dust and Ken charged over its ruins.

To face a huge dog.

Well, dog in a manner of speaking. The creature looked more like a wolf, but a wolf seen by the director of a horror movie. It was bigger than a malamute, with a huge muzzle and white, very sharp teeth.

However, it couldn't possibly be a wolf, because last I had checked, wolves did not have red, glowing eyes.

You'd think that Ken would be running back to the car, or perhaps—considering that this thing looked large enough to outrun the car, or perhaps to grab it by the back bumper and prevent it from moving—cowering behind the fence. Or at the very least pulling out the doggie bone and offering it as appeasement.

But no. In proof of the fact that he needed medications way more than I did, he was in fact crossing his arms on his chest, tapping his foot and glaring at the dog as if the dog were his puppy and Ken had just found a suspicious wet spot in the brand new rug. "I thought you knew better than that, Brent. Have you no shame?" he said.

I don't know what the wolf answered due to the fact that I don't, in fact, speak wolf. It was a low growl, deep in the massive throat over which the hairs rose, in canine fury. Its eyes looked bigger and glowed even redder, and as its looked at Ken, saliva dripped from its jaws. I knew, without being told, that he was seeing Ken as a very large chew toy.

I also knew—suddenly—what this was all about. After all, Ken had called the man by the missing artist's name. Which meant . . . that Brent Barker was in fact this huge, growling wolf. Which meant that the wet dog was . . .

The wolf's muscles bunched, as it prepared to spring. I reached into Ken's pocket, where I'd seen him put the necklace he'd used on the owner of the café.

As the werewolf sprang, I threw the necklace, just right. It went over the wolf's head and around his neck.

A naked, middle-aged man rolled to the ground, whining.

"But I don't understand," I said. "Why didn't he go back to his wife right away? I guessed that he was used to going to that house for a week a month, when the moon was full."

"Probably," Ken said.

We'd driven Brent Barker back to his cottage and he'd gotten decent before driving him back to his marital abode. There, Ken had told Mrs. Barker that Brent had been kidnapped. He'd also recommended that Brent tell his wife about the affair he'd had with Trixiebelle, the dancer in the Wet Dog Café.

"Then how come this time he didn't come back?"

Ken looked pained, as if I were forcing him to go into distasteful subjects, which I realized I, in fact, was, as he said, "Trixiebelle was in heat."

"Oh," I said, not getting it at all. "The poodle."

He looked at me as if I'd lost my mind. "The were poodle," he said. "When a were female is in heat she gives off a kind of pheromone that will keep a were male in canine form and . . . well . . . helpless. Brent couldn't leave her if he wanted to."

"Did he?" I asked.

Ken shrugged. "He seemed willing enough to go back to his wife," he said.

"But not to tell her the truth," I said.

"Well . . . " he said. "Would you believe it, if you hadn't seen it?"

Hell, I hardly believed having seen it, and I was seriously considering getting medications, just in case.

"So," I said, following my own line of reasoning and remembering that Ken was in a support group with Brent. "Does this mean you too are a werewolf?"

He looked at me so suddenly that he almost drove off the road. His expression was of pure surprise and I didn't think it was because I'd figured out his secret. "Wha—?" He asked. "No!"

"A were poodle?" I asked.

He made a sound that wasn't a growl, but might have been laughter. "No were anything."

"So this group you're in with Brent Barker . . . "

He shook his head. "Eating disorder," he said.

"Oh." Well, he didn't look either too thin or too fat, so the group must work. "Sorry."

"No problem," he said.

"But if his wife doesn't know what he is," I said, changing the subject quickly. "How is she going to prevent Brent from straying?"

Ken inclined his head and smiled a little. "Well, his wife knew that she had called psychic investigations, see . . . So I privately told her that her husband had been under a spell cast by this woman."

"And?" I said.

"And that from now on when he's out of her sight, she should make sure he wears that silver necklace, which has special powers to repeal spells."

"But that means he won't be able to change, doesn't it?" I thought, thinking of all the hair on that sofa and the chewed rawhide bone, speaking of happy doggy days. "He's not going to be happy."

Ken shrugged. "He brought it on himself. He had no business getting involved with Trixiebelle to begin with. If they didn't already have a relationship, she wouldn't have had that kind of power over him when she went into heat." He grinned at me, a happy grin. "My guess is that from now on his wife will keep him on a short leash."

Robin Wayne Bailey is the Nebula Award-nominated author of numerous novels, including the *Dragonkin* series, the *Brothers of the Dragon* trilogy, and the Frost saga, among others. His science fiction stories were recently collected in *Turn Left to Tomorrow*, and his work has appeared in many anthologies and magazines. He lives in Kansas City, Missouri. Visit him at his website: *http://www.robinwaynebailey.net*

Meet the Harrys

Robin Wayne Bailey

Mary Harry moved quickly to take up her daily post at the front door. In the crook of her right arm, she carried three brown paper lunch bags. With her left hand, she adjusted the single string of pearls around her throat and smoothed her primly starched blue cotton dress. She glanced at the clock on the living room wall, sighed, took a deep breath, and put on a bright smile.

A noisy clatter sounded from upstairs, and a bedroom door slammed. A moment later, dragging his book bag behind, little Larry Harry bounded down the perfectly polished tiger oak staircase. His brown hair sprouted outward in all directions above a ruddy, freshly scrubbed face and round, liquid brown eyes that shone with youthful eagerness. "Morning, Mom!" he called.

Mary Harry held out one of the lunch bags, and little Larry stuffed it into his book bag. "Hurry, dear," Mary Harry gently urged. "You don't want to miss the school bus again!" She tried to smooth his stubborn cowlicks, but her fourth grader wouldn't stand still for that.

"Don't!" he insisted. "It took me half an hour and half of Sis's hair gel to get it to look this way!"

As if on cue, a high-pitched shriek ripped through the upstairs hallway. A door slammed again. "Mom!" Cary Harry appeared at the top of the stairs with an open jar in one hand. "You obscene little Chihuahua!" she shouted, glaring at her younger brother. "You used it all! Do you know how much this stuff costs? It's designer!"

Larry Harry grabbed for the doorknob. "Gotta go, Mom," he said, yanking open the door. "The Doberman's barking again."

At the top of the stairs, Cary Harry gave a low threatening growl, and her eyes blazed. She raised her arm as if to throw the empty jar, but the front door slammed as Larry Harry dashed out to meet his bus at the curb. "Oooh!" Cary Harry stamped her foot in frustration. "I swear, Mom, someday I'm going to eat him!" She spun away again, sputtering and mumbling, and the door of her bedroom slammed.

A look of utter confusion spoiled Mary Harry's perfectly made-up face, but she drew another deep breath and recomposed herself, putting on a fresh smile. Just in time, too.

Another bedroom door opened and closed, this time without any slamming, and Harry Harry started down the stairs in his best dark suit with his briefcase on a strap over his shoulder. He was a handsome man, tall and thin with an erect bearing, with bright, dark eyes that gleamed over a gently hooked nose and a strong chin. His hair was neatly groomed, and the smile on his face equaled his wife's as he bent to kiss her.

However, before his lips met her cheek, a tiny wolfen shape darted out from behind a living room chair. With a warning snarl, it gave a low flying leap, caught Harry's trouser leg in fanged teeth, and worried the upturned cuff like a bad-mannered puppy.

"Stop him! Stop him!" Harry cried in alarm. "I thought you put him in his crib?"

"Barry! Bad baby! Stop that!" Mary Harry dropped the lunch sacks and tried to scoop up the furry bundle, but Barry dodged her, scampering around Harry's leg, twisting the mouthful of worsted wool around Harry's ankle. Harry lost his balance and tried to catch himself without stepping on baby Barry. His briefcase went one way; he went another. Harry sprawled haplessly upon the floor. Barry yipped and jumped on Harry's back and chewed Harry's collar.

Before Mary could grab her infant, Barry hiked one little leg and let go a golden stream. "Oh, dear!" Mary exclaimed as she finally snatched up her baby. "He's out of his diaper again. I'll have to go change him!"

"Change him?" Harry sputtered as he rose to his knees. "What about me?"

"Now dear, you're old enough to change yourself." Mary hugged baby Barry in her arms and rocked him protectively, while Barry licked her face.

Harry Harry shook himself. "That kid's a menace!" he scowled, as he started back upstairs. "Mary, you've got to do something! I'm running out of suits! He's already chewed my best shoes to ribbons!"

"Just hurry, dear," Mary soothed as she shifted Barry to one arm and bent to retrieve the lunch sacks. They only contained sandwiches, and Barry's "accident" had missed them, so no harm was done. She watched as Harry stomped up the last step. "You don't want to be late."

As her husband moved one way down the upstairs hall, a door slammed, and Cary Harry came the other way. She paused at the top of the stairs, daring her mother to say something as she adjusted a backpack on her shoulders with clawed hands. Cary wore tight black slacks and a black, navel-bearing midriff top, and sleek blond fur sprouted from every exposed inch of her winsome body. Some of that fur was dyed a punkish purple, and a spiked leather collar adorned her throat.

Mary took the bait. "Oh, no you don't!" she scolded. "You're not leaving this house in that collar! A collar, of all things! You go right back to your room and change!" Everybody was changing today, it seemed, or at least on edge. The full moon surely was approaching. "Have you no pride?"

"I have tons of pride!" Cary barked. "In fact, I'm coming out! No more hiding for me! This is what I am, and I'm proud of it!"

Mary admired her daughter's rebelliousness sometimes, even if she found it exhausting. "You come out like that, and they'll lock you up! The world really isn't all that accepting yet, Cary."

Cary struck a brazen pose. Then the air seemed to shift around her, and as she descended the stairs, she metamorphosized. Her face flattened into a more human shape and all the fur retreated until she resembled a mostly normal, if chronically angry teenaged girl again. "But I'm wearing the collar!" she snapped as she snatched one of the lunch sacks. "Alpo again, I presume."

"On whole wheat with mayonnaise, the way you like it," Mary answered, trying to sound agreeable. "And Kibbles to snack on."

"It's just so Rin-Tin-Tin!" Cary snarled. Suddenly, she slipped awkwardly on the wet floor and caught herself. "What the . . . ?" She stared downward. Then she glanced at her baby brother and crinkled her face in disgust. "Oh . . . Mother!" Wiping her feet, she jerked open the door, stomped out, and slammed the door behind.

Harry Harry reappeared at the top of the stairs and came bounding down. He had changed into his brown suit, and he cut a wide swath around baby Barry as he looked around and found his briefcase. Mary sniffed delicately. He'd showered again, too. Baby Barry squirmed, wiggled, and snarled, but Mary hugged the little ball of fur securely.

"He just doesn't like me!" Harry said as he took his lunch sack from his wife.

"Of course, he likes you," Mary said with gentle forbearance. "You're his father. You were probably chasing cars at his age." She gave Barry a motherly shake.

"I never chased cars," Harry protested as he opened the door. "I had too much dignity."

"You had a choke chain," Mary muttered under her breath as the door closed.

Alone at last, Mary gave a contented sigh. Barry fell instantly asleep, and for a brief time all was quiet. This was her favorite time of the morning, her time. She turned the lock on the door and checked to make sure the blinds were pulled.

The skin on her arms peeled back, seeming to turn inside out, and a soft auburn fur sprouted over her shapely limbs. Her face elongated; she ran a rough tongue over perfect fangs and licked her chops. Yes, it was her favorite time of the morning, before the postman appeared or the ladies called for bridge, when she could just be herself. Bouncing her baby, she glanced down at her free hand and smiled. Today, maybe she would do her nails.

Larry Harry sat attentively at his desk, watching as his teacher, Mr. Morgenstern, scrawled compound sentences on the white board in big black letters. Suddenly, something struck Larry a tiny stinging blow just behind the right ear. Clapping a hand to the back of his head, he twisted in his seat.

Tommy Thompson grinned at him from the back row.

Larry glared. Thompson was a troublemaker, a fat red-headed bully, and the worst student in the class. The two locked gazes for a moment, then Larry gave his attention back to the sentence on the board: *Squashed flat by a passing beer truck, a dog sniffed and nibbled at the remains of an old hamburger.* Larry scratched his head and frowned as Mr. Morgenstern continued to write. Larry raised his hand with a question. *If the dog was squashed flat . . .*

Something stung him in the neck. Larry twisted in his seat again only to see Tommy Thompson grinning the same innocently stupid grin. Larry glanced at the oblivious Morgenstern, who was now writing, *Flying through the air, the dog barked and caught the red Frisbee,* then back at Thompson, who shrugged and mouthed the word, "What?"

Looking around, Larry spied a small green pea on the floor. He gave a low, private snarl of annoyance, but decided to ignore Thompson. He returned his attention once again to the board. He really wanted to know how a dog could fly through the air.

Yet a third sharp sting—the hard little pea struck him in the ear this time, causing a tiny explosion of pain. Larry yipped. Forgetting himself, he sprang out of his chair, over the head of the student seated behind him, and tackled fat Tommy Thompson at his desk. A red and white striped peashooter flew through the air as the two boys crashed to the floor.

Tommy screamed. Larry let go a high-pitched howl, baring small wet fangs as he raised a hairy, clawed hand and ripped the bigger boy's shirt open. Buttons popped and clattered all around. Desks and chairs scooted as other students shot to their feet and scrambled out of the way.

Mr. Morgenstern grabbed one of the students by the shoulder and shouted, "Who let that dog in here? Get it out of here right now! Thompson, is that your mutt?"

Pinning his squirming and nearly naked enemy to the floor with his paws, Larry Harry froze. He stared at his claws, ran a slavering tongue over his teeth, and growled. Without thinking, he had transformed into his wolfen shape, something he was never supposed to do in public!

He looked around at his angry teacher and his wide-eyed classmates as his mind raced. Sally Jenkins, in her yellow dress, dropped to her knees and snapped her fingers. "Nice doggy!" she called.

Under his furry whiskers, Larry Harry flushed red. He had something of a crush on Sally Jenkins, but she wasn't important now. His dad was going to kill him! What was he supposed to do?

His teacher loomed closer. Larry gave a sharp warning bark and snapped his jaws, causing Mr. Morgenstern to recoil. However, Mr. Morgenstern stepped on one of the loose rolling peas. With an awkward yelp, his feet flew upward, and his arms spread wide. He hit the floor flat on his back, and all the students burst out laughing. "Good doggy!" Sally Jenkins cried.

Larry's heart pounded. Some of his classmates were starting to circle him, and still pinned, Tommy Thompson, the school bully, was bawling like a baby. Larry looked down at Thompson and snarled. He knew he was in deep trouble, but he didn't regret getting even at all. He licked the bully's face with the wettest, slimiest tongue he could manage, and Tommy Thompson let go a long wail.

With that, Larry looked around quickly, and spying an open window, he jumped through, over a hedge and flowerbed, and to the school's expansive lawn, running as fast as he could run.

The alley Dumpsters made a perfect place to hide and think. Behind one of the big steel containers and in boy form again, Larry Harry shivered as he sat on his haunches in the deep shadows and watched the traffic zoom by at the far end of the alley. The gray buildings towered above him, allowing only a thin shaft of afternoon sunlight to penetrate the smelly gloom.

Larry had no idea where he was. All he knew was that he didn't dare go home. His father would kill him for breaking the family's strictest rule, and then his mom would kill him all over again. It wasn't fair! He'd always been so careful not to let anybody know that he was different.

The traffic whizzed by, and suddenly police sirens screamed. The piercing sounds seemed to intensify as they echoed off the close walls. Red and blue lights flashed madly as a trio of squad cars shot past the alley entrance.

Larry Harry cowered. Mr. Morgenstern had called the police! They were looking for him! Larry's pulse raced, and he fought the urge to transform again. He was in enough trouble already. Sniffling, he wiped his nose with the back of one hand.

He would run away, he decided. He would become famous—an actor, maybe, or a singer, or a well-known interior decorator with his own home cable show. The Tommy Thompsons of the world would never pick on him again, and maybe his parents would be proud enough to let him come home someday.

It was a good plan, he told himself.

A raucous clangor of bells sounded. Startled nearly out of his skin, Larry shot to his feet. A door at the back of the alley slammed open. Five tough-looking men charged out. The first man out the door fell over Larry. The second man fell over the first. They all toppled like dominoes, and bags of cash went sliding over the greasy pavement. One of the bags broke open, scattering bills.

"Oh, cool!" Larry exclaimed as he lifted his chin. "Bank robbers!"

The man on top of him looked furious. "It's a kid, boss!" he shouted. "What'll we do now? He can identify us!"

"What dya think, Jonesy, ya idiot?" The boss got to his feet and brushed the knees of his suit. "Snatch him, and bring him along! You others, get those bags and be quick!" The boss looked down at Larry, then smiled and patted Larry's head. "We're not bank robbers, junior," he lied. "We're, uh, bank examiners. But we got a tip, see, that some real bank robbers were gonna be along any minute to rob the place, so we gotta take the cash and hide it, see? And it ain't safe to leave a kid like you hangin' around with a bunch of bank robbers on the loose!"

The one called Jonesy picked Larry up and tucked him under a muscular arm while the remaining thugs grabbed up the bags of cash. Larry felt a surge of excitement. Here was a chance to redeem himself. Everyone would forgive him if he was a hero and saved the bank. "Let me help!" he insisted. "I can carry something!"

"You can help, alright, kid," the boss said. He winked at Jonesy. "We need a place to hide the cash, and quick. Where do you live?"

Larry Harry gave his address. "Oh boy, my parents are gonna be so surprised!"

"They sure are, kid, they sure are," Jonesy answered as the goons darted down the alley with their recovered loot to a big black car parked near the curb.

Over the drone of her vacuum cleaner, Mary Harry heard the jangle of the telephone. With a frown, she glanced toward the kitchen where she also had a chocolate cake timing in the oven. Who could be calling?

She picked up the phone. "Hello?"

"Mrs. Harry, this is Mr. Morgenstern, your son's fourth grade teacher. I'm afraid we've had an incident!"

Mary Harry caught her breath. "Is Larry all right?"

"I'm afraid he's missing," Mr. Morgenstern answered, obviously distraught. "Somebody's dog leaped through the window this afternoon and attacked a student. The students were terrified. In all the chaos, Larry disappeared! I'm afraid the dog frightened him! I took a terrible fall, myself!"

"I'll call his father right now, and we'll come down!" Mary hung up and quickly punched up her husband's office number. "You have to come home at once, dear!" she explained. "Something's happened to Larry!"

Before she could hang up, the front door slammed forcefully. Cary Harry, home early from school, threw down her books, but she caught her mother's final words. "What's happened to Larry?" she demanded. "Is it that bully, Tommy Thompson?"

Mary gave her daughter a look. "Tommy who?" Then she waved her hands dismissively. She'd get the details of that later. "Never mind, dear. All we know is that your brother has disappeared. Your father and I have to go down to the school, and that means you'll have to watch Barry."

Cary shrieked. "You're leaving me with that little monster after the way he chewed my best motorcycle jacket last week?"

"You don't have a motorcycle, anyway, young lady, and there's no one else. Oh, and watch the cake in the oven. The timer should go off any minute now."

Cary's protests ended at the mention of a cake, and Mary hurriedly put away the vacuum cleaner. Drawing a deep breath, she fingered the string of pearls around her neck, as she often did when she worried. There was so much to do! It would be ten minutes before Harry got home, and she needed to look perfect when she met him at the door.

Brakes squealed suddenly outside. Car doors slammed. Startled, Mary Harry rushed to the living room window, parted the curtains, and gazed outward. Four men strode up the sidewalk as a big car pulled away again. One of the men had her son under his arm!

Mary dashed to the front door and pulled it open. "Larry!" She held out her arms to take her son. "You found him! Everybody's been so worried! How can I ever thank you?"

The boss reached inside his suit and pulled out a .45 pistol. He stuck it under Mary's nose. "You can thank us by letting us stay with you a couple of days, lady. And don't worry, we're great houseguests." He beckoned to his accomplices. "Pete, Mac, Doobie—bring in the bags, but don't bother unpacking."

Cary gave a low growl and took a step forward.

"Don't!" Mary Harry warned in a stern voice as she retreated from the doorway with Larry's hand clutched firmly in hers. "Everybody remain calm. Your father will be home soon. He'll know what to do!"

"Smart girl," the boss said. "Nice pearls, too. You look just like June Cleaver." He stepped inside and looked around approvingly. "Nice comfy place you got here. Doobie, be sure to let Jonesy in after he's done stashing the car. Mac, find some rope or cord or something, and make our hosts uncomfortable."

Ignoring the boss's gun, Cary shot forward. "Mom, let me . . . !"

Mary caught Cary by the leather collar around her daughter's neck. Cary made a gurgling sound as her eyes shot wide with surprise. "Heel!" Mary ordered. "Wait for your father!"

Larry pulled away from his mother and grinned. "It's okay, Mom. They're bank examiners! We're saving the cash from the real bank robbers!"

Cary sneered. "You moron. They *are* the real bank robbers!"

Larry looked confused. For once, he didn't have a smart comeback for his big sister, and the idea that she might actually be right scared him more than the boss's big gun.

Pete emerged from the basement with a length of clothesline. With methodical precision, he tied Mary, Larry and Cary up in neat packages and dumped them on the living room sofa.

Larry looked crestfallen. "I really screwed the pooch, didn't I, Mom. I don't know what that means, but Dad always says it."

Cary muttered under her breath. "Just let me change! I can eat these guys for dinner without even breathing hard!"

Mary shook her head and tried to remain calm. The robbers had actually done an efficient job of tying them up, and the clothesline with its nylon core would be tough to break. However, she had bigger worries. The robbers had not gone upstairs yet. They had not discovered Barry.

A car pulled into the driveway. The robbers quickly hid themselves. The boss waved his gun meaningfully at Mary, and then hid behind the door just as it burst open. Harry sprang over the threshold. "Honey, I'm home! What's this about Larry?"

The boss brought the butt of his pistol down, and Harry hit the floor like a twenty-five-pound sack of dry dog chow. The crooks wasted no time, and in short order they tied Harry hand and foot and deposited him on the now very crowded sofa.

"Well, Dad's home," Cary muttered, glowering in disgust. "Is there a backup plan?"

Mary chewed her lip and tried to think. She worried about her baby in the crib upstairs, and she worried about her husband's poor head. Harry wouldn't be in a good mood when he woke up. Most of all, she worried about the family secret. Everything depended upon secrecy—Harry's job, their idyllic suburban life-style, even their lives. There were still too many people in the world that considered folks like the Harrys abnormal, perverts, abominations.

Mary had always done everything she could to hide who she really was, for her husband's sake and for her children's.

Maybe her daughter was right.

The crook called Doobie rattled around in the kitchen. Mary heard the oven door open and bang closed. "Cake!" she heard the robber call. Pete and Mac immediately went to join Doobie. At the same time, the doorbell sounded. The boss cautiously cracked the front door open and admitted Jonesy. "About time," the boss murmured. "After dark, we're getting outta here. Let's get some cake before the others eat it all."

Despite herself, Mary gave a low snarl. She had worked all afternoon making that cake from scratch for her family. She hadn't even iced it yet. Now there were five crooks, instead of four, and they were tracking the carpet she had just vacuumed. It was just more than she could bear.

With all five robbers in the kitchen, Mary lost control. Her body contorted, grew, and sprouted thick fur. Her face elongated into a snout, and her ears lengthened. Her lips curled back to reveal vicious fangs. With a determined effort, she strained to break her bonds.

Yet the clothesline around her wrists and ankles held firm.

With a yelp of disappointment, Mary quickly reverted to human form before any of the robbers could come back into the living room and see her. All she had managed to do was get hair on the sofa. "Let me try!" Cary offered, but Mary shook her head again. "Wait," she said in a tight whisper as her gaze turned toward the stairway.

Barry stood on the bottom step—and he looked hungry. Dark hair covered his tiny, diaperless body, and his little jaws drooled. He twitched his ears, wiggled his nose, and yipped.

Licking crumbs off his face, the one called Jonesy stepped out of the kitchen. "Hey boss! They got a dog! Cute little fella, too!"

Barry yipped again, then leaped upon the bags of money piled by the door. Raising one leg, he peed a golden stream. Jonesy gave a horrified look and dropped the last bite of his cake. "You crazy mutt! Stop!" He lunged at Barry as the other crooks emerged from the kitchen.

Mary screamed. Cary and Larry both growled viciously and began to transform. "Leave him alone!" Mary cried. Struggling against the clothesline, she also started to change.

The boss shot her a wide-eyed look. "What the hell?"

Barry dodged the outstretched hands that reached for him. Like furred lightning, he ran straight for the boss and sank his fangs into the leg of the robber's suit pants. "Get him off! Get him off!" the boss yelled, shaking his leg. Barry clung tenaciously. "What the hell are you people?"

Jonesy picked up one of the pee-soaked bags of money and held it out with a disgusted expression. "Boss! They're . . . ! They're . . . !"

Fully transformed, Cary snapped her bonds and sprang for Jonesy. Her claws flashed. With one stroke, she slashed open the bag of money he held, and bills fluttered everywhere. "We're what?" she demanded, as she pinned Jonesey back against the wall.

Larry wiggled out of his bonds, too. "We're rich!" he shouted, as he pounced upon another bag of money. "I won't have to be an actor, a singer, or even an interior decorator after all!"

A gunshot exploded, and a bullet dug deep into the carpeted floor. Barry growled viciously as he climbed up the boss's leg, his tiny claws digging deep, doing damage. "Get off! Get off!" the boss continued to scream as he danced around in a circle. He tried to aim the gun again—straight at Barry.

Free at last, Mary leaped across the couch, colliding with her daughter as Cary also sprang to her baby brother's rescue. Their combined weight smashed the crook back into the kitchen. Cary snatched Barry as Mary knocked the gun away and rolled on top of the boss. "You want some cake?" she demanded as they sprawled across the kitchen table. The remains of her chocolate cake were nearby. She raised it over the boss's face. "Well, do ya, punk?" She pressed it down with a firm splat, grinding it into eyes and nose and mouth as the crook sputtered.

Cary finally pulled her off. "Enough, Mom! He's had enough! They've all had enough!"

Panting and salivating, Mary stood back. Larry stood close by, rocking Barry in his arms. One of the robbers lay stretched across the money bags by the door. The three others lay draped indecorously across various pieces of furniture. "I got one of 'em," Larry bragged.

"It didn't take a lot," Cary admitted. "I just growled, and they rolled over and played dead."

Mary resumed human form again and picked up the gun. "Tie them up, and let's call the police." She sighed as she glanced at Harry who finally showed signs of stirring on the couch. "And for heaven's sake, let's try to act normal."

They did not have to call the police. One of the neighbors had heard the gunshot and saved them the trouble. Sirens screeched outside and flashing lights lit up the entire block as Larry yanked open the front door. The Harrys' neatly manicured lawn was rapidly filling up with officers and assorted gawkers. Mr. Morgenstern came rushing up the sidewalk right behind the police, but the officers held him back. Larry, in boy form once again, gave a yelp as he spied Sally Jenkins while Cary, also in human form, preened in self-satisfaction.

Harry, finally awake, looked dazed as the police untied him. He looked at Mary. "Is it bondage night already?" he mumbled.

"No dear," she sighed with an amused expression. She turned to the officers and to all the people pressing through her front door for a look. Then she winked at her daughter. "I baked a cake. It's a coming-out party."

Slowly, deliberately, for all to see, Mary Harry began to change.

Jim C. Hines has sold six novels, forty-plus short stories, and one bumper sticker at the time this bio was written. His latest novel is *The Stepsister Scheme*, best described as a mash-up of fairy tale princesses and *Charlie's Angels*. He is also the author of the humorous goblin trilogy from DAW Books. His shorter work has appeared in *Turn the Other Chick*, *Realms of Fantasy*, and *Sword & Sorceress*, among others. Jim and his wife live in Michigan with their two young children, both of whom would probably be scarred for life if they knew what he had written for this anthology. Online, he can be found at *www.jim-chines.com*.

The Creature in Your Neighborhood

Jim C. Hines

IMAGINATIONVILLE SEASON 8, EPISODE 6

"The Creature in Your Neighborhood"

Today's Special Guest Star: The Man in the Moon

[INT. MISTER JOHNSON'S RESTAURANT. NIGHT.]

(The restaurant is full of boxes, with cans and other food items spilling out onto the floor. Bobby Bunny, Gobbler, Grumpus, and the Mall Rats are sorting more food into various boxes.)

MISTER JOHNSON: Thanks for your help everybody. I think we've collected even more than we did in last year's food drive.

GOBBLER: One for poor. One for *me*! (Stuffs a box of spaghetti into his mouth.) Yum, yum, yum. One for poor. One for—

BOBBY BUNNY: Gobbler, no! *All* of this food is for the poor!

GOBBLER: But me love spaghetti! (Pulls box and broken spaghetti noodles out of his mouth) Hm . . . me think maybe this spaghetti not done yet.

GRUMPUS: Spaghetti? Yuck! Unless it's moldy old noodles in rancid garbage sauce, like Mama Grumpus used to make back in Grumpusland.

MISTER JOHNSON: Don't worry, Grumpus. Mrs. Johnson baked you a special mildew mud pie to thank you for helping.

GRUMPUS: I hope it's got plenty of dust and dirt in it.

MISTER JOHNSON: (Laughs) It does. She made apple pie for the rest of us. Then after we're done, I thought we could go outside and use my telescope to learn about the moon. We might even get to see the Man in the Moon.

GRUMPUS: (Ducks into his trash can) Here, I saved these old banana peels for your food drive, and some green cheese with fuzz growing on it. At least I think that's cheese.

MALL RATS: *Cheese!*

MALL RAT #1: Oh no. The cheese is *totally* moldy!

MALL RAT #2: That is *so* gross!

MALL RAT #3: A moment of silence for our fallen cheese.

(The Mall Rats bow their heads.)

BOBBY BUNNY: Nobody wants to eat that stuff, Grumpus!

MISTER JOHNSON: Thank you for offering, though. It's always nice to share with people who are less fortunate.

(Confetti and trumpets herald today's Word of the Day. A banner reading "SHARE" drops into view.)

BOBBY BUNNY: Congratulations everybody! We found the Word of the Day!

GRUMPUS: I hate the Word of the Day.

BOBBY BUNNY: But Grumpus, the Word of the Day is how we—

(Rolly runs into the restaurant carrying a ripped puppet arm. Threads, stuffing, and tufts of brown fur trail from the arm.)

ROLLY: Mr. Johnson! Mr. Johnson! Rolly was going to camp out in the backyard with Rolly's friend Bobo Bear, but when Rolly got there, Bobo was . . . he was . . . .

MISTER JOHNSON: What happened, Rolly? What is it?

ROLLY: (Wails) Bobo Bear was *dead*! All Rolly found was Bobo's arm.

MISTHER JOHNSON: (Worried) I'm sure Bobo is all right. Maybe this is a game, like when Rainbow steals Leslie's nose.

ROLLY: No, no, no, no, no! There was stuffing every-where and torn felt and fur and now Rolly needs to sing the therapy song. (Singing)

Therapy, therapy, therapy for me!
Rolly's letters of the day are P, T, S, and D!

BOBBY BUNNY: (Takes the arm from Rolly) Look at the felt. This arm was bitten off.

MALL RATS: (Scream)

GOBBLER: Hey, no look at me! Me not sicko. Me eat only *healthy* foods from food pyramid. Grains and vege-tables, fruits and milk and meat. And sometimes cake. Not people.

BOBBY BUNNY: Whatever did this, we have to find it . . . before it strikes again!

[EXT. LESLIE AND RAINBOW'S BACK YARD. NIGHT.]

(Leslie is sitting on the back porch, feeding the squirrels who have gathered from the woods behind the house.)

LESLIE: Now, now, little friends. You do not have to argue. I have plenty of nuts for everyone.

(Squirrels form a circle around Leslie.)

LESLIE: That's better. Isn't it nice to relax at the end of the day by sharing a nice, healthy snack with your friends?

(Squirrels stiffen, then flee up the nearest tree.)

LESLIE: What is wrong, little friends? I bought these from Mr. Johnson's restaurant. Is something wrong with Mr. Johnson's nuts? Come back, and—

(From the trees comes a sinister growl.)

LESLIE: That does not *sound* like my squirrel friends.

(A shadowy form steps out of the woods. Only the eyes are visible: glowing yellow ping pong balls with slitted pupils. The shadow changes shape, dropping to all fours.)

LESLIE: That does not *look* like my squirrel friends.

(Leslie stands, dropping her bag of nuts, which spill across the porch.)

LESLIE: Hello there Mr. Wolf. Have you come to sh-share with the squirrels? Maybe you would like a d-different snack. I will go inside and look for wolf food to share. (Turns and opens the door.)

(The wolf charges across the backyard.)

LESLIE: Aaaah! Rainbow, there's a monster in the yard!

(Leslie starts to go inside, but the wolf catches her by the foot and yanks her back. Leslie and the wolf disappear into the darkness. Screams fill the air, along with the sound of ripping felt.)

RAINBOW: (Opens the upstairs window and peeks outside) Leslie? Is that you?

(Squirrels leap to the roof and race in through the window.)

RAINBOW: (Comes downstairs and steps onto the back porch) Leslie? Oh, boy! It looks like it's time to play "Follow the Rainbow!" That's the game where I hide and Leslie tries to find me. But tonight it looks like Leslie is hiding, so I get to—

LESLIE: (Weakly) Rainbow? I'm over here.

RAINBOW: (Sniggering) You'll never hide from me like that, Leslie!

(Leslie drags her mangled body from the trees. Her clothes are shredded, her limbs torn, and she carries her nose in one hand.)

RAINBOW: What happened to you? Don't you know puppets are supposed to be dry-clean only? (Sniggers again)

LESLIE: Monster . . . attacked me. I called, but you—

RAINBOW: Hey, you're really hurt. (Runs to Leslie) I'm sorry, Leslie. I was in the tubby with my rubber bath toys. Which monster did this to you? Was it Cepi Monster? Rolly Monster? Leemo Monster?

LESLIE: Those teeth. Those eyes. This was no ordinary monster, Rainbow. This was evil. Evil! It changed into a wolf, and—

RAINBOW: Oh, Leslie. Don't you remember the stranger song? Come on, everybody. Sing along! (Singing)

Strangers with puppies and strangers with candy,
Strangers who act like they're all nice and dandy,
Strangers who tell you your mother is near,
These are the strangers we always should fear.

LESLIE: (Regains her strength long enough to throttle Rainbow one last time) I tried to share with the wolf. "Share" is the word of the day. It's the word of the day, Rainbow! The word of the day failed! (Collapses) The word . . . failed.

(Leslie dies.)

RAINBOW: Leslie? Leslie? (Slowly bends down to pick up Leslie's nose)

[INT. IMAGINATIONVILLE LIBRARY RESEARCH ROOM. DAY.]

(Googol the Mouse is at the computer, surrounded by Bobby Bunny, Grumpus, Gobbler, Mall Rats, Mister Johnson, and the Mathmagician. Bobby Bunny still carries Bobo's arm.)

GOOGOL: (Races about on the mouse pad, clicking madly) The computer says the bite marks appear to be from a large canine.

GRUMPUS: It's Woofers! I knew that giant mutt was rabid. I say we put her down!

BOBBY BUNNY: You leave my dog alone! She was safe in her kennel all last night!

MISTER JOHNSON: Let's calm down, Grumpus. We don't know Woofers did this.

GRUMPUS: That crazy canine is going to eat us all.

(Rainbow bursts into the room, carrying Leslie's nose.)

RAINBOW: It's not Woofers! Leslie said it was a monster, a puppet who changed into a big bad wolf.

GOOGOL: A werewolf!

RAINBOW: Where wolf? In our backyard!

(Rainbow sniggers, then looks down at Leslie's nose. Her laughter changes to low sobs.)

GOOGOL: (Still clicking on the computer) The werewolf is a creature who changes into a wolf under the light of the full moon. They are strong, fast, and deadly. They can only be harmed by weapons made of silver.

GRUMPUS: So it's the Man in the Moon's fault? Who invited him to be today's special guest star?

MALL RAT #2: It's morning now. We should be like, totally safe, right?

GOOGOL: I am afraid not. According to this almanac—

BOBBY BUNNY: How do you spell "al-man-ac"?

GRUMPUS: Shut up.

GOOGOL: The almanac says the full moon is tonight.

MALL RAT #1: But Bobo and Leslie were eaten, like, *last* night.

GOOGOL: The moon must be full enough to trigger the change on the day prior to the full moon, which means it will likely do the same on the day after. So this werewolf may be among us for three days.

MATHMAGICIAN: Three! (Waves his wand, drawing a 3 in the air) Count with me, my friends. One! Two! Three!

GOOGOL: There is more. Now that the werewolf has tasted puppet, it will be hungry for more. I fear the creature will hunt us all.

(Everyone panics and runs away.)

[INT. ROLLY'S ROOM. NIGHT.]

(Crayon-drawn boards cover the windows and doors. Rolly and his pet gerbil Mo are hiding behind the bed. Rolly is busy coloring.)

ROLLY: (Singing)

It's time to play in Rolly's Room.
Hooray, hooray for Rolly's Room.
Rolly loves Mo and Rolly loves you.
And now let's all learn something new!

(Rolly holds up a bullet in one hand and a silver crayon in the other, studies the bullet, then colors the very tip.)

ROLLY: Hello, boys and girls! Today, Rolly is learning about *werewolves*. Like the werewolf who met my friend Bobo Bear. Googol says you have to have *silver* to stop a werewolf, so Rolly is making *silver bullets*.

(Rolly picks up a handful of colored bullets and begins loading them into an oversized revolver.)

ROLLY: Rolly is also learning about *handguns*. This is a Henson & Oz .45 caliber special. (Whispers) Rolly's Daddy thinks Rolly doesn't know the combination to the gun safe!

(Rolly finishes loading, spins the barrel, and sights the gun at Mo.)

ROLLY: But Rolly wants to know *more* about werewolves.

(The window rattles behind the boards. Rolly leaps to his feet and points the gun at the window.)

ROLLY: You stay the fuck out of Rolly's Room, Mr. Macaroni! Rolly will fucking kill you! Rolly saw what happened to Rolly's friend Bobo, and Rolly's not going down like that. That's right, Mr. Macaroni. You stay over there in your pasta world. Touch those blinds again and Rolly will blow your goddamned head off!

(Rolly picks up Mo, who's trembling. They sit back down behind the bed.)

ROLLY: (Muttering) Always peeking through Rolly's window. Rolly thinks Mr. Macaroni is a fucking pervert.

(Rolly eyes Mo.)

ROLLY: Now Rolly wants to know if *gerbils* can be were-wolves. Maybe Rolly should ask the computer.

(Rolly sets Mo down and points the gun at him, slowly backing toward the computer. A knock at the door makes him jump.)

ROLLY: Who's there?

DEEP VOICE: I'm today's special friend! I've come to—

ROLLY: (Shoots at the door) Nooooooooo! Rolly is too young and too popular to die! (Continues shooting) Eat silver-colored death, werewolf! You want more? (Reloads) Rolly will show you! Rolly will kill you, you fucking bastard! (Resumes shooting)

(Rolly runs out of bullets. The revolver clicks as Rolly continues to pull the trigger. Smoke rises from the barrel.)

DEEP VOICE: (Groans)

ROLLY: (Panting) That's right!

(Rolly rips down the bullet-ridden boards and opens the door to reveal Tommy the Talking Tuba standing against the far wall of the hallway. White stuffing pokes through numerous holes in the tuba puppet's body.)

ROLLY: Oh, *shit*! (Sets gun down) Tommy Tuba, are you all right? Those holes don't look so bad. Rolly bets Mrs. Johnson could sew them right—

(Tommy falls, landing facedown on the floor. His back is a mess of shredded stuffing and felt.)

ROLLY: Uh, oh. Rolly forgot Rolly was firing *hollow-points*. (Slams door, grabs gun, and runs back behind the bed.) Now Rolly wants to learn about *disposing of evidence*.

[EXT. MAPLE STREET CUL DE SAC. NIGHT.]

(Bobby Bunny is standing with Peter the Pretendisaurus under the light of the street lamps.)

PETER: I don't know, Bobby. I'm afraid of the dark.

BOBBY: There's nothing to be afraid of, Peter! Remember, I'm the only one who can see or hear you. That means the werewolf won't be able to see or hear you either! All these years everyone has said you weren't real. Well, when we take care of that werewolf, they'll have to admit you're real. Won't that be fun?

PETER: I'm not sure. I heard the werewolf got Leslie and—

BOBBY: You're a giant purple dinosaur. You've got nothing to be scared of. And when it's all over, we can *share* some of my delicious carrot cake.

PETER: I do like carrot cake.

BOBBY: I know you're scared, but we did a whole episode about being afraid. Remember?

PETER: That's when you brought me my night light. (Smiles) You said, "When you're feeling all afraid, just smile 'til those feelings fade!"

BOBBY: That's right, Peter! This will turn things around for both of us. Everyone will know you're real, and I'll be the hero who figured out how to stop the werewolf. I'll be the star again, like in the old days before Rolly came along.

PETER: I'll do it! I'll face my fear. (Glances around) But . . . you're going to come with me, right?

BOBBY: I wish I could, buddy. But the werewolf can see me, remember? Don't worry, all you have to do is sneak up on him and *pow!*

(Bobby swings a fist, spinning himself around.)

PETER: Okay, Bobby. I'll do it for you, because you're my friend.

BOBBY: That's great! Thanks, friend!

(Bobby scampers away, disappearing into one of the houses. The door slams and locks behind him. Peter begins trudging down the street.)

PETER: Smile 'til those feelings fade. (Forces a smile) All right. If I were a werewolf, where would I be?

(Peter reaches the end of the street and turns the corner. Dogs bark as he passes.)

PETER: This isn't so bad. The moon is like a big night light . . . a big scary night light that turns people into werewolves. Maybe a song will help me keep my smile. (Singing)

If I were a werewolf, where would I be?
Where would I be, oh where would I be?
If I were a werewolf, where would I be?
Could a werewolf be hiding from me?

And if I were a werewolf, what would I wear?
What would I wear, oh what would I wear?
If I were a werewolf, what would I wear?
Do werewolves wear more than just hair?

PETER: Gosh, it's awfully quiet out here. Hey, I've got a joke. What do you call it when two dinosaurs crash their cars? Tyrannosaurus Wrecks! (Laughs) And what do you call a dinosaur who snores? A Stegosnorus! (Laughs louder) It's working! I'm not afraid anymore!

(A shadow lumbers across the street ahead.)

PETER: (Whispers) Was that the werewolf? (Louder) Oh, right. I forgot it can't hear me. I wonder where it's going. It ran down Oak Street, toward the post office. Maybe the werewolf wants to mail a letter!

(Peter wanders into the empty parking lot. He peeks around the mailboxes, then approaches the rows of parked mail trucks behind the building. He stretches his neck past one of the trucks.)

PETER: I found you! Pretendisauruses are good at hide-and-go-seek. Boy, you're a scary looking monster. Bobby said to get you. Hm . . . Pretendisauruses are herbivores. That means we eat plants, and we don't have sharp teeth or claws like you. I guess I'll just have to—

(From behind the truck comes the sound of sniffing.)

PETER: Uh oh. Bobby Bunny said nobody could see me or hear me. He didn't say whether anyone could *smell* me. Maybe I should—(Screams)

(Cloth tears, and stuffing flies into the air above the trucks. Peter staggers back, his head torn from his neck. He runs several paces, crashes into the back of the post office, and collapses.)

[EXT. IMAGINATIONVILLE SCHOOL PLAY-GROUND. NIGHT.]

(Everyone has gathered in the soccer field. Most carry improvised weapons, including baseball bats, letter openers, shovels, axes, and in the case of Bobby Bunny, a giant silver tuna.)

MISTER JOHNSON: Everyone settle down. This is the third night, and the moon will be rising soon. As long as we stay together—

BOBBY BUNNY: We're going to *share* the danger.

GRUMPUS: You mean we've brought the danger here!

MISTER JOHNSON: Now Grumpus, we don't know the werewolf is one of us.

GRUMPUS: What werewolf? I'm talking about that freak Rolly. I heard what he did to Tommy Tuba.

ROLLY: (Wearing a straightjacket) Rolly didn't do nothing! Don't listen to Mo. He's a lying bastard snitch!

RAINBOW: (Still holding Leslie's nose) Leslie used to play the tuba in marching band.

ROLLY: You hear me Mo? You can't prove anything! Rolly will kill you, you little rat!

MALL RAT #1: Hey, that's like totally racist.

MISTER JOHNSON: I know we're all frightened. I'm frightened too. Maybe if we *share* our feelings, we won't be as frightened anymore.

GRUMPUS: Shut your man hole. Your kind is always trying to tell the rest of us what to do, and we're sick of it.

MISTER JOHNSON: My kind?

GRUMPUS: You know. Fleshies! You and your fleshy family ought to go back where you came from and leave the rest of us alone!

GOBBLER: No, no, no! Mrs. Johnson make delicious pies. Strawberry, apple, key lime . . . yummy, nummy pies!

BOBBY BUNNY: Stop it, all of you! We have to concentrate on the werewolf problem!

GOOGOL: Imaginationville has never been troubled by werewolves before. We should figure out how this creature came into our midst.

GRUMPUS: Let's see, who do we know with strange occult powers? Someone whose magic never does what it's supposed to?

(Everyone turns to stare at the Mathmagician.)

MATHMAGICIAN: It wasn't me, I swear!

MALL RAT #3: Your unnatural magic totally could have brought that thing here.

MATHMAGICIAN: "Unnatural?" You're a *talking rat*! (Draws his wand) Stay back! Don't make me draw upon the power of He Who Must Not Be Counted!

MAN IN THE MOON: Hello, everybody!

ROLLY: This is all your fault! When Rolly gets Rolly's gun back, Rolly's going to put some new craters in the Man in the Moon!

MAN IN THE MOON: Don't blame me! I just shine my beautiful light and—

RAINBOW: Hey, what's wrong with Gobbler?

MAN IN THE MOON: Oops. Sorry. . . .

GOBBLER: (Doubled over in pain) Me hungry. Me hungry . . . for *bunny*!

(Gobbler's body twists into the form of the werewolf. He jumps through the air, impossibly high, landing on the fleeing Bobby Bunny.)

BOBBY BUNNY: Help me! Somebody help meeeee!

GOBBLER WOLF: Yum, yum, yum! (Sound of ripping cloth)

ROLLY: Rolly bets you all wish you'd let Rolly keep his gun now! Now all Rolly can do is sing the dismemberment song!

MATHMAGICIAN: One, two, three, four, turn this wolf into . . . a drawer!

(Glowing numbers 1, 2, 3, and 4 appear from the Mathmagician's wand and begin marching toward Gobbler Wolf. The numbers scream as Gobbler Wolf tears them apart.)

GRUMPUS: A *drawer*? You're such a putz. (Ducks into his trash can and pulls the lid shut.)

ROLLY: (Singing)

Arms and legs, arms and legs,
Flying through the air.
Screams and screams and screams and screams
And corpses everywhere.

MISTER JOHNSON: (Swings his shovel, knocking Gobbler Wolf back) We have to work together!

MALL RATS: Charge!

GOBBLER WOLF: (Pops Mall Rat #1 into his mouth, swallows, then belches.)

RAINBOW: Hey, Gobbler! You're still hungry? Taste the Rainbow, you son of a bitch!

(Rainbow throws Leslie's nose, hitting Gobbler Wolf in the face.)

RAINBOW: This is for you, Leslie!

(Gobbler Wolf charges. Rainbow grabs Grumpus' trash can and whirls around, clubbing Gobbler Wolf and knocking him down. Before Gobbler Wolf can rise, Rainbow screams and raises the trash can overhead.)

RAINBOW: Take that! (Pounds Gobbler Wolf.) And that! And that and that and that!

GRUMPUS: Hey, knock it off! I'm trying to hide in here!

RAINBOW: None of you understand! (Continues to bludgeon Gobbler Wolf.) Leslie's dead and I never had the chance to tell her how I—

GOOGOL: We need silver. Grumpus' can will not be enough. Even now the monster rises again.

RAINBOW: (Determined) I don't think so.

(Rainbow slams the can to the ground and rips off the lid. She lifts Gobbler Wolf from the ground and stuffs him headfirst into the can.)

GRUMPUS: (Muffled) Hey, what are you doing? Get out of my can! Beat it, you! Argh!

MISTER JOHNSON: Come on, everybody!

(The Mathmagician picks up the lid and hammers Gobbler Wolf into the can. The survivors throw themselves onto the shaking can, trying to hold the lid in place. Slowly, Grumpus' shouts die down, and the can goes still.)

MISTER JOHNSON: Grumpus? (Starts to lift the lid)

ROLLY: Nooooooo!

MISTER JOHNSON: The can is empty.

MATHMAGICIAN: Doesn't Grumpus' trash can lead to Grumpusland?

(The others stare into the can in silence)

ROLLY: Yaaay! Rainbow *shared* the werewolf with the Grumpuses!

MISTER JOHNSON: Grumpus might still be alive. We should try to rescue him. That's what friends do.

MATHMAGICIAN: You go right ahead, buddy.

ROLLY: Grumpus wasn't *Rolly's* friend. Grumpus was an asshole to Rolly.

RAINBOW: (Panting and crying) I've got tools back at our . . . at my house. I could rivet the lid shut.

GOOGOL: We should plate the can in silver, too. That will seal the werewolves in Grumpusland.

MISTER JOHNSON: Where are we going to get that much silver?

(Rainbow picks up a torn ear, all that's left of Bobby Bunny.)

RAINBOW: Puppet insurance.

[INT. MISTER JOHNSON'S RESTAURANT. DAY.]

(The survivors of Gobbler Wolf's rampage are gathered together at the front counter, drinking milkshakes and eating pizza. Most are armed. They jump nervously at the slightest sound.)

MALL RAT #2: (Softly) Isn't this the part where Grumpus tells a totally lame story to his pet slug?

ROLLY: Rolly hated those stupid stories. Rolly thinks *Rolly* should tell the story. Everyone likes Rolly best anyway.

RAINBOW: No.

MALL RAT #3: But we *have* to tell a story. Otherwise we can't—

RAINBOW: No! Stories won't change what happened. Evil doesn't care about the word of the day. (Looks at her hands.) Some things don't wash away in the tubby.

GOOGOL: Has anyone stopped to think about what will happen if the Grumpuses find another way into our world?

MATHMAGICIAN: (Waving his wand) If Gobbler infects even one Grumpus, then there will be two. If they infect two more Grumpuses, and those werewolves infect four more, that makes eight. Eight werewolves! If those eight werewolves . . . (Wand begins to smoke)

MALL RAT #2: Poor Gobbler. I don't understand how he became a werewolf in the first place.

GOOGOL: He must have been bitten some time since the last full moon.

MISTER JOHNSON: But who bit him? None of us changed when the moon came out.

MATHMAGICIAN: There have been one, two, three, four special guest stars since the last full moon. It must have been one of them.

GOOGOL: We must find them and figure out which is the werewolf. Once we do—

ROLLY: (Slams a silver-bladed survival knife into the counter.) Then the Word of the Day will be *kick ass*!

MALL RAT #3: (Whispers) That's, like, two words of the day.

(Rolly glares at Mall Rat #3, who cowers. Everyone gathers their weapons and heads out, leaving the empty restaurant behind.)

THE END

About the Editor

Esther M. Friesner dearly loves working in a field that has no trouble reconciling her role as the creator of the wildly popular *Chicks In Chainmail* series of anthologies, her Nebula Awards for some decidedly serious stories, and her latest vocation for YA novels (including *Nobody's Princess* and *Nobody's Prize* for Random House, *Temping Fate* for Penguin, and more on the horizon). Originally from New York until the siren song of Yale brought her to Ph.D.-land, she's been living in suburban Connecticut ever since and knows whereof she writes.

The Following is an excerpt from:

DRAGON'S RING

DAVE FREER

Available from Baen Books
October 2009
hardcover

Prologue

The dragon flew above the rage of the elements. Above the tumultuous maelstrom of ocean swirling into the void. Above the sheet lightnings and vortexes of dark energies released as the tower fell, with the vast granite masonry shattering into swirling dust.

A fierce delight filled his dragonish heart as he looked down on it.

The narrow—and, to Fionn's strange vision—coruscating band of twisted and constrained elsewhere that was one of the seven anchors of the place of dragons, stretched. Torrents of energy, shimmering fountains of it, across all the spectra, crackled and shrieked away into parallel planes. Great gouts of paramatter appeared briefly to interact with here-matter, before reaching an implosive null-state, destroying more and more of the magical foundation of the guardian tower.

The tower fell at last, into the endless void . . . and the threads of constrained elsewhere parted.

The dragon, his work done, fled.

Even a dragon could be destroyed by that cataclysm he'd caused. Pieces of here and elsewhere roiled in the backlash wave, a tsunami of water and debris that bore all before it.

Nothing could live through that wave.

Except . . . something did.

Something small, soft and terribly fragile, which was torn from a desperate mother's arms. A mother somewhere on the other side of elsewhere.

The dragon, winging his way south, was not aware of it, in all the chaos he had caused.

This was beyond the babe's understanding too. She only knew that she was suddenly cold, wet and frightened. But the sea would not hold her, nor could the wild surge warm and caress her. She screamed, demanded that it be changed. She did not understand how or what was happening. But she wanted it to stop, NOW.

And it did. Her kind could not drown. The wave cast her up on the broken shell shingle. She wanted warmth, and she wanted a breast. For comfort, as much as anything. So she called for it.

"It's alive!"

"Leave it. It's no mortal child, Hallgerd. Let the sea take it back to where it belongs."

"It's a baby, Wulfstan. I know a human baby when I see one," said Hallgerd, picking up the girl-child up. It burrowed into her arms, nuzzling. She knew right then that she'd never give it up, no matter what the headman said. It filled the hole her own lost child left in her heart.

"It's ill luck to cheat the sea of its meat," he said, crossly.

"The sea spat it out," said Hallgerd, unbuttoning her blouse.

Wulfstan spat too, onto the wet shingle. "Nothing good will come of it, mark my words."

Chapter 1

A few yards in front of Meb, the green headland dropped away to the sea far below the fractured basalt of the cliff. The wind carried the shriek and mew of the gray-backed gulls swooping out from their cliff-nests. That should have been a warning to her.

But Meb was too busy. Dreaming, and lost in her dream.

When the boats came in on the morrow's tide, she'd be working too hard to dream. Along with every other woman in the fishing hamlet, she'd be gilling and gutting fish, as fast as her hands could work. A person had to concentrate when they had a razor-sharp knife in their hand. She still had the scar from learning that lesson. Today . . . well, today the East wind had kept everyone home, with not as much as a coble out on the bay. A cold mist clung to the water out there, as it did when the wind was in this quarter, hiding reefs and landmarks, muffling the warning sounds of surf.

She sighed. There had to be more to life than fish-guts. She turned the focus of her attention inward again, not sure what had disturbed her. In her mind, she rode a dragon across the sky of Tasmarin. His scales gleamed obsidian . . .

Being precise by nature she tried to get the details of the dragon right, but it evaded her. Of course, there was no such thing as a black dragon, but the basic shape was the same for all dragons. Their overlord, the dragon Lord Zuamar, flew seldom, but if only he would appear and take a turn over the bay, and land on the fang-rocks across the inlet.

She looked out across the sea, her gaze drifting unseeing across the black ship clawing its way inwards across the bay. Another, and then another, followed it, sliding out of the cloaking sea-mist, long oars raking her-ringbone patterns on the still water. Meb was not truly aware of their presence. They were not what she was looking for.

And then, to her delight, she saw the dragon spin down from heaven in a tasseled and spiky spiral of shimmer of sable, flaring its wings to land on the rocks across the water from the ships.

Suddenly her mind registered the shrieking gulls . . . and the ships. Her first thought was that the fleet must be in early—the gulls were flying off to feast on the scraps. And here she was idling on the cliff-top! She stood up hastily, wiping her hands on her patched skirts.

But . . . but they hadn't gone to sea today!

A second, incredulous look told her that this was some-thing far worse than being late for the gutting. The gulls might be fooled into believing that all ships were fishing-boats, but Meb wasn't. She knew a galley from a fat-bottomed fishing smack, no matter what her adopted family said about her.

A bare second's hesitation and she lifted her skirts and began to sprint back, frantically screaming "raiders!"

The broken basalt of the cliff curved high above the bay. From time to time pieces fell off, down into the hungry waves that ate at its foot. Running along its edge Meb was gasping for breath already. If she'd stopped to think for a moment, she'd have realized that she couldn't both run and yell, but she wasn't thinking, right then. Still doing her best to sprint, she cut as close to the curve of the rotting cliff-top as she dared. She had to get to the village before them.

Too late, Meb realized that she'd dared too much.

A curl of white-hot steam drifted away from Fionn's mouth. His talons dug into the sea-etched basalt. He twitched, sending a shimmering shiver through his ebony scales. He'd always been a bit wary about the vast surge of salt water. It was even more relentless than dragons.

You had to see the funny side of it, he thought, grinning wryly to himself. He was aware that the force lines of everything from water to earth had been badly twisted and torn here by some adept's bungling magics. That was not surprising. Magic workers usually used magic, without understanding how—or what—they were doing, simply following a rote. He was used to having to adjust objects and tweak forces after their bungling. But it was the first time he'd actually been a part of the crude tangle. Well, the balances out here near the edge of the world were unstable anyway. There was a seasonal flux, something you got so close to the edge of existence, where matter had been twisted and abused. Still: Yenfar was one of the largest and most stable of the islands. He had not expected it here.

Fionn blinked his huge scarlet eyes, adjusting his vision to the entire spectrum of energies, not just the visible spectra, but all of them. Now he saw the world as a swirling soup of complex patterns, not merely as reflections of light. And the weave here was indeed twisted, dented and torn. Water, sky and earth energies swirled well away from the true shape of their physical being. Chaos and misery! He sighed. A planomancer's work was never done. He'd rather be sitting in the shade, drinking cool wine, with a platter of crispy fried whitebait and baby squid on the side—which was exactly what he had been doing before the summonsing—than wrestling with this mess. He chuckled. Ah well. It had got him out of paying for the earlier bottles of wine and platters of food rather neatly. Saved him a bit of trouble.

It was odd, though. The summonsing had felt like human magic. But there were no human magicians in Tasmarin.

Dragonkind had hunted down and killed all of them.

Falling takes a long, long time, thought Meb. It was either that, or time itself that stretched. The first idea was somehow easier to deal with. Like the scream that came from her mouth, falling to her death seemed to be happening to someone else. Even if she survived the fall, the sea would kill her. The villagers knew perfectly well that it killed men, let alone women. Women didn't even go out on the fishing boats, never mind into the sea. The blue water was full of sharks, rays, whales and merrows.

She'd never actually seen one of the merpeople. She had, somehow, a time for regret and to try and imagine what a half-fish half-man really looked like before she hit the water.

It was a lot harder than she'd thought it would be.

Fionn shifted his weight uneasily. There it was again. Just as he'd worked out what would need re-alignment, something plucked and twisted at the water energy lines, changing them. The cliff on the far side of the bay was re-aligning itself, cascading in a shower of rocks and turf into the foam-edged blue. That could not account for this tweak, however. It was more like a great, clumsy hand pulling fatelines, with no care for what it did to water or earth or even fire. He frowned.

Humans!

Fionn paid more attention to humankind—the lice, as the others put it—than most dragons in Tasmarin did. They were an unusual interest for a dragon. But then, he was an unusual dragon. Unique on this plane, possibly the last of his kind on any plane, anywhere.

That didn't mean that he interfered with human affairs, any more than other dragons who merely taxed them.

It would have been a great deal too much like hard work, for a start.

He paid no attention to the raider-galleys whose keels were crunching onto the shingle. Instead, he reached a long-taloned forepaw into his front-pouch and hauled out a wad of folded parchment. He looked around and grimaced. These rocks were not a good spot. Nowhere flat to lay out the diagrams. In truth he didn't really need them, but he loved the detail and intricacy of them. They helped him decide. He spread his wings, unfolding the joints, extending them. It was a lousy place to launch from, but it was either fly from here or swim. The water looked cold, and might get at the charts. There was much labor in the drawing of them, and didn't feel like doing it again. The way things were finally falling apart on this plane of existence, he didn't think that he'd have enough time to, before the end.

He'd done enough work to get it into this dire state.

He launched. A trailing tip of his vast wings just touched the water. It was, indeed, cold.

Meb found that the water was not only hard, but also icy. The sudden shock of the cold broke the odd unreality of her falling trance. She was going to die! DIE!

Eyes wide open, all she could see was trailing bubbles and blue. She thrashed wildly, panic overwhelming thought.

Her head broke through into the air. She gasped for breath, frantically flailing at the water to stay afloat.

A wave hit her in the face, tumbling her.

And then strong, web-fingered hands seized her, dragging her under.

She fought them with all her remaining strength as they hauled her down into the watery darkness.

She was so busy struggling that she took a while to realize that she could breathe. And hear.

"Will you stop all this thrashing about, woman!" said someone irritably. " 'tis hard enough swimming with you, without that."

Part of Meb was unwilling to let go of her panic. *This was the sea. You died in the sea.* Another part of her, the odd rational bit that poked fun at the rest of her, that also dreamed dreams that rose along way above fish-guts, said: *Don't be afraid. Be terrified. And breathe deeply.*

As usual, the ordinary village Meb listened to the inner voice, after a while. She was stiff with fear, but at least she could breathe . . . And cough. It was amazing that there still was any sea left out there. She seemed to have swallowed most of it. And now she was dead.

The rational part of her mind said: *so why are you still breathing?*

"Sit here. There's a bit of a shelf," said the voice. "I'll need to make a light so that we can inspect the damage."

The "shelf" was narrow and rough with barnacles. The current plucked at her as she sat on it. But at least she was half above water, on something solid. She tried to dig her fingers into the very rock. The place reeked of drying sea-life: seaweed, dead crabs and a hint of fish.

Then she saw a greenish-white spark glowing in the darkness. It grew into a globe of light of the same color, held in a webbed hand. The hand had rather more fingers than was normal. It was also blue and scaly, like the rest of the merrow it was attached to. He smiled at her. His smile revealed white teeth. They weren't square and blunt like human teeth. No, his teeth were pointed and sharp. He held the light up, looking her over thoughtfully.

"Well, you don't appear to be bleeding too much," he said, sounding a little regretful. "Any other injuries besides those that I can see?"

She stared at him. At his tasseled fins and the toothy smile.

"Shark got your tongue, maybe?" he said, sardonically. "I asked you a question, human wench. Are you all right?"

*** End Excerpt ***